RESERVED

South Bay Billionaires
Book 2

ASHLEY JACOBS
S. S. RICH

Shelf Indulgences LLC

A note on content and language

Reserved is an MF romance with explicit content intended for an 18+ audience only. This book contains content that some readers may find sensitive. If you'd like to review these topics before reading, you can find them at: https://shelfindulgences. com/sbb#reserved

Van, our male lead, is Italian American and a second-generation immigrant whose family hails from Naples. He speaks Italian phrases throughout, mostly to fluster and worship the object of his affection. We've done our best to do the language justice and appreciate your grace for any creative liberties we may have taken in this work of fiction. You can use your e-reader's translate feature or reference the Italian-to-English glossary at the back of the book for definitions.

If something seems off with our use of Italian, you find a typo, or you'd like to suggest additions to the content warnings, please contact us: hello@shelfindulgences.com.

We appreciate you! Enjoy.

To anyone who has ever had a partner neglect your needs—Van is for you. He's the over-the-top, jealous, possessive billionaire you deserve.

Prologue

It felt good to find my voice. After a lifetime of censoring myself for the benefit of others, the confidence to put words to my wants was a gift. Even though I was hollow inside, darkness rising to swallow all the softest parts of me, I stood confident in my power for what felt like the first time.

I was no stranger to betrayal. My dreams had been a casualty of others' actions more than once. But to be betrayed by him? To know the one who had dismissed me and my goals was the same person who had built me up and made me feel seen and cherished? Suffering his duplicity felt like a rebirth. It had broken me, then reforged me–and I was emerging stronger than before.

As I walked away from him, I was resolute. If I survived this–survived him–then rebuilding my future on my own terms would be simple. I could almost thank him for the clarity his mistakes had given me. Almost.

There was more to navigate, I knew. One searing moment of realization didn't solve the challenges I faced, but it gave me the motivation I needed to stop being a passenger on my own journey. It was time for me to take control.

I took a deep breath as the black SUV pulled up, centering myself once more. Yes, I was grateful he had broken through the wall I'd built around my dreams.

I just wished my heart hadn't been collateral damage.

Chapter 1

Van

"Did you order from the trolley?"

I looked up from my monitor to see Miles Davenport, my business partner's executive assistant, leaning in the doorway to my office. I squinted in annoyance and his eyebrows flew up.

"I don't think so, Mr. Grumpypants," he snapped, holding a finger out in admonishment. "I am not here for your particular brand of alphahole today. Answer the question and I'll leave you alone."

I scoffed at his over-the-top antics. "No."

He rolled his eyes heavily, as was his habit, and muttered under his breath as he turned to leave. "Heaven forbid I try to help a man out." He threw a hand up in the air in a haughty wave and called back to me without turning. "Sorry I care about you missing lunch, boss man! Won't happen again."

A chat pinged on my screen, drawing my attention.

> Lex: Stop antagonizing Miles.

How dare she.

> Me: I did no such thing.

> Lex: I could hear you two bickering from my office.

I pressed two fingers to my temple in exasperation.

> Me: It's not my fault you hired an unprofessional assistant.

Her reply was swift, and I could tell she was amused. Because of course she was. The woman knew me too well.

> Lex: He keeps this place afloat and you know it. Apologize, publicly, even if he is being dramatic. We don't need any dissension in the ranks.

Isn't that the fucking truth.

Athena Ventures, the venture capital firm Lex had founded and brought me on to help her build and run, had a stellar reputation in the Bay. But we were also under the microscope for a few reasons, including the fact her father's global investment firm had opened its first venture capital firm right down the street. The competitive relationship between the family was well documented and had received media attention thanks to a few highly public recent events, so Lex was on alert about ensuring things stayed as level as possible for our team. We didn't need any manufactured tension to cause any challenges for our people.

I had no desire to chase Miles down for an apology he would immediately know was performative, but if Lex asked... I'd do it. *He knows it, too, the little shit. Probably baited me.*

> Me: Fine.

I stood and pulled my suit jacket from the closet behind my desk, settling it back on my shoulders as I strode for the door. Suits weren't a requirement in the VC world; in fact, they were often seen as overkill amongst the casual tech startups we often worked with. But I had worked hard to earn a salary that could outfit me in custom Italian craftsmanship. And, after my humble beginnings back home in New Jersey, I was damn well going to enjoy the luxuries I could afford.

I felt the team's eyes on me as I passed and nodded to those bold enough to make eye contact. I had a reputation in this town, and this industry, for being ruthless but respectable, and I wore it like armor every day–even here.

"Miles," I called, approaching him. He'd paused to chat with a junior associate in the busiest area of the office, right in the middle of the open collection of desks where our junior and operations team members sat.

"Yes, Mr. Costa?" he replied, turning to me with an accusatory eyebrow raise. His eyes flashed mischievously and the corner of his mouth quirked ever so slightly up.

Little shit-stirrer, I was right. I gave him a tight smile, refusing to call him out for his performance in front of our staff.

"I believe there was a miscommunication."

"Oh, was there?" He gave me an overly innocent look, batting his lashes. "Please, do tell."

"My short reply was not in response to anything you did," I said. "I was merely concentrating on my work and found context switching difficult in the moment."

"Apology accepted," he responded primly, knowing full well that I had in no way apologized.

"Good," I gritted out, even though "thank you" might have been the more polite response.

I could tell he was fighting back a laugh, and I rolled my eyes to the ceiling and sighed. I was already out here, with an audience. I might as well make Lex happy and try to seem more human for the troops, as she was always asking me to.

"You mentioned a trolley?" I asked, immediately regretting the question when Miles's eyes lit up in delight.

The man was nothing if not conniving, and I knew he was going to play this situation to his advantage. Even if only to get maximum entertainment out of it.

"That's right," he smirked. "Jax, the mail boy, started ordering from there last week."

"He says they have the healthiest lunch options; everything's gluten-free and vegan," the young junior associate Miles had been chatting with added. "He's getting in shape for a shoot or something. You know, for his modeling side gig."

I raised an eyebrow at her, surprised she was indulging in office gossip with me, of all people. Miles grinned, clearly thinking the same.

"Right you are, Rebecca! And, well, it's all delicious, so he's got the whole Pit ordering from her now," he continued, gesturing at the many desks around us.

"Her?" I asked, glancing around.

"Cami," Rebecca said brightly, "the trolley girl."

Just as I was about to ask for more information about this trolley girl, I caught sight of her. She was on the far side of the office, having delivered food to the row of offices opposite mine first. She had her back to us as she chatted animatedly with Jax, our resident mail boy/model. She was average height, maybe 5'6", with luscious dark brown hair that cascaded down her back. It was long enough to wrap around my fist, I observed. She looked at home amongst the more casually dressed members of our team, with her well-worn high-rise jeans beautifully framing an ass I'd love to sink my teeth into.

I blinked at myself, surprised at my errant thought. About to turn back to Miles and excuse myself, I heard the woman–

Cami–laugh. She leaned toward Jax as she did, throwing her head back to send her hair dancing across her oversized white linen shirt and filling the room with the most joyous, melodic sound. It hit me in my chest, my whole body tightening in response. *She is exquisite.*

She was. She laid a friendly hand on Jax's arm before moving back to continue pushing her cart, and I heard a rumble start in my chest. If that overgrown surfer boy was doing anything other than paying for his lunch, I'd–

"You alright, there, sir?" Miles interrupted my wildly inappropriate, but completely justified, train of thought.

I whipped my gaze toward him to find a look of surprise etched into his features. *Ah, shit. He heard that.*

I cleared my throat gruffly. "Fine, Miles. I'm fine."

"Mmhm," he taunted, that infuriating smirk reappearing. "I can see that."

I fought my eye-roll and turned back toward my office. It just so happened Cami was headed that way as well. It was clear she'd been here a few times, as she greeted most people with a friendly smile and a hello, many of them by name. I followed slowly, thinking through my options. Jax saw me passing and raised a hand to catch my attention, opening his mouth to no doubt call my name, but I shut him down with a look. The kid was a character, I'd give him that, but if he tried to get between me and the angel in front of me right now, I'd tear his head clean off.

"Excuse me, I don't think we've met," a sweet voice called.

I looked up and realized both Cami and I had reached my office, which was ultimately a dead end for her.

"I haven't had the pleasure." I offered her a hand.

Her eyebrows rose, but she accepted my hand, the soft press of her calloused fingers sending shockwaves across my skin. Her handshake was gentle but not weak, and her hand slipped from mine slowly.

The play of light in her warm brown eyes mesmerized me. "Van."

"Cami," she replied, a bright smile taking over her features. "Of Camellia's Kitchen," she continued, gesturing to the happy floral logo on the side of her trolley.

"*Bellissima*," I murmured and was rewarded with a gentle rush of pink to her freckled cheeks.

"Um, thank you." She tucked a strand of hair behind her ear nervously. "Do you have an order today, Van?"

"No." I looked down at the orderly pile of sandwiches, salads, and bowls she had with her. "Is everything accounted for?"

"I have a sun-dried tomato pesto veggie sandwich or a quinoa bowl if you want one of those?" She offered both, one in each hand, with a hopeful glint in her deep eyes.

"Lucky me. The quinoa." I went to fish my wallet out of my pocket.

"Oh no, it's okay," she protested, waving away the card I was retrieving. "Jax always over orders. They're already paid for. He told me to find them a home."

I grunted, both surprised and not, and accepted the bowl she handed over with a nod.

"This is my favorite," she whispered conspiratorially. "It's got pickled onion and this absolutely gorgeous kale I found at the market this week."

"Do you make them?" I asked, finding myself desperate to keep her talking, just so I could keep her with me.

She nodded enthusiastically, "Sure do, every single one. It's a small business but fulfilling work."

"Well, Jax apparently has only good things to say. I'm looking forward to trying it."

Her smile turned sheepish, almost self-deprecating, and she gave a little shrug. I could feel frustration rising in me. Not at her, but at whoever had made her feel like she had to reject praise or soften her shine. I wanted to buff and burnish her–mind, body, and spirit–until she glowed more powerfully than the sun.

"Have dinner with me," I blurted, unable to hold back any longer.

She gasped quietly, her eyes widening. I could see her pulse thunder in the hollow of her neck, could see the effect I was having on her. We stood close enough my six feet, five inches loomed over her, and I loved the way she looked as she craned her neck to meet my gaze.

"Um, well," she muttered, taking a tentative step back and turning her trolley. "It was, uh, nice to meet you, Van."

"Tonight," I pressed, intent on seeing her again.

Her gaze flew to mine again and that flush crept back up her cheeks. "You sure are a forward one, aren't you?"

"I'm a man who knows what he wants, Cami." I flashed a grin. "And I'm unafraid to pursue her."

Her mouth dropped open a fraction, her breathing heavier than it had been a few moments before. Her reactions were stunning, and I was glad my suit coat and the quinoa bowl in my hands obstructed her view of exactly how much I was enjoying the conversation.

She blinked at me and shook her head slightly, as though gathering her wits. But I didn't want her to gather them. I wanted them to stay scattered so I could slowly, deliberately, gather them up myself and piece her back together like the work of art she was. And then shatter her all over again. And again.

"I'm flattered, Van, really," she recovered, her natural inclination to be cheery warring with the way my words had obviously affected her. "But you're a stranger to me."

"Fair." I nodded, perversely pleased she wasn't throwing herself at my feet just because I'd asked her out. I wanted her to be safe. "I'll just have to help you get to know me. Won't I, *bella*?"

I so desperately wanted to stroke the backs of my fingers along her cheek, neck, and down to the delicious swell of her breast above her neckline, but I offered my hand instead. Turning her hand in mine, I brought the back of it to my lips, pressing a chaste, but lingering kiss to her warm flesh. Her breath stuttered and she smiled softly as I slowly released her, stepping to my office door.

"*Buongiorno, bella*," I said, reveling in the heat I saw flash in her eyes. "It's been a pleasure."

"Um, thank you, Van," she replied, trying to find her footing. "Have a good one."

She pushed her trolley back toward the Pit, casting a glance over her shoulder with a tentative smile as she did.

"See you tomorrow, Cami," I called.

This is going to be fun, fiorellino. I can't wait.

Chapter 2

Cami

"You've got to be kidding me," I muttered, staring in disbelief at the administrative portal of my online ordering system.

"What?" Preston asked from across the island, her eyebrows raised in interest. "Oooh it's him, isn't it? What did he say this time?"

I took a deep breath, shaking my head at her and the entire situation. *Who is this man and where the hell did he come from?* Every day since we'd met over my lunch cart on Monday, Van Costa of Athena Ventures had been placing orders via my online system. He had also been diligent about helping me get to know him by abusing the notes section on every order.

On Tuesday, he'd ordered the veggie sandwich and a kale side salad. He'd also informed me he was "from the East Coast and came from a huge Italian family." He'd ended the note with a question: *Where are you from, Cami?*

Before I could second guess myself, I'd scribbled my brief response on the paper wrapper of his sandwich: *Ukiah, farm country.*

Wednesday, it was the Thai peanut bowl with tofu and a

ginger citrus immunity shot. The notes had mentioned how he'd always wanted to explore more north of the Bay, then named his favorite park in the city. He claimed to spend most weekends out with his German Shepherd, Duke. I'd melted a bit at the mention of his dog; I'd always wanted one growing up.

The answer to that day's question was also an easy one. He'd asked if I had any pets, to which I scrawled, "Not anymore, but I had a cat as a kid. Maggie McGonagall–Mickey to her friends" on his receipt in reply.

Thursday, he'd ordered the hero and a green juice. Preston read his note over my shoulder and collapsed into giggles at my reaction.

A Harry Potter fan, I take it? Don't give me too much credit– I looked it up. Are you a reader, bella? I rarely indulge in fiction, but when I do, I reach for adventure or thrillers. Something about the escapism is...soothing, no?

"Your face!" Preston snickered. "You look like a deer in the headlights, Cam. You good?"

"Good? What even is good?! The hottest, wealthiest, most successful human being I've ever met in my entire life is talking about looking my cat's name up on the freaking internet. What is *happening* right now?!"

My complete inability to grasp the situation only made Preston laugh harder. When she managed to recover, she shook her head in amusement. "There's a lot to unpack in that statement, sister. Let's start with the whole success thing–what do you know about Van's career?"

I tried to hold back my smile and shrugged at her. "I've heard your brother talk about him plenty."

Preston's twin, Parker, was a close friend. He was also our most frequent guest since Preston bought the place right out of undergrad. Not only did he work for Athena–he worked directly for Van.

"And," I mumbled, looking away, "I may have looked him up online."

Preston cackled. "You did not! Oh my God, Cam, you are too adorable. I can't. I can't!"

"What else was I supposed to do?! He's this gorgeous, growly mystery," I gestured wildly, as though I could physically illustrate my point. I thought back to the moment I'd first seen Van at Athena; he'd taken my breath away. Tall, dark, and Italian–from his tanned skin to the confident way he carried himself–he was the kind of man you'd notice in a crowd of thousands. But more than his captivating amber eyes or his impossibly sharp jaw, Van's sheer physicality was imposing. *Like he could toss me around for hours without breaking a sweat.*

"Men like that don't pay attention to people like me, let alone demand I join them for dinner." I'd rubbed my forehead, exasperated. "The man put me on my back foot, Preston. It's not a familiar position!"

"First of all, what do you mean 'people like me'?" she asked, her gaze narrowed in accusation.

I gestured wildly again. "You know! Normal people! Farm kids from the country who weren't born with silver spoons in their mouths. People who are not considered society darlings or photographed for the gossip pages."

Preston was all of those things–modelesque, wealthy, and a media favorite amongst the upper-class elite in the Bay. She and Parker ran in the same circles as people like Van, while I watched from the sidelines with popcorn and wine.

My best friend and Camellia's Kitchen's angel investor gave me a hard look. She was no stranger to my argument about not fitting in. "What I know, Camellia Maria Rivera–"

"Seriously?" I drew back and placed a hand on my chest, affronted. "You're going to full-name me right now?"

She held up her hand and kept talking, ignoring my

outburst. "...what I know, Cami, is that you deserve to have someone sweep you off of your feet."

I didn't know if sweeping me off of my feet was Van's aim, but the man sure was smooth. *And smelled like heaven, if heaven was full of bergamot, cigar smoke, and whiskey.* And maybe I was a little tempted to find out where this note-based conversation would go. In the interest of my burning curiosity, I'd scribbled a short reply on the wrapper of Van's sandwich: *I read romance.*

Then, Friday morning arrived. His lunch order–quinoa bowl and another green juice–was accompanied by the shortest note yet.

Hmm, a romance reader. Why am I not surprised? You'll have to tell me your favorite authors at dinner this weekend, bella.

I re-read the note as Preston watched, her eyes twinkling with amusement. I spun my laptop around so she could read it for herself. She leaned forward, eager, and looked up at me with a mischievous grin moments later.

"So?" she prompted, her tone expectant.

"I don't know!" I exclaimed. "I'm out of my element with this situation, Pres."

"What, because he's not someone you've known your entire life? Newsflash, Cam, most people don't end up with the boy next door."

"Hey now, this has nothing to do with Gabriel," I admonished. "Anyway, bringing my ex into the conversation feels like a low blow." It was also the perfect reminder of why I should be reluctant to get involved in any romantic situation. *Trust doesn't come easy for me anymore.*

Preston shrugged, never one to pull punches. "If the shoe fits, babe."

I sighed. "That's all you're going to give me? A reminder

that I'm broken in the romance department? I need good advice for this one, missy, not snark."

"But that's who I am, Cam!" she laughed, throwing her arms wide. "I am snark. Snark is me."

I shook my head at her with a laugh; she wasn't lying. "Fine," I sighed dramatically. "Be snarky if you must."

"Anyway, get that shit out of your head," she snapped, pointing at me. "You're not broken. You just made the mistake of letting a douchebag walk all over you because you have a warped view of what love is. But you have the power to prevent that from happening again."

"I know," I said, quietly, not wanting to go down that particular lecture-filled road. "Just tell me what to do. Should I go out with Van this weekend?"

She gave me a long look, knowing I was ducking the bigger conversation about relationships, love, worthiness, and past trauma. She read my unwillingness correctly and dropped the Gabriel point, but I knew it was only a matter of time before she revisited it.

Preston and I had known each other for years. We became friends in undergrad at Berkeley, where we'd been paired as roommates freshman year. When I met her on move-in day, I was in awe. She was a force–confident, aggressive, ridiculously smart, and stunning.

It felt at the time like she was my opposite in every way: the society darling from one of the Bay's wealthiest families paired up with a fourth-generation farmer's daughter who was also a first-generation college student. The fact she'd even given me the time of day had been a surprise to me, but she saw the potential for friendship and wasn't deterred by my shyness. She may have ended up my business partner and roommate, but she was first and foremost my best friend. I knew I could count on her for literally anything–including pushing me out of my comfort zone at every opportunity.

She licked her lips salaciously. "It's Van Costa, Cam. He's got that whole alpha male vibe nailed, which is fucking delicious. And he's mature with plenty of experience?" She fanned herself enthusiastically. "Honestly, given the chance, I'd climb him like a fucking tree because that shit is hot as sin."

I choked on a laugh. No matter how much time I spent with Preston, she still managed to surprise me.

"You've been so focused on the Kitchen for the last few years," she went on, "I think you forgot this is also your chance to be free from all the bullshit. It's dinner, not marriage." Her gaze hardened. "You want my advice?"

I nodded, giving her my big, innocent eyes. Even Preston couldn't say no to me when I pulled out that expression.

"Good. Here it is...Girl! Go! Get! That!" She punctuated each word with a firm slap to the kitchen island.

I laughed, her enthusiasm and bluntness doing exactly what she knew I needed it to–loosening the tight knot of nerves and indecision that had formed in my chest.

"You're right. I deserve a night out!"

It had been a while since I'd gone out on a date; it was too easy for me to use my business as an excuse. Preston wasn't afraid to call me on it from time to time, but I usually ignored or put off her challenges.

"Fuck yes, you do," she agreed. "And it should be with someone new."

"It should," I conceded.

"And because *you* want to, not because you feel some weird sense of obligation to your parents or their friends."

I gave her a pointed look, still not willing to take the bait. She raised her hands in defeat and sighed.

"Fine, I won't keep harping on the Gabriel thing."

"So generous of you, Pres. Thank you!" I batted my lashes at her.

She twirled her hand through the air with a flourish and gave a little mock bow in reply. When she straightened, her intent gaze snapped to mine. "For now. Just know, missy, that reckoning is coming."

I groaned dramatically and dropped my head back to stare at the ceiling while she cackled in delight at my discomfort.

"Fine," I whined, drawing the word out. I heaved a sigh and looked back over at my friend with a smile. "Okay then, help me pick a place. If I'm doing this thing, it's gonna be on my terms."

"Damn straight!" she cried.

You can do this, Cami. It's just one date.

Chapter 3

Van

"*B*uongiorno, Mamma," I greeted as I walked into my kitchen, phone in hand.

"Giovanni!" her warm voice rang through my earbuds. "It has been too long, *tesoro*. When are you coming home so I can feed you?"

I set my phone aside and began pulling ingredients for ragù from the fridge and pantry. "I'm a grown man; I feed myself just fine."

She tutted in reply, and I knew she was shaking her head. We had this conversation every time we spoke, whether on the phone or in person.

"I feed you better," she insisted.

"Of course you do, Mamma," I agreed. Pulling a knife from the block and a cutting board from the drawer, I busied myself with chopping. "What's the news from the family?"

"Oh, my sweet boy. It's been busy here," she gushed. "Elena and the girls were over last weekend; we made cookies. And Lucia and her boys stopped by for dinner last night. And Enzo– well, you know your brother, Giovanni."

I hummed my confirmation that I did, in fact, know my

flighty and indecisive youngest sibling. She prattled on as I prepared the sauce, filling me in on all the happenings in my old New Jersey neighborhood. I didn't have to contribute much to keep the conversation going—just a grunt here and a "yes, Mamma" there. It was part of my Saturday ritual, this call to check in on the family back home.

Most Saturdays started with a run with Duke. He was still a young dog, and the more I did to work off his energy, the happier we both were in my condo. Once home, I'd work out and shower while he napped off our run. My groceries were delivered mid-morning, at which point I'd call to check in while I prepared some meals for the week.

The kitchen was home. It was where I'd learned my family history and my nonna's recipes, where I'd helped my madre teach my three younger siblings how to cook. I felt more at home in front of a stove and cutting board than I did in most conference rooms—a fact my colleagues and clients would be surprised to learn.

Cooking reminded me of where I came from, the blue-collar New Jersey neighborhood where most people stayed for their entire lives. I'd clawed my way out of that future tooth and nail, determined to write a new story for my family along the way.

"You're lonely, Giovanni." My madre's voice brought me back to the present.

I stirred the sauce, turning the burner down to a simmer, and sighed internally. This was a familiar conversation. "I'm fine, Mamma. I have Duke."

"You need more than a dog to cuddle," she chided. "Tell me you've met someone."

"When I have something to tell, you'll be the first to know," I assured her.

An image of Cami flashed in my mind's eye, her warm brown eyes full of life and joy. She surprised me yesterday. I hadn't expected her to give in after my question-and-answer game. Her responses had been brief and to the point. Then, yesterday, she handed over my quinoa bowl with three things scribbled on the lid: *Saturday, 7 pm, Taverna.*

"You're not a young man anymore, you know," my madre pressed.

"And yet, you're a young woman. Mamma, tell me how that works. What is your secret?"

"Psh. Your tricks are wasted on me. You need a good woman in your life, Giovanni. Someone to feed you."

"I told you, Mamma, I feed myself. And I have to go–the sauce is done and I need to stop by Cece's before I head out for the evening."

"Oh, sweet Cece! Give her our love."

"I will."

"*Ti voglio bene*, Giovanni."

"*Ti voglio bene anch'io*, Mamma."

We hung up, and I pulled the earbuds from my ears. Duke wandered into the kitchen and sat by my feet, grinning up at me as he did.

"Finally done napping, I see." I reached down and stroked his head as he panted, clearly pleased. "Let's package some food up for Cece and take you over for a visit, hm?"

At the sound of her name, he jumped to his paws and turned a quick, excited circle before going to the door and sitting to wait, his tongue lolling out. I huffed a laugh and turned back to the stove, pulling the pot of pasta off to strain. It was a simple menu–ragù and homemade pappardelle. I'd made enough for six meals, half of which I'd be delivering to my across-the-hall neighbor.

I first met Cecelia Rutherford in the hallway of our building. She was headed down to meet her driver as I came home from the office one evening. The model of old Hollywood glam, she'd paused to give me a long look as I opened my door.

"Oh my. I didn't think they made them like you anymore, gorgeous. Are you my new neighbor?" she'd teased, a mischievous glint in her eye.

Her over-the-top persona amused me, and I invited her over for dinner sometime. She'd accepted immediately, calling down to dismiss her driver and brushing past me to let herself into my condo.

Over cacio e pepe and a bottle of wine, I'd learned she was a widow, living alone in her large condo. She'd been surrounded by staff for most of her life, the trophy wife of a prominent Hollywood producer for decades. They'd retired together in the Bay, but he'd passed away shortly thereafter. Childless, with no nearby family, she was all too happy to find a friend in the building. And when she found out I could cook? Well, I'd been bringing her weekly home-cooked meals ever since.

I finished portioning out the ragù and stacked three take-away containers in a bag before placing the rest in the fridge. Duke cocked his head expectantly, eager to go visit Cece. From the moment I brought him home, she adopted Duke as hers. When I was caught up at the office or had evening commitments, he'd spend time with Cece, and when I went on business trips or visited home, Duke stayed with her.

Her support and friendship had been unexpected and welcome. Unlike others in the Bay, Cece held no pretense or agenda, and I didn't have to keep my guard up with her. And it didn't hurt she loved my cooking. I often turned to the stove when I needed to let off steam, and Cece was more than happy to help me ensure the product of my stress management didn't go to waste.

"Alright, Duke, let's go see her."

We walked across the hall, and Duke scratched lightly at

Cece's door. She swept it open moments later, no doubt expecting us after my text the day before.

"There's my boy! Come in, come in," Cece said, motioning to me as Duke slipped past her and darted into her cozy living room and the brand new bone I could see waiting on his bed.

"Cece." I bent down and kissed first one cheek, then the other. "Thank you for watching him this evening."

"Don't mention it, love, please," she tutted. "Is that my compensation?" She eyed the bag in my hand and reached out, wiggling her fingers.

I smiled and handed it over. "Beef ragù with pappardelle."

"You perfect man," she crooned, patting my arm as she took the bag. "I have your containers from last week waiting on the island."

I wandered toward the kitchen as she busied herself putting the food into the fridge.

"Another business dinner tonight, hm?" she asked, back to me.

"A date."

She whipped around, her blue eyes sparkling. "Do tell. It's been a while, if I'm not mistaken."

I chuckled. "Observant of you, Cece. Mamma says hello and sends her love."

She pursed her lips, suggesting she saw right through my evasion tactics. "Your mother is simply a doll. Please send all my love and appreciation for her and her perfect son right back."

She winked, and I shook my head in amusement. "I'll tell her."

"I know you will, love. Now go on, I've got our boy from here. Do I get to keep him overnight, then?" She turned her smile on Duke, an indulgent lilt to her lips.

"I won't be out too late, Cece. I can collect him tonight if you're up."

"Well, that's a pity. But, you know me; always burning the midnight oil. Drop in for him anytime before one."

"You should get more sleep."

"And you should go on more dates, find yourself a nice girl," she teased, that pointed brow returning.

"On that note, I'll take my leave. Thank you."

"Anytime, love, you know that."

I kissed her cheeks in farewell, then glanced at Duke. He panted happily from his bed, bone wedged between his paws and tongue hanging out.

Chapter 4

Van

A few hours later, I was on my way to Taverna. The restaurant was a short walk from my place, and I was grateful for the opportunity to forgo a driver, preferring to walk whenever I could.

As I made my way, I thought back to each interaction I'd had with Cami over the last week. On Tuesday, she'd been timid. She had a bright smile fixed on her face as she handed my lunch over, but her gaze barely met mine. I'd said thank you, and she'd nodded, then turned to go. "See you tomorrow, *bella*," I'd called.

I suspected I made her uncomfortable, but a little discomfort wasn't a bad thing. The more she worked through it, the more comfortable she'd be with me. My theory was proven when she returned on Wednesday and met my eyes immediately as she knocked on my office door.

"Hi there, Van," she said, her plastered-on grin from before softening to something genuine.

"*Buongiorno, bella*," I greeted her with a smirk. I stood, buttoning my jacket as I did, and walked over to meet her at my office door.

"You know, I kind of pegged you for a dog person."

My smirk turned into a grin, and she swallowed thickly in response. "Oh? Do tell."

"Just a vibe," she murmured as I drew closer, shrugging one shoulder.

"Want to expand on whatever's written on my lunch today?" I nodded toward the items in her hand.

She huffed a laugh, nervous, and handed it over. "Nothing more to say at the moment. Thanks for ordering again."

"Of course. I look forward to seeing you tomorrow."

Her gaze lingered on mine as she leaned against the door-frame, looking moments away from saying something else. After a few seconds, she blinked and shook her head, then flashed me a shy smile and a nod before turning to go. I let her, but it took more restraint than I wanted to admit to stop myself from attempting to coax more out of her.

Later that night, I researched more than her childhood cat's name, desperate to know more about the beguiling caterer who I knew so little about. I looked into her hometown, Ukiah, and found what I assumed was her family's farm. They'd been working the land for generations and had a well-established presence within the community. Cami was all over their website and featured heavily in photos and on the page detailing their story. It appeared she was the heir apparent to their operation, despite running a catering business two and a half hours away. *I bet there's a story there.*

The urge to learn and understand more of her story was strong, but I didn't want to overwhelm her by leaving an interrogation in my order notes. No, I needed to play this carefully because there was only one acceptable outcome–her saying yes to a date. The few moments each day over lunch weren't enough. I craved her sunshine with an intensity that both surprised and emboldened me.

Romantic relationships typically played a transactional role in my life—they were something I invested in when a mutually beneficial arrangement would help further the goals of both parties. But my attraction to Cami was different, and I wasn't looking for anything more or less than her. All of her.

Thinking of her brought a smile to lips as I neared the restaurant. She'd been magnificent yesterday morning; she was nervous, but her determination had won out over her trepidation. Her fingers had brushed mine as she handed my lunch over, and that gentle touch had once again been nothing short of electric.

"I hope you like Mediterranean fare." She'd smiled and blinked rapidly a few times as she slowly drew her hand back.

My grin broke free immediately, and my heart swelled at the way her eyes lit in response. "Of course, I do."

"Good," she squeaked, then cleared her throat. "That's good, then."

I glanced down at the note on my quinoa bowl, and my smile softened.

"Can't wait to see you tomorrow, *bella*." Her eyes flashed to mine, her cheeks flushing.

She let out a forceful breath and looked away, a soft laugh falling from her lips. "You're good at disarming people, Mr. Costa."

"You're not the first to mention that talent, Miss Rivera, though I've taken far less amusement—and pleasure—from my effect on others."

Her giggle made my smirk grow into another grin.

"You might just be the death of me," she mused playfully.

"I certainly hope not."

The flush that bloomed on her cheeks hit me right in the gut. I was a glutton for her reactions, hungry for every smile, blush, and laugh. I wanted to collect them all.

"I look forward to tomorrow." I stood to escort her to my door, feeling victorious over the fact she'd lingered long enough for me to do so. It was a first.

She glanced up at me as we headed to the door. "You know what? So do I."

"You sound surprised."

"Maybe a little." She shrugged and her smile turned sheepish.

I slapped my chest in mock pain teasingly. "I'm choosing to not be offended by that."

She coughed a wild laugh and shook her head. "Oh god, no, I didn't mean it like that!" Her cheeks flamed. "I don't have a lot of practice with, uh," she gestured between us, "this. Dating."

How can that possibly be? She was gorgeous, yes, but she was also kind, warm, and so fucking talented. That I didn't have a line of men to fight off for her attention was a minor miracle.

"I can't say I'm disappointed about that," I admitted, and she bit her lip. "But let's dive into that more tomorrow, hm? Once I have your undivided attention, *bella*, I intend to make the most of it. I fear you'll be far too distracting if we explore that comment now." I glanced down at my watch. "After all, the weekend is still hours away."

"Right," she gulped, nodding. "Yes, of course. Tomorrow." She paused at the door and turned to me, just inches away, and her eyes held mine for a long moment. "I really am looking forward to it, Van."

I couldn't hold back the urge to touch her any longer. Reaching out and tucking a piece of hair behind her ear, I brushed a thumb along her cheek. Her lips parted on a sharp inhalation of breath as she gazed up at me, her body swaying closer to mine.

"I wouldn't miss it for the world, *bella*." I reluctantly dropped my hand and stepped back.

Cami blinked, still looking mildly bewildered, then nodded. "Have a lovely rest of your day, Van."

I'd been replaying those brief moments of contact in my head ever since. They weren't nearly enough to satisfy my craving for her, though I hoped to get slightly further than a casual brushing of our fingers tonight. I wasn't known for my patience.

As I neared Taverna, I noticed Cami up ahead, approaching the door from the opposite direction. She was easy to spot, her exuberant energy and natural beauty setting her apart from the crowd. Her flowing green dress was just long enough to show a flash of the flat gold sandals on her feet. Warmth settled in my gut at the sight of her.

"Cami," I called, catching her attention as she grabbed the door handle.

"Van, hi." She released the door and turned her perfect smile toward me.

Walking right up to her, I placed a hand on her arm–just above her elbow–as I leaned in to kiss first one cheek, then the next. When I drew back, her expression was dazed and that endearing flush was creeping up her neck.

"You are *bellissima,*" I murmured, squeezing her arm gently.

"You're too kind, Van, really."

"I make a habit of being only as kind as necessary," I teased. "And I always speak the truth."

She glanced up with a grateful smile and ducked a nod. "I can respect that."

"Good." I moved my hand from her arm to the small of her back as I opened the door with my free hand. "After you."

Walking up to the host station, the young woman immediately beamed at us both.

"Cami! We have your table all set. Come on back."

"Perfect, Julie. Thanks," Cami replied with a warm grin.

"How's Henry doing at his new camp?"

Julie started walking toward our table as she answered, waving us both along. "Oh, he's loving it! You're so sweet to ask. Thanks for that suggestion about the local honey, too. His allergies have been so much more manageable this summer."

"I'm so glad! A little local honey on a consistent basis is like magic."

"It really is." Julie turned to beam at us as she stopped at a small table by the window. "How's this?"

"Perfect, thank you," I answered.

"Excellent! Well, I'll leave you both with these," she placed menus on the table, "and Niko will be by soon to get you some drinks. Enjoy!"

"Thanks, Julie!"

"Anytime, girl. I mean it!" Julie flashed a final grin as she squeezed Cami's shoulder and turned to walk back to the host stand.

When she'd gone, I looked up from my menu to study the woman before me. The interaction between the two had been brief, but elements of it were very clear: Julie thought the world of Cami, and Cami cared deeply for those she knew. After a moment, Cami glanced up from her menu.

"Can I help you?" she teased, that sparkle back in her eyes.

"Do you know her?"

"Who, Julie?" Cami glanced toward the host stand with a smile. "Yeah, I'm kind of a regular around here. Her son sometimes comes in with her. He's a sweet kid."

"A regular, hm?" I looked down at the menu, giving her a reprieve from my gaze. "What's good?"

She laughed, quick and bright, and I had to look up at her again. "Everything? I've had it all, and it's all delicious. Can't go wrong."

I hummed, thinking, as I perused the menu. Setting it down,

I looked back up to find her watching me. "Well, it's decided then."

"What is?" she asked, bewildered.

"You'll order for us."

She blinked owlishly. "I will?"

I nodded. "Please."

"But I don't know what you like."

"I like good food."

"Oh," she looked down at the menu, then up at me again. "Um, any allergies?"

"None. Do you like wine?"

She swallowed, then cleared her throat. "Yes, I do."

"I'll get us a bottle."

"Yes, okay. Thank you."

As her frantic gaze went back to the menu, I reached out and placed a steadying hand on hers. Her eyes snapped to mine and she hitched a breath.

"I trust you, Cami," I said softly, squeezing her hand. "No pressure, just pick what you like, and I'll be happy." *I'd eat my menu if it meant sitting across from her.*

The tension that had jumped into her shoulders seeped away, the tightness in her face melting into a grateful smile.

"Sure, Van," she murmured. "I think you'll love it all, really."

"I'm sure I will." I squeezed her hand again before reluctantly releasing her and picking up the wine list. I had no desire to let her go, but I also knew my desire to move quickly needed to be tempered for her comfort. *For now.*

The server, Niko, stepped up to our table with glasses of water and a basket of bread.

"Welcome to Taverna," he greeted. "Lovely to see you, Cami." He cast her a warm smile, which she returned, before turning to me. "Sir, have you been in before?"

"First time."

"It's a pleasure to have you. Can I get you anything else to drink?"

"Please. We'll do a bottle of the Alphonse Mellot Sancerre."

"Of course, sir. I'll be right back with that."

"Thank you." Cami and I both said, our eyes catching as twin smiles crept across our faces.

"What are you ordering for us, then?" I asked.

Cami glanced back at the menu. "Well, I love the dolmathakia and halloumi appetizers, so maybe those. But the crispy zucchini cakes are delicious, too–"

"Get them all."

She looked up, wide-eyed. "That's so much food."

I shrugged. "Leftovers."

She tilted her head and stared at me. "I'm sorry, Van, but you are such a surprise."

I chuckled and placed my forearms on the table, leaning toward her.

"And why is that, *bella?*"

Her blush made my cock stir. "Well, you're letting me order and encouraged leftovers, for starters."

"I'm not letting you order. I asked you to order for us." I cocked an eyebrow at her. "There's an important nuance there. And it's a smart move–you know this menu better than I do."

"Sure, yeah, I–"

"As for leftovers, why does that surprise you?"

She was flustered, but I was willing to wait it out. "I...well, in my head, once you reach a certain level of wealth, leftovers are beneath you."

I huffed and shook my head. "My madre wouldn't hesitate to smack me upside the head if I threw away food solely because it wasn't made fresh." I met Cami's eyes and gave her a small smile. "But I know what you mean. There are plenty of pompous assholes in this city who wouldn't be thrilled by the prospect of leftovers. Good thing I'm not one of them."

"A pompous asshole?"

My laugh was quick and sharp. "No, I am that. Just not about leftovers."

She giggled, and my chest warmed at the sound. There was so much I wanted to know about her, so much I was curious to understand. I felt this fierce drive to get as close to her as I could, and I wasn't about to ignore it.

"So, we'll get the dolmathakia, halloumi, and the zucchini cakes. What else?"

"A salad, and then we should split the souvlakia and the moussaka."

"Excellent."

"And for dessert—"

"Is it too bold of me to request you?"

Her eyes snapped to mine, eyebrows comically high. "Excuse me?"

"For dessert."

"M-me?" she squeaked.

My grin was wolfish, but I wasn't going to rein it in. The flush rising from her décolletage to her cheeks was far too delicious to dismiss. "Yes, *bella*. You."

She surreptitiously fanned herself with her menu. "Um, well—"

"Here's that wine," Niko said as he waltzed up to the table.

I smirked as Cami let out a relieved huff, grateful for the interruption. After I approved the tasting he poured for me, Niko served us both generous glasses.

"And do you know what you'd like for dinner?"

"Yes," I replied, gesturing gently to Cami.

She flashed me a grin before ordering everything we'd discussed, except dessert.

"Lovely choices," Niko praised, gathering our menus. "I'll get those starters out soon. Enjoy the wine."

"Thank you," Cami called as he left.

When she turned her gaze back to me, I could feel my insides heating. She was captivating, but there was also an openness and earnestness to her that was incredibly refreshing. I had no doubt the woman I saw before me was the real Camellia Rivera, nervous ticks and all. There was no performance to her demeanor, no element of her behavior that suggested she was pretending to be something she wasn't.

In the industry I worked in and the social circles I was a part of, few people wore their hearts on their sleeves and showed up as their true selves. I was surrounded every day by people who played the game to achieve their next goal, whether a promotion or a fat payout. I was one of them because I'd learned at an early age things don't come easy to those who aren't born into privilege.

But Cami–she was exactly who she seemed to be. And I wanted to bury myself in her, figuratively and literally, and bask in her authenticity. I wasn't a patient man, but I could try to hold myself back for her. I didn't want to scare her away, but I sure as fuck wasn't going to lose her, either.

I raised my wine glass. "To delicious food and even better company. And to you."

Cami smiled softly and mirrored my action, then tapped her glass lightly to mine. "To saying yes."

My cock woke all the way up at those words on her lips. I was surprised at the vehemence with which I wanted to hear her say yes to me. Yes in the throes of passion, yes to another date, yes to a question it was way too fucking early to even consider asking. *I want every single one of this woman's yeses–today, tomorrow, and forever.*

Chapter 5

Cami

Van Costa was an enigma. Seriously, I didn't know what to make of the warm, intense, vibrant human being who sat across from me at dinner. He was nothing like I had pictured from our brief interactions at his office or from what little Parker had shared. Yes, he was more than a bit domineering and I wouldn't describe him as verbose, but...the saying "still waters run deep"? That was Van. There was an incredible depth to the man that both surprised and intrigued me.

We talked through dinner and laughed more than I thought we would. The time flew by so quickly I didn't realize how late it was until Niko stopped by with the baklava we'd ordered.

"Can I get you two anything else? The kitchen is closing soon." He deposited the plate full of glistening pastry between us with a flourish.

"Oh! I'm sorry, Niko, we lost track of time."

Niko grinned. "Don't apologize, please. The laughter from this table is infectious."

He gave Van a bright smile and a nod, then slipped away.

"I'm sure you light up every room," Van murmured.

I felt my cheeks heat in response to his words, warmth

threading through me. He'd peppered me with compliments relentlessly, and I'd been flushing like a teenager all evening.

"You might be a little biased," I teased.

He shook his head, expression serious. "No, *bella*. Just the lucky fool persistent enough to finally catch you."

"Is that what you've done, then?" I asked, feeling emboldened by his attention. "Caught me?"

His intense gaze met mine and flared with want, and my core clenched in reply. "Have I?"

My throat was suddenly parched. *How can two little words and one look have such a physical impact?* I took a sip of wine, willing my racing heart to settle, before responding in a hoarse voice. "I think you have. My attention, at the very least."

His slow, devilish grin did unspeakable things to my insides. I felt my body respond and fidgeted in my seat, squeezing my thighs together.

"I'm pleased to hear it."

I grabbed my fork, eager for a distraction and the sweetness of the baklava. But before I could take a piece of our dessert, Van chopped off the corner of the flaky pastry. Turning his fork around, he held it up, level with my mouth.

"Ladies first," he commanded, his voice husky.

Suddenly self-conscious under the weight of his attention, I licked my lips before opening my mouth. He gently pushed the fork forward, and I closed my lips around the bite, leaning back to draw it off the tines. His gaze was intense on my face the entire time, and I could feel it like a caress on my heated flesh.

A soft groan of appreciation broke free as I chewed my bite, the richness of the honey and nut mixture nearly overwhelming. Across the table, Van shifted slightly, and I had the wicked thought he might be as affected by me as I was by him. The confidence and desire that swelled in response was a heady thing.

"Good?"

I gave him a satisfied smile and nodded. "Delicious. Here—"

I speared the bite I'd intended earlier and held my fork up for him, returning the surprisingly intimate favor of feeding him. His dark gaze never wavered from mine as he accepted the bite, but when he started to chew, his eyes dropped closed and he gave a sigh of contentment.

"This place is *fantastico*," he muttered as he patted his mouth with a napkin. "Thank you, Cami, for bringing us here."

The honesty in his gaze made my heart squeeze. The plus side of his intensity, other than wreaking complete havoc on my libido, was I believed every word he said. I had the sense Van wasn't going to give me platitudes or say whatever I wanted to hear. He was going to say precisely what he meant, and only that.

"Of course," I replied. "It's my favorite restaurant in the Bay. I've known the owners for a while; I met them at the farmer's market. They've even consulted on some Mediterranean recipes I use when the right ingredients are in season."

"Smart. Do you have many connections in the restaurant community?"

I nodded. "I don't know everyone, of course. I'm not sure anyone could, really. But I know a lot of the smaller, local chefs and restaurateurs in the Bay. Before I started buying my produce from the same suppliers, I sold to them from my family farm. In Ukiah."

"Ah, yes. I may have looked Ukiah up after your... brief...reply."

My laugh was sheepish. "When I got your note, I wasn't sure what to say or, honestly, if I should say anything."

"You should," he insisted. "Please, always say something. Say everything. I want to hear it all."

My heart thumped because I believed him. And that was

surprising. Most people I'd chosen to believe had used that faith and trust to their advantage, and I'd rarely come out on top.

"Thanks," I murmured, finishing my last sip of wine. I was desperate to move the conversation off of me. Though he hadn't been interrogating me by any means, I felt Van had learned a lot more about me than I had about him. "Tell me, Van...is your name really Van?"

He chuckled, taking another bite of baklava. "Giovanni. It's a mouthful. Van is more practical."

"Giovanni," I mused, testing out his full name. I liked it. It rolled off the tongue beautifully.

"If everyone said it like that, I just might do away with Van for good," he growled, his eyes fixed on my mouth.

I did my best to ignore the desire that flared in response to the lust in his tone and gaze. "It's a lovely name. Giovanni Costa. I like it."

"Thank you."

I tilted my head at him, considering. "Why not Gio?"

He made a face that suggested the thought wasn't worth considering and shook his head. "Too cutesy."

I snorted. "Excuse me? Did you just say 'cutesy'?"

He pointed his fork at me and raised an eyebrow. "I did, and I stand by it."

My belly laugh was inevitable. He was adorable, but I suspected I might be the only person in the Bay to think so, given his reputation. "I like it. Gio. It suits you." I gave him a mischievous grin.

"You can call me whatever you like, *bella*." He shot me a heated look, almost in challenge, and I flushed. Again.

Niko swung by then, the bill in hand. Van didn't even look at it, just held up a finger to indicate Niko should wait, then pulled his wallet out of his pocket and handed over a black card. Niko thanked him and walked quickly off to the register.

"Thank you," I said, reaching over to grasp Van's hand briefly. "Truly. It's been a lovely evening."

He squeezed my hand back with a warm smile, making my stomach flip. There were promises in that look I wasn't ready to acknowledge or accept.

"The pleasure has been all mine, Camellia."

I went to release his hand, but he held on. There was a challenge in his eyes, daring me to try and take my hand back, but I willingly gave in and let him keep it. He stroked a thumb over my knuckles and hummed his approval, and I swear I could feel the vibration of that sound between my thighs.

"Did you walk here?" His question caught me off guard, but I nodded quickly. "So did I. I'll walk you home."

I suspected any protest would be ignored, and I honestly didn't feel like refusing him. "I'd like that."

That hum of approval rumbled from his chest again, and I squirmed in my seat. Niko reappeared with his card, but Van still didn't let me go. He sorted the receipt and tucked his card back away, entirely one-handed.

"Ready?" he asked, fierce amber eyes meeting mine.

I nodded and he released me so we could both stand. Van diligently pushed his chair back into the table, then did the same to mine before offering me his arm. I took it graciously and with no small amount of butterflies in my stomach. That one simple move screamed so much about his character. I badly wanted to believe he was the person he seemed to be, but I had been wrong about judging character and intent before. *So very wrong.*

"So, Camellia, I have a very important question for you," Van whispered as we began our walk toward the condo I shared with Preston.

"What's that?" I looked up at him, absently recognizing–and adoring–how his height and size made me feel both small and safe.

"Am I going to have to keep communicating with you through the notes in your online ordering system?"

I laughed loudly and squeezed his arm. "I mean, I have grown rather fond of your notes."

"I see." His pleased smile felt like a gift all its own. "What if I promise to continue leaving you notes, but you also give me your number?"

That imperious brow raise made another appearance, and I giggled again. "I think I can live with that compromise."

"I'm glad."

I shivered as we walked, my dress doing little to stop the late-night chill. Van noticed–*because of course he did*–and immediately stopped to remove his suit jacket and drape it over my shoulders. He faced me as he did, looking down into my eyes as he straightened the collar to make sure I was covered, then rubbed his hands along my upper arms.

"Thank you," I said softly, captivated by his gaze.

"You're welcome."

He reached up, brushing a gentle thumb along my cheekbone before cupping my face in one large, warm hand.

"I've wanted to kiss you since the first moment I saw you in my office, with your head thrown back while you laughed."

"Oh," I breathed.

He'd asked me out that same day, so I'd known he was interested. But hearing him mention that moment as though it was seared into his memory gave it considerably more weight.

Van's hand was heavy on my neck and jaw. He stepped closer, bringing our bodies flush together, his gaze never wavering from mine.

"I'm going to kiss you now, *bella*."

"O-okay," I managed before his lips collided with mine.

I've made out with a handful of people, but all of those experiences paled compared to the masterful way Van owned my body with a single kiss. His hand on the side of my neck directed me as he pressed our lips together, his other arm winding around my waist to hold me firmly against him. I reached up and grasped his biceps, anchoring myself as his tongue swept across my lip and I opened for him.

He groaned in approval as he explored my mouth, and my knees went weak. I sagged against him, and he held me up as he deepened the kiss, tilting my head for better access as he did. It was as though I was clay in his hands, and he was more than willing to shape me to exactly what he wanted. *How is this so fucking hot?!*

I was breathless, my chest heaving and my fingers clutching onto him for dear life, by the time he slowly released my lips. I stared up at him, no doubt flushed and kiss-swollen, as he drank in my features.

"You are simply breathtaking, Camellia," he whispered. "I don't think I can get enough of you."

"I'm okay with that," I murmured, pressing myself more firmly against him. Whether I did so out of sheer desire or because my legs still weren't working, I wasn't sure.

I could feel his arousal like a steel rod against my belly, and it inspired far too many salacious ideas. He groaned, bringing his forehead down to rest against mine.

"Tell me I can take you out again this week."

Um, yes, please. I need more of this in my life. "You can take me out again this week."

He growled–*seriously, I always thought the growling was just a thing that happened in romance novels*–and kissed me again, this time slower, more deliberately. He fitted our lips together and teased first my upper lip, then my lower, his teeth putting just enough pressure to make their presence known. There was dominance in that kiss, and I liked it. Maybe too much.

When he pulled back, he studied my face before tucking my hair behind my ear, his fingers lingering on my neck before falling away. He pressed a kiss to my forehead and dropped his hand from my face, but kept his other arm tight around me as he fished something out of his pocket. He held his phone up to unlock it, then handed it to me.

"Add your number, then text yourself so you have mine," he ordered.

I found myself all too willing to comply. I quickly typed in my number, then shot myself a text. When I was done, I boldly slipped the phone right back into his pants pocket. Van growled again and leaned down to kiss my neck, his stubble feeling delicious against my skin.

"Are we close to your condo?" he asked, face still buried against my neck and one hand rubbing my back through his coat.

"Just another couple of blocks."

He straightened reluctantly. "Perfect. I'm going to get you home before you freeze, then I want you to text me when you get up to your place."

"Okay."

I felt conflicted over how much I liked him telling me what to do, despite typically hating that kind of behavior from men.

With Van Costa wrapped around me, it just hit differently.

Chapter 6

Cami

"One sec!" I shouted toward the door as I rushed down the hall, still settling my sundress on my hips.

I'd been getting dressed when a delivery person buzzed the condo a few moments ago. I'd let them in the building and, based on the knock I'd just heard, they'd reached the condo door faster than expected.

"Coming!" I called again, swinging the door open quickly. "Oh, holy crap."

"Yeah, this one's a stunner," the *floral* delivery guy agreed over the top of the largest flower arrangement I'd ever seen. "You C. Rivera?"

"Sure am. Who are these from?"

"Bayview Floral." He motioned to the logo on his shirt. "You want more specifics than that, you'll have to read the card."

"Oh, right. Of course. Um..." I stared at the arrangement of flowers he held, not entirely sure I could take them from him without making a complete fool of myself. It was oversized, to say the least.

"I can put them somewhere for you?" he offered. "Just show me where."

I huffed a grateful sigh. "Yeah, okay, that would be great. Thanks so much." I turned and led him into the condo, calling over my shoulder, "They'll look good on the island, I think."

He followed me in and set the arrangement on the island gently, stepping back to check the placement. He tweaked the position of the large ceramic vase–a statement piece of its own– then smiled sheepishly.

"It's one of the best I've seen, honestly."

"You're not kidding. It's gorgeous." I leaned closer to catch the sweet fragrance of the flowers, recognizing camellias and peonies.

"Well, I'll see myself out." The delivery guy pointed over his shoulder at the door.

"Oh, thank you!" I trailed after him as he headed toward the door, glancing back over my shoulder at the arrangement as I went.

After I closed the door and locked it, I whipped my phone out as I spun back toward the kitchen.

> Me: Did you send me flowers?

> Pres: Um, no. Why? Do we have an anniversary I'm unaware of? If so, rude.

I snorted and shook my head at her ridiculous and incredibly speedy reply. *Who the heck is sending me flowers on a random Sunday?* There was an envelope on a bamboo stick nestled in the mass of pale pink and white flowers. I plucked it out and removed the card inside. It was thick cardstock with a luxurious feel and had "Bayview Floral" embossed on the front in metallic gold. Inside the card was one line, the handwriting elegant and vaguely familiar.

See you soon, fiorellino.

The lightbulb went on in my head and I released a surprised laugh. *Talk about going overboard! This guy is too much.* My phone buzzed from where I'd left it on the island. I saw a text notification pop up and went to grab it.

> Van: I would have been more specific, but we didn't set plans last night.

How the fuck...

> Me: Good morning!

> Van: Good morning, bella. I got a delivery receipt from Bayview; did you get my gift?

> Me: They're gorgeous! 😍 Thank you so much

> Van: YOU are gorgeous. They are simply flowers.

> Me: Gorgeous flowers 😚

> Van: I'm glad you like them.

I bit my lip and shook my head. My stomach flipped, as though I needed another reminder of how charmed I was.

> Me: I do, very much

> Van: Excellent. I'll pick you up at 7pm on Friday.

I blinked at my phone. While I remembered agreeing to go out with him again next week, I had zero recollection of setting a time or date. *Didn't he just say we didn't set plans?* Regardless, I was free Friday.

> Me: Friday's perfect

> Van: Good. I'll see you tomorrow at lunch.

Before I could fully process what he meant, my phone rang. Preston's face flashed across the screen just before I answered.

"Do you have a stalker?" she asked immediately.

"We really need to work on your phone manners, Pres."

"Hi, Cami, great to see you. I'm fab, thanks for asking. Now, are you being stalked?"

"Why would you think that?" I laughed.

"You sent that cryptic question about flowers and I saw the delivery guy on the security camera. That arrangement was fucking huge." Her voice was rising and falling as she spoke; I guessed she was at the gym.

"I don't have a stalker. Why is that your first thought? Should I be worried?"

"God, I hope not. You know, just comes with the whole media darling territory. I've had to deal with a few."

"What the hell, Pres, how did I not know about this? Recently?"

She blew out a heavy breath and the background hum reduced, as though she'd stepped away from a treadmill or something. "Yeah. I mean, I don't want to freak you and Parker out. There's a reason I have security."

"You mean the cameras and stuff?"

"Yeah, and a security team member or two."

"Preston!"

"What?"

"This is information your *best friend and roommate* should know."

"I pay them to keep us safe and I ask them to stay out of sight because fuck that drama. The point is, we're safe. Besides, it's been a little while and all the former creeps were dealt with."

"Well, that sounds ominous as hell. What does *that* mean?!"

"Don't worry about it. I just wanted to make sure you didn't have a stalker issue."

"No, Preston, I don't have a stalker issue. But I might have a best friend issue if you don't spill."

"Huh, as your best friend, I can confirm there's no issue. So I guess we're good!" She was a master of deflection, and she pressed on in a sing-song before I could interject. "Were those pretty flowers from Van, Cami?"

"Maybe," I mumbled through my grin.

"OH. EM. GEE!" she squealed. "Girl, did you climb that and not tell me? You clearly made an impression."

"For fuck's sake, Pres, *no*," I choked on a laugh. "I did not climb that."

"Pity." I could hear the pout in her voice.

"You *would* think so," I chuckled, rolling my eyes.

"Does this mean you're going to see him again?"

"Friday." I picked up the card from the arrangement and rubbed my thumb over the note, feeling the indentations left behind by the pen. "I think he went to the florist and wrote this card himself, Pres."

"What? Why?"

"I've seen some of his files in his office. The handwriting is the same."

She whistled. "That's some next-level shit, Cam. I fucking love it. You deserve someone over the top."

"Do I?" I murmured absently, staring down at the card. I'd read plenty of over-the-top characters in my romance novels and I could admit they held a certain...appeal. At least on the page.

"Yes. You do. I gotta go to pilates class, so I'm gonna run. Don't get all in your head about what this shit with Van means, Cami."

"I–"

"Nope, don't protest or whatever. I don't want to hear it. There's nothing to get in your head about yet, anyway. Enjoy his ridiculous affections and just let it happen."

I scoffed and nodded. "Okay, I'll try."

"Do better than try. Bye, babe."

She hung up before I could respond, as was her way. I glanced at the notifications I hadn't seen while I'd been on the phone and noticed I had a new order in my online system. *Van, you persistent man.* I clicked open the order and smiled like a fool when I noticed there was plenty of text in the notes.

Thank you for a lovely evening. Did I mention I'm the oldest of four? They all live in New Jersey–Elena, Lucia, and Enzo. You strike me as an oldest sibling, too. But the real question, bella... what do I get if I'm right?

As though simply mentioning my family could summon them into existence, my phone buzzed once more and chased away the tingle of anticipation Van's question had inspired.

> Cris: We're 15 out. You setting up?

I glanced at the time and yelped–if I didn't get a move on, I'd be late. Helping my family at the farmer's market on the weekends was a nearly sacred tradition. I had only missed setup once or twice since I had moved away for undergrad, but my father would never let me forget every infraction.

> Me: Of course! I'll meet you there. Tell Dad to drive safe

All I got in reply was a thumbs-up emoji, but that was my

little brother for you. I grabbed my *Rivera Family Farms* apron off the hook in the hall and shoved it into my oversized purse, then hustled out the door.

While it was tradition, the farmer's market wasn't necessary for my family's business. We had established buyers in the area who accounted for most of our sales, but the market was a great way to connect with others in the community. It was also the Rivera family training ground–every single one of my aunts, uncles, and siblings had all spent time leading the stand, myself included.

It was a bright, breezy day as I made my way toward Gilman Street. The better the weather, the busier the outdoor market would be. The further I got from the condo and Van's beautiful gift, the more I questioned my memory of the night before–getting in my head just as Preston knew I would. Yes, he'd been a complete gentleman, despite his occasionally naughty remarks, and he'd kissed me–more than once–and sent me flowers. But would someone like me be the best fit for someone like him?

I tried to picture Van Costa, in his immaculate and likely custom-made suits, at the market. I almost snorted at the image of him sampling peaches and plums, bent at the waist to let the juices drip to the ground. It was a favorite pastime of mine and the best way to enjoy stone fruit when it was in season. I couldn't picture him being comfortable in that environment, let alone helping run the farm stand with me. By the time I neared the market, the feeling our worlds were far too disparate to be united had deepened.

"Camellia!"

I snapped out of my musings and looked toward the sharp voice that had called out. My father waved from the truck, pulling up to the market as I arrived.

"Morning, Dad!" I called, giving him a wave. "Morning, Cris."

"Hey, Cami," Cris mumbled, throwing me a couple of fingers in greeting. *So generous, little brother.*

"We'll see you at the stand. Check-in for us," my father ordered.

"Of course!" I waved again as they pulled away.

My parents were hard-working people. They met in Ukiah when my mother started working on my dad's family farm. Despite the power imbalance and resistance from both of their families, they persevered and married young–both barely in their twenties. As their firstborn, I was taught the business from the time I was a toddler. Some of my earliest memories were of tractors or picking fragile fruit in the fields. My life had always revolved around food, whether I was helping my father plant and harvest it or cook it in my mother's kitchen. When I went to college, they expected me to get my degree, and then return to Ukiah to begin taking over the family business.

But undergrad, and meeting Preston and Parker, had opened my eyes to a whole new world of possibility I never had the freedom to consider. I told Preston about my family and the farm and even took her home for some holidays. She knew what was expected of me, but she was also the first person to hear the story and then immediately ask me what I wanted.

I could still remember how that question had affected me. The panic and fear that had filled me, coupled with the over-whelming excitement of what could be, was chased by a twinge of sadness at the realization she was the only person who had given me the opportunity to answer for myself.

I loved my parents dearly. They were honest, good-hearted people and loved me and my two siblings dearly. But they both came from cultures where children were expected to respect and serve their elders. They had never dreamed of something other than what they knew, so they never thought their children might do otherwise.

"Morning, Cami!" a bright voice called.

I smiled warmly as I walked up to the registration desk at the market office. "Hey, Becky! Just checking in for Rivera."

"Of course, love, I've got you all sorted. Saw you coming a mile away." She beamed up at me.

"Thanks, girlie. Give my best to Aaron and the kiddos, yeah?"

"You got it. Say hi to that pops of yours. Remind him he can check in sometimes too, yeah?"

I laughed. "Oh, I'll let you remind him of that one."

She snorted knowingly and waved me off, turning to the next person in line. I moved through the people setting up their stands and made my way over to where Cris and Dad were setting out our offerings for the day.

"The eggplants are still in the truck, Cami," Dad called by way of greeting.

"Okay, Dad." I pulled out my apron and put my bag under the table where Cris was setting up the register. It was always my job to take care of the transactions, while my dad and siblings would bag produce and answer customers' questions.

I hustled over to the truck to start unloading the eggplant, quickly falling into a familiar rhythm. We'd all done this dance so many times it came as naturally as breathing.

"The avocados are lovely this week," I commented to my father as I helped him set up the final crate.

He grunted. "The trees are faring well. I'm disappointed in the lemons right now, but your mother says they're improving."

"They look a little small, but they're dense." I lifted one, feeling the heft. I rubbed a thumb along the rind to test the feel and try to determine thickness. "They don't feel dry or anything."

"They could be better."

That was my father's mantra–it could be better. And my mother's, ever since I could remember–it could be worse. They were a mildly infuriating pair to be sandwiched between, as we kids often were. But they typically balanced each other out, in the end.

"Customers incoming," Cris called from the front of the stand.

I patted my father's shoulder and moved toward the register, smiling at the people who wandered up to inspect what we had on offer.

"Try a plum." I nodded at the small basket to the side of the table, topped by a "free samples" sign. "They're in season and absolutely divine."

The woman grinned. "Oh, I'll definitely take you up on that." She moved over and picked up a plum, then took a bite. Her eyes widened, and she immediately leaned forward as the juice dribbled down her chin.

I laughed and held out a paper towel. "The best way to enjoy them, right?"

She giggled and nodded as she wiped her face. "That's amazing. I'll take two containers. My kids will go through them in a day."

"Wise choice. Anything else strike your fancy?"

She nodded and pointed out a few more things as Cris dutifully gathered everything up.

"Need any bags?" I asked.

"Nope!" She held up a couple of canvas bags.

"Perfect. Cris will get you all bagged up while I check you out."

"Thanks so much."

I totaled her order and processed her card, then sent her on her way with a smile.

"You're so good with them," Cris muttered as he fiddled with the avocado display.

"The customers?"

He grunted, sounding so like my father I almost did a double take.

"It's called politeness and being kind, Cris." I nudged his shoulder with mine. "It's not hard."

"People are hard," he retorted. "Peopling is harder."

I wrapped my arm around his shoulders and sighed, giving him a squeeze. He'd always been a quiet kid, more at home with his nose in a book than in any social situation. I knew market days were a mild form of torture for him, but maybe it wasn't as mild as I'd thought.

"The plums will be popular. Maybe go organize the refill produce so we can get at them easier?"

He shot me a grateful look and a tiny smile, then ducked to the back of the stand to work in peace.

"Six months to go, Camellia." My father came up behind me and clapped a hand on my shoulder.

I nodded. That ticking clock was loud in my head, too. "Yep! A whole half a year."

"You could come home earlier," he offered.

"Thanks, Dad, but I want to see this time through. Camellia's Kitchen is important to me." I knew he'd offer, and he knew I'd refuse.

"How's your little trolley doing?"

While I was familiar with his dismissive tone, it still made my heart pinch to hear it.

"Really well, actually. I've broken into a few high-profile businesses recently and orders have ramped up a lot. I might have to hire someone—"

"Doesn't make sense to hire someone for only six months, Camellia. Don't be silly."

I snapped my mouth shut and took a calming breath.

"Your mother and I have indulged your big city dreams enough," he said, his voice hard. "It's time for you to come home and start stepping up at the farm. We agreed to give you five years after you graduated for you to do what you wanted down here. Five years, Camellia." He pinned me with a stern look. "Not a day more."

My eyes burned, hot tears threatening. I swallowed and blinked them back with a watery smile, turning to the customer who had just stepped up and putting my father's conversation to the side. He wouldn't begrudge me the choice–he only took the time to talk to me because there was a lull in traffic to the stand. I knew what my parents wanted and expected of me, but I couldn't help but wish they would care enough to ask me the same question Preston had.

Here, in the farm stand, with my father's expectations front and center, Van felt a million miles away. Last night was fun. Wonderful. Magical, even. But a man like Giovanni Costa lived a life essentially incompatible with mine. My father had delivered an ice bucket of reality to counter the fantasy Van had conjured. *How could a man like that fit in a world like mine?*

Chapter 7

Van

I had never been one to note the passage of time. What was the point? The minutes ticked by the same way every day, regardless. And yet, time had never moved as slowly as it did on Monday morning.

"Is that an excuse?" I barked at the associate who had called to give an update on their latest pursuit. While he stuttered an answer, I drummed my fingers against my desk.

"Take a breath, Stephenson. Regulatory changes happen. It's your job to pivot, not panic. Call me back when you have a plan."

I hung up before he could respond, then caught myself checking the time on my laptop to find it had been a mere three minutes since the last time I'd looked. I scoffed at myself, frustrated. *How did she get under my skin so quickly?*

Needing a distraction, I walked from my office and headed to the kitchen. To my chagrin, Miles was busy at the espresso machine. He glanced up as I entered and shot me a wide grin.

"You know, boss man, this is your most significant contribution to this place." He patted the Italian espresso machine fondly. "Lex told me this baby was your doing."

"It was. Lex is too practical; she was going to buy one of those single-serving machines."

He clutched his chest in dramatized horror. "No, not a single-serving coffee machine!"

I side-eyed him but didn't call him on the drama. "I can't work without espresso. It was an obvious solution."

"Of course, very obvious. Why wouldn't we drop ten grand on a coffee maker?"

My side-eye turned to an outright glower. "To be clear, because you like to stir shit and I'm not in the mood, I paid for this. Me, Davenport. Not Athena."

He choked on the sip of coffee he'd just taken. "You're shitting me." Wide-eyed, he looked back and forth between me and the machine. "That's some serious dedication to caffeine, Van."

Moving to the cabinet, I pulled out an espresso cup and grunted. "Worth it."

"I certainly hope so." He patted my shoulder and waltzed out of the kitchen.

I pinched the bridge of my nose and set my cup under the spout before selecting a double espresso and starting the machine. As the cup filled, my mind wandered to Saturday night. I'd submitted my lunch order Sunday morning while texting with Cami, hoping she'd answer my question right away. But she'd been silent since our brief exchange about the flowers. I was annoyed at myself for being ruffled by it.

Women didn't tie me up in knots. The few relationships I'd maintained in the past had been almost contractual in their specificity. We each had something we were looking to accomplish, whether professionally or in terms of public image, and we'd been able to achieve that together. Dates had been high profile and intentionally visible, carefully curated to serve our social agendas. If we slept together, then it was just that. Two consenting adults meeting their baser needs, nothing more.

My madre hadn't met any of them either, at my insistence. *But I want her to meet Cami.* I could picture the two of them in the kitchen, talking about food and family. My madre would adore her. She'd look at me with a knowing smile and nod, congratulating me on my perfect choice. The imagined scene was so idyllic I could feel emotion sitting hot and uncomfortable in my chest.

Clearing my throat, I found my coffee ready. I picked up the cup and turned back toward my office, checking my watch as I did. *Only ten minutes? This is fucking ridiculous.* I was going to have to find more associates to berate to distract my mind until lunchtime.

———

A soft knock drew my attention away from the article I was reading about an exceptionally interesting startup. I looked up to find Cami leaning against my door with a smile too wide to be natural, my lunch in hand.

"Cami, come in."

She did, but something was...off. Her usual energy was muted, her smile forced. I had thought after our date and text exchange the day before, she would have been as happy to see me as I was to see her.

"Are you alright, *bella*?" Walking around my desk to close my office door, I turned back to watch her set the sandwich and salad I had ordered next to my laptop.

"Long day." She shrugged.

"I see." I slid my arms around her, pulling her to me. Her quiet gasp reached my ears as she raised her arms to make room for me. She froze, arms raised, as I wrapped myself around her.

"Give in," I murmured into her hair. "Let me hold you."

Her breath shuddered out of her as she rose on her tiptoes

and wrapped her arms around me, finally returning my embrace. I hummed my approval, bending to press my face into the curve of her neck, inhaling the sweet vanilla scent of her. She was stiff for a few more moments, then melted against me, molding her body to mine.

"Thank you," I mumbled, my lips against her skin.

She shivered in my hold, her head moving to the side to give me more access. I made a slow path up the side of her neck, pressing open-mouthed kisses to her warm skin between gentle nips and light flicks of my tongue. By the time my lips met her jaw, she let out a quiet whimper.

"Van..."

"Yes?"

"Please..."

The fire that poured through me at that word on her lips was an inferno. My cock, which started to swell the moment I had her in my arms, hardened instantly as I groaned.

"Tell me what you want, Camellia," I breathed between light kisses.

She whimpered again. I knew being decisive was difficult for her, but I needed her to tell me. I needed to hear what she wanted so I could make her every desire come true.

"I can't give you what you want unless you tell me, *bella*. And believe me," I pressed a kiss to the corner of her lips, then leaned back to bring both hands up to cup her face, "I want to give it to you."

Her arms slid down from around my neck to settle on my waist as she stared up at me, those giant chestnut eyes of hers swimming with too many emotions to name. Her fingers flexed against me as I cradled her face in my hands, waiting. She opened her mouth, and I stilled.

"Kiss me, Gio. Please," she begged, her voice thready.

Fuck. Me. The nickname I hadn't used since middle school

rolled off her tongue like pure sex. I crashed our lips together, dominating the kiss from the start. She opened for me instantly, earning a pleased groan in response. I swept my tongue into her mouth, desperate for her taste. Her fingers clutched against me, pulling me closer, and I released her cheeks so I could run my hands down her sides. I knocked her hands off of me in the process, but as I bent my knees and hoisted her up, she wound them around my neck and her legs around my waist. We stood there, lost in each other, long enough for my arms to tire. Cami pulled back from me, staring down into my eyes as she held my face in her hands.

"Thank you," she whispered.

I shook my head. "Don't thank me for giving you what you want. What you need."

She smiled genuinely then, and something clicked into place. If I hadn't already realized how invested I was in this woman, the rightness in my chest when her happiness shone through would've been all the proof I needed. As I held her there and gazed up into her eyes, I knew there were very few things I wouldn't do to keep Camellia Rivera smiling.

I gently released my hold on her ass, giving her cheeks a squeeze before I did. She giggled as she slid back to her feet, her breath hitching as she pressed against my hard cock. I smirked at her and adjusted myself while she bit her lip, her eyes sparkling in amusement.

"When I'm a bit more presentable, I'm going to take you for a coffee."

She glanced down at my lap quickly, then back up, cheeks rosy and head nodding. "I'd like that. Athena was my last stop today, so I have time."

"Good," I murmured, cupping her face in one hand. I couldn't keep my hands to myself around her, and she seemed willing to let me satisfy the irrational urge for constant contact. "I'm very happy to see you, *bella*."

"I noticed." She looked down again as I laughed.

"Minx," I teased.

She gasped, throwing a hand up to her chest in fake indignation. "Well, I never!"

I chuckled, running my hands down her upper arms and then pulling her to me for another hug. *I've never hugged anyone this much in my life. Who the fuck am I?*

She leaned right into it with a happy little sigh and my heart panged.

"I think it's safe." I pulled back and winked at her, then moved to grab my jacket from the back of my chair.

"Where do you go for coffee around here?"

"Well, usually the kitchen. We have an espresso machine."

"Fancy!" Her eyes lit up.

"Miles would agree with you," I grunted. "Let's go to the place across the street. Parker speaks highly of it."

"Parker's the furthest thing from a coffee snob, but sure," she quipped.

I raised an eyebrow at her. "You know Parker?"

She smiled. "Yep. Remember the business partner I mentioned? That's Preston, his–"

"Twin."

"Yes! Have you met her?" she asked eagerly.

I nodded as I held the door for her, directing her to the elevator bank. "Briefly, at the Feed the Bay gala and a few other events."

"Oh, that's right. So you must know all about Parker and LB."

"You could say that."

The way she looked up at me from beneath her lashes made

me want to stop the elevator and ravish her. "Someday you'll tell me all your stories, Gio."

My cock liked that name on her lips a bit too much. "Only if you tell me all of yours."

That flush flared in her cheeks again, but I was prevented from doing anything about it by the elevator doors opening on the ground level. I held a hand out to keep the doors open as she exited, then settled my hand on her lower back as we crossed first the lobby, and then the street. She smiled as I held the door open for her at the coffee shop, ducking under my arm to enter before joining the modest line.

When we were still a few people back, someone bumped into me from behind. Putting a steadying hand out to make sure Cami was secure, I looked over my shoulder.

"Van Costa?" the middle-aged man asked. "Well, I'll be. What are you doing here?"

"Ethan," I greeted the potential client I'd been courting for months, turning to offer him a hand. "Our office is across the street."

He glanced at my hand briefly, then beamed at Cami.

"Cami, is that you?" he said, clearly pleasantly surprised. *What the fuck?*

"Oh, hi, Ethan! It's been a while; how are you?" Her expression was friendly, and part of me was secretly glad it looked nothing like the ones she gave me in greeting. *But why the fuck do they both look so pleased to see each other?*

"Well, right at the moment, I'm a bit baffled. Are you two here together?"

Cami flashed one of her warm smiles up at me and nodded. "Yes, Van's buying me a coffee. Then I've got to go back up to Athena to collect my trolley."

"Ah, how is the catering business?"

I looked back and forth between the two of them, trying to

piece together their connection. Ethan Masters owned a couple of different businesses in the Bay, and he'd recently started a new project Athena was very interested in. But he had yet to give me the time of day, so I hadn't been able to broach the terms of a deal, let alone close one.

"Really well!" Cami answered. "I've been just busy enough lately."

"That's great news. I'm probably headed up to Ukiah for a visit here soon. Do you make it home often these days?" Ethan asked.

Cami glanced my way, then reached down and took my hand in hers, squeezing it as she replied. "Every few weeks. I was at the market with Dad and Cris yesterday, like usual."

"It's been too long since I've been to the market. I'll have to stop by." Ethan looked shrewdly between the two of us for a moment. "I have to say, Cami, I'm surprised to see you with someone like Van Costa."

Her brow furrowed, and I wanted to punch him for it. I didn't care what he said about me; the man was notorious for instigating arguments for the fun of it. Unfortunately for me and everyone else in the industry, neither class nor tact were required to succeed in business.

"What do you mean, someone like him?"

Ethan laughed as though it was obvious. "A suit." He gestured at me, as though my very existence was explanation enough as to why we shouldn't be there together.

Cami laughed off the insult, but I could tell she was uncomfortable. "I think you forget who my business partner and her brother are, Ethan. I've been in with the 'suits' for years." She snuggled into my side and wrapped her arm around me, placing a hand on my torso. "And I happen to think Van's one of the best of them."

I wrapped my arm around her and squeezed her to me, smiling down into her eyes.

"I've certainly never seen that expression on his face," Ethan taunted. "I must say, Van, she does bring out the best in you."

I shrugged. "You're not wrong."

He narrowed his gaze for a moment, assessing me. I was comfortable in silence, so I waited him out, my arm still around Cami.

"Tell you what, Van. I know you've been trying to get on my calendar for a while." He looked between the two of us again, a calculating smile on his face. "Let's do happy hour sometime soon. Bring Cami."

I looked down at Cami, waiting for her answer. She tightened her arm around me, giving reassurance, then turned to Ethan with a bright smile.

"Sounds great, Ethan. It'll be fun to catch up."

I squeezed her to me then bent to press a kiss into her hair, uncaring we had an audience. If he was going to drag Cami into something that should be just business, I was going to make it very clear what she was to me. *Mine.*

Ethan eyed me as I straightened, the claiming gesture not lost on him. "It will, indeed, Cami. It will, indeed."

Chapter 8

Cami

"Go with the green one," Preston instructed, pointing over my shoulder at the dress in my closet.

"Can't. That's the one I wore last week."

"Never mind," she mumbled, flicking through the options. She narrowed her eyes in suspicion. "Isn't this technically your second date in a week?"

"Technically?" I pretended to think about it, then grinned at her. "Yes."

She nudged her shoulder against mine. "You like him."

"I barely know him," I demurred.

"You guys talked for literal hours on your first date. And you've seen him almost every day at Athena. He's no stranger." She pulled a black jumpsuit from the back of my closet and held it up. "Where the hell did this come from?"

"You," I laughed, taking it from her and shoving it back in the closet. "It's itchy."

She snorted. "No shit, it's lace. And not the good kind. Why do you still have it?"

I shrugged. "You gave it to me."

Her look turned incredulous. "It was a cast-off from a shoot."

"Yeah, but still."

"You are too kind for this world, sweet girl," Preston scoffed, diving back into my closet.

"If you say so."

"This one!" She pulled a floral sundress out with a triumphant shout. "It's perfect. He sends you enough flowers that you could make a replica with the real thing."

I giggled, blushing. Her suggestion, while farfetched, wasn't as impossible as it sounded. Van had sent another massive floral arrangement this morning, with an almost equally brief note in what I was 90% sure was his handwriting: *Can't wait to see you.*

The feeling is mutual, Gio.

"Okay. Think it's nice enough?" I asked, giving the dress a critical look.

"Where's he taking you?"

"He hasn't said, actually. Just mentioned cocktail attire."

"Hold up, he volunteered the dress code?" She turned to face me, eyebrow arched in surprise.

I nodded. "I was as shocked as you are. I didn't even ask."

"Weird," she muttered. "Well, that's more summer party than cocktail. Do you have an LBD?"

I cocked my head at her.

"Little black dress, Cami, come on. It's like you're an alien sometimes."

"Being from the country does not make me E.T." I pinched her arm, making her squeal.

"Okay, okay! I take it back!"

"You better. What about the navy one?" I pointed at a simple blue dress.

She pulled it out and held it in front of me. "Nice cleavage, but not short enough to be slutty. Luxe material. It's cute. Where's this from?" She held it up in front of herself. "I like it."

"Also you." I scowled playfully and snatched it from her. "No take-backsies."

"Fine, fine." Preston threw her hands up in surrender and stepped back. "You have shoes, or do you need me to dig through that pile, too?"

I looked at the dress for a long moment. "Would my black pumps work?"

"With that? Totally."

"Then I'm good. But you're on hair and makeup duty in twenty when I get out of the shower."

"Ugh!" Preston sighed and flopped dramatically back onto my bed, one arm flung over her face. "You're such a taskmaster! How am I supposed to work under these conditions?!"

I laughed and smacked her feet. "You're ridiculous. Get up, go on, get outta here. I gotta get ready."

"Fine," she whined, rolling off the bed and dragging herself out of the room.

Hurrying into the bathroom, I started the shower and stripped out of my work clothes. It had been the biggest week ever for Camellia's Kitchen. My orders at Athena had steadily been growing, as were the ones at several other offices on different floors in their tower. My lunch business was now exclusive to their building because the sheer volume of orders per office meant I couldn't possibly serve them all *and* add another stop to my route before the lunch rush ended. I still had room to grow my evening and weekend catering business, but lunches proved so lucrative I'd invested little time in expanding that customer base. I adored my few regulars and wanted to keep it that way.

As I stepped under the water, I thought back to Monday. I'd been ready to tell Van he should move on from me after the wake-up call my father had delivered. But, somehow, Van had instantly known something was wrong and had wrapped himself around me so thoroughly that all I could smell, see, or think about was him. And it had been all too easy to give in when he held me and asked me so earnestly what I wanted.

We still came from different worlds and I still had the ticking clock of my familial obligation in my head, but I was cautiously willing to put it all aside for the moment. I loved being around him, loved being the center of his attention. Having a man like Van interested in me was a unique and thrilling experience, one I knew I needed to make the most of. How long our moment would last, I didn't know.

From what I'd seen online and what Parker had shared, Van didn't do long-term relationships. He'd had a few very public, brief dalliances with society darlings and powerhouse businesswomen in the Bay, but none had seemed to progress past a few public appearances. And Parker was certain there was no secret love in his life. Knowing that, I was curious where he saw us going–would I be something to show off, then cast aside? He hadn't given me the impression he was manipulative, but I'd been wrong enough about men in the past to have little faith in my ability to judge character.

I stepped out of the shower, thoroughly clean, though my mind was still spinning. As I toweled dry, I tried to find equilibrium within my thoughts. There was plenty I didn't know about Van and where we were headed, but I could only anchor on what I knew: I felt seen, heard, and valued when I was with him. And that would have to be enough for now.

"Pres! Get in here! I need you to beautify me!" I called.

"Shut up," she snapped, breezing into my bathroom so quickly I knew she'd been lurking in my room. "You could go like that and you'd still be one of the most beautiful people there."

"Sopping wet and in a towel? Really Pres?"

"Whatever. Take the compliment or leave it. You know I only speak truth."

My lips twitched. "You know what? Van said something similar last week."

Preston's gaze flew up to meet mine in the mirror. "So, the Italian Stallion has game. Lucky bitch."

I barked a laugh as she started blow-drying my hair. "You're ridiculous."

"You love me."

"True."

"What fear spiral were you processing in the shower?"

I choked on my saliva. "Excuse me?"

"Girl, we've been roommates for almost a decade. I know you process pretty much everything in the shower, and you're a worrier under that shiny, happy exterior. So, there's always plenty to process."

"Sometimes having you as a friend is exhausting," I complained.

"Don't I know it. So, did you talk yourself back into seeing Van?"

I reached around and smacked her hip. "Stay out of my head. Some things should be internal."

"I mean, okay. But you and Parker are the same. You think you can figure it all out by yourselves, so you don't bring me in until things have already gone to shit. And then it's a big old mess I could've prevented in the first place." She worked quickly while she talked, curling my hair with a round brush while she dried it.

I rolled my eyes at her. "Let me guess, Parker would've saved himself a lot of pain if he'd come to you sooner about his relationship."

"Exactly. So much unnecessary angst. Don't be like my brother. Put me to better use."

"I maintain that you're ridiculous."

She sighed heavily and shook her head. "The world's just not ready for me."

"That's the damn truth," I agreed.

I appreciated her offer, but everything with Van felt too new. And my processing, as Preston put it, was also wrapped up in my family stuff, and I knew where she stood on all of that. As much as she loved and supported me, Preston would never understand why I would consider putting my dreams to the side for my parents. She'd told me numerous times I should just tell them to take their five-year deal and shove it. If I told her I was having a hard time reconciling my future with Van's present, she'd roll her eyes and tell me there was an easy solution. And maybe for her, with her broken family and challenging parental relationships, that would be true. But it wasn't going to be easy for me to navigate my wants and my parents' expectations.

"Earth to Cami. Am I going full glam or glam light with the makeup?"

I blinked up at her. "Sorry, spaced. Um, is there a natural option?"

She groaned and poked my side. "You. Are. No. Fun."

I shrugged. "I yam who I yam."

"You and the food puns, I simply cannot." She shook her head as she grabbed a makeup brush.

"It's not like I'm raisin them every day. I don't know what the problem is."

"Stop it. And you call me ridiculous."

"You are. But olive you anyway."

"You! Say one more ridiculous thing and I'm accidentally stabbing your eye with the eyeliner."

"Doesn't sound like much of an accident," I accused through my smile.

She grinned at me, and I felt some of the tension ease from my shoulders. We may have been from opposite worlds, but Preston knew me better than most. Maybe better than anyone.

"Alright, that's it. You look one hundred percent fuckable."

"Preston!" I snorted.

"What? You do! And you didn't even need me to get there, but I certainly helped." She teasingly fluffed her hair. "When is Romeo getting here?"

"Um, he said seven."

She glanced at her phone and grimaced. "You've got approximately two minutes to shimmy that ass into your dress."

"Shit!"

———

I fidgeted in my seat next to Van in the back of his hired car. After rushing around my room like a headless chicken, I'd had to send Preston to greet him at the door when he arrived perfectly on time. He'd patiently waited the few minutes it had taken me to throw on jewelry and slip on my shoes, and Pres had hustled us out the door with an exaggeratedly mouthed "OH MY GOD" of appreciation. I had to admit, he looked exceptionally gorgeous tonight in yet another tailor-made suit, his dark hair freshly cut and styled to perfection.

"Where are you taking me?" I asked, peeking out the window as we paused at yet another light.

"Atelier Laurent, have you been?"

I couldn't stop the surprised laugh that tumbled from my lips. I'd heard of the place, because it was the latest restaurant opened by a local celebrity chef, and it had just earned its third Michelin star.

"Uh, no. Isn't the waitlist like six months long?"

His smug smile made my belly flip. "More like a year. I called in a favor."

"You know Maxime Laurent?"

He nodded. "He's a client."

"Oh, wow. I didn't realize Athena invested in the restaurant scene."

"We manage a diverse portfolio. Potential is everywhere." He smiled warmly and reached down to thread his fingers through mine. "Especially in the kitchen."

I flushed, pleased by his subtle praise. Not everyone saw the value in a small, food-based business. It was refreshing that someone who made a living out of finding diamonds in the rough did.

"Ah, here we are. Thank you, Antonio." Van nodded to the driver as he pulled up to the curb. He reached over and unbuckled my seatbelt, whispering into my ear as he did. "Wait right there."

I did as instructed, watching him step confidently from the car. He walked around the trunk and stopped at my door, opening it and offering me a hand.

"Watch your step, *bella*."

The whole charade felt strangely formal, and I swallowed through my discomfort, doing my best to play along.

Van held the glass door open, leading me into the dimly lit establishment. Immediately, I knew this was the nicest restaurant I had ever been to. The dining room was crowded with the types of people you'd see on Wall Street or the Upper East Side in New York City, all seated at white-clothed tables and being served by suited waitstaff.

A slim gentleman in a suit and tie greeted us. "Hello Mr. Costa, Miss Rivera. How are you this evening?" *How did they already know my name? I guess Van told them when he made the reservation?*

Van stepped beside me and nodded. "Yes, we're well, thank you."

"Excellent. Please, allow me to show you to your table."

Once we were seated and given menus, personalized at the top with our names no less, the waiter walked us through the 10-course tasting menu. Van proceeded to order a bottle of red wine for us to share after I insisted he choose. There was no way I was signing us up for a $400 bottle of wine. *How is that the cheapest option on the menu?!* The meal had already added up to more than the city's average rent payment.

"Van, this is all too much! You didn't need to go to such lengths to impress me. I'm pretty sure I'd have to wash dishes in the back for a month to pay for this meal myself!" I hissed in a stage whisper once the waiter left.

Across the table from me, Van only chuckled. "Camellia, you don't need to concern yourself with the cost. We're here because I thought you would enjoy it, and I wanted to bring you." Pausing, he reached across the table and began tracing his fingers up and down my arm comfortingly. "And besides, there isn't an amount I wouldn't spend to have your attention for the next...ten courses," he said with a wink.

At that moment, our waiter approached, holding what looked like a tiny cauldron, complete with smoke rolling out the top. I shot Van a bewildered look before pulling my hand away.

Gesturing to the dish, our waiter explained. "An amuse bouche from the chef this evening to welcome you. You're going to have caramelized foie gras with smoked eel and green apple in the middle. On the bottom, we have a spring onion and cilantro foam."

"Wonderful, thank you," Van replied.

Not wonderful. Not even slightly wonderful.

I swallowed. *What a way to start a meal. How am I going to explain this...*

"Gio. Van, I mean..." I stuttered as I met Van's eyes.

He smiled back at me and small laugh lines appeared in his cheeks, which only flustered me further. "What is it?"

"Um, so it's this small, silly thing you're totally going to judge me for," I muttered sheepishly.

"If it's important to you, it's important to me."

"It's just...I had a pet duck growing up on the farm who was practically my best friend, and there's no way I can eat one now," I rushed out, mortified I had brought Daisy up to this man.

"Oh." Van stared expressionlessly as he processed my words before looking from me to the dish in front of us. "Oh, I see."

I winced. "I'm sorry. Please don't let me stop you. Go ahead."

Van shook his head. "No, absolutely not. Let me get this cleared away." He motioned to the waitstaff and pointed at the dish. "We're done here."

The waiter looked at Van, confused. "Are you certain, sir?"

Van's brows furrowed. "Do I sound uncertain?"

"No, sir. My apologies." The waiter jumped into action to fulfill Van's order.

With the dish removed, Van looked at me apologetically. "Let's hope the next course is more to your liking."

I scrunched my nose. "No other pets, and we'll be fine I'm sure. I promise I'm a total foodie!"

Van barked a laugh at my joke, and I admired the way his normally serious expression shifted. "Yes, no more pets."

The waiter appeared once more. "Sir, miss. For your next course, we have a wild salmon roe in a crust of dried lamb's blood."

Van looked between the dish placed in front of us and my

horrified expression before clearing his throat. "We're done here. You have my card on file, correct?"

I pulled my eyes away from the table and saw the waiter scrambling to figure out what to do next.

"Ah, um, well yes sir, we do."

"Perfect, charge that. Our compliments to the chef, and we'll see ourselves out." Standing, Van held out a hand to me. "Shall we?"

Unable to form words, I nodded and bolted from my chair, allowing Van to lead us out of the restaurant.

What on earth just happened?

Once outside, Van started laughing. Meeting his eyes, he gave me a look that said *"What the fuck was that?"* through his laughter, and my tension melted away as I giggled. *He isn't mad we just wasted a car payment? Who is this man?*

He swiped his hand through his hair before taking his suit jacket off and draping it over his shoulder. Then he held his free arm out for me to take. "I think I've had enough dinner for the evening. How about we skip straight to dessert?"

Taking his arm, I tilted my head up to meet his twinkling eyes. "I'm not sure I trust your food recommendations anymore. What did you have in mind?" I teased.

His lips quirked. "Fair enough. Is ice cream safe?"

"Do I get to pick the flavors? Ooh, I hope they have honeycomb. It's my favorite!"

"Anything but cotton candy."

I stuck my tongue out. "Only a monster would choose cotton candy."

"Right you are. There's an excellent gelateria down the block. We can sit in the park across the street."

Squeezing Van's bicep, I smiled up at him. "That sounds perfect."

I felt Van's answering hum rumble in his chest. "Good. I

was worried you were going to faint if I didn't haul you out of there."

I inwardly cringed. "Faint? No. But I don't frequent fine-dining restaurants and can't say I'm the right person to appreciate some of the more...adventurous dishes on the menu. The best meals I've ever had were served family-style, with produce from the garden, no cauldrons or foam in sight."

Van leaned down and buried his nose into my hair. I felt him smile before he kissed the top of my head. "I completely agree, *fiorellino*."

Chapter 9

Van

"Thank you, Ms. Thompson." I stared out the window in my office, one hand in my pocket and the other holding my phone to my ear. "I'd like to be the one to tell the owner, if you don't mind."

"Oh, sure. That would be...Cami Rivera?" Cassandra Thompson, reporter for the Bay Bulletin, asked.

"That's right. She's stopping by Athena later today; I'll be able to tell her in person."

"That's great, Mr. Costa, thanks. And thank you for sending through the nomination. We'll tag Camellia's Kitchen and the other honorees on social media when we launch the List later this afternoon."

"Perfect. Thanks again for the good news. I look forward to seeing the rest of the List."

"I'll have the courier drop off a few extra copies for your lobby."

"Excellent."

I ended the call and slipped my phone into my pocket. Telling Cami about the little surprise I'd pulled together was going to be the highlight of my day–no, my week. When I'd gotten a deeper glimpse of who Cami was during our first date, and again during our second the other night, I knew I'd do anything in my power to help her succeed. She was the best kind of person and an investor's unicorn–dedicated, passionate, ambitious, with a clear vision for what she wanted to build. She hadn't shared everything with me yet, but I looked forward to hearing and supporting every single dream.

The ping of an incoming email interrupted my thoughts. *I seriously need to turn those notifications off.* I walked back over to my desk and took a seat, mildly surprised to find an email from Ethan Masters at the top of my inbox. After running into him at the coffee shop with Cami, I'd expected him to forget about his happy hour proposal. Instead, it appeared he was reaching out to get the event on the books. His message, with the oh-so-subtle subject line "Happy hour w/ Cami", was brief: he offered two times that worked for him over the next two weeks and suggested a location downtown. Inviting us to what he saw as his turf was no surprise, but I scoffed at the posturing.

As I'd walked Cami back upstairs from coffee the day we'd run into Ethan, she'd explained he had family in Ukiah. He visited regularly for most of his life and knew Cami's parents through his aunt and uncle, who owned a local supply shop. I had no doubt he'd try to make their connection seem deeper than it was to grate on my nerves. The man was addicted to competition, even when it was uncalled for. I, for one, despised that kind of worthless machismo. But I certainly wouldn't mind adding Ethan to Athena's portfolio, so I'd let his antics slide if it meant we'd close a deal.

This could work out nicely, though. I had two things for Cami when she stopped by with lunch: an ask and a gift. I glanced up at the clock and smiled. If I left right then and called Bayview on the way, I'd just have time to sign the card for another flower delivery to her condo before she left to start her deliveries. *After all, congratulations are in order.*

———

A soft knock on my door at 1:03pm had me grinning and immediately rising to my feet. "Come in," I called.

My door opened and Cami stepped through with a smile. I reached her a moment later and swept her into my arms, completely ignoring the sandwich in her hand and crushing her against me. Her soft body against mine was a balm for my soul.

"Gio!" she gasped, laughing. "What's gotten into you?"

"You," I quipped, then captured her mouth in a fierce kiss.

Her answering moan was music to my ears. The way she went completely pliant in my arms made me want to lock my door and lay her out on my desk. I was hungry, but not for the sandwich she held for me. But realizing I was mauling her with the door open, I slowly released her and reached out to push it closed.

"Hi," she whispered, breathless. Her lips were rosy and swollen, and the sight of them made my cock thicken.

"Hi, *bella*."

She blinked and swallowed, visibly gathering herself. "You have some explaining to do, mister."

I smirked. "Oh, do I?"

"Yes. I didn't have time to text you before I left for the lunch rush, but why did I receive another massive, over-the-top Bayview arrangement with a card saying 'congratulations' this morning?" She propped one hand on her cocked hip, the other still casually holding my lunch.

"Hmm, I like this question. I'm going to ask you one before answering, though."

She pouted, her pink lower lip jutting out. I immediately

stepped into her space and bent to grab it gently in my teeth, drawing it out slowly as her breath hitched and she pressed up and into me. I followed my teasing love bite with a slow kiss, then a peck on the nose. When I pulled away, her eyes were glassy and pleasure-drunk.

"You're rather fond of scrambling my brain, aren't you?"

"Quite." My answering grin was feral, I knew, but I couldn't stop it. "You like it."

"You know what?" She gave me a wry grin as her gaze cleared. "I do."

I chuckled and touched my forehead to hers, soaking up her closeness. "Are you free a week from Tuesday?"

She hummed while she considered it. "For you? Yes."

"Remember bumping into Ethan Masters at Daybreak the other day?"

She leaned back and looked up at me, mild confusion on her face. "Of course."

"I didn't expect him to follow through on that offer of happy hour, but he has. While it's a business meeting, he wants you there." I leaned back and ran my hands lightly up and down her upper arms. "Would you be willing to join us?"

Her expression softened as she smiled. "Of course, Gio. If it'll help you, I'm happy to. And Ethan's nice enough." Her casual shrug tamed the jealous beast threatening to rise in my chest.

"Thank you," I murmured, pressing a gentle kiss to her brow.

She wrapped her arms around me and snuggled close, sighing in contentment. I barely heard her reply. "Anything for you."

"Careful, *bella*. Words like those could give a man like me...ideas."

Her eyes sparked in response to my heated look, and she licked her lips. "What kind of ideas?"

Her husky voice went straight to my groin. I wanted to swallow the tiny gasp she gave when my cock hardened between us, pressing firmly against her.

"Ideas we don't have time for right now." I nuzzled her neck. "How about you come to my place for dinner on Friday?"

"Hm, I'd like that," she hummed.

Reluctant to lose the heat of her body but excited to tell her my news, I pulled slowly away and straightened.

"Good. It's a date."

Her answering grin warmed me from the inside out. I held out my hand for my lunch, and she released it with a laugh.

"Can't forget about that," she teased. "It's the reason I'm here!"

"Well," I cocked an eyebrow at her, "not the *whole* reason."

She flushed, that rush of pink in her cheeks sending an answering heat through me. "No, Gio. Not the whole reason."

I cast her a wink, then quickly moved over to deposit the wrapped sandwich on my desk. "Have you gotten any social media notifications recently?"

"What an odd question." I heard the amusement in her voice as I turned to face her, finding her almost close enough to touch already. *As though she wants to be as close to me as I do to her.* "I don't know. I've been making deliveries. Let me check."

She pulled her phone from the pocket of her Camellia's Kitchen apron, her eyebrows shooting up immediately.

"What on earth...?" her voice trailed off as she stared down.

I stepped up so I could see her screen as she opened her profile. There were already dozens of notifications for comments and likes and, buried under the deluge, was a tagging notification from the Bay Bulletin. She clicked it and gasped.

"What...how did...I can't believe..." She glanced up, her eyes wide in what I hoped was excitement but seemed a bit like panic. "The Kitchen–my Kitchen–is on the Best in the Bay list."

"Congratulations, Cami. It's a huge accomplishment."

"It really is," she croaked, staring back down at her phone.

"Are you pleased?" I asked gently, touching a hand to her elbow.

She looked back up at me. "I think I'm still in shock. I didn't even apply. How did..." Her eyes widened in realization. "Did *you* do this?!"

"You have an amazing business, Cami. It deserves recognition."

Her eyes swam with emotion as she sniffed. "Thank you," she choked out, wiping under her eyes quickly. "I appreciate that so much. I do. But it's not an answer."

I tilted my head, wondering if there was a landmine I should be aware of in this conversation. "I sponsored your nomination, yes. And I may have convinced them to extend the deadline a bit so I could."

Her eyes bugged and she gave a shaky laugh. "That's...Gio, that's...wow."

I stepped forward and gripped her upper arms in my hands. "You deserve this, Camellia. It was me who got you on their radar, but it was your product and the testimonials of your customers that got you on the list. I should know–I offered to pay, and they turned me down." My lips twitched up, as she gasped a wild laugh at that bit of information.

"The List is something we target for all our clients in the culinary space. It changes people's careers, launches their businesses." I squeezed her arms and then gathered her in for a hug because I desperately needed to close the distance between us. "You should be so proud of yourself and what you've built."

Her body shuddered, and she sniffled. "Thank you," she

whispered, arms finally rising to wrap around my waist and hug me back.

I shook my head and pressed my lips to her hair. "No thanks necessary, *bella.*" Then, I uttered words I knew it was too soon–by normal standards–to say. *"Farei qualsiasi cosa per te, fiorellino."*

"I don't know what that means." Her voice was quiet and further muffled by my body.

"I know." *You're not ready for that truth.* I stepped back and gave her a soft smile, feeling my heart squeeze in response to the emotion in her gaze. She looked both excited and conflicted, and I had to tamp down my frustration that she wasn't comfortable enough with me to explain her reaction. "What do you need?"

She huffed something that could've been a laugh. "I...I mean, honestly," she stammered, "I need to finish my route and get home to share the news with Pres."

I noticed two things about her response. First, she struggled to frankly communicate her needs. We'd have to work on that. Second, my reaction to her saying she needed someone other than me was completely illogical and unwarranted. Jealousy flared through me, hot and uncomfortable. I wanted her to need me. Wanted it bad enough I felt a physical ache in my gut when she didn't acknowledge that she did. Forcing down the irrational surge of emotion, I nodded and turned to open the door for her. I was mildly surprised to find it cracked. As I pulled it open, Lex stepped through.

"Van." She nodded, then turned to Cami. "Ah, Cami. Lovely to see you. Thank you for dropping my quinoa bowl off."

Cami chuckled and sniffed again, smiling at Lex as she put on a bright smile to mask her emotions. "Of course, Lex. Thanks for being such a loyal customer."

They both laughed at the teasing tone in her voice. Cami

reached out and squeezed my hand, giving me a watery look. "Thank you, Gio," she said, ever so softly.

I returned the squeeze. "You deserve it, *bella*."

With a little wave to both of us, Cami slipped from the room. As Lex turned toward me, I gently pushed my office door closed and leveled her with a hard look.

"Eavesdropping, Lex?"

She leaned against the wall, crossing her arms and nailed me with a pointed look. "I knocked gently, per usual, and opened it when I didn't hear a response. Also, per usual. You were a bit preoccupied with your *guest*, so I shut it most of the way and waited, seeing as we have a meeting you're already late for."

I sighed and scrubbed my hands over my face. "You're right. That was uncalled for."

Her only response was a mild head tilt of agreement, followed by a look of askance.

"How much did you hear?"

"Enough to realize you speak Italian. Are you fluent?"

"I am."

She blinked. "How did I not know that, Van?"

The question was rhetorical, but I answered it anyway. "It hasn't been relevant to our business. My mother and grandmother taught me. I speak it regularly with family."

"Is Cami family?"

She zeroed in exactly where I suspected she might and hoped she wouldn't. I wasn't sure I was ready to crack that internal can of worms just yet. I looked to the closed door, remembering the brush and squeeze of Cami's fingers before she left, and sighed.

"Not yet."

Those expressive eyebrows of hers climbed her face, and she straightened, her arms falling to her sides. "Well, would you look at that."

I scowled, sensing a line of conversation I was not interested in following. "Look at what?"

"You. Feeling something real for someone. For once." A tiny smile started at the corner of her mouth. "Catch me up, Van."

"Not much to share," I huffed. Breaking eye contact was only going to give her more ammunition to push or tease me, but I couldn't help it. My gaze dragged over to the door again, then snapped back to Lex. "We've gone out a few times."

"You've gone out enough to be telling her sweet nothings in Italian in the middle of the workday?"

"How do you know they were sweet nothings?"

"You may have forgotten to share with me you're multilingual, but the languages I speak are in my fucking bio, Van."

I grunted. "Reviewing bios is what we pay the PR team for, *Lex*."

She scoffed a laugh and shook her head, as though she couldn't believe my audacity. I couldn't blame her–I wasn't exactly winning any gold stars as a business partner or friend. And I hadn't decided if I was grateful or annoyed that her exasperation was entirely good-natured.

"You like this girl."

"Was that a question?"

She ignored my attitude, which we both knew I used as armor. "I think it's great."

"You think it's great," I deadpanned.

"I do."

I stared at her for a moment, waiting for her to expand. When she didn't, I knew she was using my own tactic against me and waiting for me to fill the silence. *Touché, boss.*

"And why is it great, Lex?" I played along.

"Because this is a job, not a life, and there has been more life in you for the last couple of weeks than in all the years I've known you. And I can only assume it all started when you spotted that sunshine of a girl across the Pit."

I could feel my eyes widen, surprised I'd been that transparent, before I quickly schooled my expression. Usually, I was the one stripping others bare with my words. So far, Lex was the only person I'd found who could turn around and do the same to me. Her ability to see me, and others, in a way few could was a significant reason I'd agreed to partner with her to open Athena.

Her knowing look in response was gentle. "She's different from your other...arrangements. Isn't she?"

"Fuck off, Lex," I muttered, looking away.

The last thing I wanted to do was get into a detailed conversation about my past relationships. None of them could hold a candle to what I felt for Cami and what I could see building between us.

Lex chuckled and shook her head, knowing me well enough to know pressuring me wouldn't get her anywhere. "Look, Van, we both know I'm no relationship expert. I've had even fewer than you have in the last decade, and that's saying something. But even I can recognize when a good thing comes around. And Cami? For you, she's a very good thing."

Swallowing roughly, I nodded. "I agree. About your qualifications for giving advice, and about Cami." I shot her a wry grin, breaking the tension.

She barked a laugh. "Fair play, my friend. I won't offer advice I'm not qualified to give. But I will tell you one thing."

"What's that?"

Her expression sobered, and she leveled an intense look in my direction. It was her "I mean business" face, and it was effective on just about everyone, including me. I straightened, ready to hear what she had to say.

"That smile you wear around her is something special." She

moved toward the door, clapping a hand on my shoulder as she passed. Once there, she paused, fingers on the door handle, and met my gaze. "You both deserve something good. Don't fuck it up."

Chapter 10

Cami

"Explain to me again why you're so cranky about all this?" Preston stared at me, incredulity painted across her features.

"Because!" I snapped, throwing my arms wide in exasperation. "I don't... Ugh. He had no right!"

"Cam, honey, help me understand this. The hottest man you've ever met–your words, not mine–believes in you and your business so much he pulled strings to get you in the running for one of the most prestigious award lists in the Bay." She paused, eyebrow raised in question and waiting for my confirmation. At my nod, she threw her hands up in the air. "Why is this not a good thing?! We should be popping champagne!"

I wasn't sure I could articulate the emotions running through me in that moment, but I knew Preston wasn't going to let it go. She'd squealed in excitement when I'd rushed home and told her the news, literally jumping up and down in our kitchen while I read off the mini profile published in the List.

The article praised my healthy, flavorful dishes while highlighting our partnerships with local growers. And recognizing the Kitchen's commitment to zero food waste, the author celebrated our program to donate any unsold meals to community shelters. They ended the article by writing that Camellia's Kitchen was "a revolutionary example of how fast food should be done."

"I know I should be excited, Pres, I do. This is amazing."

"It's life-changing shit, Cam."

"I know." I groaned in response to yet another pointed glare. "I know! I do. This is something I would've put on my vision board for the next five years, no question."

Preston scoffed. "But of course, you didn't because you're still going to bottle up your dreams in favor of your parents' backward expectations."

My sigh was internal because I knew this was one thing Preston would not get. "Forget that part of it, Pres. It's just...the Kitchen is...it's mine. It's the one thing I've had and done that's *mine*."

"Ours," she pouted teasingly.

"Oh my God, Preston, of course. Sorry, *ours*."

"Okay," she whined, flinching away from my guilty look. "It's yours. I just bankrolled it. Once. And pay the rent."

My answering chuckle was rewarded with a soft smile. She was talking me down indirectly, and I appreciated her for it.

"The Kitchen is my dream, my baby, you know? I would've worked toward the List when I was ready. But I didn't do any preparation for this, Pres. My orders for this week and next are already through the roof, higher than they've ever been. And I'm drowning in inquiries about menu items, delivery zones, and every detail imaginable–and complaints that I don't have more information on the website or haven't answered them on social media."

The stress those complaints caused was going to chip steadily away at me, I knew. There was a reason I hadn't tried for the list yet–I hadn't decided if I wanted to subject myself to the pressure.

Preston's eyes widened, and she shot around the island to look at my laptop screen. "Holy shit, would you look at all those orders. Girl! That's amazing!"

I choked on a laugh. "It is, right?! I mean, I don't know what I'm going to do to meet the demand, but these numbers are unreal."

"If you need me to front you more money to cover ingredients or whatever, I will." She shrugged like it was nothing. *Because it is nothing, Cami. She's a freaking billionaire.*

"That's not..." I worriedly chewed my lip. Taking advantage of Preston was the last thing I wanted to do, but the years we'd spent as friends had taught me fighting her generosity would only piss her off. "Thank you, Pres. Really. I hate to ask."

"You didn't. I offered."

That's how most things were for Preston–black and white. Sometimes I wished I could see the world the way she did because it seemed so much simpler. Scary, too, though. Good luck to anyone who saw things differently than she did.

"Thank you."

She eyed me, clearly assessing my state of mind and finding it lacking. "Come to lunch with me and Parker tomorrow. He'll have some perspective on all this."

"On all what?"

She twirled her finger in a circle in front of my face. "On the spiral you're going down about his boss."

The heat that flared in my cheeks was instant. "What spiral?"

My best friend said nothing. She just crossed her arms under her chest and cocked an eyebrow and one hip, then waited. It took less than a minute for me to fold.

"It feels too much, too fast, Pres," I said quickly, feeling a strange sense of desperation rising through me. "I like him, but we're not too far into this thing, you know? It feels like it could get messy. I'm not his client and I have no desire to be."

"Girl, you need to take a deep fucking breath. He's not treating you like a client."

I huffed, an unpleasant pinching sensation forming in my chest.

"Seriously, Cam. The man dotes on you. The flowers? The dates?" It was her turn to huff at the look I shot her because our last date had been a disaster until Van pulled the plug and changed it up. "I know he didn't hit the note perfectly, but he was trying to impress you. As a woman, not a business owner. I really don't think he meant anything nefarious by doing this. Didn't you say he asked you to go to a business thing with him and the one dude?"

I bit my lip, nodding. "Ethan, yeah. Happy hour."

"He's a businessman, Cam. He asked you for something, but he gave you something at the same time. Transactional."

"So what is it, Pres?" I fired back. That pinch in my chest had turned into an itch under my skin. "Is he impressing me as a woman or treating me like a transaction?"

She stared at me, dumbfounded, for a moment. Then exclaimed, "Oh, my GOD, is this what it's like?!"

I started. "Is this what...what's like?"

"Dealing with me! With my drama!"

I blinked at her. "You've lost me."

She smirked. "You are normally the most easy-going human on the planet. I sweep into your space with my drama and disrupt everything, talk in circles, annoy the shit out of you–"

"You don't–"

"Sh." She held up a finger. "Still talking. That's me–a fucking tornado of bullshit most of the time. I know, I own it.

But *you*. You are the calm in the storm, the rational one, the first one to give the benefit of the doubt."

She paused, waiting for confirmation. "Um, sure?"

"You are. Very drama-free, it's honestly annoying. But right now, at this moment? Girl, you are bringing the drama, and I. Am. Here. For. It."

I flushed and wrapped my arms around my middle. "I didn't think I was being all that dramatic," I mumbled.

"Honey, you are drama-full right now. You don't know how to react to someone doing something good for you, something you didn't ask for, so you're trying to figure out how to vilify Van. But the thing is, the man's just being himself. He can't separate his business mind from his romantic mind–men aren't that complex."

I snorted. "I don't think that's a compliment."

"It's the truth. He's not treating you like a transaction, and you know it. But he did have something to ask of you related to his business, not his courting of you *as a woman*."

Though I didn't want to admit it, I knew she was right. I was jumping to the worst possible interpretation of things because... because I felt out of control. Not that control was something I needed or thrived on, necessarily. There had been many decisions in my life made for me. But Camellia's Kitchen wasn't one of them–that one was mine. And a man had almost destroyed it before.

"I guess...it feels like he took something from me, in a weird way, that I *know* isn't rational. Something I could've achieved for myself."

Preston grabbed my upper arms in her hands, holding me firmly. "Cami, he didn't *take* anything from you. He told you he couldn't pay for your spot on the list, right?"

"Right..."

"You earned that spot. He just put you on their radar. He

elevated you enough for them to take notice, and they did." She shook me gently. "Your hard work, your brilliance, your customer service, your recipes...that's what won you that recognition. *You* got the Kitchen on that list, Cam. Van just made sure they didn't miss you."

"Ugh," I groaned, leaning forward and smacking my forehead into her shoulder.

Preston wrapped her arms around me. "I know. It sucks being wrong." She patted my back. "So I'm told, anyway."

"Oh, whatever!" I pulled back and gave her a playful shove. "You're full of it."

She cackled and pushed me back. "You love me."

"Alas," I teased, "it's true."

"Lunch tomorrow, babe. We'll make it a late one so you can come after your deliveries. You can pick Parker's brain about Van."

"Okay, okay. Lunch tomorrow."

She nodded as though we'd settled a deal. "Good. Now, how the hell are you going to fill all these orders for the next few weeks?"

I stared at my laptop screen for a moment, thinking. "I mean, I know all my suppliers personally. I could make a few calls, see what the farmers' market crew is willing to do for me."

Preston's eyes lit up. "Oh my god, they're all going to be so fucking excited."

"About what?"

She just grinned and swung around the island to the fridge. "They all love you, Cam, and you've helped every single one of them in some way, shape, or form–haven't you?"

"I mean, probably." I shrugged. Helping out was kind of my thing; if you looked up acts of service in the book of love languages, you'd probably find a picture of me.

"Have you ever gone to them asking for help?"

"Of course, I have–"

"Nope, don't just answer. Think about it. When was the last time you asked any of those people for help?"

I took a moment and thought through all the regulars at the market, the suppliers back home in Ukiah, and the staff I worked with every week. Preston's grin didn't falter for a second.

"I mean, I guess I've never directly asked for help..."

"I know you haven't because you don't. You never do. Just you wait, little miss. They're going to trip all over themselves coming to your rescue. This little supply chain issue that has you in knots is going to be solved in an hour. Don't believe me? Prove me wrong."

Grabbing my phone, I eyed her as she pulled a pitcher of strawberry basil lemonade–a favorite of my trolley regulars–out of the fridge. I sent off a few texts as she poured a glass, asking some of my connections if they could reserve more produce for me or knew of anyone who might be able to help if they couldn't.

Before I'd even finished the fourth text, my phone buzzed with responses.

"Told you," Preston smirked. "You've got this, Cam. You've got an entire network of people who would give their left kidney before they let you fail."

I glanced down at the enthusiastic and supportive replies I already received, my smile impossible to hold back.

"Don't forget Leilani," Preston said, pointing at me.

I bit my lip, knowing she was right. If I activated the community without reaching out to my family, I'd never hear the end of it. "Good call."

> Me: Hey sis. The Kitchen's in a bit of a bind.
> Any chance you've got extra of my usual
> produce this week?

Her reply was swift.

> Lani: Is the bind because you're on the
> FUCKING BEST IN THE BAY LIST!? What the
> hell, dude! I didn't even know you applied!

> Lani: Anyway, we have a few things. Kale,
> corn, maybe berries? Gimme 5

I smiled at my phone. *Maybe you do have this under control, Cami. Maybe this will all be fine after all.*

———

"Do you two always come here for lunch?"

We sat in a back booth of a retro diner, the red vinyl seats and decor screaming 1950s. Preston and I perused the laminated menu while we waited for Parker to show.

Preston snorted in response to my question."No, our lunches are all over the place. This is just the venue of the moment. Parker was craving their onion rings."

Before I could comment about how delicious onion rings sounded, Parker pushed through the front door. His eyes swept around the restaurant, then brightened with his smile when he caught sight of Preston as she waved.

"Hey, you two!" he called as he drew near before plopping himself into the booth opposite us. "Hope you haven't been waiting long."

"Do you own a watch?" Preston sniped.

Parker just rolled his eyes, choosing not to engage his twin's tyranny about time.

"I've got a short window today, ladies. Have a few things to wrap up before I meet LB for dinner."

"If you were on time–" Preston started, leaning forward.

"Pres, do you want to waste our limited time giving me shit, or do you want me and Cami to have time to cover the topics you felt were so pressing?"

Preston huffed and sat back in the booth. "Go ahead, Cam," she mumbled.

I looked from one twin to the other, wide-eyed. "Um. Well, see..."

Parker nodded, giving me an encouraging smile. "I hear congratulations are in order."

"Thank you, Parker, really. But that's sort of part of the problem. What can you tell me about Van?"

Parker's eyebrows rose. "I've worked with him for a few years now. He's one of the best in the business and I've learned a ton from him; honestly, he and Lex are the only reason I'm still playing the VC game for now. But...you're going to have to narrow the question if you want any useful intel."

"They're dating," Preston piped up.

"Oh." Parker blinked, the wheels turning. "Oh, shit, yeah. That makes all sorts of sense." He looked over at me, as though he was studying me anew. "Yeah, okay. Got it. What do you want to know, Cami?"

I wrung my hands together in my lap, unsure where to take the conversation. When Preston had insisted I join them yesterday, it had made so much sense. But now that we were talking about Van, it just felt uncomfortable.

"He's a good guy?" I asked, my voice sheepish.

Parker smiled at me and nodded. "Yeah, Cami. He is. He's got a reputation, and he's earned it, but what people don't talk about is what I get to see. He cares. Deeply."

"This whole list business," Preston chimed in. "Do you

think he did that to be manipulative or to try and get a hold of the Kitchen somehow?"

Parker leaned back as though physically repulsed by the idea. "Fuck, no. That's not Van at all." His eyes found mine, and he leaned his elbows on the table. "Van says exactly what he means, Cami. That's important for you to know. He doesn't mince words. He doesn't sugarcoat. It's part of why he has the reputation he does. You don't have to go looking for hidden meanings with him. If he did anything to get you on that list, it was because he thought you deserved it and would appreciate it. Nothing more."

Preston knocked my shoulder with hers, giving me an "I told you so" look, even though she'd said nothing of the sort.

"And the only time I've seen Van fired up," Parker continued, "is when he's protecting his people. He fights for every member of his team the same, whether it's our mail guy or Lex. I respect the hell out of him. Fuck, I still want to be him when I grow up." He leaned back in the booth again, a wistful look in his eyes.

Preston snorted and kicked him under the table. "You're ridiculous."

Parker flinched and leaned down to rub at his shin. "Ow, twinkie. Why you gotta be so vicious?"

She shrugged. "Born that way." She turned to me. "Feel better?"

I smiled sheepishly, glancing first at her and then at Parker. "Yeah, I think so. It's not that I thought ill of Van or anything, it's just..."

"He's a lot," Parker offered with an understanding smile.

"Yeah," I agreed. "He is."

"He's poured most of himself into Athena, Cami. I've never seen him in a real romantic relationship, so this is probably unfamiliar territory for him." Parker shrugged a little. "He's going to make mistakes, but he'll listen if you talk to him. I've never known him to shut anyone down. Communicate with him, and he'll do whatever he can for you."

"Thanks, Parker," I said softly.

He grinned at me. "Anytime, Cami. I'm excited for you guys."

"Aw, you're both adorable. Now mind your ears, I'm going to whistle for our server."

Chapter 11

Cami

I'd never been more excited to reach Friday. The days following the List's announcement were the most intense of my career. And if I was honest, they'd also been some of the most rewarding.

My farmer's market community had rallied around me without hesitation, and my family had hustled to get me the ingredients I needed to fulfill my orders. I was even able to open order capacity a bit, eager to sell out all the beautiful fresh produce that stuffed our fridge.

Sleep hadn't been much of a thing, though. I stayed up late making dressing, aioli, and bread, and prepping ingredients. Preston offered to hire a sous chef, but I'd refused. Part of the magic of my Kitchen was that I made everything by hand. There was something extra special about food made with love, and no amount of logic could change my mind.

I sighed deeply as I sat back in my office chair. Orders had steadily streamed in all week, and I'd just finished prepping my shopping list for the weekend. Preston was at a photo shoot, so I had the place to myself. It was quiet and a little lonely, and I found myself wishing Preston had caved and let me adopt something furry to snuggle.

I glanced at the clock and blinked in surprise. *Van's going to be here in fifteen minutes.* Gasping, I jumped up and rushed down the hall to my room. He'd mentioned dinner at his place and hadn't sent a dress code this time (*thank goodness*), so I assumed casual would do. I snatched the floral sundress Preston had suggested the week prior and threw it on. I'd showered and shaved after my busy day of deliveries, so I didn't have much more to do to get ready. Preston was my official hair and makeup person; in her absence, I just fluffed my hair and put on a soft pink gloss.

There was a soft knock on the door as I slipped on a pair of neutral slides.

"One sec!" I called, checking myself in the mirror.

After rushing down the hall, I pulled the door open and froze. *Oh, fuck me.* Van was in dark jeans and a tight, white button-up shirt, his hair–longish on top and tight on the sides–slightly damp as though he'd recently showered. The barest hint of a five o'clock shadow dusted his jaw, and I swore I'd never seen anything hotter in my life.

"Hi, *bella*," he said with a small smile, as though he knew exactly what he was doing to me standing there in casual clothes.

"I–um, hi. Gio, hi," I stammered, stepping forward to give him a hug.

His arms, strong and corded, wrapped around me, and I was surrounded by his scent. *Why does he always smell so delicious?!* I felt him press his lips into my hair and wanted to melt into a puddle of goo at his feet.

"I have a car waiting. Are you ready?"

I leaned back to look at him and nodded. He slipped his hand to the small of my back and directed me out of the condo, pausing for me to lock up before guiding me to the elevator.

"How was your day? I missed you at lunchtime."

"I know," I pouted. "Jax said you were meeting with a client last minute."

He stepped closer and leaned one arm over my head, nearly pressing our bodies flush together as he crowded me against the elevator wall. "Jax, hm? You two...catch up?"

I glanced up to find his expression fiery. My core quaked in response, even though my rational brain knew jealousy wasn't necessarily a positive trait. *Is it that bad, though?*

"N-not really," I stammered. "I didn't have time to linger. He just explained why your office was empty."

He hummed, leaning down to kiss me almost chastely. Then he buried his face in my hair, his lips ghosting over the pulse at the base of my throat.

"The idea of you talking to or touching another man makes me feel irrationally violent, *bella*," he confessed against my skin.

My pussy throbbed as he kissed me once, twice, three times up my neck. He was still physically crowding me against the wall, his hard weight making my breath catch. *I know I shouldn't find that sexy, but oh my god I do. I so do.*

"He's just a customer," I eked out.

Van raised his head to peer into my eyes, and it was like he was gazing into my soul. He dipped down to kiss me properly, his lips demanding but gentle on mine. His free hand came up to cradle my face, his thumb exerting just enough pressure to turn my jaw and angle me for better access. I moaned as his tongue dipped into my mouth, and he groaned in response.

The ding of the elevator brought us both back to ourselves. I stared up at him, chest heaving, as he peered down at me.

"As long as you remember whose you are," he said softly.

He straightened and took my hand, leading me out of the

elevator. I trailed after him, my mouth agape as I processed his words. When we reached the curb outside, a black town car waited for us. Van opened the door for me and got me settled– even buckling me in–before walking around to the other side to join me. He quickly buckled, then reached for my hand again, his thumb stroking over my knuckles.

"Gio?"

He looked over at me, humming to acknowledge I'd spoken.

"Whose am I?" I asked, needing to hear him say it.

Fire flared in his eyes again, and I clenched my thighs in response to the pulse I felt between them. Slowly, without breaking eye contact, he brought my hand to his lips and ghosted them lightly across my skin. That single, gentle, barely there touch sent goosebumps rising across my arm. My nipples hardened in arousal, and it took a concerted effort not to pant. He drank in every small reaction, his pupils dilating as he watched me combust over the slightest kiss on my hand.

"Mine," he growled.

I did pant, then, at how that single word rolled over and through me like an electric current. Being claimed by Van was perhaps the most dizzying experience I'd ever had in my twenty-nine years on the planet. I wasn't sure I would survive it.

"Oh," I breathed, captivated by his gaze.

I don't know how long we sat there, lost in each other's eyes, but the next thing I knew we were stopped at another curb and Van was climbing out of the car. His presence was so over-whelming, I felt almost cold in his wake. But moments later, he opened my door and smiled warmly at me, the intense passion from the elevator and car ride set aside.

"Come, *bella*. I want to show you something."

I took the hand he reached for me, welcoming the heat of his tanned skin against mine. Van was greeted by every single person we met as we entered the building and crossed the lobby to the elevators, our passage marked by a chorus of "Mr. Costa". I smiled to myself as I peered up at him out of the corner of my eye, imagining how he looked to others. His expression was stern to everyone but me, his response a simple head nod. No smile, warm or otherwise, graced his lips. I realized some of my favorite expressions were ones Van saved just for me. *And, oh, what a dangerous realization that is.*

Van pulled me around to stand in front of him in the elevator. He leaned against the back wall after pressing the button for the top floor, then pulled me to lean against him. He bent his head and nuzzled through my hair to my neck, breathing me in as he held one of my hands and pressed his other flat against my stomach.

"Can't get enough of you," he whispered against my skin, placing another light-as-air kiss behind my ear.

I couldn't help it; I shivered. I could feel his smile as his fingers flexed against my stomach, pulling me momentarily closer before the elevator smoothly stopped and the doors opened. We stepped into a hallway with two doors, one on each side. Van stepped toward one and nodded to the other.

"My neighbor, Cece. Duke's with her tonight."

Who is Cece? I pushed down the irrational surge of insecurity. *He wouldn't casually mention another woman like that if there was something romantic between them to worry about...would he?*

"Oh. Alright. I, um," I fidgeted, internally pouting at the lack of puppy cuddles awaiting me.

Van paused, watching me. "Go on, Camellia."

"Uh, sure. Well, I was just..." I shrugged, then decided to leave any questions about the mysterious Cece for another time. "I want to meet Duke someday."

He smiled. "You will. Thank you for telling me."

I flushed, though I wasn't sure why, and followed him into

his condo. My jaw fell as I took in the open floor plan–it was incredibly luxe, modern, and so very *masculine*. Rich hardwood floors accented dark furniture in leather and earth tones. The space was minimally decorated and tidy, but spoke of someone who knew exactly what they liked. Black and white photographs decorated the living room's walls, and an immaculate album collection and record player occupied one corner. Floor to ceiling windows made up the far wall and showcased the setting summer sun. *Where am I and how did I get here?*

Van kicked his shoes off at the door, and the sight of him in socks for a moment before he pulled them off was almost comical it was so casual. I'd only ever seen the man in a suit, but now he was in jeans and barefoot. I never knew someone could be so thoroughly clothed and still seem incredibly indecent. I followed his lead and toed off my slides, then padded after him as he drew me through the open living room to a drool-worthy chef's kitchen.

"You cook." The words tumbled out of me unbidden, as it was obvious his kitchen was well-loved and well-used.

He turned to me with a smile. "I do."

"This kitchen....Gio. It's amazing."

He nodded. "I knew you'd appreciate it. It took a while to get right, but I'm happy with it."

"I'm desperately jealous of that range."

He glanced over at his impressive six-burner stove and nodded. "It's the crown jewel. Imported from Italy. Damn thing took nine months to arrive. Take a seat, Camellia."

He gestured to the stools at the kitchen island, then moved through the space with practiced ease. He opened the fridge and pulled out a gorgeous charcuterie board, already prepped with a selection of meats, cheeses, olives, and grapes. After placing it on the island in front of me with a soft smile, Van turned back to the cabinet to fish out two wine glasses. A decanter was already set up on the counter, and he brought it over to fill both glasses with a generous pour.

"I hope you like carbonara."

"Well, Gio, it's only my favorite pasta dish ever, so. Yes. I do."

He grinned and handed me a glass of wine, then held his up to clink. "To the date we should've had last time."

I giggled. "You're definitely making up for it already." I popped an olive into my mouth with a cheeky grin.

"Good. Enjoy your charcuterie while I get the salad together."

He turned away, and my chewing paused. I looked down at the impeccably done charcuterie board. *Wait, did he make this? He didn't order it?* I glanced up as he pulled pancetta, eggs, mozzarella, and a plate of beautiful uncooked fresh pasta from the fridge, then turned to a cutting board full of heirloom tomatoes. On the stove sat a pot of water at a low temperature.

"I..." my voice trailed off, a lump in my throat.

Van stopped immediately, turning back to me. "Yes, *bella*?"

"Sorry, I just...did you make this?" I pointed to the charcuterie.

His brow furrowed. "Is something wrong?"

"No," I said, raising my hand. "God, no. It's perfect. I just..." *Oh, god, get it together, Rivera.* I swallowed roughly. "It's just, this is a first."

He gave me a quizzical look. "Charcuterie?"

I laughed. It sounded a bit wet, but I did my best to ignore it. "No, having someone cook for me like this. Usually, it's me doing the cooking." *And the caretaking.*

His smile was gentle and knowing. *What do you know, Van?* "I'm glad to turn the tables on you. You deserve it." He turned back to the tomatoes, snagging a towel from next to the cutting board and tossing it over his shoulder.

I watched shamelessly as he rolled first one sleeve, then the other, up to his elbow. My core tightened at the sight of his strong hands and their practiced movement. The cords of muscle that shifted under the skin of his forearms gave me far too many filthy visions of what he might look like with fewer clothes on. I shifted on my stool, desperate for friction. Van glanced up at that moment, checking on me.

"Are you alright?" he asked, a smirk on his lips. "You look flushed."

I choked out a laugh. "Just enjoying the view."

He grinned as he looked down and began slicing tomatoes. "I'm happy to be your viewing entertainment anytime."

I flushed and took another bite of my appetizer. "You'll have some of this too, yeah?"

He looked up and smiled, nodding, then went back to work. "This won't take long. Caprese salad, carbonara, then honey-comb gelato for dessert."

I whipped my eyes up from the piece of prosciutto I'd been about to devour. "You remembered."

He nodded. "Of course." He glanced up and shot me a mischievous look. "I'm not *that* old."

I sputtered, and he chuckled as he placed alternating slices of tomato and mozzarella in a ring on a white plate. I could feel the blood rising to my cheeks, but I took a deep breath to calm my nerves. Van had a good thirteen years on me, but I didn't mind. Age was a number, and like Preston had pointed out—experience could be a very good thing.

"Old enough to have the most beautiful condo I've ever seen," I quipped, looking around. "This place is stunning, Gio. Seriously. I don't know that I've been in a place this nice." I scoffed a little laugh, then muttered, "And I thought Parker's place was fancy."

Van snorted. "Parker's just a kid. He's still developing his taste."

"Hey now, watch who you're calling a kid. Parker and I are the same age." I narrowed my eyes in challenge.

Van set down the balsamic he'd drizzled over the salad and looked up to meet my eyes. "Parker was born with a silver spoon in his mouth. I'm not saying he hasn't worked hard, because I know better than most he has, but it's different. You and he are not the same."

He picked up the plate and placed it in the fridge, then wandered back over to me. Popping an olive into his mouth and chewing it slowly, he studied my face.

"You've built something from nothing, and you've done it well. I admire your work ethic and tenacity. I see what you've given of yourself to make your dream a reality. You should be proud of yourself, Camellia."

My heart squeezed at his words, emotion pricking at the back of my eyes. How this man could see me so clearly after so little time, I didn't know. My parents thought me flighty and indecisive, Preston thought I lacked the spine to fully chase my dreams, and my ex had run roughshod over my heart and my future.

Van picked up a ball of mozzarella and wrapped a piece of prosciutto around it, then offered it to me with a tilt of his head. I leaned forward and took it from his fingers, my lips brushing over his skin as his eyes flared.

"There is nothing childlike or immature about you, *bella*," he rasped.

Chapter 12

Cami

I wasn't going to say it out loud, but I suspected Van was the better cook. He might not beat my gluten-free biscuits or vegan pancakes, but there was no way I'd go head-to-head with him on Italian cuisine.

"Van, that may have been the best home-cooked meal I've ever had." I set my spoon down, savoring the lingering flavor of honeycomb on my tongue.

Van grinned at me from across the table. "I'm glad you enjoyed it. It was a pleasure to cook for you."

I flushed. It was a simple thing, but the way he said it made my pussy clench. After he fed me, every other look between us was utterly filthy. It was clear we were both hungry for something a bit more...carnal. I couldn't stop picturing Van leaning over me in the elevator or holding me so effortlessly in his arms in his office earlier in the week.

Van rose from his chair and collected our gelato dishes, taking them to the sink. I relaxed at the table, taking the last few sips of the white dessert wine he'd served with my favorite frozen treat. His sleeves were still rolled up, and I was uncomfortably turned on just from watching him rinse the dishes.

"Can I help?" I offered.

He looked up with just his eyes and scoffed. "You're helping."

"How?" I laughed, leaning my forearms on the table.

"Motivation," he said. His rough tone had a direct line to my clit.

"Oh?"

"The faster I go, the sooner I can enjoy my second dessert."

The dark promise in his eyes made my whole body flush. I leaned back in my seat and gulped, wishing I had more wine. Something told me sex with Van would not be quick or forgettable. I was as nervous as I was aroused, but whatever happened next—I knew I was in good hands.

Van finished up in the kitchen before walking back to the dining table. He moved with such calm, assured confidence—it was striking. I found myself matching his pace when I was with him, as though he had his own gravity pulling me in. Pulling me closer.

"Will you let me taste you, Camellia?"

My lips parted with a quiet gasp as I gazed up at him, frozen in surprise but also flush with want. I watched, without answering, as he set a small bowl of ice on the table, and then walked behind my chair. Without warning, he pulled it back from the table. I gasped again, scrambling to hold the arms as he moved me, chair and all, with ease. Dropping to his knees in front of me, his big, warm hands slid up my thighs as his amber eyes pierced through me.

"I've been thinking about tasting you since the moment I saw you," he growled, his fingers flexing against my dress. "And I know you find me disarming."

I huffed a laugh, my pulse fluttering oh-so-rapidly. "Just a little."

He smiled, and I felt like I could melt into nothingness. "But

I'm going to need you to talk to me, *bella*. What I have planned for you...."

He bent his head, placing a kiss on the inside of one knee, then the other. My brain stopped working for a moment, addled by the sight of this massive man on his knees for me, his head in my lap. He slid his hands further up my thighs to hold my ass and took a deep breath. His fingers flexed as he squeezed and inhaled me.

"I need to know you can tell me what you want and what you don't."

I nodded frantically, ready to give this man whatever he asked for if it meant he'd keep touching me like that. Like he wanted to claim me. Mark me. *Consume me.*

"It's important, Camellia." He looked up and my heart stuttered at the sight of him. "I need to hear your voice." Pausing, he waited.

"O-okay," I managed, my voice cracking.

His lips curled into a smirk and I squirmed, so turned on I could barely think.

"Okay, what?"

I swallowed, then licked my lips. "I want you."

He growled and surged forward, gathering me up in his arms as he came to his feet. Whirling around, he set me gently on the table as he claimed my mouth. I moaned, so glad for the contact, for the slide of his lips on mine. He kissed me like he needed to, like he wouldn't survive another moment without his tongue tangled with mine. When he drew back, I whined, not ready to lose his touch. He chuckled, and the sound of it sent goosebumps rising on my arms.

"I'm glad you want me, *fiorellino*. I want you, too. But I'm going to need you to be more specific."

I stared at him owlishly and nodded slowly, willing to do whatever he wanted.

"I want to own your pleasure, Camellia," he breathed, cupping my face in his hands. "I want to wring every drop of it out of you until you're sobbing and delirious with need."

The heat that flashed through me was intense, my pussy throbbing and breasts feeling heavy on my chest as my nipples tightened. My mouth and throat dried out as I stared up at him, wide-eyed and transfixed.

"I want to break you apart bit by bit." He dipped his face toward me and trailed his nose along my cheek, his stubble scraping my skin. "And put you back together again." He kissed my lips, then trailed kisses along my jaw. "And again," he murmured, between kisses. "And again."

He drew back to look me in the eyes. "Are you ready for me to do that, Camellia?"

"Please," I gasped breathlessly, without hesitation. My voice was gone, along with my inhibitions. Whatever Van was selling, I wanted it whole-heartedly.

He chuckled again, the deep dark sound coiling around me and pebbling my flesh. "I don't think you are, but I'm not selfless enough to let that stop me." His eyes flashed as he studied my face. "I need to know what you'll say if you can't take any more, Camellia."

I licked my lips and racked my brain. "Like...like a safe word?" My core clenched, and I felt the ridiculous amount of moisture between my thighs.

He nodded once, waiting for my reply. I felt dumb as I looked up at him, my vocabulary reduced to nothing in an instant. I'd never considered a safe word before, but I wanted to answer Van. Wanted to see what he did once he had it and stopped holding himself back. Because he was holding back. His body nearly vibrated with tension, his cock hard between us.

I licked my lips and swallowed again. "Truffle."

He hummed, his thumbs stroking over my cheekbones.

"Truffle. If you say that word, no matter what we're doing, it stops. You understand?"

I nodded.

"Words. I need your words." His persistent eye contact was a physical caress.

"Yes, I understand."

He smiled softly. "Good. I want you to tell me when you like something and when you don't, Camellia. Now," he paused, looking down at my dress. "Arms up."

I obeyed, lifting my arms over my head. He slipped his hands around my back to my zipper, sliding it down with a sensuous brush of his fingers on my skin, then gathered my dress in his hands and pulled it over my head. His gaze intensified and his nostrils flared as he stared at me sitting on the table in nothing but my mint green bra and thong.

"You are a masterpiece, *fiorellino*."

He began unbuttoning his shirt in short, quick movements. I sat on the table, quivering in want and lust, as I watched him bare more and more of himself to me. He was muscular, thick–his tanned shoulders impossibly broad and his chest deep. I bit my lip as he slipped his shirt off and folded it before setting it neatly aside. He looked like a wet dream come to life, standing before me in a pair of dark jeans and nothing else, his dark hair lightly mussed and his expression fierce.

"Lie back," he instructed, stepping toward me.

I did as he asked, gently lowering myself until I was flat on my back, my legs still hanging over the table's edge. I jumped when I felt his light touch on each calf, then bit my lip to hold back a whimper as he slid those impossibly large hands up my legs, lifting them and setting my feet on the table so my knees were bent. He stepped between them, leaning against the edge as he loomed over me.

"Close your eyes."

I did, my pulse thundering. I didn't know what was going to happen next, but I was so beyond ready to find out. The nerves had given way to wild excitement, a desire I had never felt before raging through me. Losing my sight had heightened my other senses, and I heard my own breaths as though they were bellows in the open space.

"Keep them closed, Cami," Van warned. "Do I need to blindfold you?"

I shook my head quickly, not because I was worried or scared, but because I didn't want him to delay any longer. Before he had to remind me, I remembered he wanted my words.

"No. No blindfold," I rasped, my voice raw.

That dark chuckle floated between us again and I tried to squeeze my thighs together, but Van's hips were in the way.

"*Brava ragazza,*" he crooned, and I melted into the hard surface of the table at the praise in his tone.

I felt him shift against me as though he was reaching for something off to the side, and then something cold touched the space between my breasts and slid down my stomach to the top of my thong. I gasped, sucking my stomach in to try and escape the harsh temperature.

Before I could protest the cold, something warm and wet descended on my skin, teasing where the lace of my underwear sat on my lower belly. I moaned at the feel of Van's mouth on me, the heat of him chasing away the shock of the ice. He licked and kissed the same path up my body, and it was as though every nerve woke up and started singing under my skin. The brush of his stubble, the lush softness of his lips, the slip of his tongue–it all combined into one heady symphony of sensation rushing through me. The tension in my body was exquisite, almost distracting.

I nearly yelped when the ice descended once more, this

time teasing across one lace-covered nipple, circling it slowly before sliding across the valley between my breasts to the other peak.

"I want to hear you, *bella*," Van reminded me. "If you want to scream…" He swirled the ice around my nipple again, then his fingers brushed my skin. I arched into his touch and he gently grasped my nipple between his fingers, then twisted lightly and pulled. "Then you should scream."

My back arched as I let the sound rip from my throat, the sharp pain followed by a rush of insistent pleasure that had me tightening my legs around Van. My hips thrust up, seeking friction where I needed it, but he ignored my lower half. A moment later, he descended on my breasts, again following the path of the ice with his lips, tongue, and teasing nips of his teeth. Soothing licks and kisses chased the small bites of pain, lighting my skin on fire.

"Gio…" I whimpered, fighting to keep my eyes closed.

"Tell me."

Ice touched me again, this time starting in the middle of my stomach, sliding down to my underwear, and sweeping out to first one hip, then the other. I gasped and writhed, sensation flooding my brain and making it hard to think.

"Gio, please…"

"Tell me what you want, Camellia," he rasped.

His lips and tongue were on me again, and my head rolled back as I arched toward him, desperate to feel him between my thighs.

"I-I need…" my thoughts scrambled, words evading me. "Please, touch me."

He hummed against my skin, the soft vibration making my thighs clench as I squeezed him between my legs.

"Touch you…here?"

His fingers slid down my calf to my ankle, caressing lightly before skating back up to my knee.

"Or...here?"

He trailed a featherlight touch along my jaw. I turned toward him, a heat-seeking missile, and pressed my cheek against his hand. I kissed his skin, opening my mouth to try and capture one of his fingers, needing something to suck, needing to be filled.

"Touch you where, *bella*?"

I moaned in frustration, thrusting my hips up again. *He's really going to make me say it.*

"Between my legs," I whined. "Touch me, let me come."

He hummed, and I could hear his smile. I whimpered as he stepped away until his hands found my hips, and he pulled me to the edge of the table, dragging my thong off in the process. My heart rate increased at the thought of being bare to him and unable to see his reaction and at the promise of pleasure that came with the simple act. He moved my legs and draped them over what could've only been his shoulders. He was quiet as he maneuvered us both into position, and I soon found out why.

The first touch of his ice-cold tongue, precisely placed against my clit, had me bowing violently off the table. I screamed, my hands grappling for purchase and finding his head. My eyes flew open, and I moaned aloud at the sight of him between my thighs. He looked up at me and dominance flared in his gaze. I slammed my eyes shut again, breaths heaving violently out of my chest as I tried to relax back. But relaxing was impossible when Van's tongue was warm again and the soft pulses of pleasure each lick and suck sent through me ratcheted me ever closer to that peak.

I whimpered, my fingers flexing in Van's hair, as he speared his tongue into me. My hips thrust against him gently, seeking more, always more, and he groaned in pleasure. His teeth scraped gently across my tender, swollen flesh and I shuddered, little lightning strikes of bliss shooting off across my skin. Just as my breaths quickened, and I was nearly there, Van pulled away. I whined, almost opening my eyes again.

"What's your safe word, Camellia?"

My eyes popped open. "What?"

"Your safe word. What is it?"

He was still between my legs, and he leaned forward and ran his lips along the crease of my thigh, distracting me. My eyes fluttered closed. When I didn't answer for too long, he nipped me.

"Cami."

"Truffle," I huffed, hips writhing.

He rewarded me with one long lick up my seam, and I contorted in his hold. He sucked my clit into his mouth and I saw stars, my hands clenching around his hair as my body tensed. Again, just before I tumbled over the edge, he changed his approach, teasing my labia with his teeth and sucking them into his mouth. I groaned in frustration, needing to come with an urgency that felt almost painful.

"Please, Gio," I half-sobbed. "I need to come."

He hummed in approval and returned to my clit, circling it with his tongue in a steady rhythm. I whimpered in appreciation, my skin feeling hot and tight. His fingers teased at my entrance lazily, stroking my wet flesh, and I twitched against Van's face, feeling suddenly so very empty. As though he could read my mind, he pressed two fingers slowly into me, and I groaned in ecstasy.

He curled them inside me as he continued to lick and suck my clit, his fingers stroking steadily along my inner walls. My building orgasm was two-fold, warmth and heat sending shockwaves from both my clit and G-spot radiating out through my body. I trembled, overwhelmed with sensation, and bit my lip, holding back a sob as my body tensed. Van sucked on my clit again, his fingers hitting that perfect spot inside me, and everything shattered. Wave upon wave of pleasure raced through me as I cried out my release, my pussy clenching around Van's fingers as my thighs closed around his ears. My eyes opened as I threw my head back and let the orgasm rage through me, turning me inside out as I shook.

"Again," he demanded, the word muffled against my body.

I was oversensitive, everything feeling raw and exposed, but Van didn't stop. He'd slowed his assault as I came, but as I went boneless in the wake of my pleasure, he ramped right back up. He pressed more firmly against my G-spot with his fingers, swirling them in a circle as he stroked. His tongue flicked against my clit once, twice, and he sucked it hard into his mouth, white hot pleasure shooting down my legs to the soles of my feet. A second orgasm caught me by surprise, barreling through me with an intensity that stole my breath and left me wordlessly moaning.

Van finally slowed, then stilled between my quivering legs. He placed a soft kiss on my clit that had me twitching as though I'd touched a live wire, then slid his fingers slowly from my pussy. I wanted to cry at the loss of him, but I held it together. Barely.

He rubbed his hands along my hips comfortingly, kissing my inner thighs with astounding tenderness. *I don't know if I'll survive this man.*

"You are stunning, *fiorellino*," he murmured against my skin, pausing to stand and look down into my face. "I love the way you fall apart for me."

I shivered at the raw desire in his gaze, and watched, transfixed, as he unbuttoned his jeans and slipped them off his hips. He was before me in only his boxer briefs, his erection reaching out of the waistband. I swallowed roughly and knew I was more than willing to be destroyed by all that was Giovanni Costa.

"Are you ready to come on my cock now, *bella?*"

Chapter 13

Van

S he stared up at me, eyes wide, skin flushed and dewy with her sweat, lips swollen. I took a mental picture of her and filed it away, tempted to take a real one. *Someday, Giovanni. There will be time for that and so much more. Nessuna donna è mai stata così perfetta.*

Cami started to scoot back on the table, as though she expected me to rut into her like an animal right there. I chuckled and shook my head. She deserved far more than that. I'd selfishly indulged in the fantasy that had been plaguing me ever since our first date–laying her out and feasting on her–but now it was time to cater to her.

"Come." I extended my hand.

She sat up slowly, still languid in the wake of her pleasure, and slipped her fingers in mine as she peered up at me. I pulled her firmly into my chest when she was on her feet, wrapping one arm around her and sliding the other into her hair. I crashed our lips together, needing to feel her mouth on mine, needing to share the taste of her so she knew how delicious she was. She moaned, opening for me without hesitation, melting into my kiss so perfectly. My hard cock flexed toward her and she pressed more firmly against me in response, her hips moving slowly side to side. I pulled back and drank her in, still stunned I had her in my arms.

"I want you, Gio," she breathed, her hands pressing against my chest where they were trapped between us.

Heat and no small amount of satisfaction blazed in my chest. "Tell me exactly," I demanded, bending to kiss her neck.

She tilted her head to the side, ever so accommodating, and I rewarded her with a lick along the hollow of her throat. She shivered and my grin was slow and decadent as I kissed the sensitive spot again. I wanted to bask in every sigh and moan, revel in the most minute flush of her skin and twitch of her muscles.

"Tell me what you want, Cami," I whispered, continuing my assault on the other side of her neck.

"You," she whimpered. She went to reach a hand down toward my cock, but I stopped her progress.

"Words."

She bit her lip and looked down and away. *That won't do.* I didn't want to change a thing about her, but I did want to empower her. She was a bright light in a very gray world, the sunshine cutting through the fog, but she had no idea how she blessed those around her. For all my talk of owning her pleasure, she would always be the one in control. If she ever realized the power she had over me, she'd be astonished at what I'd be willing to do at her command.

"Look at me, Camellia." I still cradled her head in my hand, our bodies flush.

Her eyes snapped back up to mine, and her lips parted. I pressed a gentle kiss to her lush mouth, then bent and grabbed the backs of her thighs, lifting her up into my arms. She gasped as she pitched forward and held onto my neck, her legs winding around me.

"Do you know what I want, *bella*?" I asked, turning to walk toward my bathroom. My voice was husky with lust, my arousal prodding at her exposed entrance.

"No," she whimpered, clinging to me.

I hummed, flexing my fingers to grip more of her ass cheeks. I could picture sliding myself between them, disappearing into her tight little hole. My cock throbbed and I let out a shuddering breath. I walked us into my bathroom and set her on the countertop, smirking when she gasped at the coldness on her bare skin. Her cheeks flushed, and I hoped she was remembering the kiss of ice on her most sensitive parts.

"What I want," I said pointedly as I unhooked her bra and slid it off her arms, "is to give you everything you've ever wanted."

She trembled in my hold, staring up at me with innocent eyes. I couldn't resist kissing her again, long and slow.

"You could ask me to lay the world at your feet," I murmured against her lips, moving to trail kisses along her cheekbones. "You could ask me to burn it all down." She shivered, her hands rising to wrap around my wrists as I held her head in my hands. "You could ask me to hand over all of my riches, and I would. Without hesitation."

I straightened, peering down at her. "The greatest pleasure I have ever known came in giving you what you want, and I will stop at nothing to feel it again and again."

"Gio," she whispered, reaching up and around my neck, pulling me down to her once more.

She led the kiss this time, her touch almost frantic in its intensity. Her arms wrapped around my shoulders and she clung to me, pulling herself up off the counter to get closer. I hauled her up into my arms as she devoured my soul through my mouth, thoroughly erasing the taste of any other woman who had come before. They didn't exist for me anymore. There was only this perfect creature, *bellissima fiorellino*. I'd known it the moment she'd bowed off the table, the moment the first hint of her orgasm rolled through her and all her nerves and concerns had fallen away.

I meant every word I'd whispered against her skin moments ago. Whatever she asked of me, I would do, if only to see the flash of surrender and delight in her eyes when she saw me on my knees for her–literally or metaphorically. *She doesn't know it yet, but Camellia Maria Rivera owns me.*

I backed up, Cami secure in my arms, and leaned against the massive free-standing tub. She whimpered when I pulled away briefly to turn on the water, but her eyes brightened when she realized what I was doing.

"You'll join me?"

"I will."

She hummed a happy response, her fingers playing in my hair as she gazed up at me, still wrapped around me. *There's nothing I won't do for you.* She wasn't ready to hear the thoughts running through my head. I'd share them with her someday. The tub filled quickly, and I helped her slide down from my lap and slip into the water. She gasped at the heat, then sighed in contentment, looking up at me expectantly.

"Will you tell me what you want now?" I urged.

"Get naked and get in here, handsome," she ordered, her eyes sparkling.

I paused. "Before I do, let me ask you something. Do I need to get a condom?" *Please say no.*

Her eyes widened, her cheeks flaming hot as she worried at her lip. "I'm on the pill," she blurted. Then, in almost a mumble, "And I'm clean. It's, uh...it's been a while."

I felt like an asshole for being pleased about that, but I never claimed to be anything else. "Me, too. I got tested a couple weeks ago." *The day after we met. I wonder if she'll do the math.*

She drew a shaky breath, her expression full of anticipation. "Then, no, Gio. You don't need to get one." She eyed my groin, then dragged her gaze back up to mine. "Do I need to ask again?"

"No, *bella*," I grinned and followed her orders, shucking off my briefs and loving the soft exhalation of surprise that left her lips. Her expression was both hungry and apprehensive.

"Problem?" I teased, stepping over the tall edge of the tub. The move brought my hard cock within inches of her face.

"Christ, Gio. I don't know if you'll fit."

I smirked as I settled into the tub, my back leaning against the edge. She drifted closer, slipping her arms around my neck, while my hands settled on her hips and I pulled her against me, trapping my cock between our bodies. I chuckled as she bit her lip and glanced down.

"I'll fit. I was made for you."

Her lips parted in surprise as she stared at me. She reached out and cupped her hand against my cheek, a look of wonder in her eyes.

"Who even are you, Giovanni Costa?" she whispered.

"*Il tuo futuro marito.*"

"I don't know what that means."

"I know."

She huffed a laugh, her expression soft as she accepted my reply. Her wet fingers traced light lines along my cheekbone, sending sparks of pleasure across my skin. I reached over and turned off the water, never breaking eye contact.

"I want you inside of me, Gio," she breathed. "Please."

Keeping her in place with one hand on her lower back, I dropped my other hand to her core, my fingers sliding through her soft folds. She bit her lip, a small gasp and moan breaking free as I dipped my fingers inside her. I didn't want to hurt her and was pleased to find she was still slick with her cum.

"Not your fingers," she complained, gasping.

"Fingers first," I insisted.

She kissed me in lieu of a response, and I pushed both fingers inside her. She whimpered into my mouth, her hips writhing as she worked against me, seeking more. I stroked in and out a few times before working a third finger in. She shuddered and clutched at my shoulders, her lips slipping from my mouth to drag along my jaw. She was impossibly tight as she squeezed my fingers, and my cock strained between us.

"Are you ready for me?" I whispered, nipping at her earlobe.

"Please, Gio," she begged. "I need you."

I slipped my hand from between her thighs, trying to ignore the whine that escaped her as I did. *Her eagerness will be my undoing.* Wrapping my hand around my cock, I squeezed the base to stave off what had been building from the moment she looked at me with those glossy, emotional eyes in my kitchen, so shocked I was cooking for her. I slowly dragged the swollen head along her folds, groaning as she whimpered and writhed, trying to push down onto me. Notching my head at her entrance, I pressed the barest amount in, then looked down and got drunk on the sight of my flesh disappearing into hers.

Her eyes fluttered closed as she sank down another inch, her pussy stretching so perfectly around me, swallowing me in soft, silken heat. She trembled as she leaned her forehead against my shoulder and worked herself further down my length, her whole body tensing.

"Breathe," I soothed, stroking my wet hand up and down her back.

"God, I'm so full," she panted.

She bore down again and my hips flexed, driving deeper. Her moan was the sweetest sound as she shuddered against me.

"That's it," I encouraged, reaching down between us to stroke her clit. "Look at how well you take me, *bella.*"

She obeyed, looking down and whimpering at the sight of us.

"You can do it." I kissed her, my fingers circling her clit as she lowered herself more, nearly seated in my lap.

I was already out of my mind with my pleasure, lost in the heat and smooth feeling of her wrapped impossibly tight around me. Her body was finally flush with mine, and we both moaned as we settled against one another. I kissed her again, my fingers still working her tight bundle of nerves. Her breathing quickened as she stiffened against me, her inner walls squeezing deliciously.

I lifted my face away from hers and flexed my hips up, reveling in the look of sheer ecstasy that crossed her face as her eyes rolled back. Her fingers dug into my shoulders, holding me desperately.

"Eyes on me, Camellia," I murmured, determined to see her come apart for me.

Always willing, she looked up at me, her lips parted on another moan as I thrust up into her once more. She threaded her fingers through my hair and pressed her forehead to mine. It was intense, our closeness and connection, and just when I wasn't sure if I could last, she unraveled.

Her whole body shuddered as she moaned, her pussy clamping down so hard my jaw clenched as I struggled to keep my own orgasm back. Her eyes were wild on mine, then sex-drunk as her body started to relax, the aftershocks still twitching through her.

"Hold on," I said, running one hand up her back to cradle her head and neck, and planting the other on her hip.

I thrust up into her roughly, and she cried out and buried her face against my neck. She began to move, matching my rhythm, pushing down against me as I surged up and into her perfect cunt. We were surrounded by a cacophony of us—my harsh breaths and her desperate moans amplified by the room's marble. Water sloshed over the tub's edge, but I was undeterred. She felt like heaven around me and I was lost to her reactions, the shift of her muscles as she clenched, the shiver of desire through her core, the rise of goosebumps across her skin.

"I want to fill you with my cum," I growled, tightening my hold on her neck so I could pull her back and see her face. "Do you want that, *fiorellino*? Want me dripping out of you?"

Her answer was more a moan than yes, but I heard enough to take it as permission. I pounded up into her, my head swimming at the thought of filling her to the brim, of seeing my cum on her skin. I was desperate to make that vision a reality. *Next time. And every time after this.*

"Oh, god, Gio, please," she whimpered, her hands clutching my shoulders once more. She bucked against me, leaning forward again to change the angle and nearly screaming when I thrust into her again. "Right there, please. I'm close."

I growled and held her in the right position, pistoning up and over that perfect spot again and again. Her pussy clamped down around me, throttling my cock. I could feel my balls drawing up tight, that tingle in my spine starting. I was going to get her over the edge once more, desperate to see that blissful look on her face when she flew away.

"Come for me, Camellia," I ordered.

She cried out and tightened around me so firmly I lost all control, my thrusts turning staccato as my orgasm rushed up through me. I grunted, claiming her lips in a bruising kiss as I eased us both through the aftershocks with long, gentle thrusts.

Cami collapsed against me when our kiss broke, her breaths coming harsh as she trembled in my hold.

"*Brava ragazza.* You did so well for me, *fiorellino*," I murmured, stroking her hair as we breathed together.

I was loath to separate from her, but I could tell she was

exhausted and the bath was no place for her to rest. I shifted and she whimpered, holding on to me. Smiling, I placed a kiss on the top of her head.

"Let me take care of you."

She sat up and leaned back, looking slightly dazed.

"I'm going to start the shower, then I'll come get you."

I lifted her off of me, both of us hissing at the loss of contact as I slipped from her. Glancing down, I saw my cum stretching between us in the water and my brow furrowed.She waited for me, eyes sleepy and head resting against the tub, as I flipped on the shower and pulled two huge, fluffy towels out of the linen closet in the corner. I draped them over the glass wall of the shower, where I could easily grab them.

"Ready?" I asked.

She peered up at me through squinty eyes and nodded, slowly moving to rise. I wrapped my arms around her, lifting her to her feet before helping her out of the tub. When she was steady, I bent to kiss her as I ran a hand down her stomach to her core. I could still feel a bit of my cum at her entrance, and I swooped two fingers over it, then gently pushed it back inside of her. She moaned into the kiss, shifting her hips closer to my possessive fingers. A deep sense of satisfaction settled in my chest as I drew back and leaned my forehead on hers, my fingers slowly slipping from her. She rested a hand on my chest and laughed breathlessly.

"You're a possessive man, Gio."

I hummed in agreement. *And you are too perfect for this world, bellissima ragazza.*

I led her the few feet to the oversized steam shower, and she stepped under the warm spray with a grateful sigh. As she raised her hands to run them through her hair, I reached out and held her wrists, gently stopping her.

"Let me."

She paused, searching my face for a moment, then let her arms fall back down. I reached up and gently angled her head under the water so it ran through her hair, wetting it thoroughly. I pumped some shampoo into my hand, feeling absurdly smug at the thought of covering her in my bath products, my scent.

She sighed happily as I massaged the shampoo into her scalp, her eyes closed and body relaxed. I took my time with her, thoroughly washing and conditioning her hair. Her pleased hum as she pressed her cheek to my chest and loosely looped her arms around me had my chest tightening. I lathered a wash-cloth, then took my time gently scrubbing every inch of her skin. I lingered here and there, pressing kisses to her pulse points as I worked her over.

I ran the cloth over my body in a quick swipe before we rinsed off together, her hands trailing smooth patterns across my shoulders and down my arms, over my hips. Never had I shared this kind of intimacy with someone, never had I joined them in the tub or washed them. Sex had been transactional for me before this, before Cami. It had been enjoyable, and I had always appreciated the expression of female pleasure, but I had never been filled with the driving need to care for my partner's every physical and emotional need. But with Cami, it was as instinctive as breathing. As long as I had her, I'd put her plea-sure, her comfort, her...everything...first.

Emotion rose hot and prickly in my throat, and I turned to grab our towels. I bundled Cami up first, then slung mine low on my hips.

"Give me just a moment."

She followed my instructions, holding her towel around her. I pulled a few things from the cabinet, then offered her my hand. She took it, and I drew her out to my bedroom. Her eyes widened as she took in the expansive, luxurious room, and I smiled. I loved seeing her in my space.

"On the bed." I motioned toward my king bed and she climbed up, then turned to look at me.

"Relax, *fiorellino*," I murmured, crawling up to sit behind her. I kissed her shoulder gently, then gathered her hair into my hand.

She drew her knees up in front of her and looped her arms around them, her head tilted back for me. She hummed a happy sound as I began teasing my fingers, then a wide-toothed comb, through the tangles.

"It's been years since someone's done this for me," she muttered, her voice thick. "Not since I was a kid."

"Kids aren't the only ones who need tenderness. You deserve to be taken care of, too."

She sniffed, then expelled a shaky breath. "I feel like I can turn my brain off around you, Gio, and it's a little scary. I've never been able to do that with anyone before."

"I've got you, Camellia." I kissed the juncture of her neck and shoulder, my lips lingering. "You can let me be your brain."

I'll let you be my heart.

Chapter 14

Cami

I woke slowly on Saturday morning, more comfortable and content than I had been in a very long time. Maybe ever. Van was a warm, heavy presence against my back, his body molded to mine. My eyes fluttered and the hand on my stomach flexed, pressing us closer together.

"*Buongiorno, bella,*" he murmured, his voice rough with sleep.

I loved the sound of it, loved the feel of him. He destroyed me the night before, slowly took me apart just as he promised, then put me back together in a new configuration—one that was incompatible with any other man. Sex had never been like *that* before. I didn't even know a person could legitimately sob with want, even though I had read it plenty of times in my romance novels. But when Van teased me with the ice and his mouth, getting me so close to an orgasm then backing me off of it, I had been moments from tears. *And I fucking loved it.* Orgasms had always been fun, but the orgasm that had burst through me after *that*? It had been earth-shattering. *Would it always be like this?*

Van's lips met my shoulder, then moved toward my neck,

kissing every inch of skin as he went. My core clenched at the mere thought of us being intimate together, and I flushed.

"Morning," I whispered back.

Needing to see him, I rolled over to face him. He smiled as I did, slipping his arm down for me to use as a pillow as I wiggled closer to him. He tangled his legs with mine and settled a claiming hand on my hip, his fingers drawing little patterns on my skin.

"You're something else, Gio." I studied his face, drinking in his masculine beauty.

His mouth twitched up in one corner in amusement. "Oh?"

"How are you still single?"

He barked a laugh. "Why do you ask?"

I gestured to him as if to say "all of that" and his eyes twinkled with amusement. "That, and your cooking is criminally delicious. And, well." I shifted my hips closer, feeling his morning wood hard and heavy between us. "That thing is ridiculous."

He laughed again, and I loved everything about it–the way his Adam's apple bobbed, the deep sound, the crinkling smile lines that appeared on his often stoic face.

"I assume you were pleased with our makeup date?"

I scoffed. "Assume away. That was the best date of my life."

His hand flexed on my hip, his eyes flaring. "Was it, really?"

I nodded, and a pleased growl rumbled through his chest. He touched his forehead briefly to mine, then kissed the spot where our skin had met.

"I like that more than I can say, Camellia."

"Well, you cooked for me. That automatically puts you in top five territory."

"I see." His eyes lit with mischief. "The way to your heart is through your stomach, hm?"

"That's what they say," I teased back.

"Well, that means my next move should be breakfast."

I groaned in anticipation. "My mouth is watering already."

He chuckled. "It would be a disappointment if I cooked breakfast for you. I've heard Parker rave about your quiche, and I can't claim to have mastered the pancake flip."

"Oh, Gio, that's okay!" I moved to sit up, but he held me down firmly. "I'll cook for you..." my voice trailed off as he shook his head.

"You cook all the time. For me and everyone else." He raised a pointed eyebrow, and I shrugged a little. *He's not wrong, especially these days.* "When you're with me, *bella*, you relax. Rest. Let me feed you."

My mind wandered to something hard, thick, and long he could satisfy me with. It was pinned between us, still standing at attention. He groaned a laugh and rolled onto his back.

"Stop looking at me like that. We'll never make it out of bed if you don't."

"That doesn't sound like much of a threat," I mused, following his retreat and lowering my head to his shoulder. As I settled a leg over his and reached for his needy cock, my stomach rumbled. Loudly.

"Ah, ah, ah," Van admonished, catching my hand before it could venture far and threading his fingers through mine. "You need food, and I need to feed you. It's a Costa thing." *What does that even mean?*

He pulled my hand up to his mouth and kissed my wrist, reminding me of when he'd done the same in the shower last night. He'd lavished each of my pulse points with open-mouthed kisses as he washed me. It had felt decadent, worshipful. His eyes met mine, and they flared at the desire he saw.

"I'm going to go out and get us something from the bakery down the street."

I started to pout, but he reached a hand out and placed a finger on my lips.

"Don't. Please. I'm not strong enough to turn you down, *bella*. Use that information with care."

He kissed me lightly, then rolled quickly away. As he stood, I watched him without shame. He was the perfect combination of rugged and gorgeous–thick with muscle, but not overly chiseled. Powerful and strong. His thick thighs alone could stop traffic.

"You should take a picture," his amused voice broke my reverie.

I looked up at him and grinned, unembarrassed by my ogling. Holding my hands up, I pantomimed taking a photo of his bare backside. He chuckled as he drew black boxer briefs up over his very biteable ass.

"You could take a real one, if you wanted." He cast me another look over his shoulder, the heat in his eyes enough to make me sweat.

My phone was in his kitchen, tucked into my purse. I just smiled at him, my head propped on my hand as I watched him slip on a pair of joggers and a t-shirt, all in black. My mouth dried at the sight of him, sleeves stretched over thick biceps and his perfect forearms bare.

"You're such a snack, Gio," I sighed.

He laughed. "I can't say I've ever heard that compliment before."

"It's a good thing," I explained. "Means you look good enough to eat."

His nostrils flared, his gaze heating as he pointed at me. "Stop that. You'll make me imagine too many filthy interpretations of that statement and I won't leave."

"Again...not really a threat," I teased.

Van surged toward me and I yelped and giggled as I fell

back on the bed. He climbed up and hovered over me, bracing himself above me in a filthy promise of what could happen between us again soon. *Really soon, I hope.* He leaned down and kissed me, pulling back before I could wind my fingers in his hair and urge him to settle his full weight on me. I wanted him to press me into the bed, smother me, cover me head to toe.

"You are a temptress," he growled, nipping at my jaw, then my earlobe. "But I won't let you distract me. Anymore."

He pressed a fierce kiss to my lips, then left the bed as quickly as he'd returned. Pausing by the door, he smiled back at me.

"I won't be long. Rest, relax."

I grabbed the covers and pulled them over me, burrowing until just my face peeked out at him. His expression softened before he turned and headed down the hall. As silence descended around me, I bit my lip to hold back the grin that tried to rise. I flopped onto my back and threw my arms out wide, staring up at nothing as I replayed the last fourteen hours in my head. I hadn't been exaggerating when I'd told Van it was the best date I'd ever had. And the more I thought about how he played my body so perfectly and the romantic things he'd said, the lighter my heart felt in my chest.

Just as I was about to let my emotions out in a girlish squeal, I heard a door opening. I sat up, surprised he could be back so soon. Hurriedly, I walked over to the walk-in closet, looking for something to cover my nakedness. A pale pink button-down shirt caught my eye, and I smiled. *Of course the man wears pink.* I pulled it down and slipped it on over my bare body, buttoning it as I wandered over to the bedroom door. I wouldn't call myself petite, but the shirt swallowed me whole, covering all the necessary parts and falling to my knees.

I could hear a voice that definitely wasn't Van's as I walked toward the kitchen. As I drew close, I slowed, taking a few steps into the open space before meeting the bright blue eyes of an older woman.

"Well, look at you. Aren't you just a lovely creature!" she exclaimed.

Before I could respond, a dark streak of fur barreled into me and I stumbled back, laughing.

"You must be Duke!" I giggled as he licked at me, jumping up to put his paws on my hip.

"Oh, you silly thing! Let the poor girl be, Dukey. Come."

The sweet dog listened immediately, trotting over to her. She turned to pet him in reward, and I took a moment to study her as I walked closer. Though she was old enough to be my grandmother, she looked nothing like any grandmother I'd ever met. Tall, svelte, and toned, she radiated sophistication and wealth. She wore a brightly patterned caftan cinched with a narrow belt at her waist, gold glinting from her bangles, earrings, and heavy necklace. Her makeup was impeccably done, her hair covered in a silk wrap matching her flowy dress.

"Um, hi," I said, waving timidly as I drew near.

She grinned mischievously at me. "So, you're the date."

"Cami," I offered. "And you are?"

"What! That perfect man didn't tell you all about me? I'm just shocked," she drawled, tossing me a wink.

I flushed and smiled, liking her already.

"I'm Cecelia, dear. Cece to my friends, and any friend of Van's is a friend of mine." She winked again. "I share custody of Duke with your man, though I don't think he sees our arrangement quite the same way."

She grinned back at me, then gave me the same long once-over I'd given her. I fidgeted, very aware I was bare under Van's shirt and our clothes from the night before still laid over a nearby chair. Duke decided he too needed to investigate me further, and he padded over to sniff at my hands.

"Hey there," I smiled, crouching down to his level to pet him.

He panted in delight, pushing into my space and wagging his tail as I roughed up his fur and stroked his head.

"He likes you."

I looked up at Cece and smiled. "He's a sweetheart."

She chuckled. "I was talking about Van. But yes–Duke is a doll."

I stood back up and gestured toward the kitchen. "Can I get you a drink or make you something to eat? It's the least I can do to thank you for keeping Duke last night and letting us have the place to ourselves."

Her smile widened. "Oh, no wonder he likes you. You're cut from the same cloth."

My eyebrows rose. *What on earth is this woman smoking?* Van and I couldn't be more different.

"Ah. I see. Yes, I'm sure he hasn't told you much has he?" She tutted and shook her head. "That ridiculous man. Come, I'll put on the kettle, and we can have a seat at the island and chat."

"Oh, um, well, that sounds lovely. I should really go get changed first."

"Oh nonsense, you're perfect just the way you are. Come on now!" She swept into the kitchen and I trailed after her, Duke trotting over to a dog bed in the corner and settling in with a large chew toy. I took the same stool I'd perched on while Van made our feast the night before.

"Did he tell you more than my name?" Cece pulled an electric kettle out from a lower cabinet, plugging it into an outlet on the island. This clearly wasn't her first time in Van's kitchen.

"Only that you had Duke last night. And you live across the hall."

She took the kettle over to the fridge to fill. "Yes, that doesn't surprise me. Man of few words, that one. But that doesn't mean there's not a million things going on behind that quiet, cool exterior."

I huffed a laugh. "That's the truth."

Cece nestled the filled kettle back on the base, pressed a couple buttons, then turned to me. She placed her hands flat on the counter, arms wide, and leaned in.

"The first time I met Van, he invited me in and cooked the most incredible meal. It was simple, cacio e pepe, but it was divine. Partly because he's talented in the kitchen, but more because he didn't hesitate to extend a welcome and a home-cooked meal to a lonely old woman."

I made a small noise of protest and she just smiled at me.

"I'm an old woman, Cami, and I embrace it. The things I've seen! The life I've lived!" She threw her hands out and looked up at the ceiling, then turned her eyes back to me. "I feel fortunate to be an old woman. Wouldn't change it for the world."

"I love that outlook, Cece."

She nodded. "I do too, honey. But of all the people I've met, there's no one on this earth who cares as deeply for the people in his life as Van does. He doesn't talk about what he does for others because he doesn't do it for recognition. He does it because, for him, it's just the right thing to do."

I was puzzled, feeling like I only had part of the story.

"Let me explain," Cece continued, reading my expression. "Van meal preps on the weekends; it's his therapy. And ever since we met, he makes more than he needs and brings me no less than three meals. Every week. For years. And why does he do that? Because in our first conversation, I mentioned being sick of takeout and asked him for a recommendation for a personal chef."

The smile that crept across my lips was involuntary.

"He calls his mother every weekend. Sends money home. Pays for his nieces and nephews to attend the best schools, even relocated his sister when her daughter got into a competitive music program so they wouldn't have to commute. And I only know this because he made the mistake of introducing me to his mother, and that woman is a font of information."

My eyes felt hot. I looked down at my hands, willing the emotion to ease back. Van was a caretaker, that much he'd proven to me last night. But to know how deeply he valued family? That spoke to something ingrained in my soul.

Cece reached out and patted my hand, her expression kind. "He's intense, and he never elaborates on anything with words, but he loves bigger than the sun. And food isn't just his love language, it's his first language. You offering to cook me something and get me a drink?" She pointed a manicured finger at me and chuckled. "That's exactly what Van would do. Well, he'd just pour the drink and make the food, but you know what I mean."

We both laughed then because it was so true. I could picture Van as a host, welcoming people into his home with nothing more than a nod. I could see him handing them a beverage and directing them to sit, then busying himself in the kitchen with no more than ten words spoken between them.

"Thank you for telling me all this, Cece, truly. I appreciate knowing more about him. We have so much more to learn about each other."

"Just the fact you're here tells me you're something special."

I flushed, shrugging. *How special could I be this soon?* "Oh, I'm sure you've met plenty of Van's girlfriends, having known him as long as you have."

Cece scoffed and turned back to the kettle to pull mugs from the cabinet below it. "Honey, I haven't met a single one. You're the first I've ever seen him bring home."

My eyebrows drew up in surprise. "Oh! Well, maybe they

enjoyed getting dressed up and going out. I'm much more comfortable staying in."

Cece slid a steaming mug over to me and met my eyes with a smug smile. "Van has to be pushed out of his condo anytime there's an occasion requiring a dress code. Don't let the man's looks fool you. He may wear a suit like he was born in one, but he's happier anytime he can stay home with Duke. You and he have plenty in common, just you wait. You'll see."

Chapter 15

Van

Having Cami in my home, my bed...it had shifted something for me. I felt like my brain chemistry had been altered, tweaked, attuned to her. Waking up to her, feeling her skin against mine, being surrounded by her scent–they no longer felt like options, but like biological imperatives.

"I understand you're frustrated by the FDA's pace, Henry, but there's nothing we can do to speed the approvals short of bribery." My client sputtered, trying to interrupt, but I plowed on. "And last I checked, that's still illegal. We're following the proper steps and the timeline is well within average."

"Van, of course I'm not saying–"

"It doesn't matter what you are or are not saying. Right now, we wait. It's all we can do. Don't hound us for something you know we can't change. We'll reach out when we have an update."

He sighed. "Fine. But I don't like waiting–"

"Neither do I. But I'd argue wasting time is worse. Goodbye Henry."

The moment I hung up, my thoughts turned back to Cami. The brief glimpses we got of each other over her lunch deliveries weren't enough. I'd made sure my calendar was blocked over lunch for the foreseeable future, as I didn't want to go a day without seeing her smiling face if I could help it. But with how much her orders had ramped up, she barely had time for a peck and a wave. Then Thursday arrived, and, instead of spending time with her one-on-one, we had drinks planned with Ethan Masters.

A soft knock on my office door frame drew my attention from my thoughts.

"Lex," I greeted her, rising from my desk chair.

My friend and business partner stepped into my office, swinging the door shut behind her. She walked over to the bar cart in the corner, pouring two glasses of scotch.

"Devina just sold. 374 million."

My eyebrows rose. "That's a hard-fought win, Lex. Congratulations."

She turned and handed me one of the cut crystal tumblers she'd gifted me for Athena's five-year anniversary. "And to you. Quite the joint effort, that one."

"Indeed." I tapped my glass against hers and took a long sip of the smoky liquor. "Can't say I hate any excuse for a mid-afternoon drink."

Lex chuckled, folding herself elegantly onto my couch. I settled into the armchair to her left, one ankle resting against my other knee. She tapped my shoe affectionately with the pointed black toe of her signature stiletto.

"You've been quieter than usual, Van."

I glanced over at her, my brows furrowed. "Is that so?"

"It is." She gazed at me, waiting. "Talk to me."

"I've had a lot to think about."

"Cami."

Just the sound of her name made something stir in my chest. I raised the tumbler to my lips. "Among other things."

Lex rolled her eyes. "Right."

"Ethan Masters, for one."

She sighed, leaning her head back against the couch as her eyes closed. "When are you going to let that one go, Van? He's got something against me, you, the firm...hell, maybe all three. I know he has plenty of connections in the Bay and some seriously stellar businesses, but is it worth the runaround?"

"We're having drinks tonight at Bar Albert."

Her head lifted, and her eyes snapped to mine. "You're having drinks tonight. With Ethan Masters."

I nodded. "And Cami."

Her eyes narrowed. "Context, Costa."

I caught her up on our run-in at Daybreak, and the confusion in her gaze turned to thoughtfulness.

"Tread carefully, Van. This could get messy–mixing personal and professional. And you have to know he might be baiting you."

"I do know. I have it well in hand, Lex."

She sighed and reached forward, patting my knee once, then squeezed it briefly. "I know you do. I just...worry."

"No, you don't." Lex's calm, steady demeanor in the face of any challenge had been a significant contributor to her success. It was a hallmark trait of hers, known through the Bay.

She snorted. "Outwardly, no. Not much." She eyed me. "But about you, whom I love like a brother? I do. This relationship seems different for you, and I'd hate to see something go wrong."

A knot settled in my chest, and I reached up and rubbed at it absently. Lex and I were excellent business partners–both decisive and opinionated, with a willingness to listen and grow. Work had been our myopic focus for the duration of our partnership, and I trusted her implicitly. But we rarely ventured into personal matters, largely because neither of us had much to share. We both had family back East, but neither of us had put down roots other than Athena.

"I'll tread carefully, Lex."

She hummed, finishing her scotch. "You've been quieter, but you've also been killing it–with clients and the team. She's clearly good for you."

I huffed and shook my head. "Don't meddle."

Her laugh brought a small smile to my lips. She threw her hand up in defense. "An observation, Costa. No meddling here. I wouldn't dream of it."

The sparkle in her eye suggested otherwise, and I just grunted in response. She took my empty tumbler from my fingers, then rose and placed both glasses on the lower shelf of the bar cart. She turned back to me, thoughtful once more.

"Ethan has a new venture in the data privacy space for digital health. I'd explore that with him tonight–it would be the best fit for the portfolio and seems to have the greatest potential."

I smirked. "I agree. What was it you said earlier about letting go?"

She pointed at me. "Do as I say, not as I do."

My laughter brought a wry grin to her lips and followed her out of the room.

———

"I hope he doesn't show," I murmured against Cami's hair.

We'd arrived at the bar a few minutes prior after I'd picked her up from her condo. She was wearing a floral blouse and an infuriating pair of high-waisted pants that hugged her hips and ass. I wanted to peel them off of her far more than I wanted to spend the evening with her and another man.

Cami huffed a laugh and tried to look up at me. "No, you don't. This could be good for Athena, right?"

I nodded, my face still in her hair.

"Then we're right where we need to be."

I sighed and kissed the top of her head again. She sat at the bar, a gin and tonic before her. I'd ignored the open stool next to her in favor of standing as close to her as possible. She'd leaned back against my chest the moment I was within reach, and a feeling of rightness washed over me. *I've got it bad.*

I sipped my scotch, my free hand trailing down to lightly stroke her upper arm. The need to be in contact with her at all times was insistent.

"Van, Cami, there you are," an unwelcome voice called from behind me.

Sighing internally, I turned and gave Ethan a welcoming nod. I extended my hand, and he took it for a vigorous shake. He squeezed hard enough to cause a weaker man no small amount of discomfort, but I just tightened my grip until his grin cracked into a wince. *Nice try, asshole.*

"Ethan," I greeted, placing my arm back around Cami.

He surreptitiously shook out his hand before turning to Cami with an exaggerated grin. "And the lovely Camellia, it's so wonderful to see you again."

He leaned forward to kiss her cheek. I stiffened, my grip on her side tightening. She turned her head at the last minute, making the attempted kiss a one-armed hug. *Thank fuck. Almost had to punch a prospective client.*

"Great to see you, too, Ethan. Should we move to a table?"

"We have one reserved," I interjected, as Ethan opened his mouth to respond.

His eyes flashed to mine, full of challenge, and I stared him down. I jerked my chin toward the host stand, but he didn't budge.

"After you, Ethan. The host will take us to our table."

He huffed, his expression clearing as he blinked. "Righto, of course. Let's do it."

"Let's," I drawled, and Cami giggled beside me.

I squeezed her gently to me, then placed my hand on the small of her back and encouraged her to follow Ethan. She obeyed the direction immediately, and I had to fight not to adjust my slacks around my thickening cock. Her obedience did things to me.

The host took us to an intimate booth in the bar, just big enough for four people. Upholstered in leather and high-backed, it offered a modicum of privacy from those on either side. Cami stepped up to settle on one side, and I followed, snaking my arm low around her waist to rest on her opposite hip. Ethan sat across from us, eyeing first my arm and then our drinks.

"Got started without me, I see," he quipped.

"We were on time."

Cami choked on her sip, then settled her hand on my thigh and squeezed. "What Van means is we couldn't find any seats other than at the bar while we waited, and we didn't want to be rude and not order anything."

"Is that what Van means?" Ethan pressed, sarcasm rising in his tone.

"Hm," I mused, taking another sip of my scotch. I looked away from the annoyance across the table and caught the eye of a server. At my slight nod, she headed our way.

"Hi there, folks," she said as she got closer. "What can I get you?"

"Do you have any 25-year single malt scotch?" Ethan asked, too eagerly.

"Of course, I'm happy to–"

"Whichever is most expensive," he interjected, smirking at me. "My friend is paying."

The server looked to me in question, and I nodded my confirmation. "Right away, sir."

I could see the vein in his forehead pulse at her clear deference to me, and I had the suspicion Ethan had avoided Athena up to this point because he found me intimidating. *It wouldn't be the first time an asshole with an inferiority complex tried to give me the runaround.* It was an effort, but I fought back my frustration with his attitude and focused on the business side of our conversation.

"I was pleased to get your invite, Ethan."

Cami squeezed my thigh again, and I smiled to myself.

"Were you?" he challenged.

I nodded. "You have quite a few irons in the fire, but we're particularly interested in what you're doing in the digital health space. What can you tell me about that venture?"

His eyes flared with interest, and he set aside some of the posturing. "That one's a passion project of mine, actually. Few have asked about it. I'm surprised it's on your radar."

"We look for the rare and impactful at Athena. We leave the mundane to our competition."

He barked a laugh, and I glanced over to find Cami grinning up at me. I squeezed her hip, then turned my attention back to Ethan.

"What do you know about digital humans?" Ethan asked, leaning forward to place his forearms on the table.

"Admittedly, very little."

His eyes widened minutely. "I'm surprised to hear you admit that so freely."

Before I could answer, Cami interrupted. "Why?"

Ethan turned his gaze to her, his expression placating with a hint of condescension that made my eye twitch. "You must know he has a reputation."

"I do. It's stellar," she replied matter-of-factly. "He's invested in more successful ventures than anyone in the Bay, other than Lex, and his portfolio's rate of return is actually higher than hers." She glanced up at me.

"Sure," Ethan shrugged off her compliments while I felt something balloon in my chest. *This incredible woman; what is she doing to me?* "But he's also known for being ruthless. An asshole."

Cami frowned. "According to whom, exactly? Because everything I've read about Van credits him as decided and to-the-point. A man of few words, but meticulous in his decision-making. For some, maybe that's ruthless; to me, it just sounds like good business."

She looked up at me briefly, a smile on her lips. "And from what I've experienced firsthand, Van's the kind of man who says exactly what he means—nothing more or less." She squeezed my thigh again, and my heart soared. "It's refreshing."

Ethan stared at her, slack-jawed. "Refreshing."

She nodded. "Refreshing. And it's also why your comment about being surprised is misplaced. It's not surprising Van would be honest about his knowledge. It's exactly what you should expect."

I couldn't help it. I leaned over and kissed the top of her head, closing my eyes briefly as I inhaled her warm vanilla scent. She snuggled closer to my side, and I wanted nothing more than for Ethan to disappear and for us to be alone.

"I see," he said, looking between us. "Interesting observations, Cami."

She shrugged. "I just thought you should know, Ethan."

"Know what, exactly?"

"The kind of man you'd be doing business with."

"And, pray tell, what kind of man is that?" Ethan asked, his head tilted to the side as he studied her.

"The trustworthy, brilliant, successful kind." She looked up at me from beneath her lashes, her fingers flexing against my thigh. "The best kind," she finished, looking back at her childhood friend.

Ethan slowly dragged his gaze back over to me. "I value her opinion pretty highly."

I inclined my head. "As you should. I do, too."

He leaned back in the booth, looking between us for a moment. "Maybe I've misjudged you, Van Costa."

"The past is immaterial, Ethan," I retorted. "The correct question is: what can we achieve together in the future?"

He huffed a surprised laugh. "This is not what I expected this evening."

"Lively discussion and excellent company?" Cami chimed in. "Why ever not?"

A chuckle rumbled up through my chest as Ethan barked a laugh, a rueful smile on his lips. She grinned when my eyes met hers, and I felt a foreign lightness in my being. Never had someone stood up for me in that way; often, I was the protector. I protected Lex from her family and our more nefarious competitors, my team from the worst of our clients, my family from the various bad actors back home in Jersey. I did it because it needed doing, and I'd rather bear the burden of the fallout than subject any of them to it.

But Cami stepped in on my behalf without hesitation, against someone she'd known for far longer. Through her actions, I could see a glimmer of what we could be together. The pair we'd make—her kill-them-with-kindness bubbly nature matched with my blunt directness.

We would be magnificent. She is the sun, and I am all that craves its light—forever at her mercy.

Chapter 16

Cami

"What time is Romeo getting here?" Preston asked. She was draped facedown haphazardly across my bed, her chin propped in her hand as she watched me assess my outfit in the mirror.

"Quarter 'til, so we can get there by eight." I picked at my blouse, debating changing it. Again.

Preston huffed. "He's seen you naked, Cam. You could wear a burlap sack and he'd be happy."

I knew she was right, but that didn't stop me from wanting to look worthy of my spot on Van's arm. *I have a spot on a billionaire's arm. What even is this life?!*

"Not the point," I muttered, checking my angles one last time. "It'll do though!"

My dark hair was piled in a messy bun, a few tendrils framing my face. I'd gone for a simple tank top and fitted jeans, which was my typical market attire. But looking at myself in these clothes, and comparing it to the luxe trousers and blouse I'd borrowed from Pres for drinks a couple of days prior...I couldn't help but worry the real version of me didn't exactly fit in Van's world.

"Stop overthinking. I can hear the wheels turning in your brain." Preston rolled off the bed and stood behind me, bending down slightly to rest her chin on my shoulder. "You like him, huh?"

I nodded. "I think I do."

"You know you do. You're just afraid to admit it because of the absolute shitstorm it would make of your life."

"Gee, thanks, Pres. Please, no need to soften the blow or anything."

She grasped my shoulders and turned me to face her. "Cami, my darling platonic life partner, please listen to the words I'm about to say."

My lips twitched, but I held back a grin and nodded for her to go on.

"You need to live in the moment and enjoy this summer for what it is. Your parents and their asinine ultimatum can wait. Your concerns about the different worlds you and Van live in," she gave me a pointed look, "can wait. All you need to worry about is today. And, honestly, sometimes you need to let life happen, or you'll miss the little magical moments because you're too focused on what could be."

I bit my lip. "Quite the speech. That's easier said than done, you know."

She smirked. "Oh, you know it. But you're a bad bitch and I have faith in you. Now go, get out of here. Your man's painfully on time and I'm dying to see him lose his shit over your tits in that top."

Suddenly self conscious, I glanced down at the ample, but contained, cleavage visible in the scoop neck of my tank. "Oh crap, is it too much? Why haven't you said anything? I wear this all the time!"

"I know," she laughed, pulling me toward the front door.

"And you slay all day in it, so stop worrying." She tossed me a suggestive wink. "He's gonna love it."

Right on cue, and perfectly on time, a firm knock sounded on the front door. Preston shoved me toward it and snatched my tote bag from the kitchen island, thrusting it at me.

"Have fun!" she sing-songed.

I stuck my tongue out at her before turning and hurrying to the door. When I opened it, the sight of Van in designer jeans and a black t-shirt had my mouth going dry.

"*Bellissima*," he said, a heated look in his eyes as he took me in.

I vaguely heard Preston cackle in triumph, her voice fading as she returned to her room.

My cheeks flushed, and I smiled up at him. "Good morning, Gio."

He stepped toward me and invaded my space, winding one hand to press firmly against my lower back and sliding the other up to cradle my face. A moment later, he pressed his lips to mine and overwhelmed my senses as I drowned in his bergamot-and-tobacco scent.

He drew back slowly, as if he didn't want to put any distance between us. "You are simply stunning, Camellia."

"You're pretty handsome yourself." I grinned up at him. "Let me grab my market bags and we can go, yeah?"

He gave me one more brief kiss, then reluctantly released me so I could gather a handful of canvas shopping bags from the peg by the door.

"I'm looking forward to seeing your home away from home," he said, threading his fingers through mine as we walked toward the elevators.

Van's notes in his daily lunch orders had continued, much to my amusement and delight. After sharing that Athena and his kitchen were his favorite places outside of Jersey, I'd mentioned the market. He'd been quick to insist I take him at the next opportunity. And, as luck would have it, my sister had texted the next day to let me know they had extra help for the weekend and I didn't need to work the stand.

"It'll be so fun to be a customer today," I mused aloud as we walked. "The blueberries are going out of season soon, so they should have some good deals on those. And lots of the stone fruits will be at their peak ripeness." I gave him a mischievous look and squeezed his hand. "I can't wait to see you test the plums."

"Test?" He arched an eyebrow at me.

I saw my face reflected at me in the lenses of his aviator sunglasses as I glanced up at him. "It's a thing the growers do at the market. They'll have samples of their ripest fruits to entice customers, and the stone fruits are always decadently juicy."

"I see. And you want me to try a plum?"

"Or a nectarine, a peach. A pluot if you're feeling feisty."

He chuckled. "Something tells me I'm fortunate to have you as my guide today."

"Not used to produce shopping, oh mighty Van Costa?" I teased.

"Not like that, I'm afraid. And I'm a better judge of vegetables than fruits, if I'm honest."

"Ah, so you're a savory chef."

"You could say that." He tossed his arm around my shoulders and pulled me closer. "We make a good team. I'll leave the desserts and baking to you, hm?"

My answering laugh was breathless. *We make a good team.* That simple statement had my mind whirring with possibilities of what we could be–in the kitchen, the bedroom...even the board room. Every time Van had me in his physical orbit, I had a hard time remembering the ways we didn't fit; I could only see all the ways we did.

"I like that plan," I murmured, shoving back the thoughts that were evolving far beyond our reality. "What are you making for you and Cece this week?"

He looked thoughtful for a moment before answering. "It's been a while since I made gnocchi, and Cece loves it. I usually add in a vegetable or two, though–brighten it up."

"Sounds delicious." *And I know just what to find for you.*

We'd reached the entrance to the market, and I was already getting waves and shouted hellos from the growers and vendors I knew. Some I'd met as a kid and had known throughout my childhood, but many were connections I'd made after moving to the Bay.

"Everyone knows you," Van commented, his arm tightening a fraction around me.

I knew I shouldn't find his possessive tendencies attractive, but I couldn't help it. There was something about him claiming me that set all my nerves on fire in the most delicious way.

"Cami! What a treat to see you on the other side of the booth!"

I turned toward the friendly voice and grinned. "Gloria! How are the boys? Are they here?"

Steering Van with a shift of my body against his, we walked up to my friend's stall. I peered around, looking for her seven-year-old twins.

"They're not, thank goodness. Hector kept them home so I'd have some peace."

I laughed. "Because there's so much peace at the market, of course."

"Sometimes all you need for a break from your chaos is *different* chaos," she crowed, drawing a soft laugh out of Van.

"Gloria, this is Van."

He offered a hand, which she shook warmly. "It's a pleasure to meet you, Gloria," he said.

Her eyes widened, then she looked over at me with a teasing grin. "Where on earth have you been hiding him, Cami?"

My blush was instant and Van chuckled.

"No hiding, I assure you." His voice was like melted chocolate as he settled his arm more firmly around me. He pressed a kiss into my hair before continuing, "I'm grateful our schedules finally lined up so Cami could bring me down."

"Oh, I'm grateful, too." Gloria gave me a wink.

"Okay, introductions are over!" I said, throwing my hands up in the air. I peered over at her greens and made a happy sound. "Can I have double my normal kale, please? If it's okay, I'll pick that up at closing. But in the meantime..." I reached out and snagged some summer squash. "I'll take these now and you can add it to my bill?"

"Of course! Doubling again, hm? That business of yours is taking off." Gloria smiled fondly. "Proud of you, Cami dear."

"It's thanks to all my amazing suppliers and supporters, really," I demurred, wrapping my arm around Van's waist to give him an appreciative squeeze.

"And your talent for blending flavors, finding stellar produce, and reliably delivering a superior product," Van added. "Don't sell yourself short, *bella*. You deserve the praise. Accept it."

"Oh, yes. I like this one." Gloria's smile was wide and knowing. "Listen to him."

I gasped out a strangled laugh, squirming under their attention. "You're both making me uncomfortable! Gloria, thank you for the kale. I'll stop by just after noon?"

"That'll work well, dear. In the meantime, enjoy your shopping." She eyed Van, then winked at us both.

The heat in my cheeks could have powered Preston's condo for a month, and Van's loaded chuckle didn't help the situation. *Now I'm the color of a tomato and my panties are drenched.*

Great. I needed to get this trip back on track, and fast. I deftly steered him toward a local butcher's stall, knowing they'd have Italian sausage that would pair beautifully with the squash and gnocchi.

As we wound our way through the market, pausing to talk to the many people I knew and loved, a feeling of contentment settled in my chest. Van had surprised me. In his domain, like at happy hour the other night, he was all business. Every word he spoke was weighed, considered. Even his expressions and body language were tailored to drive the conversation where he wanted it to go. That kind of formality was foreign to me.

The market was where I thrived–it was organic, wild, tumultuous. There were people from all walks of life, loud noises, and any attempt at a plan was quickly thwarted by the sheer energy in the place. I had worried, as I got ready that morning, that Van would struggle in such an environment, so counter to what he chose to surround himself with at work and home. And yet, he seemed to fit as easily in the chaos as he did in the order of his office. He smiled at my friends, chuckled at their jokes and teasing, and let me lead, seemingly happy enough to follow me through my territory.

He also couldn't keep his hands off of me. His arm was wrapped around me, or my hand was tucked in his at all times. He stood close when we stopped at a stall, pressing kisses to my hair or stroking my arm with light fingers. With unspoken insistence, he carried the bags of food I gathered as we went, giving me a dismissive look when I offered to help.

While giggling in response to one of Van's teasing comments, our idyllic morning was shattered with one simple sentence.

"Cami, what are you doing?"

I whirled in surprise, my eyes widening. "Gabriel."

We were almost to my family's stall, and as I looked past my ex to my sister, she grimaced at me. Suddenly, her reason for telling me I didn't need to help at the stand this week became clear.

"Why are you here?" I asked, attempting to gently draw my hand out of Van's.

He refused to let me go, his fingers tightening around mine. Gabriel zeroed in on our joined hands, then assessed Van from head to toe.

"Who's this guy?" Gabriel sneered, his lip curling as he gestured rudely at Van.

"Van Costa. Her boyfriend."

Boyfriend?! It was Van's turn to be on the receiving end of my incredulous look.

Gabriel's sneer flickered with shock. "Her what now?"

"Boyfriend," Van insisted while I gaped up at him. "Partner. Significant other. Take your pick, the meaning is the same. She's with me."

"Cami, what the fuck–"

"Don't." Van's tone was arctic, his expression hard. "Speak to her with respect, or don't speak at all."

Gabriel's nostrils flared and he stepped back a bit before he caught himself. Dismissing Van outright, he turned to me. "Cami, please. Can we talk for a minute?"

Van's fingers tightened around mine again, and I knew it was a warning. Taking a steadying breath, I turned to look up at him.

"I'm sorry–"

"Cami..." he started.

"Van, please. Just give me a minute," I whispered. "I don't know why he's here, but if my sister's look a second ago is any sign, he came to work at my family's stall. As much as I want to ignore him, I can't."

"Why not?" he bit out, his jaw clenching. "He's an ex, I take it?" His gaze searched mine, and he scoffed a laugh. "He's *the* ex, isn't he?"

I chose to ignore his uncanny ability to see straight through me. "He and his parents are also very close friends of the family. Please, Van. Five minutes."

A muscle in his jaw ticked as he looked from me to Gabriel, who stood a few feet away watching us with a smug look. Van narrowed his eyes at my ex, then looked back at me.

"He hurt you?"

"I...it's complicated."

The vein in his temple throbbed as he leaned toward me, eyes dark. "Camellia, if that man laid hands on you, there's no way–"

My eyes widened as I shook my head. "No, Gio, of course not. Nothing like that."

He grunted, then released my hand and grabbed me firmly by the back of the neck, pulling me roughly into his chest. My eyes widened as my hands hit his pecs and he gave me a heated look, then pressed his lips to mine in a searing kiss. My eyes fluttered closed as I melted against him, opening my mouth when his tongue demanded entrance. A whimper rose in my throat and he growled in response, his hand flexing on my neck. He pressed his forehead to mine when we broke, his breath rough on my lips.

"I didn't do that because of him. I did it for me. Five minutes, *fiorellino*."

"Just five," I whispered my agreement, voice shaky.

He released me slowly, his fingers trailing down my arm to curl briefly with mine. "I'm going to wait right here."

"Thank you."

I turned quickly to Gabriel, knowing Van would suck me back to his side with nothing more than a look if I didn't. Glowering at Gabriel as I passed, I marched to the side of a nearby stall. We were still in sight of Van, but no longer blocking the walkway.

"What do you want, Gabriel?"

"Who is that guy, Cami?" he snapped, gesturing toward Van.

"If that's what you want to talk about, this conversation is over."

His eyebrows rose. "Oh, is that so?"

"It is." I cheered internally when the surprise didn't leave his face. He wasn't used to me standing up for myself.

He huffed and looked away, crossing his arms. "When are you coming home?"

I blinked, confused. "Home to Ukiah?"

"Home to me." He tapped his chest. "I know I fucked up, but are you really going to make me keep apologizing? It's time we started planning for our future."

The incredulous laugh burst forth unbidden. "Excuse me? Gabriel, you *stole* from me, never mind all the bullshit you put my heart through. And you haven't once apologized."

"Cami, don't be dramatic. We've talked about this, remember? What's mine is yours and what's yours is mine."

I ignored his asinine interpretation of events–I'd heard it all before–and eyed him, trying to figure out his angle. "Did my dad put you up to this?"

He looked off to the side, then back to me. "I know your five years are almost up. Our parents have been talking a lot about transitioning the businesses to us. And to be honest, I'm tired of waiting for our lives to start."

"You have got to be kidding me," I muttered, rubbing my forehead in frustration. "Me coming home or taking over my family's business is none of your concern, Gabriel. It used to be. It's not anymore. And I'm sure as hell not standing in the way of your life starting. By all means, go ahead; it would be refreshing to watch you take responsibility for something for once."

"Cami, baby–"

I cringed, the sound of that old pet name grating. There was a time when I would swoon at Gabriel calling me baby, but that time had come to a gut-wrenching close when I realized he'd raided my savings account mere weeks before I planned to launch Camellia's Kitchen.

His expression soured and he rolled his eyes at my reaction. "Seriously? Come on, I made a mistake. How long are you going to hold it over my head?"

"As long as it takes for you to get the picture, Gabriel," I snapped. He reared back, not used to hearing that tone from me. *Thank you, Preston. About time you rubbed off on me.* "We're over. We've been over for a long time."

I glanced over at my family's stand, catching sight of Leilani as she helped a customer. My dad wasn't there, likely home to keep things running smoothly with the harvest. With a sigh, I turned back to the man I had once considered my best friend.

"Thank you for helping with the stand. Did Cris stay home?"

Clearly unwilling to accept the change in subject, Gabriel's jaw ticked as he stared at me. Finally, he huffed and looked away. "Yeah, he had a study group or something. My dad suggested I take his place."

"I appreciate you supporting my family, Gabriel, but this conversation is over."

"So you can run back to Mr. Moneybags?"

I glared at him.

"What? The guy oozes money, Cami. I didn't think you were into guys like that. And how old is he, even?" His tone was hard-edged and cruel.

Before I could respond, Gabriel's face went white and he

stepped back. Van loomed close behind me, a claiming hand falling on my hip.

"I believe she said the conversation was over." Van's voice could've frozen a fireball. And, though I didn't need saving, I was grateful for his presence.

Gabriel took a readying breath, clearly delusional about which fights he could win, but Van just shook his head.

"We're done here." His hand firm on my hip, Van turned us away.

"Oh, so you speak for her now, huh?" Gabriel taunted.

Van paused, his pulse visible at his temple. Then he dropped his hand from my side and stepped into Gabriel's space, nearly close enough for their chests to bump, before staring down at him. He had a solid five inches on my ex, and Van was twice as wide. Gabriel shrank back and Van gave a low, menacing chuckle.

"Don't start fights you can't win, kid," he warned. "I was tempted to put you in your place, but seeing you cower in fear is just as satisfying. This time."

Gabriel's Adam's apple bobbed as he swallowed roughly, taking another step away. I reached out and took Van's hand, reassured when he squeezed it gently.

"Let's go, Gio," I murmured. Then, to Gabriel, "Take another five for your break, yeah?"

"Whatever." Gabriel turned and stalked off.

"What do you need, Cami?" Van asked, his voice low and just for me. "Do you want to go? See your sister?" His arm around me was an anchor, holding me up and fortifying my scattered emotions.

"I want to pretend that never happened," I muttered, leaning against him briefly. I was beyond grateful he wasn't pressuring me for an explanation. *But I know that reckoning is coming.*

Recentered, I heard a welcome voice call my name and turned to find Lani standing behind our family's stall, an empathetic smile on her face. Keeping Van's hand, I steered us over to the booth.

"Hey sis, you okay? Sorry you had to run into Gabriel like that," Lani greeted. "I tried to warn you away without mentioning that cretin and bringing up old stuff, but here you are."

I shrugged, not wanting to unpack how I felt while standing in a busy crowd. "All good. You in charge today?"

Lani began restocking bunches of carrots and celery as she nodded. "Yeah, I offered so Dad could focus on the harvest. You know how it gets this time of year. Everything's ripening faster than we can pick it."

I winced internally knowing how hectic peak summer was and immediately felt guilty I wasn't there to help. Van's gentle squeeze of my hand pulled me back.

"I know you're busy, Lani. I just wanted to stop by and introduce you to my...Van." *Good one, Cami. We really need to discuss that boyfriend comment.*

Van noticed my discomfort and stepped in to introduce himself, reaching his free hand over the produce to grasp Lani's. "Leilani, hi. Van Costa. Good to meet you."

Surprise flashed across her face before she answered Van's introduction with a bright smile. "Yeah, likewise. First time at the market?"

Van chuckled and looked at me. "I've been once or twice, but never with such an expert guide. It's a whole new experience."

Before Lani could respond, someone from a neighboring stall popped their head into the tent. "Lani–do you have change for a hundred? I'm short on small bills."

Meeting my eyes and mouthing "sorry," Lani paused her

restock and dusted off her hands. "I gotta go help with the cash drawer, but thanks for coming and saying hi. Van–it was a real treat." She tossed me a wink.

I shook my head and gave her a wave goodbye. "Of course. Give me a call this week and we can catch up."

Turning to leave, Van wrapped an arm around my shoulders, squeezing briefly before meeting my eyes with a smile. "So, what was it you said earlier about stone fruit?"

Chapter 17

Van

"You busy?" Cami's voice drew my attention from the email I was drafting.

My lips curved before my eyes met hers, pleased to be in her presence. "Never too busy for you, *bella*. Close the door."

I met her halfway across the room, pulling her to my chest and kissing her hard. She smiled into my kiss before softening in my hold. "I'm in a rush today, so I can't linger." Her words put a slight damper on my spirits, but I pushed that aside.

I cupped her face in my hands and studied her for a moment. "Did you sleep?"

Her flush deepened and she gripped one of my wrists in her hand comfortingly as she glanced away. "I slept enough."

"Hm." I didn't believe her, but I wasn't going to push.

"I brought you something extra, though!" Her tone brightened and she turned back to the trolley sitting outside my door. She picked up a bowl, a green juice, and a small cellophane bag tied with a blue ribbon.

"What's this?" I looked at the small bag, seeing several heart-shaped cookies inside.

"They're for Duke." Her smile lit her eyes as she looked up

at me. "I didn't have a bone-shaped cookie cutter, so hearts will have to do. I don't think he'll mind. They're full of organic goodness for him, though. Low-grain and all."

The feeling in my chest that only she caused tightened around me like a band. "Thank you." I kissed her forehead gently. "I'm sure he'll love them."

"And a green juice for you. I know you didn't order it, but this is an exceptional batch. I used Gloria's kale, some lemons and celery from home, and the citrus-infused honey from Marta's stall."

"You spoil me."

I couldn't help kissing her again, but we were interrupted almost immediately.

"Hey, Van–oh! Sorry–"

"Parker!" Cami grinned. She set my things on my desk, then turned to give him a hug.

He glanced up at me over her shoulder as they embraced, his wide grin faltering at my hard expression. *Knowing they're friends doesn't make it any easier to see another man wrapped around her.*

Parker released her quickly and chuckled. "It's good to see you, Cami. You sticking around for a bit? I can come back for Van."

"Oh, no." She insisted, tossing a rueful smile over her shoulder. "Your timing was actually perfect. I have to get going. These lunches won't deliver themselves!"

She turned back to me for another hug, and I soaked up as much of her warmth and vanilla scent as I could.

"I'll see you later," she murmured against my chest, rising to her tiptoes to quickly peck me on the lips.

"Can't wait, *fiorellino*."

She squeezed my hand in hers, then turned to exit. "Bye, Parker!"

She gave us both a little wave before disappearing down the hall. Parker watched her go for a minute, then turned back to me.

"I came by to chat Ethan Masters. Now work?"

I grunted in response, nodding toward the couch. Having worked with me for years, he needed no further instruction. Parker quickly closed the door, settling on the couch and flipping open his laptop. I grabbed my lunch, then took a seat in the armchair.

"Before we get into the boring stuff," he quipped with a smirk, "how are you?"

My eyebrows furrowed. "What are you doing, Parker?"

"Small talk. It's a thing colleagues do."

"I'm aware." I waited him out, knowing he'd fill the silence if I didn't.

"Well, Van, we have some friends in common now."

"Some."

"Okay, one," he conceded easily.

"That's true," I mused, opening my quinoa bowl. If he was going to offer up information, I wasn't going to turn it down. *I want to know everything about her.* "You and Cami are close?"

His eyes widened, as though he hadn't expected me to take the bait. *Give me credit, Parker—you know how much I like knowing the details.*

"Not as close as she is with Preston, but yeah. She's been a big part of our lives for going on a decade."

"You've met her family." It was clear family was important to Cami as it was to me. Even though our run-in with her sister at the market had been cut short, I'd seen the care and love between the two of them.

He nodded, studying me as he answered. "A few times. She and Preston go up to Ukiah a couple times a year, but I don't make it as often."

"Anything I should know about any former...relationships?" I had to force the words out through gritted teeth, hating the idea of her with anyone else. The image of that worm, Gabriel, rose in my mind, and I had to fight back a sneer. She had treated him with more respect than he deserved, and I had despised every moment.

The lightbulb went on in his head, and he chuckled. "Wow, boss. I walked right into that one."

I shrugged, unashamed, and took another bite of my lunch. *So damn good; she's fucking talented.*

"The story of her ex is one Cami will have to tell."

As much as his diplomacy annoyed me, I respected it. I would've tossed him out on his ass if he actually caved.

"Just the one ex then?"

"Maybe we should talk about Ethan Masters," Parker suggested, his eyes sparking in amusement.

He was right, but I was loath to admit it. Cami needed to be the one to share what had gone down between her and Gabriel. Knowing that didn't stop me from considering hiring a private investigator anyway. I dismissed it quickly, but the thought was tempting.

I glanced at him, reluctant to depart from my favorite topic.

"She's working too hard, Parker."

He stilled, as though I'd surprised him again. "She's always been passionate about the Kitchen," he offered.

"I can see that, and I admire the hell out of her for it. With a few tweaks for efficiency, she could double it overnight."

Parker was holding back, I could tell. He tilted his head at me, waiting for me to continue. *That's right, kid. Use my tactics against me.* I couldn't even be upset at him for it–I was proud, but he didn't need to know that.

"She has so much to learn, Parker. I can help her."

Parker cleared his throat. "Cami loves her business, Van. She's always seemed very happy with its growth."

"Hm, but the List surely changed things." I could see what the future could hold for Camellia's Kitchen so clearly, and it was grand. But she couldn't continue as she had been the last few weeks. I could see the effort wearing on her as clearly as I could envision the changes that would set her on an accelerated path.

"I know she's busier, but I also know she's working it out. She's smart."

I scoffed. *Smart doesn't cover it.* "She's brilliant."

Parker's mouth twitched up into a smile. "She is."

I grunted, then nodded at his laptop. "Ethan Masters."

He chuckled at the sudden subject change and shook his head, turning to his laptop and pulling up the projections. "I looked into digital humans, as you asked. Researched the technology his firm has patented, and reached out to a few of our contacts in healthcare and life sciences."

"There's demand?"

"It's still early, but the total addressable market could grow to hundreds of billions. The major challenge is overcoming the regulatory and compliance hurdles, but we have the right connections to help with that–and the privacy focus of Ethan's business is a big plus. I think our connections alone could get Masters to sign a deal."

"Got it. Barriers?"

"He's an early actor. There's a lot yet to test and prove, which is a hard sell for highly regulated industries. They want some proof the juice is worth the squeeze, and I think we can help with that. But the possible upside is massive, and all signs point to this being game-changing technology. Few are considering it now, but it'll be the norm soon enough."

"Your take?"

"Green light. Huge opportunity, we have the team and part-ners in place to help him overcome the challenges, and the path to an exit is clear. Projections show there's potential for one of the largest exits we've seen."

"Very good. Thank you."

Parker studied me for a moment. "You're welcome, boss."

I stood, taking my bowl to the compost. Parker rose to his feet and tucked his laptop under his arm.

"Well done, Brooks."

He smirked, and I gave him a hard look. My unspoken "don't push it, kid" had the desired effect, and he just nodded.

"Good luck at dinner with Ethan. Not that you need it." His smirk turned into a grin. "With Masters or Cami."

My expression darkened into a glare, and he laughed, raising his hand in surrender.

"There's a line and I found it," he chuckled. Pausing at my door, he considered me. "Preston and I love that girl, Van; she's family. I trust she's in good hands with you."

"She is," I confirmed. "Always."

Chapter 18

Cami

The best way to describe the restaurant Van led me into for dinner with Ethan was opulent. The place screamed wealth, with low lighting accenting dark, luxe fabrics, and exposed wood beams. It was busy, but quiet in that way high-end restaurants were–like the acoustics had been intentionally designed to create a feeling of intimacy despite the place being packed to the gills.

Entering the restaurant, Van drew the attention of nearly every woman in sight. He wore what I assumed was a custom-tailored suit in a green so dark it looked black. But when the light hit just right, the fabric's color accentuated his striking amber eyes.

"We'll wait for our guest," Van directed the host.

She blushed as she nodded and suggested we take a seat on the couches at the edge of the bar area. I was grateful Preston had once again helped with my wardrobe, finding a copper-colored silk dress that was just the right mix of sexy and profes-sional. Van had growled when he saw me earlier, a noise I now interpreted as the highest form of his approval.

Before I could ask about Van's day, Ethan swept into the restaurant.

"Van Costa!" he called, his voice booming in the intimate space.

Van rose to his feet immediately, pausing for me to do the same, then led me with a gentle touch to greet Ethan.

"Ethan." Van offered his hand, which Ethan eagerly shook.

"And Cami, darling. Look at you!" He held his arms out in front of him, as though framing my body. "Just stunning!"

Before I could reply, he swept in to place a kiss on each cheek. Van stiffened next to me, and I laughed awkwardly as I took a step back.

"Ethan, it's good to see you," I squeaked.

Van cleared his throat and placed a possessive hand on my hip, pulling me into his body. Ethan noted the move with a rakish grin.

"Sorry, old chap. Couldn't resist." He winked at me, and I fought the urge to react with the repulsion I felt.

Van's grip around me tightened. "Let's sit."

The host reacted swiftly to his pointed look, leading us to a table for four in the back corner of the restaurant.

"Ethan, I'd love to hear more about your partners in the digital health venture."

"All work and no play makes Van Costa a very dull boy," Ethan quipped, shaking his head. "Drinks first, then business."

Van blinked at him, then slowly inclined his head. He signaled a server, and someone was at the table moments later to collect our order.

"Now starters," Ethan demanded when the server left, winking at me again.

"Something in your eye, Ethan?" I smiled and innocently batted my lashes.

Van's rumbling chuckle put me at ease, and I smirked to myself.

"Oh, ho! She has jokes!" Ethan laughed. His cheeks were flushed, and I had the lingering suspicion he'd already started on the drinking part of his evening. "Cami, tell me. Have you been home recently?"

"No, it's the busy season. Why do you ask?" Something about his demeanor nagged at the back of my mind.

His eyes flashed with something, then he shrugged. "Curious. My aunt and uncle send their best."

There it is. "Oh, did you visit recently?"

"Just caught up with Gabriel earlier."

Van stiffened at the mention of my ex, and I winced. We hadn't discussed the run-in at the market yet, though I knew the conversation was overdue. I turned to him, reaching out to take his hand in mine.

"I was remiss in not mentioning this before, but Ethan and Gabriel are cousins."

Fire blazed in Van's eyes for a moment before he turned to Ethan. "I see."

Ethan dismissed his comment with a wave of his hand. "Gabriel's a hothead. Didn't deserve her."

Van cleared his throat, his fingers ratcheting tighter around mine. "Perhaps business would be a more prudent topic of discussion."

Ethan's laugh was sharp and loud. "No doubt it would, Van. Fine. Let's talk business."

Some of the tension that had filled me drained at his easy acquiescence. The server stepped up with our drinks, distributing them with a smile.

"Thank you," I murmured as she placed my gin and tonic in front of me.

"You're welcome," she answered. "Are you ready to order your meals?"

"We need appetizers," Ethan announced. "Pick your two favorites."

She blinked, then glanced at Van. I noticed Ethan flush when she did, no doubt frustrated she didn't take his word as gospel. When I glanced back at Van, she'd left, and I assumed he'd confirmed Ethan's order.

Van raised his glass. "To business," he said simply.

"Here, here!" Ethan agreed, tapping his glass to Van's.

As I watched Ethan take a long sip of his whiskey, I realized why his behavior seemed so similar. *This is exactly how Gabriel would act when he was tipsy and upset about something.* Unease filled my gut, and I set my drink down. I knew a clear head would likely be the better option if things took a turn.

While my mind had wandered, Van and Ethan had started talking about some of the technical aspects of Ethan's patent. The conversation was largely Greek to me, but I smiled and nodded along, encouraging them both. Ethan would glance at me occasionally, and Van's hand was a comforting presence on my thigh.

Ethan laughed at something he'd said, and Van's fingers dug into my flesh as he took a sip of his scotch. The server appeared at that moment with our appetizers.

"Ah, excellent!" Ethan clapped. "Please, another round." He gestured to the drinks, though Van's was still half-full, and mine was barely sipped.

"Not for us," Van interjected, shaking his head at the server.

"Oh, come on. Join me!"

"We're with you, Ethan," Van answered. His tone was cool, but not unkind.

Ethan huffed, rolling his eyes. The server hovered, unsure of what to do. Van gave her a nod and gestured briefly to Ethan, and she gratefully turned to get him another drink. When I looked back to face Ethan, I found his eyes on me.

"Gabe said he saw you last weekend."

"He did–"

"This is a business dinner, Ethan," Van interrupted, his grip tight on my leg.

Ethan's eyes flashed, and he turned to Van. "And you brought your date, who I've known most of my life. Are you going to stop me from talking to her?"

"I'm going to keep us on topic."

"Ha! Of course you are."

"Ethan, please," I urged. "We can catch up another time."

Ethan took another long sip of his drink before pointing his index finger at Van over the glass. "Van–you're a very lucky man. My cousin may have gotten there first, but a looker like her always deserved better. There's not much I wouldn't have done to give it to her." Licking his lips, he shifted his attention back to me with a lewd look before adding, "Just a little information for you, Van. Now you know what you can offer to sweeten this deal to a sure thing."

At that moment, it was as if time had stilled. I felt Van's entire body stiffen next to me, the hand that had been tracing circles on my thigh freezing. Glancing up, I saw the muscles in his jaw twitch and his chest rise with a steadying breath.

"Cami, excuse us. I need to have a word with Ethan," Van ground out, palpable anger rolling off of him.

"Gio, that's not necessary, I'm sure–"

"Don't move," Van commanded, his voice low.

Van reached across the table, plucking the whiskey tumbler from Ethan's hands and setting it on the table with cold precision. He stood, calmly buttoning his jacket before leaning over Ethan, his face inches from the other man's.

"Let's go."

Ethan's answering smirk–shot across the table as he stood–turned my stomach, the arrogance and entitlement evident in his casual attitude.

"Looks like the men need a moment alone, doll. Won't be but a minute I'm sure," Ethan drawled.

Van's hand clapped Ethan's shoulder as he led the man towards the restaurant's bathrooms, down a darkened hallway. While the gesture could have been mistaken for friendly to any casual observer, from my view I could see Van's knuckles whiten from the force of his grip and Ethan's answering wince. I didn't know whether to be angry at or worried for the man.

Shifting in my seat, I contorted my body to keep them in view. While they were too far away to overhear and the dim lighting forced me to squint, I could just make out what was happening. I may have respected Van's wishes to not interfere or make a scene, but I had the right to know what was going on.

They came to a stop opposite the kitchen, and I watched Van release Ethan's shoulder for a moment before slamming him against the wall, his hand fisted in his shirt. Van's massive frame towered over him as he said something I couldn't make out.

Oh my god. Is he going to hurt him?!

Ethan held his hands out in front of his body as if in surrender, his head shaking from side to side while speaking animatedly in what looked like pleading–his expression pained. Van's hand clenched into a fist by his side before punching the wall inches from the man's head.

My hand flew to my mouth, a gasp escaping my lips.

I watched as Van stabbed a finger at Ethan's chest, his face contorting into a sneer as he spoke. Ethan nodded animatedly, and I could read the words "I'm sorry" on his lips. Van shook his head as he stepped back, pointing at the restaurant's illuminated exit sign at the end of the hallway. Ethan straightened up from the wall before staggering down the hall and through the doors.

Across the restaurant, Van's eyes found mine, his expression tight. He held up a finger in a silent request for patience, then turned and headed through the kitchen's double doors.

Blinking back to the table, I took a deep breath, realizing I hadn't done so through their entire exchange. Slowly, I grabbed my drink and swallowed back its contents, my mouth suddenly dry.

"Camellia–" His voice was gentle, soothing. I looked up from my drink and saw Van standing beside our table, not a hair out of place.

"Where's Ethan?" I croaked.

"Gone. He apologized for his behavior and for cutting dinner short." Van sat next to me, his body turned towards me and his hands finding mine and pulling them into his lap.

"*Bella*–are you okay?" Van stared down at my face, searching for an answer.

Looking away in an attempt to gather myself, my eyes caught on Van's hands.

"Gio! Your knuckles!" I gasped, grabbing his hand and pulling it closer to inspect the swollen, broken skin.

With his free hand, Van swept the hair from my face, tucking the loose locks behind my ear and cupping my cheek. "Nothing but a scratch, *fiorellino*. Now, tell me–are you alright?"

Nodding, my head in his palm, I let out a breath.

"Van, I'm fine. I'm so sorry my history–"

Gripping my chin, Van locked eyes with me.

"Never, and I mean never, apologize for someone else's behavior, especially not when they are entirely unworthy of your kindness or respect," he demanded.

"But, I...I know that business deal was really important for Athena, and I–"

"Fuck the deal, fuck Athena." His voice was hard, unyielding. "I don't care what it costs me, you come first. Do you understand me? You will *always* matter more."

I flushed under Van's intense gaze. "Yes, I understand," I murmured.

"Good. Now, the kitchen has boxed up our meals. We're going to mine."

———

Van hadn't waited for a response back at the restaurant. He simply took my hand, drew me to my feet, and marched me out the door. He was as stoic as ever, but I could tell there was something roiling under the surface.

When he let us into his condo, he went straight to the kitchen, setting the bag of takeout containers on the island. He laid his hands flat on the counter and leaned against it, his shoulders moving as he took several deep breaths.

I approached him slowly, wanting to offer comfort but also unsure of how he'd react.

"Gio, are you–"

He whirled toward me so quickly I gasped, stumbling back in surprise before his arms wrapped around me and roughly pulled me into his body, holding me tight.

"I'm sorry," he said, his voice raw and still full of anger. "What he was suggesting–"

"I know," I murmured, soothing my hands anywhere I could reach. There was a sharp, frenetic energy humming between us. Goosebumps pricked on my skin in both warning and promise.

Suddenly gentle, Van cupped my cheeks in his large hands and tilted my head back, searching my eyes. There was a fierceness to his gaze that went straight to my core, tightening my muscles and dampening my underwear. His nostrils flared as he watched the desire flush across my face, and he bent to kiss me.

It was aggressive, his kiss. There was no slow buildup or decadent teasing of his lips and teeth, no tenderness. There was just raw need, hot and bright between us. It was as though the situation with Ethan had upset our balance, and we were both fighting to get back to equilibrium.

We broke apart, and he breathed deeply, as though he was gathering himself, then straightened and gripped my forearms.

"Do you remember what I told you the last time you were here, Camellia?" His voice was gravel, and my pussy clenched.

My lips parted, but I had no reply.

"I told you I'd burn the world down for you, if you wanted. Lay all my riches at your feet. Do you remember?"

"Yes," I breathed, memories of that night making my skin flush and my nipples pebble.

Van lowered himself to his knees before me, his hands trailing down my body to land on my hips. "They weren't just pretty words to make you wet, *bella*."

My breath caught in my chest and my eyes widened as he slipped his hands down to the hem of my skirt, beneath it, then back up to my waist. Keeping eye contact with me, he hooked his fingers in my thong, then drew it down.

"They were a promise."

He discarded my underwear, then shoved my skirt up around my hips, baring me to him. Leaning forward, he pressed his face against me, inhaling deeply. He groaned, then kissed my pussy lips.

"They were a vow."

His tongue delved between my folds, and I whimpered, clutching his wrists as he held my dress up against my hips. Lazily, he circled my clit once, twice, then retreated.

"Whatever you want, Camellia," he murmured, looking up at me with an expression both demanding and yielding. "Whatever you need. It's yours. *Al cuore non si comanda. È dato.*"

"I–I don't know what that means," I said breathlessly. I knew what his response would be; I'd grown so used to hearing it, I almost craved it.

"I know."

He stood slowly, unzipping and pulling my dress off as he went.

"What are you doing, Gio?" My voice was a quavering, insubstantial thing.

Goosebumps freckled my arms as he slowly removed my bra until I was completely bare before him. There was something incredibly arousing about being here naked, while he was still in his three-piece suit. He stepped closer to me, taking my wrists and pulling my hands up to clasp behind his neck, then slowly trailing his fingertips down the underside of my arms. I shivered against him, my eyes fluttering closed.

"Does it scare you to know that I want to destroy you?"

My knees wavered, and wetness coated my inner thighs. I drew a ragged breath, the tight bundle of nerves between my legs aching for his touch.

"Talk to me *bella*," he pressed. "Does it scare you?"

"No," I breathed. "You don't scare me."

He groaned, leaning in to kiss me deeply. "If you knew what I was envisioning right now, you might change your mind."

I looked up to meet his eyes, captured in the heat and emotion of the moment. There was a dark promise there, along with unbridled need. Dinner had rattled him, I knew. He needed me, needed to sate his desires and soothe his anger with proof I was safe and we were whole.

"Show me."

Chapter 19

Van

Show me.

The fire that lit my blood with those two words was unlike anything I had ever experienced. All pretense of toning down my want flew out the window, and I hauled her into my arms. She squealed in surprise and tightened her grip on me, but otherwise didn't protest. *She has no idea what she's doing to me.*

When Ethan had suggested her role in our negotiation was anything more than a friendly courtesy, I had seen red. My whole world had narrowed to the singular purpose to protect and care for her, and that meant getting rid of him. I had wanted to do far more than threaten him and punch the wall, but the thought of her horrified expression stopped me from crashing my fist into his face. *I'm not sure the wall was the better choice.*

My hand still burned, but the naked figure in my arms was proving to be the perfect salve. I brought her into my bedroom and settled her on the bed.

"Don't move," I ordered, before disappearing into my walk-in closet. Visions of the pleasure I would wring from her body filled my head, my cock already rock hard.

At the back of the closet waited a discreet black bag. After her first night here, with the memory of her coming apart for me ever-present, I had gone shopping. I selected an item from the bag, picked up a bottle of cleanser, and took both through to the bathroom. When I emerged just a few minutes later with the gift tucked away in my pocket, my cock flexed at the sight of Cami on my bed, exactly where I'd left her. *She didn't move an inch. What a good girl.*

Her eagerness to please was a heady thing. She watched me with wide eyes as I removed my suit, gently placing each piece on the bench at the foot of the bed. When I was down to just my slacks, she bit her lip, her breaths coming harsher as she took me in. I crawled into the bed with her, tucking my body alongside hers.

She turned and reached for me, and I kissed her thoroughly, craving her taste. I slid one hand down to grip her hip, pressing her to me as I sucked on her tongue, then nipped at her lips, jaw, and neck. Slipping my hand into my pocket, I withdrew the bullet vibe, pressing the button to start it before trailing it along her hip and thigh. She jumped when it made contact, looking up at me in surprise.

"Do you have toys at home, *bella?*"

She nodded, and my stiff cock throbbed. *Someday, I'll have her show me.*

"Have you used them since you were here last?" I stroked the vibrator from her hip to the middle of her stomach, then back, delighting in the way she quivered.

"Yes," she murmured.

I hummed and nuzzled her neck, kissing that sensitive spot that made her back arch. "And what did you think of when you played with yourself? What made you come?"

Her breathing quickened as I drew the vibrator down into the hollow of her hip, then ghosted it over her mound.

"Y-you, Gio," she gasped. "I thought of you."

I growled at the overwhelming mixture of pleasure and desire her words stirred, claiming her lips again as I slowly pushed the little pink vibe against her clit. She stiffened at the initial contact, then writhed against me, finding that perfect angle. She threw her head back against the pillows and I kissed along her neck and collarbone as she whimpered. My pressure with the toy was light, and her hips bucked up to increase the friction. When she started to stiffen, I withdrew. Her eyes snapped to mine, faint panic in her gaze.

"Tell me your safe word." I kissed her nose, her lips, her forehead.

She blinked a few times. "Truffle."

"*Brava ragazza.*"

Pushing her flat onto her back, I slipped the vibe back between her glistening pussy lips. When she moaned and fisted the sheets, I knew the placement was just right. Keeping it there, I leaned down and sucked one taut nipple into my mouth, teasing the flesh with my lips and tongue. Cami started babbling, her hips pressing up as her muscles tightened. Every twitch, every sound, every tiny reaction was motivation to get her to that peak again and again. Her body locked up and bowed toward me, her heels bracing against the bed as she started to shake.

"Ohhhh, Gio–fuck, fuck, fuck," she chanted, her orgasm arcing through her.

I smirked against her breast, not slowing my assault, as she flinched away from the unyielding vibrations. Giving her a brief respite, I drew it back slightly, my mouth never leaving her.

"Gio," she sighed, reaching up to thread her fingers through my hair.

Humming my contentment, I switched the toy's setting from the persistent vibrations to one that pulsed. Just as I bit gently into her breast and nipple, I placed the toy back against her over-sensitive clit.

"Fuck!" she yelped, involuntarily twitching away.

"Shhh," I murmured. "You can do it, *bella*. Give me another. Show me how you break for me."

She whimpered, her skin flushing, but she stopped trying to evade the toy.

"That's it," I praised, leaning over her body to lavish her other breast.

Her body shuddered as sensation overwhelmed her, her hips writhing against me as she drew close to that cliff once more. I increased the pressure, circling around her clit slowly. She tensed all over, her legs shaking, and gasped out a harsh cry as her second orgasm washed through her.

"*Bellissima*, Camellia," I whispered, kissing her lips once more as I drew the vibe away. "You fall apart so perfectly."

"Gio, please," she whimpered, clinging to me with weak hands in the wake of her pleasure.

"What do you need?"

"You, please," she panted, her words stilted.

"Hm. You'll have me, but not yet." I pressed a kiss to the corner of her mouth, then her jaw, and then the hollow of her throat. "We haven't tried all the settings."

I drew back and smiled softly at her panicked eyes. She licked her lips, swallowing roughly.

"How–how many settings are there?"

Good question. She bit her lip at my answering voracious grin. "Seven."

Her whimper made my cock strain painfully against my slacks. I adjusted myself, unwilling to speed my own release at the cost of hers.

"Gio, I–I don't think–"

"I know you can," I interrupted, moving so I could sit back on my heels between her spread thighs.

Her perfect rosy pussy was on display for me. I pressed a hand against my straining erection, squeezing the base and willing it to settle. I clicked the button on the vibrator again, and the pulses changed to rapid-fire.

"Reach down and spread those pretty lips for me, *bella*. Show me what's mine."

Her hands trembled as she obeyed, reaching down to gently prise her pussy lips apart. My breath caught in my chest at the sight, and I took a moment to simply appreciate her.

"You are perfect, Camellia," I whispered, touching the toy to her clit again.

Her body spasmed, and she nearly withdrew her hands, but I tutted at her and she froze. Her lip was wedged between her teeth as she squirmed, eyes watching me obsess over her every movement. I soothed a hand along her thigh, gently stroking and kneading. From my vantage, I could see her muscles fluttering, could see how her pussy clenched in pleasure in response to the vibration. It was mesmerizing, the flinch of her skin and the undulation of her body, but I needed more.

Abruptly, I leaned forward and settled my chest against the bed, burying my face in her core. Her gasp only urged me on, and I steadied the vibe against her clit while I licked at her slit. Her thighs closed around my head as I teased at her, drawing me closer.

"Gio, I–oh, god, I'm going to come."

Pulling back just enough that she could hear me, I encouraged her. "That's it, *fiorellino*. Come for me, shatter for me. Show me what I do to you."

She cried out, her hands grasping at the sheets as her back bowed. Her orgasm was faster this time, and she jerked away from me in sensitivity all too soon.

"No more, Gio, I can't–"

"You can," I insisted, letting the vibe fall away.

Not waiting for her response, I licked a broad stripe up her opening, then thrust and stroked my tongue inside her. She moaned loudly, her fingers threading into my hair and roughly pulling at the strands. I growled in approval, sucking her clit greedily into my mouth as I did. Her thighs squeezed me tightly, and I placed one hand on her stomach to steady her.

I clicked the vibe again; the vibration changed to one that slowly ramped up, fell away, and repeated. Glancing up, I felt my cock leak at the sight of her–head thrown back, neck taut, body bent backwards. *Fucking stunning. Can't get enough.*

Keeping one hand on her lower body, I continued my sucking and lapping at her clit as I teased her folds with the toy. She shivered, her legs opening to give me better access.

"*Brava ragazza,*" I praised against her tender clit, her answering moan making my cock flex painfully.

Gently, I pushed the toy and one finger inside her. The squeeze of her warm, drenched cunt was almost punishing as I slid in, making my eyes roll back in my head. I kept up the attention on her clit as I pushed the vibe just far enough inside to angle it up against that little patch of nerves at the top of her channel.

"Oh my GOD," she screamed, her body bucking in my hold. "Gio, fuck–"

Wanting desperately to encourage her but knowing I couldn't stop, I kept my mouth on her. As I sucked on her clit, I made small circles with the vibe against her G-spot. Her whimpers turned to short gasps, then a low, long moan that radiated out through her limbs. She shook, her body tensing head to toe, as the most powerful orgasm yet racked her body.

She convulsed as the vibe reached its peak just as she started to go boneless, a sob of pleasure and overstimulation breaking free. I withdrew it from her, my hand and the toy covered in her cum.

"Gio, that–fuck. I..I–"

"*Bellissima*," I growled, desire pounding through me so hard I could barely think. The scent of her was overwhelming, and I couldn't resist the urge to lick my finger clean.

Her eyes fluttered open, catching me with my finger in my mouth, and widened. "Oh, god, Gio..."

The sight of her, the taste of her, the scent of her–I was at her mercy. My plan to bring her to ruin crumbled as my desire rose through me like a beast with its own mind.

"*Bella*," my voice cracked as I discarded the toy and crawled up and over her, bracing above her as I kissed her. "*Bella, ho bisogno di te.*"

She returned my kiss with what eagerness she could muster, her muscles weak. I nuzzled the soft skin of her neck and kissed her wherever my lips could touch, my body vibrating with tension.

"Gio, wha...what's it mean?" she gasped, breathless.

"It means I need you." I let my hips drop, pressing my hard length against her lower body.

She whimpered, arching into me. "Please," she begged. "I need you, too."

"What do you need, *bella*?" My teeth nipped at the hollow of her throat, her collarbone, then her breast.

"I need you..." her fingers gripped my hair, pulling my mouth away from her dusky flesh. "–to fill me."

As I rose from the bed to shove my slacks and boxer briefs from my body, kicking them onto the floor, I asked for clarification. "With my cock? Or my cum?"

"Yes," she moaned, the sound of her voice an aphrodisiac all on its own. "Please."

Breathing heavily in anticipation, my cock leaking precum, I wrapped a tight fist around my base to stave off my orgasm. *Not until I'm buried in that perfect cunt.*

"Rollover, Camellia. Face down for me."

She obeyed, her movements sluggish, and looked at me with dazed, lust-filled eyes as she pressed her cheek into the sheets. I moved up onto the bed, positioning myself between her spread thighs. Bracing myself over her, I placed open-mouthed kisses along her spine, from the nape of her neck to the top of her perfect ass. She was panting, her skin flush and dewy, physical evidence of her pleasure that was slowly tearing me apart. *She'll destroy me before I can destroy her.*

"I'm going to fuck you now, *bella*." I gripped her hips in both hands, drawing her up to her knees. Clenching my jaw against the electricity building at the base of my spine, I dragged the head of my cock through her wet folds. She used what little energy she had to push back, inviting me in. *Who am I to deny her anything?*

Surging forward, I sheathed myself in her tight heat with a single thrust. Our twin groans filled the room and I stilled, gathering myself as currents of sheer ecstasy ran over my skin.

"Gio, please," she whimpered, squirming.

Anchoring her hips to keep her flush against me, I sat back on my heels, then snaked my arm under her to lift her up. She gasped, her hands flying back and around my neck as her back pressed against my chest. My hand wrapped around her throat, and her wildly thundering pulse felt like a taunt as it thrashed against my fingertips.

I thrust slowly into her as we both adjusted to the position, her grip tightening on my neck as she moaned. Feeling her body against mine, her throat in my hand, was the most exquisite pleasure.

"Hang on," I murmured, drawing her earlobe gently between my teeth before quickening my pace.

She arched her back, helping me drive deeper, and the wicked sounds of our bodies slapping together echoed in my head as I pistoned into her roughly. Her pussy clamped down on me, threatening to wring me dry in moments.

"Touch yourself, *fiorellino*. I need one more–show me what only I can do to you while I fill you with my cum."

"God, Gio." She reached down to circle her clit with two fingers, and my grip tightened ever-so-slightly around her throat.

Her pussy squeezed me in response, and I groaned as my balls drew up tight.

"I'm so close, *bella*. Will you come apart for me one more time? I need it. Need to see you shatter." I bit gently on her shoulder and she shuddered, her inner walls fluttering. "That's it, *fiorellino*. You take me so well. So perfect."

She cried out as another orgasm seized her, the grip of her pussy drawing my release to the surface. I groaned and buried my face in her hair, against her neck, my hold on her hip and throat loosening as we both slowed. I continued to rock into her through the aftershocks that pulsed through her pussy and around my cock. Finally, my hand slipped down to her chest, keeping her against me as I kissed where my fingers had pressed.

"You did so well, Camellia. You break so beautifully."

Her breaths came deep and ragged as her hands slid down, her body limp and drained. I wanted to lay her out and see my cum dripping out of her so I could push it back in, claim her, keep a part of me within her. But she was exhausted, her eyes heavy-lidded as her head lolled against my shoulder. *Another time. There will be another time–there has to be.*

As we sat there on my bed, both sweating and trembling, I wished she didn't have to leave in the morning. I wanted her here, in my sheets, then in my kitchen tomorrow. I wanted to wake her with my head between her thighs, then watch Duke greet her when Cece brought him home. It had only been a short while, but she was embedded in the heart of me, had taken up residence in the very core of my being. She was so much more than her sunny personality, beauty, and kind disposition; she was talented, driven, loyal–brilliant and compassionate in equal measure. *I stand in awe.*

"*Il mio cuore è tuo,*" I whispered against her skin.

She hummed in response, a soft sigh of contentment falling from her lips. I would tell her what it meant eventually, when she was ready to know. *My heart is yours.*

Chapter 20

Cami

"Okay, I've been patient enough. Explain," Preston demanded.

We sat in side-by-side chairs at the salon, our feet soaking in the warm baths. Van had surprised me with a weekend away to Napa, and Preston would leave for a European adventure while I was gone, so we were taking advantage of our last few days together.

"'Scuse me?" I looked over at her in confusion.

"You've been going through the motions like a damn puppet since you finished work. What is your deal? Where's my shiny, happy Cami?"

I closed my eyes and sighed, leaning my head back against the chair. "Ugh, I know. I've been in my head all day."

"Is it the whole thing with Ethan? Because I can make that problem disappear."

Giving her some severe side-eye, I shook my head. "You scare me sometimes."

"Don't dodge–"

"I know, woman, I know," I muttered. "It's not Ethan, I just..."

Her stare was like a physical touch, but not a soothing one. It was like she was poking my face, trying to get a reaction out of me.

"Did Van do something? Was he too rough? Get all possessive and claim the shit out of you?"

My flush was instantaneous, as I remembered that night. Van had claimed me all right, but I had enjoyed every moment. My panties were getting damp just from the memories.

"Seriously, Cam, do I need to kick his ass?"

"No!" I laughed. "No, it's nothing like that. I'm just...it was intense. The whole thing. Ethan behaving the way he did was awful–"

"I'll say," she muttered, her expression fierce.

"I thought I knew him, you know? We hung out as kids and were friends as teenagers. There was never anything between us, at least not for me. I had no idea he felt that way."

"Fuck him. Any man who doesn't make his move when he has the chance isn't worth a woman's time."

There it was again, Preston's black-and-white view of the world. Couldn't say I disagreed with her on that one though.

"Van was so..."

"Alpha? Violent? Hot as fuck?"

I snorted and eyed her. "You certainly have a type, don't you?"

She shrugged and grinned. "I'm a simple girl."

"That's a fucking lie."

"Go on, you were saying."

"He's...there's so many layers to him, Preston. He was ready to kill Ethan, I swear."

"I knew I liked him," she whispered under her breath. *Oookay, she is terrifying. Ignoring that.*

"But, seriously, I think he would've beat the crap out of him if I hadn't been there."

Her wince was almost comical. "That doesn't do it for you, huh?"

I blew a slow breath out. "It didn't use to. But...it was hot, Pres."

She squealed and reached over to slap at my arm, drawing the attention of the other salon patrons. I shushed her and mouthed "sorry" to our largely amused audience.

"And then he took me back to his place, and girl..." my voice trailed off and I bit my lip, my gaze unseeing as I lost myself to the intoxicating memories playing out for me.

"I want details," she hissed, poking me in the side. "I bet he's hung, isn't he? The man radiates big dick energy. Into a little spanking, hm? Likes calling you dirty things?"

"Preston!" I gasped, laughing.

"What?! I want the goods. Sue me."

My blush was bright, and I squirmed uncomfortably in my seat. "It was hot, that's all you're getting out of me while we're in a public place." My grin slipped into something smaller, more intimate. "It's the after that's throwing me, Pres."

Her eyebrows arched. "After?"

I nodded. "Bath, shower." Rolling my head against the chair, I turned to look at her. "When was the last time someone brushed your hair?"

Her jaw dropped just enough for her lips to part, her eyes widening. "That giant alphahole *brushes* your damn hair?"

"And rubs lotion all over me, fingertips to toes."

She blinked. "After you bathe and shower together."

I shook my head. "After *he* bathes and washes *me*."

Her brain was doing double time to process that information, I could tell.

"He likes to feed me, too," I murmured. "By hand."

"AND he cooks?" She choked on nothing, shaking her head and clearing her throat. "Cami!"

"I know."

"No, I mean, *Cami*."

"I know, Pres."

She blew out a breath. "Well, now I get it."

"Get what?"

"Why you're in your head."

I arched an eyebrow at her again.

"He sounds like your dream guy–and a total daddy, I might add." I coughed a laugh, but she ignored me, forging on. "But he's here, not in Ukiah. And he's Van, the hot shot VC billionaire." She studied me for a moment, then sighed. "You shouldn't try to fit him into your parents' vision of the future, Cam. But it's probably worth seeing whether he fits into yours."

I closed my eyes and leaned my head back. "It's annoying how well you know me."

Preston wasn't wrong about any of it. After the other night, Van was constantly in my head. It was hard for him not to be–there had been yet another massive arrangement of flowers delivered to our condo the morning after the Ethan incident, the sweet scent of camellias still lingering in my nose. The accompanying handwritten note had been brief, yet again: *Il mio cuore è tuo.* I refused to look it up, much to Preston's chagrin, but I wanted him to be the one to tell me. It seemed important I looked into his eyes when he did.

As if the visual reminder of him wasn't enough, Van was also texting me regularly. He never shared much, mostly checked in, but the fact that I was so top-of-mind for him was something entirely new. Gabriel rarely instigated communication and if he did, it was to ask for money or a favor. But Van texted me every morning asking how I slept, checked in mid-morning to see if my day was off to a good start, set aside time so he'd see me when I delivered lunches to Athena, and always messaged me when he got home for the day. No one had ever shown that much interest in my day-to-day life. It was a strangely foreign experience to be the one cared for, instead of the one doing all the caring.

"You like him," Preston's soft voice brought me back to the present.

I drew a halting breath, then nodded. "I like him a lot, Pres. Too much. Because you're right, our worlds don't fit."

"Don't put those bullshit words in my mouth; I said no such thing."

Groaning, I closed my eyes. "Hot shot VC guy in contrast to small-town caterer, whatever. The meaning is the same."

"You're one of the top private chefs and caterers in the Bay, bitch. You haven't been small town in years."

Her matter-of-fact words startled me. *Holy crap, she's right.* I'd never thought of it that way, but Preston was spot-on. I'd been born into farm life and raised in a small community, but I had made a name for myself and my business in one of the most saturated markets in the country. The family farm had been such a significant part of my identity for my entire life, and I needed the reminder I was more than its heir.

As though sensing the nearness of a revelation, my phone buzzed in my lap. My fingernails were dry, so I grabbed it, grimacing at the name on the screen. Preston winced and shook her head as she caught sight of the caller ID, but I couldn't ignore my parents.

"Hi, Mom," I answered quietly. It wouldn't be my dad—he avoided phone calls like the plague.

"Camellia, honey. Is now a good time?" My mom's voice simultaneously warmed me through and turned my stomach. She rarely called and never for idle chit chat.

"Of course! Everything okay?"

"Well, your father and I are a bit concerned, Cami. Lani said you're not going to be helping at the market this weekend?"

"Oh. No, I can't. I'm actually, uh, going on a weekend trip with, uh, with a friend."

Preston smirked, knowing full well I hadn't revisited the boyfriend conversation with Van.

"We're concerned, Cami. It seems like you're not treating the commitment to the stand or the business seriously."

My stomach dropped like a stone, guilt creeping in. Preston's eyes narrowed, and she shook her head, raising a finger at me.

"You have barely missed a weekend in years, Camellia," she hissed, knowing what my mom was saying without even hearing it. "You deserve a weekend off!"

"It's one weekend, Mom. I'll be back at the stand next week, I promise."

"You have a big responsibility ahead of you, Camellia." She paused, the sighed. "We just want you to be ready."

My steadying breath shook, but she probably couldn't tell. "I know, and I appreciate that. Give Dad, Lani, and Cris my love, okay? I'll see them soon."

"I will, Cami. Love you."

As I ended the call, Preston launched into her defensive tirade.

"You deserve a day or two off every once in a while as much as the next person, Cami. Don't for one second let her guilt you into bowing out of this trip with Van."

"I won't, I promise. I'm going." *After how the other night ended, I can't wait...even if I am nervous as all hell about how I'm starting to feel and what it means.*

"Napa with Daddy Van, huh?" Preston grinned, deftly refocusing the conversation away from my family obligations.

"That'll be a far cry from the ex who couldn't find your clit. I'm almost sad I won't be here when you get back."

I scoffed, choosing to ignore her entirely accurate dig at Gabriel, who took my virginity and never once went down on me. "Oh, I'm sure a little gossip is totally making you regret your decision to spend a month in the south of France."

She smirked indulgently. "I said almost."

Chapter 21

Van

I straightened my shirt sleeves absently as I waited for Cami to answer her door. It was Saturday morning, and I couldn't wait to have her to myself for the entire weekend. Her eyes had lit up when I'd suggested the getaway. I had been wrapped around her the morning after the incident (I refused to even think of the man's name, the worthless piece of shit), kissing her shoulder when I suggested she let me take her away, just us. It had felt so blissfully right to wake up with her body molded to mine, and I was a selfish man. I couldn't wait to have her to myself, to go to sleep and wake up with her where she belonged: in my arms. Plus, taking her away would give me what I wanted–Cami's undivided attention.

Duke had happily trotted into Cece's condo as I'd left that morning, curling up on his bed in the living room. Cece had still been sleeping, but I'd gotten up early to feed Duke and take him for a run, so I knew he'd be passed out for his very long morning nap as soon as I left.

The door swung open, and my breath caught. Cami was absolutely radiant. Her dark curls shining, eyes bright, and smooth, golden brown skin exposed and glistening. I wrapped a hand around the back of her neck and pulled her close for a deep kiss before she could respond, giggling against my lips after a moment.

"Good morning to you too, Gio," she murmured, leaning back to meet my eyes.

"Now it is. You ready?"

"Um, I think so? Are you sure I don't need to bring *anything*? Not even a toothbrush?"

"Not even a toothbrush. It's all taken care of." Grabbing her hand, I pulled her into the hallway, pausing to let her lock up.

"So...a road trip! How fun! I wonder what kind of music is on your road trip playlist, hmm?" she exclaimed as she grinned up at me.

I barked a laugh. "No road trip this time, *bella*. We'll be taking a more...direct route. I should ask, how do you feel about small planes?" I opened the car door, letting her slide into the passenger seat of my Maserati.

Catching sight of Cami's jaw dropping in surprise as I closed the door, I held in my amusement and made my way around the car. I had decided to hold back the minor detail I preferred to travel by private jet rather than drive whenever possible. It seemed safer to surprise her with the news when she was already with me.

Settling into the driver's seat, I turned to gauge her reaction, and her visible swallow made me smirk. "You okay over there, *fiorellino*?"

"Yup," she squeaked. "Pres and Parker both travel private. I just didn't think...I don't know, I guess it hadn't crossed my mind you would, too."

I pulled the car out of the parking space, setting a course for the airport, and slid my hand over her thigh, giving it what I hoped was a comforting squeeze. Having her here by my side and able to touch was irresistible. I doubted I could keep my hands off of her for the duration of our trip. So I wouldn't try.

"It's nothing. More time to enjoy our weekend."

I caught Cami staring at me out of my peripheral vision. "This car...a plane. Your penthouse. You really are every inch the bachelor billionaire, huh?"

I pulled my eyes from the road to meet her gaze for a moment. Her expression was open, with no contempt to be found. *How to answer this....*

I took her free hand in mine and kissed each of her fingers before answering. "I like the finer things in life. What can I say? I didn't have a lot growing up, and I swore to myself when I did, I would enjoy the money I earned. The plane? With all the travel VC life demands, it gets me from point A to point B faster so I can focus on the things that matter." *Like family. And you.*

I glanced over at Cami again to see how she was taking my reply. She gave me a soft smile and nodded for me to continue.

"As far as bachelorhood is concerned, I don't welcome the title. It was never a choice I made, I just...spent the last two decades building a career, and hadn't met someone I wanted to build a life with."

"Oh. Hadn't?"

"You heard me."

"I guess that makes sense, then," Cami whispered.

That felt like enough of a confession for now. I wouldn't scare her by telling her I would start building that life with her today, if she was willing. I knew my decisiveness would startle her. For me, our age gap and career differences–her just building her business and mine already established–didn't concern me. It only made what was growing between us feel all the more right. Thanks to my age, I knew what I felt with Cami was special; I'd never experienced such a connection before. And with my business already built, I could give her whatever she needed, whatever she dreamed. I only had to slowly chip away at any reservations she held.

———

"Van! This place is stunning!" Cami exclaimed from the passenger seat of my car. The weather in Napa was warm, sunny, and beautiful, and I couldn't have been more pleased to have Cami there with me.

The short half-hour flight had gone smoothly before we touched down in wine country. The vintage convertible I kept for these types of trips was a touch ostentatious, but I was fine with the attention this weekend. Cami was a vision in her floral sundress and the wind in her hair. Watching her tilt her face towards the sun, smiling, as I drove us to the winery made my heart clench. She looked so happy, so relaxed. I wished for this to be our normal.

Pulling down the long, palm tree-lined drive, I grinned at Cami's excitement. The property was truly stunning. I was lucky enough to have had a hand in the winery's start as an investor and was thrilled to be sharing it with Cami for the weekend. While open during the day to visitors for tastings, tours, and lunches, the owners' villa was only accessible to a select few. We would have the entire property to ourselves overnight, and I couldn't wait to get Camellia in the hot tub under the stars later that evening.

I pulled into the brick-lined cul-de-sac, and saw Juliette, one of the winery's founders, heading down the tasting room steps to greet us.

"Mr. Van Costa finally decides to grace us with his presence!" she called by way of greeting, as Cami and I stepped out of the car.

"Juliette, it's good to see you. This is my partner, Cami." I didn't miss Cami's sharp inhale at the distinction. I decided I would just have to keep using it, so she could get used to hearing it. Because that's what she was–my partner–whether or not she believed it.

Juliette grasped both of Cami's hands in hers and smiled warmly. "Cami! It's so lovely to meet you! I've been begging Van to take advantage of the villa for years now. I'm so glad the two of you could enjoy it this weekend."

Cami returned her enthusiasm two-fold. "Thank you. This is my first visit to Napa, and this property, the garden!" She turned in a circle, taking it all in. "It's so beautiful!"

"Van is a big part of what's here. We never would have been able to make it happen without his investment. He saw the potential in the land, and our vision, and helped to make it a reality." Juliette shot me a wink before clapping her hands together. "So the two of you must be ready to eat, huh? I've had the chef prepare your lunch and set you up with a picnic and tasting in the vineyard. We'll take care of your bags, so you can go ahead and get settled. You'll head down that hill and through that middle row of vines. You can't miss the set-up at the end."

"Juliette, I appreciate it," I thanked her.

"You two enjoy your afternoon! We'll see you for dinner."

I wrapped my arm around Cami's waist, smiling at the way she snuggled into my side. Looking down, I kissed the top of her head. "You ready, *bella*?"

She flashed a grin. "Race you?"

"Huh?"

"Loser has to feed the other lunch," she squealed before ripping out of my hold and tearing down the grassy hill, her dress catching air behind her. I stood there, momentarily stunned by the bewildering woman, before coming to my senses and giving chase. Her punishment for coming in second wasn't exactly a hardship, but my competitive nature–and the visceral, animal-like desire that spiked through me at the thought of chasing her down–kicked in and demanded I fight to win.

It didn't take long to come up behind Cami, and I easily snatched her by the waist, hoisting her into my arms as she laughed between gasps for air.

"Caught you," I growled.

"That's because I let you," she smirked.

My dark chuckle in her ear made her shiver, much to my satisfaction. "Is that so?"

She leaned her weight back against my chest as she settled back on her feet. "Mmhm."

"You want to feed me, *bella*?" I murmured in her ear, dragging my nose up the long curve of her neck. "Want me to lick and suck your fingers clean after every bite?"

Her breath hitched and I could just imagine that luscious bottom lip getting trapped between her teeth. "Something like that," she breathed.

I hummed my agreement, very fucking much wanting that, too, and–without letting her go–walked toward the open-sided tent set up for us.

"What if I'd rather feed you?" I whispered in her ear.

She shivered again. "I won't complain."

A flash of what she'd look like on her knees for me as I fed her my cock filled my mind, but I forced the image away. *This weekend is about her.*

Before I could respond, an attendant greeted us with a wave.

"Welcome, Mr. Costa, Ms. Rivera," she said with a smile. "We have a picnic lunch packed for you here. I'll give you some time to enjoy your lunch, then we can start your tasting. Sound like a plan?"

"Sure does!" Cami quipped, her voice a touch squeakier than normal.

The tent was set up over a lush rug and piled with large floor pillows leaned up against a massive antique trunk. An overflowing picnic basket sat off to one side, with a small table holding a pitcher of water, glasses, and a plate of chocolate-covered strawberries. I barely noticed the attendant leave as I released Cami and watched her walk into the middle of the space, a look of awe on her face.

"Gio, this is lovely. Do they treat all their guests this way?"

I shrugged, nonchalant, and walked toward the side table. "Only the VIPs."

"I've never been a VIP before," she murmured, trailing her fingers along a cashmere throw as she knelt on an oversized pillow.

"I imagine Preston and Parker would both join me in disagreeing with you."

Her eyes snapped to mine, her lips parting on a sharp inhale. "How do you do that?"

I glanced over at her as I poured us two glasses of water. "Do what?"

"Just...say exactly what you mean. Right away, like it was on the tip of your tongue."

Handing her a glass, I studied her face for a moment, then bent to sit on my own cushion. "That wasn't a difficult answer to come up with. It might come naturally to you to underestimate your value, but it comes just as naturally to me to make sure you're reminded of the truth."

"Why?" her voice was a small, fragile thing.

"Come here," I commanded, setting my water aside.

She did the same and shuffled over to me. When she was close enough to reach, I grabbed her by the hips and pulled her into my lap, her legs straddling my waist. She gasped and gripped my shoulders to steady herself, and I kept my hands on her sides. Her warmth was tangible against my chest, seeping into me and heating me through. *Time to make a few things clear.*

"I don't know who hurt you," I began as her mouth parted and a flush bloomed on her chest, "but I see their marks. Not every pain is physical, and I see the way you swallow back your pride and shrink from praise, how you minimize your impact to elevate others. And I admire and respect the hell out of you for how deeply you care for those around you. But I need you to understand something." I took a deep breath to steady us both, tension rising in my chest over the thought of anyone hurting her, past or otherwise.

"Whoever convinced you that you aren't enough was wrong, Camellia." My voice was firm, but not unkind. "Whoever made you believe your worth is only in your service to others—they were severely mistaken."

Her eyes were wide, her fingers biting into my shoulder, as her grip tightened.

"I see you," I continued, drinking in every emotion that flashed across her expressive face—surprise, awe, fear—and savoring every twitch of muscle. "I see how hard you work, how talented you are. How you shrink from praise and dismiss accolades."

She took an unsteady breath and looked away, tension radiating through her. With gentle fingers, I took her chin in hand and turned her to face me once more.

"You know and care for everyone you meet. You give pieces of yourself away like it's nothing. But it's not." I cupped her cheek with one hand, emotion swelling in my chest when she leaned into it, her eyes fluttering closed. "You're so much more than what you give to others. The light you share is only so bright because you are the sun."

Cami blew out a shaky breath, a tear spilling over and trailing down one cheek. I leaned forward and kissed it away with a gentle, lingering press of my lips. As I straightened, I swept a thumb over her cheek to catch the next one.

"You are the sun, and I am a selfish man."

"Gio, no, you're—"

I shook my head, interrupting her. "I am. Because I would take every one of your rays if I could. Do you know why?"

"Why?" she whispered.

"To reflect them back to you," I vowed. "To remind you of your worth and your power. Of the gift you are—to me and to everyone who knows you. I am a selfish man, because I would lose myself in you without remorse and take all the light you have to give."

I slid one hand around to grip the nape of her neck, squeezing just enough to make the tension drain from her body and her eyes flare with lust. My cock thickened beneath her. "I want all of you, *bella.*"

She blinked, as though clearing her vision. "No one else in the world sees me like you do, Gio."

"Good," I grunted.

One corner of her mouth twitched up. "Why is that good?"

My fingers flexed on her neck, blood rushing south as she bit her lip in response. "Selfish, remember? I want to be the only mirror of your light. No one else; only me."

"Only you," she whispered, then leaned her forehead against mine. "Gio?"

"Hm?"

"Kiss me. Please."

As you wish. I pulled her lips to mine with a firm hand on the back of her head, directing her so I could devour her more completely. The whimper that rose from her was sweet encouragement, my head swimming with the desire that poured through me. I broke the kiss, cock twitching at the mewling sound of protest she made.

"Later, *bella*. When I can have you to myself."

Her startled blink as she realized we weren't exactly alone made me chuckle.

I looked toward the picnic basket. "Now, let me feed you–"

"No."

My eyebrow arched as I glanced up at her. "No?"

"You won." A satisfied smirk crawled across her face. "I get to feed you."

She moved to get off my lap, but I grabbed her hips, keeping her in place. "You can feed me just fine from here."

"But, I–"

I flexed my fingers on her hips and my cock against her core. She gasped, her cheeks flushing as she fought the urge to look down.

"Oh."

"Mmhm, oh," I confirmed, a wry smile on my lips. "I can reach the basket from here. Teamwork."

She giggled, the sound breaking the tension while the jiggle of her body against mine did nothing to quell the situation in my lap. Ignoring it as best I could, I tugged the basket over to where she could better inspect its contents.

"Oooh, hummus! And zucchini; those look gorgeous."

"I didn't know a vegetable could be gorgeous," I muttered.

She stuck her tongue out, and the silly, childish action drew a sharp laugh from my chest. Grinning, she turned back to the basket.

"Zucchini grows fast and can get huge," she explained, poking around in the basket, "but they need to be picked earlier than most people realize for full flavor and the best texture."

"I see." I listened to her words, but my eyes were locked on her face. *She captivates me without effort.*

"Oh, look!" She pulled out a small dish full of prosciutto-wrapped mozzarella balls drizzled in balsamic and sprinkled with basil. "It's like they know you."

I couldn't help my grin, perhaps sheepish for the first time in years. "They're delicious. I may have learned a thing or two from meals here."

"Stealing ideas from the chef. I see how it is." Her eyes sparkled as she teased me, the tension from earlier discarded. "It's okay," she said absently as she looked back at the basket. "I encourage such thievery. Everyone deserves delicious food, no matter where the inspiration comes from."

I smoothed my thumbs along her hips, glad for the excuse to touch her as she leaned over to grab a bowl of melon.

"Alright, I think we can start with this." She looked up at me shyly. "Any preferences?"

Shaking my head, I licked my lips, waiting. She bit her lip, staring at my tongue for a moment before snatching up a mozzarella ball.

"As a salute to our first night together," she murmured, that blush rising faintly once more.

She placed the bite in my open mouth, and I closed my lips around it and her fingers before she could withdraw her hand. I released her slowly, kissing each glistening fingertip after I did. Her eyes were wide, pupils blown as she watched me, then stared at her fingers for a moment.

"O-okay." She took a deep breath and picked up a piece of melon. After regarding it for a moment, she flicked her eyes to mine. "I propose we play a game."

The way my entire body tightened in response to those words on her lips was apparent.

"Not that kind of game," she said in a rush, placing a hand on my chest. "We can save that for, um, later."

"I see," I drawled, amused.

"You're not a big talker, Gio, and I want to know more of

you." The tentative look from behind her lashes hit me in the chest. How she could still be shy after the things we'd done, I didn't know. *But I fucking love it.*

"I want to know you, too." I rubbed my hands along her upper arms. "What's this game?"

Her lip disappeared between her teeth briefly. "Well, what if we do This or That? And alternate feeding and answering."

I simply nodded and gave her a soft smile. *She could ask me to play pin the tail on the donkey and I'd agree.*

"Okay, me first. Um...beaches or mountains?"

Gently prising the melon from her fingers, I offered it to her so I could answer without my mouth full. She accepted it, eyes on mine.

"Beaches. For you...sweet or savory?"

Her lips twitched up as she offered me a piece of melon. "This may come as a surprise, but savory. Give me umami over sugary sweet any day."

I hummed in agreement and squeezed her hip.

"Night owl or early bird?" she asked.

"Early bird. You?"

"Same." She grinned. "Drives Preston up the wall. Typical night owl, that one."

"I believe it. Stay home or go out?"

"Oh, I'm a homebody for sure. Give me a full kitchen and a glass of wine over a nightclub any day."

"Me, too." Each question and answer painted a more detailed picture of the us that could be and I wanted it. Perhaps more than I had ever wanted anything, which was no small admission.

"How about...who are you closer to, your mom or your dad?" After she finished her question, she happily took a piece of mozzarella from my fingers.

"My madre, now. Before he passed, my papà."

Her eyes widened as she swallowed, then stilled. "Gio, I'm so sorry. I didn't know."

"Please don't be, *fiorellino*. It's been many years; I was just a boy when we lost him."

"No wonder you take care of everyone," she murmured, touching my cheek gently. "I bet you've done that for a long time, haven't you?"

"Cece's been telling stories, I take it." I gave her a reassuring squeeze so she knew I wasn't upset; I expected nothing less from my meddling neighbor. "Losing him was one of the hardest things I've ever lived through, but the grief that seized my madre after...that was worse. Death is cruelest to the living."

Cami wrapped her arms around me and leaned her face into the crook of my neck. I returned her embrace, beyond pleased to have her in my arms despite the somber topic that drove her there. It was clear she needed more of me, as hard as it was for me to talk about myself. My past was just that–I was far more interested in my present and our future. *I'll give you what you need and nothing less than everything you want. And it's increasingly apparent my heart is part of that promise.*

"I stepped up at home because I had to. My grandparents did what they could, but they couldn't keep up with the four of us. I had to grow up fast."

She sighed, snuggling closer. "I'm sorry. Kids deserve to be kids, even if their parents experience trauma."

"Deserve? Yes. Get the opportunity? Not always. But I don't regret those years, Camellia. They shaped me, forged me into the man I am."

She leaned back and looked up at me. "Van Costa, VC hot shot?"

I chuckled at the sparkle in her eye. "Successful. Capable. Stable. All things I knew I would need to be for my family."

Her gaze searched mine. "No one could replace your father, Gio. Not even you."

How she could see through me so clearly was a mystery. I had never been an open book, but Cami could seemingly leaf through my pages at will. "You're right. I tried to for a long time. Thought it was my duty as the eldest. But I know no one could replace him, and I have no desire to try anymore. To my family, I'm just Giovanni. The brother who fixes, the fun uncle–"

"*Fun* uncle?" She laughed.

I growled at her mocking tone and tickled her just enough to make her squeal. "You'd be surprised. Kids love me. And my gifts."

"Ah, of course. Bribery! Isn't that illegal?"

"Not in the Costa family."

Her laugh bubbled through me, lifting my spirits.

"I can't imagine you surrounded by children, Gio. Not the indomitable Van Costa."

I shrugged. "You don't have to imagine it. I'll take you home with me soon. My madre and sisters will love you."

She blinked in surprise as her breath caught. She'd reacted the same every time I mentioned a future together, but had yet to address the subject head on.

"Enzo, that's my little brother, he'll be besotted. You'll have to let him down gently."

The tension in her shoulders broke as she guffawed, shaking her head at me.

"You keep surprising me, Gio."

"Not the pompous asshole you expected?" I teased.

She shook her head and pressed her palms to my cheeks, her fingers lightly running through my hair. "I'm not sure exactly what I expected, but it wasn't this. Not a picnic lunch in a vineyard, or leftovers, or an older neighbor you take care of. I read up on you and Athena and those articles painted such a...one-dimensional picture."

"My profession is one side of me. A significant side, yes. But my professional circle only gets as much of me as I need to succeed."

"And who gets the rest?"

"My family. And you." *They're one and the same.*

She smiled, crossing her wrists loosely behind my neck. "I like that I get this version of you. The warm, playful version; the one who cooks and washes my hair and brings home breakfast." Her voice trailed off, and she cupped her hands around my neck, her fingers interlaced. "When I see you like this, how you are with me...it gives me ideas."

"Hmmm. What ideas, *bella*?" I rubbed one hand up her back, enjoying the feel of her pressed against me. It was an anomaly for me to share space with someone else with such ease.

Worry and a bit of panic crept into her gaze as she regarded me. "Like I wouldn't mind keeping this part of you, all to myself. Even if only for a little while."

"Camellia, you can have all of me." *And for more than just a little while.*

Chapter 22

Cami

I'm pretty sure Giovanni Costa likes me. Like a lot. I smiled over at the man in question as we walked up the path back to our villa. His answering look flashed with heat and desire, and I felt it everywhere.

After our picnic conversation, we'd been glued to one another. I'd remained in his lap until the attendant came back for our wine tasting, at which point Van had turned me around and nestled me back against his chest. He'd completely ignored my squeak and caged me against him with one arm, denying my half-hearted attempt to move to my own seat.

"Settle," he'd said softly in my ear, his large hand flat against my stomach. "You belong right here."

The attendant had smirked at my answering flush, though I wasn't sure she could hear what he'd said. I'm sure we made quite the scene regardless.

"Watch your step, *fiorellino*." Van's firm words and gentle tug on my hand brought my attention back to the present just before I stepped off the path.

"Oh!" I giggled and righted myself, purposely bumping into my attentive escort.

His arm snaked around me and he growled playfully in my ear. "Did you have one too many? Or are you teasing me?"

"Whatever do you mean?" I batted my lashes at him dramatically, my grin wide. Shamelessly, I leaned into his embrace, more than happy to let him guide me down the path.

His chuckle was dark and full of enough promise that my pussy woke up, clenching in anticipation. "I hope you're teasing, *bella*. I have plans for the hot tub, but not if you're drunk."

"I'm not!" I cried. "I promise, I'm not. Hot tub sounds perfect. Yes, please."

He kissed the top of my head and squeezed me with one arm. "Good."

I looked up at him briefly, then cleared my throat. "Will you tell me your plans?"

"Hmm," he rumbled, making goosebumps rise on my arms. "Why don't you tell me what you want, Camellia?"

Oh, I know exactly what I want. I couldn't stop picturing myself on my knees for him; the image had risen in my mind during our picnic, and it had been plaguing me since.

"You've thought of something," he observed, his mouth moving into a deliciously satisfied smile. "Tell me."

It was harder than it should've been to say the words. I wasn't used to voicing my wants, but I knew Van wouldn't let me get away with silence.

"I want you to feed me," I mumbled, eyes locked on his face.

His eyebrows rose. "You're still hungry?"

You can do it, Rivera. Say it. "I, um. I want you to feed me your cock."

One moment, his amber eyes were bright in the low light of the path. The next, his pupils were blown and his eyes hooded with lust. His chest vibrated with a low growl, and my nipples pebbled in response. The next thing I knew, he'd thrown me over his shoulder and was striding swiftly toward the villa, his long steps eating up the distance.

"Gio!" I squealed, laughing breathlessly. "Put me down!"

His hand cracked playfully against my ass. "Not a chance."

I yelped as I felt my wetness gather, surprised at how turned on I was by his possessive behavior. It made my head swim that he could manhandle me as though I weighed nothing at all. I whimpered and his pace quickened.

"Where are you taking me?" I asked, bracing my hands on his lower back. My fingers brushed the top of his ass, the flex and power of his muscles sending a shiver through me.

"Hot tub," was his only response as we got to the villa.

He reached back to fish our key out of his pocket, but I batted his hand away and did it for him. When I lingered unnecessarily long in his back pocket, he swatted my ass again.

"Gio!" I chastised through my laughter, pressing the key into his waiting hand.

He just huffed in response, unlocking the door and letting us through. The moment we crossed the threshold, he stopped and bent to put me back on my feet. I grinned up at him as he straightened, opening my mouth to tease him again, but he didn't give me the chance. He crowded me back against the wall of the entryway, pressing his hard body against mine, as I gasped out a breath.

"You're going to be the death of me," he breathed against my lips, then crushed our mouths together.

I moaned into his kiss, so grateful to taste him and feel him against me. The flames of my desire matched his, pushing me up onto my tiptoes as I leaned into him, my hands fisted in his suit jacket. Without breaking the kiss, he reached down and gathered the hem of the flowing dress he'd bought me, pulling it up over my hips. Following his lead, I began unbuttoning his dress shirt, my movements fumbling and frantic.

After what felt like both an eternity and no time at all, we were standing in the entryway in nothing but our underwear, chests heaving as we drank each other in. He was stunning, standing there with his hair tousled from the teasing of my fingers, lips glistening and swollen from my kisses. His gaze was wild and dark, his fingers trembling slightly, as he reached up and settled his palm against the side of my neck. I tipped my face up to stare at him as I leaned back against the wall, drunk on the knowledge I was the reason he looked so disheveled, so out of control.

"The hot tub is private," he said, his voice low and raw. "No one will see us."

"I don't care–"

The answering sound from deep in his throat made me bite back a moan as my clit throbbed and moisture slipped between my thighs.

"*I* fucking care," he growled. "You and your pleasure belong to *me* and I don't share. Ever. Do you understand?"

God, that should not be so hot. I nodded as my pulse thundered, then gave him the words I knew he was going to ask for, "Yes, Gio."

"Good," he crooned, dropping to kiss and nip the hollow of my throat. He reached down as he did, sliding my thong off my hips until it fell to the floor, then deftly unhooked my bra with a flick of his fingers.

I stepped toward him and out of the discarded clothing, reaching for his boxer briefs. Gently, he stopped me.

"Not yet."

The whine that built in my throat was cut off as he lifted me into his arms, striding toward the private courtyard at the center of the villa. I nuzzled into his neck, breathing in his masculine scent. The hot tub was ready for us, the cover off and space lowly lit. Van gently placed my naked body in the warm water, then stepped back to strip off his briefs. His cock sprang free, hard and shining with precum, and my mouth watered.

"Please, Gio." I moved to the side of the hot tub, reaching for him.

"Patience, *bella*."

He reached over the side of the hot tub and felt along the wall, flicking a switch on the control panel to start the jets.

"Come here," he directed, taking my hand and pulling me into position.

He sat on the edge of the hot tub, his legs in the water, and I surged up to wrap my hand around him. His chuckle turned into a groan as I squeezed gently, then licked a stripe up the hard length of him.

"You want this cock, *fiorellino*?" he asked, grabbing himself by the base and tapping the head against my lips. "Want me to fuck your face?"

My pussy spasmed in affirmation, and I simply nodded and opened my mouth.

"You look gorgeous like that, so eager for me," he murmured. "*Brava ragazza*. Just perfect."

I flushed, pleased by his approval.

"I want you to come too, *bella*. Find the jet in front of you."

Obeying his commanding look, I reached down to find the jet along the wall.

"Ride it," Van demanded.

I shuddered, my nipples rising into tight points despite the heat of the water. Anchoring myself on Van's spread thighs, I thrust my hips forward until the stream of water rushed past my pussy lips to assault my clit directly. My body jerked and I yelped, the sensation overwhelming.

His eyes darkened as he watched my reaction. "That's right, like that. Again."

Doing as I was told, I held onto his thick thighs and looked up to watch him take me in. His amber eyes were almost blackened by the low light and the strength of his want. The water found that sensitive spot between my legs again, and I let out a small mewling sound, pleasure washing through me.

"Open," Van directed, his fist once more around his base. "And don't stop riding that jet."

I opened my mouth immediately, eager for the taste of him and moaned as he guided his cock past my lips.

"I've fucking dreamed about this mouth," he hissed, one hand braced on the wall of the hot tub and the other tangled in my hair. "Can't wait to feel you swallow around me while you come."

My groan was reflexive, lifting through me and vibrating along his cock as I sucked him into my mouth. He was heavy on my tongue and silken smooth, the flavor of him invading my senses and my eyes fluttered closed as I worked my mouth up and down. His grunts of pleasure were just audible over the roar of the jets, and I listened desperately for them as I learned what he liked.

"The jet, Camellia," he reminded me, his voice thick.

I thrust my hips back into position and gave up a groan of my own at the hot pulse of pleasure that shot through me. Hollowing my cheeks, I dug my fingers into Van's thighs to get better leverage. Heat built low in my core, the divine feel of him in my mouth and the persistent, high-pressure throb of the jet slowly dismantling me. He filled my senses, blocking out everything else–the musky scent of him, the feel of his powerful thighs flexing under my hands, the rough sound of his sex-drunk voice. The continuous pressure of the water wound me tighter and tighter until I was nearly vibrating with anticipatory tension. I choked on Van as my concentration slipped, and he inhaled sharply.

"Look at you, choking on my cock. So perfect, so pretty."

Oh, god, why does his praise feel so fucking good? My physical reaction to his words was intense, my muscles tightening as heat blasted from my core through to every part of me. I almost cried around his cock as the wave of my orgasm crested and crashed, my body twisting in response. Dazed, I sloppily tried to keep sucking him as I twitched through the aftershocks, the jet of water surging against my clit every few seconds as I shifted.

"That's it," his voice was like a beacon, cutting through the haze. "I fucking love watching you break. You're stunning, *bella.* Let me see it again."

I popped off his cock for a moment, panting, as the jet pounded at me relentlessly. My concentration was shot, my fingers trembling as I felt another orgasm building so quickly after the first. Nuzzling my face against his hard cock, I licked and sucked at his balls as I felt that slow ratcheting in my core. Van's fingers tightened in my hair and he groaned, leaning his head back as I teased him. I was half out of my mind with pleasure as I tried to suck him back into my mouth. Just as my nose bumped against him, his cock sheathed in my throat, I shattered again. White-hot electricity raced from my pussy out through my limbs, as I struggled not to gag and instead swallowed him down.

"Oh, fuck," he gasped, his eyes snapping down to mine. "Look at you," he whispered, voice full of awe. He brushed the tears off my cheek with a gentle thumb as I went boneless, letting him slip from my mouth so I could draw ragged breaths. "*Nessuna donna è mai stata così perfetta.*"

I licked my lips slowly, and his cock flexed, almost tapping against my face.

"I don't...what does that mean?" I stammered, staring at the hard, angry dick before me.

Without waiting for his answer, I wrapped my lips around him once more. He groaned and his hips thrust up slightly, and I squeezed his thigh in encouragement. Holding on to the hot tub's wall, I stilled, giving him an imploring look and inviting him to do as he had promised. *Fuck my face, Gio. I know you want to.*

"Hold on," he rasped, steadying my head in his hands as he braced one foot on the seat next to him and the other on the floor of the hot tub. "It means–" he thrust into my mouth, then withdrew, thrusting back in with the first word, "no woman has ever been so perfect."

Tears streamed freely down my cheeks once more as he used me, my eyes closing as I held on and focused on breathing through my nose. My jaw ached, but it was the sweetest torture and a small price to pay for the sounds of satisfaction he made with every movement. Van's cock swelled, causing me to gag slightly, and I knew he was close.

"I'm going to come down your throat then fill that tight little pussy," he gritted out.

I moaned my acceptance, then swallowed frantically as he filled my mouth. It was too much, and I could feel it dribbling out of the corners of my lips as he pulsed against my tongue. Releasing his hands, he drew back and slipped from my mouth. I opened my eyes to look up at him and smiled sheepishly, knowing I looked a sight.

"You're so fucking beautiful," he breathed, reaching down to wipe his cum from my face.

The disbelieving huff escaped before I could stop it, and his eyes narrowed.

"Whatever it takes, Camellia. I'll do it," he rasped.

"What?" I asked, breathless.

He stepped out of the hot tub, then lifted me out of the water. Stepping into my space once I was on my feet, he pressed our bodies close together and gently cupped my face in his hands. Standing there in the summer night air, still warmed by the hot tub with the light breeze cooling our skin, there was nothing but the two of us.

"You deserve to see yourself the way I see you," he vowed. "Whatever I have to say or do for you to understand how brightly you shine, how beautiful you are, inside and out–even covered in my cum," his voice dipped to a growl and my greedy pussy tingled. "I'll do it. Whatever it takes. It's the least you deserve."

This man. I reached up on my tiptoes to wrap my arms around his neck, burying my face against him. He lifted me easily, forearms and hands supporting my thighs and ass as I wrapped my legs around his waist. He turned and walked us back into the villa, still soaking wet.

Kissing his neck as we went, I trailed my lips up to his jaw. I ghosted my mouth over his, then dipped back to his neck. I teased and nipped at his skin, then sucked some of him into my mouth, loving the taste of him–all salt and man. A low noise rumbled out of his chest as he suddenly stopped, releasing my lower body and gently setting me on the floor. I whined as he straightened, separating us.

Ignoring my protest, he gathered my wrists in one hand, raising them above my head and pushing them back against the wall. My body followed, and I let out a surprised squeak as I collided with it. *Oh, god, yes.*

"You're a temptress," he growled into my ear, his lips moving to tease the skin at the base of my throat just as I'd done to him. "Distracting me, always distracting me." He murmured absently, as he lavished attention to first one side of my neck, then the other. "Ever since you flitted into my office, you're all I think about, Camellia. You and your smile and that laugh..."

His free hand trailed down the side of my body, raising goosebumps as it went. When he reached my hip, his hand dipped to cup my pussy, his palm large and impossibly warm against my pleasure-swollen flesh.

"And this perfect pink pussy," he continued, slowly pushing two fingers inside me. "I think about this..." He pushed his fingers in and out, coating them in my arousal before rubbing them against my G-spot. I moaned, thrusting my hips toward him, and an answering rumble sounded from deep in his chest. "All the time, *bella*. There's not a moment in my day when I don't want you."

There was an edge to his voice, a desperate need, and I wanted nothing more than to give him everything he wanted.

"You have me," I whispered. "Take me, Gio. I'm yours."

Before I could register what was happening, he spun me around to face the wall.

"Put your hands up," he commanded, "ass out."

I obeyed without hesitation, bracing myself against the wall as he lightly kicked the inside of my ankle to widen my stance. The moment I was in position, he dragged the head of his stiff cock against my entrance, coating himself in my wetness. Despite the tension I could feel in his body, caged in as I was between him and the wall, he lingered there between my thighs and teased me until I was dripping. I could hear myself, but was helpless to stop the soft gasps and moans falling from my lips.

"What do you want? I need to hear you say it." The soft rush of his breath against my ear only heightened my anticipation.

"Fill me up," I begged, voice broken and edged in want.

My wish was his command, and he buried himself completely with one thrust. I cried out at the stretch, the heady mixture of pleasure and pain scrambling my senses.

Van grunted as he set a fast pace. "Perfect."

Thrust.

"Fucking."

Thrust.

"Fit."

Thrust.

He swiveled his hips before pulling out, ensuring he hit that sensitive spot inside me with unerring precision. My eyes closed as I lost myself in the feel of him, the slap of our bodies together, the rough bite of his fingers as he held my hips at the right angle. *I hope they bruise.* I'd never wanted to wear another man's mark before, had been horrified when Gabriel had been rough enough to bruise me, but some animal part of me relished the idea of seeing the evidence of Van's fingers in the mirror after this. I wanted that reminder of him and the way he worshiped my body.

One of Van's hands left my hip, moving around to find my clit. He circled it, slowly, and I let out a lewd moan, hanging my head as my arms started to shake.

"Just like that," he urged. "Love the way you squeeze me, *fiorellino.* Want to feel you come on this cock."

I nodded my head absently, unable to find the words to reply. We wanted the same thing. My knees shook as my pleasure spiked, and he pressed me more firmly against the wall. The wallpaper, textured and luxe, rubbed against my nipples, the roughness of it sending me spiraling higher. I could sense the cliff; I was almost there. Van's pace was faltering, and I knew he was right there with me.

"Together," I gasped, more plea than command.

Van hummed a pleased sound that ended in a groan as he kept tempo on my clit, my orgasm welling inside of me with the slow, long pull of a gathering tsunami. As it began to break, my body locked up in tension as it crested, slow and languorous, and Van spilled inside of me. He continued his rhythm and the teasing of his fingers, and I screamed as that wave ripped through me, ravaging my senses as I shook in his arms, my awareness fading.

————

When I came back to my senses, we were both on the floor. Van held me in his lap, my back to his chest and his face pressed against my neck.

"You passed out," he murmured, squeezing his arms tighter around me. "I'd prefer you do that in the bed in the future."

I huffed an amused chuckle and felt his lips curve into a smile against my skin. Then he'd bundled me up into his arms and proceeded to the bath and then the shower, taking his time as he cared for me. The ritual–because that's what it was, I finally recognized–was no longer strange to me. I appreciated it, adored being the center of his attention. My world so often revolved around others; it was a rare gift to watch someone center me.

After showering, he settled us on the bed to comb through my hair. Then he asked me to lose my towel, and I leaned back against his chest, skin-to-skin, and hummed my contentment. I could hear Van pump lotion into his hands, then he warmed it in his palms before smoothing it over my arms.

"What are you doing to me, Gio?" I whispered as my eyes fluttered closed, exhaustion making me heavy.

"Moisturizing," he answered, just as quietly, then kissed my head.

That's not what I meant, and you know it. I chuckled, and I could hear his grin. "The mighty Van Costa is lotioning me."

"The humbled Giovanni is caring for *sua regina* as she deserves," he corrected.

I turned my head and tilted it back to look up at him. "Please tell me what that means." I had an inkling, but I wanted to hear him say it. And I knew he wouldn't tell me unless I asked.

He smiled, a flare of approval in his gaze for my direct request. *I'm learning, Gio. Slowly but surely.* He placed a soft kiss on my lips.

"His queen, *bella*. The humbled Giovanni is caring for his *queen* as she deserves."

Chapter 23

Cami

"Do we have to leave?" I asked Van with a teasing whine, sticking my lower lip out in an exaggerated pout.

Chuckling, he leaned in to kiss me before drawing my lip between his teeth, tugging at it gently. I relaxed into the kiss, chasing after him as he pulled away. He rumbled in approval and kissed me again, thoroughly. When we parted, I was flushed and panting lightly. *I love the way he makes me feel.*

"We do," he said simply, answering my petulant question.

I sighed, glancing around the villa. Van had assured me no packing was necessary–just as all the beautiful clothes, jewelry, and makeup had magically appeared in the villa at our arrival, they would be packed for us and returned to the Bay. He'd called it a simple gift, but my mind was still reeling over the fact he'd planned and shopped for me.

"This was perfect, Van." I turned to him and threw my arms around his waist, hugging him fiercely. He returned my embrace readily, as he always did. "Thank you."

"You deserve more," he murmured in response.

I leaned back and beamed up at him. "You can just say 'you're welcome,' you know."

He shrugged, a twinkle in his eye. "I only speak the truth."

Playfully, I rolled my eyes and preened internally at his indulgent laugh.

"I'm glad you enjoyed yourself, *bella*," he said. "We'll visit again soon. Come," he reached out his hand, offering it to me. "Let's find Juliette before we go."

It was a cloudless summer's day in Napa as we stepped from the porch and onto the winding path back to the main tasting room. A gentle breeze swept my loose hair back and made the wide legs of my sleeveless white jumpsuit flutter. Van looked as delicious as ever in his white linen shirt and tan pants, his dark hair still damp from our shower. I bit my lip and looked down, smiling to myself as I remembered him on his knees before me.

"What's on the menu this week?" Van asked, distracting me from my salacious thoughts.

"I'm not sure yet." My anxiety spiked at the thought of all that awaited me when we got home, but I pushed the feelings down. The only reason we were leaving that morning, instead of in the evening, was because I had hours of prep work to do for the week if I wanted to fulfill the orders flooding in. "Lani promised she'd work with the market folks to get my produce delivered to the condo, so we should be good to go."

Van frowned slightly. "Do you have enough space for everything in your kitchen?"

"I think so? It's getting tight, but Preston had a double fridge installed back when the Kitchen was just an idea. She's extra like that."

"Hm," he replied, his gaze distant as he seemed to lose himself in thought.

I squeezed his hand, bringing him back to me, and he flashed me a smile.

"Van? Van Costa?"

The smile slipped off Van's face at the sound of the woman's voice. He squeezed my hand back, then turned in the direction the voice had come from.

"Victoria."

"I thought that was you." The leggy blonde whipped off her sunglasses and looked Van up and down. She completely ignored my existence in the process. "It's been a while."

"It has. Did you stop us for a reason?" His voice was flat, uninterested, but my stomach still turned.

If you looked up "Cami Rivera's polar opposite" in the dictionary, you'd see a picture of this woman. She was tall, svelte, with blue eyes as piercing as they were cold. Her impeccable clothes and shoes screamed money, as did the diamonds at her neck and on her wrist. I glanced between them, not missing the mild claim and want in her expression. *Is she seriously his type?*

Victoria's eyes flicked to mine as her lips thinned in distaste. "She's a bit young for you, Van."

Van's jaw ticked and his hand tightened around mine as I tried to draw it back. "Goodbye, Victoria."

She tutted, and I wanted to shrink under her withering stare. "Still a man of few words, I see."

He ignored her, pulling me along toward the tasting room. I went with him, trying desperately not to give in to the urge to look back at the beautiful ice queen.

"You should call me," she exclaimed, and the vein in Van's forehead pulsed.

I tried to free my hand from his, uncomfortable and feeling out of place, but he looked down at me sharply and refused to let me pull away.

"Van, who was that?" I asked, trying to keep the insecurity out of my voice as I gave up the fight for my hand.

"No one of consequence." His reply was short, clipped. *Seriously? That's it?*

I squirmed internally, hating everything about how our getaway was coming to a close. "You dated?"

The muscles in his jaw flexed again. "We had an arrangement."

What kind of arrangement?! I couldn't picture him having a full conversation, let alone sex, with someone that frigid. The Van I knew was domineering, yes, but he was also tender and warm. He liked to wrap himself up with and lose himself in me, and there was no losing yourself in someone that stiff and brittle.

"Van, I'm–"

"Juliette, I'm so glad we found you," Van interrupted, giving a professional smile as our host appeared around the last bend in the path.

She beamed at us, then frowned slightly. "You're not leaving already, are you? The day has just begun!"

"We are," he confirmed.

"Thank you so much, Juliette," I jumped in, finally freeing my hand from Van's to clasp hers in both of mine. "The villa, your vineyard, the wine...it's all been a dream. Truly. Thank you."

She gripped my hand and grinned. "You're welcome back anytime, Cami. With or without your imposing, tight-lipped companion." She cast him a knowing look.

I smiled, but it didn't feel as genuine as I wanted it to be. Our weekend had been idyllic, yes, but seeing Victoria had violently dimmed my afterglow. She and I were nothing alike, and it only brought the question of my compatibility with Van back to the forefront of my mind.

"We'll be back," Van assured her. "Thank you again."

He turned to go, and Juliette smiled and waved as we walked away. Van gave me a questioning look, offering me his hand once more, and I bit my lip. I gripped my opposite elbow instead, needing a moment. Frustration flared in his eyes, but he didn't push.

The ride to the airport started out both quiet and tense. Van rested his hand on my knee, fingers flexing, and I fought the urge to pull away. *Why won't he talk to me?*

"Van, I don't understand," I broke the silence, my voice small. *It sounds like I feel.* "Who was she?"

He turned to face me, twisting in his seat. "We saw each other briefly. She was trying to elevate her visibility in certain circles in the Bay and was my date to a few events. Nothing more." *That's vague as fuck.*

"She seemed..." I couldn't find a word that wouldn't be insulting, and my voice trailed off.

"Self-absorbed," he said, his tone softening. "I told you she was no one of consequence, Camellia. I meant it."

I nodded, knowing by the finality in his tone he wasn't going to say more. The explanation didn't feel like enough, but I tried to put it out of my mind. Van had done nothing this weekend to make me doubt his intentions or his fidelity–if anything, he'd tried to show me with his words and actions how invested he was in me, in us. But I'd believed Gabriel's intentions, too, and he'd shattered my heart without a second thought.

Van could sense my distance, but he didn't push me. We pulled up to the airfield a short time later, his hand still on my knee. He exited the car first, then offered me a hand to help me out after him. I murmured a thank you, then followed him onto the waiting jet.

We sat facing each other, a small table between us. Van's brows furrowed as he studied me, then glanced out the window as we began to taxi for takeoff.

"You were telling me about your plans for this week," he prompted.

I blinked at him, my mind still whirling. "Um, I'm not sure.

I need to get home and see what I'm working with. Kind of in the dark until then."

"Hm. How do you track your ingredients and recipes?"

"Oh, I try to be as seasonal–"

Van's phone rang with a ringtone I hadn't heard before. A look of surprise, then concern, crossed his face as he glanced at the caller ID.

"I'm sorry, Cami. I have to take this."

He rose, moving toward the back of the plane, and I sighed and slumped in my seat as the plane took off and then leveled out. It was usually so easy for me to be optimistic, to see the silver lining in any situation. Preston was always complaining about my uncanny ability to turn any situation into something good. But my optimism was failing me. How many amazing weekends in Napa would it take to bridge the differences between us?

I was pulled from my thoughts by Van's return, and I immediately sat up in concern. I hadn't seen that look of worry on his face before, and there was visible tension in his shoulders.

"Gio, what is it? Did something happen?"

"I'm afraid I'm going to have to leave you with my driver when we land, Cami," he said, clearly still distracted by the conversation he'd just had.

Come again? "Um, okay?"

"I have to take the jet." He looked at me as though that explained everything. "Antonio is very good at his job; he'll get you home safely."

The last thing on my mind was my safety. No, what I was concerned about was the fact my would-be boyfriend and partner (his words, not mine), was treating me like a task on his to-do list.

"Van, are you okay? What's going on?"

"I have something to take care of, Cami." He held up his

phone briefly, then turned his attention to the screen. "Forgive me, but I need to make some arrangements."

I think I hate the word 'arrangement'. Unsure what else to do, I pulled my phone out of my purse and tried to distract myself from my spiraling thoughts.

Chapter 24

Cami

Monday could go fuck itself. Hating any day of the week was new for me, but I could suddenly understand why so many people had an issue with Monday. By the time I had dragged myself home after the biggest lunch rush of my entire life, I wanted to curl up in a ball and cry. *And Preston isn't even here to commiserate with me, the bitch.* If she thought thousands of miles and nine hours of time difference were going to stop me from calling her in for virtual backup, she was dead wrong.

I sat on a stool at our kitchen island, a glass of wine in hand. Just minutes after I'd gotten home the day before, a courier had shown up with a rack full of the clothes and shoes Van had gifted me in Napa, a massive camellia bouquet, and two cases of wine from the winery. The printed note with "Thinking of you" in embossed letters was a gut punch reminder that Van had left me on the tarmac without another word of explanation. I glanced down at my phone, our text thread open from this morning.

> Gio: I hope your prep went well yesterday, bella. Still thinking of you.

> Me: Thank you for the gifts. How are you?

It had been hours, but my question remained unanswered. *You're ridiculous, Rivera. What are you even doing?! This pining or whatever isn't you.*

I needed to stop obsessing over Van's lack of communication. *Hope you're not busy, Pres.*

> Me: I'm spiraling

> Pres: No. Not allowed when I'm not around

> Me: Why are you answering me immediately when Van has ignored me for hours?

> Pres: What the fuck? What happened?

Before I could even start a reply, my phone vibrated with an incoming video call. I answered it, despite knowing Preston would immediately zero in on my disheveled state.

"What the fuck, Cam? Did you run a marathon?" she barked the second our call connected.

"It feels like it," I sighed, leaning my phone against the vase of Van's latest floral gift. "Today was the hardest it's ever been for me and the Kitchen."

She winced. "Worse than the time the water went out in the building for a day?"

I nodded. "I think I slept four hours last night. Maybe? After I got back, I had to do all the prep, and I realized I forgot to edit the cap on the orders, so there were way more submitted than I would usually fulfill, and–"

"Whoa, whoa, whoa. Cami, honey, you're going a mile a minute. Slow down."

"Sorry," I mumbled, dropping my forehead onto my crossed arms. "It's been a day."

"Sounds like it. Maybe start with your weekend? How was Napa with Daddy Van?"

"I don't know," I said into the counter, my head still down.

"Bitch, you called me on vacation. Talk."

"You're mean," I accused, raising my head to scowl at her.

She cocked an eyebrow at me, having none of my shit. "I'm waiting."

"It was amazing, truly. Utterly perfect..."

She scoffed. "I totally believe you, given how excited you sound and look," she deadpanned.

"...until it wasn't."

As I explained how the weekend had ended, Preston's exclamations went from shocked to pissed to confused.

"He hasn't told you where he is?"

"Nope," I popped the 'p', tempted to drop my head back onto my arms.

"What the fuck," she muttered. Then she shook her head. "We'll come back to that in a moment. You started this conversation lamenting about the Kitchen. Say more."

"It's utter chaos, Pres. I've got a rush delivery of more ingredients coming tonight just to make it through tomorrow and part of Wednesday. I sold out over the weekend, but I forgot to edit the order limit in the system because I've never come remotely close to hitting it before."

"Wait, you oversold? For today?"

I groaned. "I wish. I oversold for the *week*."

"Cami, what the fuck! That's wild!" Her excited look quickly morphed and she narrowed her eyes. "You can't fulfill all those! You'll run yourself ragged."

"I can't just piss off my customers!"

"Um, like fuck you can't. You're one person, Cam. And recognizing your limits is healthy."

I could feel the tears welling, hot and heavy. "But if I can't do this..." *Maybe my parents are right and this is all a pipe dream.*

"Nope, not a chance. Don't go there. Stop!" she snapped, raising a finger at the camera. "Camellia Rivera, you are over-tired and overworked and that's making you emotional. Which is a perfectly acceptable human response, but this self doubt bullshit is *not* acceptable. Rein it in."

Blinking away my tears, I nodded. "O-okay."

"Repeat after me: I can do this."

Swallowing, I fought back the tremor in my voice. "I can do this."

"I'm a badass bitch."

I laughed, shaking my head. "I'm a badass bitch."

"Okay, good. Now, let's figure out a plan."

Guilt rose. "Pres, no, you're on vacation. I'm okay, I just got overwhelmed like you said–"

"Girl, you were two seconds from a nuclear meltdown. Let's do this shit together now, so I can go to sleep knowing I don't have to send Parker over to check on you in the morning."

I sighed, knowing there was no arguing with her. "Fine. Honestly, I planned to ask the market network to band together to help me get through this week. I've put in the limit to cap the orders so I won't oversell for next week, but this week is going to be rough. I have no idea where all the demand came from, but maybe it's related to the List?"

Sailing right over my speculation, she focused on the action plan–as was her way. "Did you ask the market crew to help with the prep too?"

"Oh." Blinking, I shook my head. "No."

"Do that. I'm sure some of them will jump in themselves or send someone who can help."

"Good call."

"And text Parker tomorrow. He and LB barely use their

kitchen, so I bet you could use it if you're running out of storage or prep space at home. Like an overflow space or something."

"I have to prep here because of permit stuff, but they could hold pre-prepped ingredients for me. That might be handy."

She nodded, studying my face until she seemed satisfied with what she saw. "You've got this, Cam."

My lips twitched into a small smile. "Thanks, Pres."

Her brows lowered. "Now, about Van."

I tried to wave her off, already feeling overexposed. "It's okay, I'm being silly."

"You're feeling some kind of way about running into his frigid ex and that's okay. Your feelings are valid."

"I know. It's just...do you think that's what he wants? Someone like her?"

Her face contorted as she stared at me. "Are you high?"

I couldn't stop the sad laugh that burst out of me.

"Because you'd have to be high to think he preferred whatever her name is to you. She sounds about as bland as unseasoned mashed potatoes. You're fusion cuisine with a hell of a kick."

"Some people like unseasoned mashed potatoes."

She looked at me like I'd sprouted a second head. "Not if they're sane. Babe, has Van ever indicated he wanted you to be anything or anyone other than exactly who you are?"

"No, but he's also—"

"Nope, the but doesn't matter. Remember what Parker said—Van says what he means. If he wanted something different, don't you think he'd tell you?"

"Maybe," I mumbled. I wanted to believe her, but my head was resistant.

"Don't be stubborn. Send him a nude. I bet that'll get a response right away." She cackled.

"Okay, I see we've entered the unhelpful portion of the conversation."

"How dare you! I'm always helpful." She winked at me.

I chuckled and sighed. "Thanks, Preston. Sorry to make you solve all of my problems from France."

"Pssh," she waved me off. "I'll solve your problems from wherever, babe. Love you."

"Love you, too. Are you going to tell me about your trip?"

Her gaze sharpened, flashing with something unreadable. "I'm saving up my stories. I'll tell you when I get home. Gotta go live them all first."

She grinned, but I could see something wild lurking in her expression. "Okay, if you say so."

"I say so. Now go prep your sexy ass off and show this week who's boss!"

"Yes, ma'am." I mock-saluted her.

"Ugh, never call me that again." She shuddered in disgust. "Bye, babe!"

"Bye!" I called, waving, but she was already gone.

Spinning on my stool, I took a deep breath and let my brain catch up. It wasn't lost on me that my best friend and the guy I was more than a little interested in were the two most intense humans I had ever encountered. *One or the other of them is going to be the death of me, I know it.*

I glanced down at my phone, then picked it up and opened my thread with Van.

> **Me: Hey, how was your day?**

Telling myself distraction would be the best approach, I turned back to the fridge to assess how much produce I'd have to beg and borrow from my network the next day. As I dug through the meager remnants of the truly obscene amount of greens my sister had stocked in the fridge over the weekend, I heard my phone buzz with a text notification. I snatched it up and let the fridge close behind me.

Gio: Better now. I miss you, bella.

You can't melt over one little text message, Rivera.

Gio: I had to go home. Everything is fine, but I'll be here a bit longer.

Suddenly concerned for completely different reasons, I hurried to reply.

Me: Is everyone okay?

Gio: They are. Thank you.

I sighed in relief, slouching as I leaned against the island.

Me: For the record, I miss you too. Can we go back to Napa?

Gio: Anything for you.

Biting my lip, I told the butterflies in my stomach to settle.

Gio: I have to go. Sweet dreams.

Staring down at my phone, I let out a long breath, releasing the excitement that had built. The emotional rollercoaster my business and Van put me on had wrung me dry, and I still had to source ingredients and prep for the next day. My business had always been a source of joy and contentment; I loved everything from picking the produce and planning the menu to handing each customer their lunch with a smile. But I didn't love anything about the prior 24 hours–every single one of them had sucked. *This Monday is the fucking worst.*

Chapter 25

Van

"Is it going to run away?"

I glanced up from my phone, meeting my madre's annoyed gaze. "What?"

"Your phone. Is it going to grow legs and run off?"

I blinked. "No."

She tutted, then turned back to the sauce on the stove. "You've been staring at it for ten minutes. I haven't seen you move an inch."

Sighing, I locked my phone and looked up to watch her move from the stove to the fridge and back. I wanted nothing more than to pluck her out of the kitchen and into the armchair in the living room, but she wouldn't let me. She'd smacked me when I'd tried.

"Sorry, Mamma. I'm hoping to hear from someone."

She glanced back over her shoulder at me, assessing. "A girl," she announced, turning her attention back to the sauce. "Who is she?"

I pinched the bridge of my nose, my eyes scrunching closed. If I didn't give her something, she'd just ask until I lost all patience. "Her name is Cami."

Mamma froze for a few moments, likely surprised I'd shared anything, then resumed her puttering. "Tell me."

Frowning, I looked down at my dark phone screen. "She usually answers quickly, but I haven't heard from her in a few hours."

She tsked at me. "Tell me about her. Where did you meet?"

"Work."

I could hear her eye roll. "Of course," she muttered under her breath. "Where else would my boy meet a nice girl?"

"She's an entrepreneur," I clarified. "She has a catering business and delivers lunch to our building."

She turned, interest sparking in her eyes. "She feeds you?"

I chuckled and nodded. "Every day."

"I like her. Why isn't she here with you?"

"Mamma, you were hurt."

"Psh. I am fine. It would take more to take me down. You should have brought her."

I stifled my sigh. "Enzo called and said you'd been in a car accident with the girls, Mamma. That didn't seem like the right time to bring her home."

Leaving Cami had been the last thing I'd wanted to do, but my frantic brother had shared so little information I'd had no idea what to expect when I arrived in Jersey. My attention had been stolen away from Cami entirely as I made arrangements for my arrival and reached out to the local hospital to learn what I could about the condition of my mamma and nieces. Guilt over how quickly I had dismissed Cami rose, not for the first time, and I swallowed roughly.

"We're fine," her voice brought me back. "The girls were safe and snug in their seats and this will heal." She motioned toward the bandage on her face, which hid the cut on her forehead.

"I needed to be here," I grumbled.

"You've been here for days, Giovanni. I love having you here, but not when you're like this." She waved her wooden spoon at me.

"Like what?"

"Tense. Fidgety. A ball of stress. I don't like it. Puts me on edge." She gave an exaggerated shiver.

My eyebrow rose. "I didn't know stress was contagious."

"Yours is," she insisted, turning back to the stove. "You're the rock of this family; have been for years. When you're tense or worried, we feel it. Especially when you're here."

"I don't mean to stress you, Mamma."

"I know, *tesoro*. Go call your girl if she's not answering. You don't need to watch over me like a mother hen."

Taking a deep breath, I considered my options. The idea of talking to Cami, hearing about her week directly instead of through text, was too tempting to pass up. "You'll call out for me if you need help?"

"I bumped my head, Giovanni!" she snapped. "I'm not an invalid."

"You had a concussion," I replied, tone stern. "That's nothing to mess around with."

"If I was a hazard to myself, they would've kept me in the hospital. But I've been home for three days." She gave me a challenging look, then turned back to her cooking. "I'm fine. Go. Take your stress with you."

I stood from my stool and wandered into the next room, unlocking my phone as I went. Cami and I had only shared a few messages since Monday, but I knew she'd been unreasonably busy, and I hoped her silence was nothing more than that. Guilt pinched in my chest again. I'd been distracted by things with my family and hadn't reached out to her nearly as much as I usually did. I figured she had probably finished up her deliveries about an hour before, and I glanced down at our text thread.

> Me: How was your Friday, bella?

It had been about an hour since I'd sent the message. Taking a seat on the couch, I considered my next move. *It's been long enough.*

> Me: Busy day?

As I stared at the screen, my spirits lifted as the three dots appeared, showing she was typing.

> Camellia: sorry, yeah 😔

Her reply was much shorter than normal, and I pursed my lips in concern.

> Me: You okay?

> Camellia: yeah, just under the weather

My eyebrows rose. *Why didn't she tell me?*

> Me: Did you take a sick day?

> Camellia: ...no?

My jaw ticked. She needed to take care of herself; business could always wait.

> Me: Video call me.

> Me: Please

Camellia: i just need sleep

Me: Camellia

Camellia: gio

Growling to myself, I opened her contact and stabbed the video call button. *She better answer.* When the call connected, I sighed in relief.

"Where are you, *bella*?" I cocked my head, trying to decipher the dark image on my screen.

"Bed," she croaked.

Concern punched me in the gut as I watched the indecipherable image shift around before her face was illuminated. She was in bed, as she'd said, with the blackout curtains clearly drawn. Her skin was pale and shiny, as though feverish.

"Camellia, what happened?" I rose slowly, the nervous energy coursing through me making it impossible to stay in one place.

"Just sick," she muttered, laying her arm over her eyes, her voice thin and hoarse.

"You need a doctor."

"M'fine, Gio. Just tired. S'been a week."

My eyebrows crashed together. "What happened this week?"

She sighed, then started coughing before she could respond.

"I'm sending my doctor to your place. He does house calls and you need medication."

She shook her head and waved her hand at me, trying to refuse through the heavy, wet coughs.

"Get some water, Cami," I demanded, worry a tight ball in my chest. "Please, you need to take care of yourself."

The coughing fit ended, and she blinked at the phone. Tears

rolled slowly from the corners of her eyes. "It's been a rough week," she rasped. "I just need to sleep. For a few days."

"Yes, you need sleep, but you also need medical attention." She started to deny me again, but I interrupted. "I don't care how much you protest. I'm sending Dr. Landry over. Is Preston there to let him in?"

"France," she rasped, trying to hold back another coughing fit.

Remembering she had mentioned Preston's trip, I groaned in frustration. "I'll figure something out. Get some water and try to rest. He'll be there soon."

"Gio, don't–"

"Camellia," I growled. "This is not up for negotiation."

I could hear her swallow, it was so rough. "'Kay."

"Get some rest." Three other words were on the tip of my tongue, but I couldn't say them then. Not in that moment, not over video, not when she looked like death warmed over and sounded even worse. *Soon, though. Very soon.*

She just nodded at me and ended the call. I immediately pulled up Dr. Landry's number, tapped call, and put it on speaker, then reopened my messages.

> Me: Are you home?

> Parker: Hi, boss. Aren't you in Jersey?

> Me: Answer the question.

> Parker: ...yes, I'm home

> Me: You need to let Dr. Landry into Cami's condo in 15.

As I finished typing, the call connected. I explained the situation to the doctor and demanded he prioritize Camellia's case.

He agreed quickly, both willing to do me a favor and knowing he'd be well compensated for the emergency visit. After ending the call, I turned my attention back to my messages.

> **Parker:** What? Is Cami okay?
>
> **Parker:** Van, what the hell?
>
> **Parker:** VAN
>
> > **Me:** I don't know what happened this week, but she needs medical attention. Preston is out of town, but I assume you have a key?
>
> **Parker:** Of course I do
>
> > **Me:** Dr. Landry is on his way.
>
> **Parker:** So am I

I should've felt some sense of relief at Parker's assurance, but I didn't. My worry for Cami overwhelmed everything else, and I knew it wasn't enough to coordinate things from afar. Making up my mind, I strode quickly back to tell my madre. The moment I entered, she looked up at me.

"You're leaving," she announced before I could open my mouth.

"I am."

She nodded. "You clearly need to. Is she okay?"

"No."

Her brows drew low, and she stepped away from the stove, wrapping her arms around me. "Then you have somewhere you need to be, Giovanni. And it isn't here, in your mamma's kitchen." She released me, stepping back to regard me. "She's special to you, this Cami."

"She is."

"Tell me why."

I glanced down as images of Cami flooded my mind. Her laughing brightly in the middle of the open space at Athena. Her looking up at me shyly from behind her lashes as she handed over the first lunch I ordered. The way she fell to her knees and giggled in delight every time Duke ran up to her, his whole body wagging in excitement. Each vision was a balm for my soul, lifting me up and filling me with a sense of hope. I worked hard to provide for myself and my family, but being with Cami made me want to live, to experience the world through her lens.

"Everything is brighter when I'm with her." Looking up, I met my madre's knowing gaze. She had watched every emotion cross my face, but I still said the words I knew would best help her understand. *"Senza di lei, la mia vita non avrebbe senso."*

She took in a sharp breath, emotion welling in her eyes. Those words had been special to her and my papà, a phrase they shared to acknowledge and celebrate their love. *Without her, my life would be meaningless.*

"Then do whatever you need to, *tesoro*. And don't you dare let her go."

Chapter 26

Cami

I felt like I had attempted a triathlon without training. With a cold. My chest was heavy, my brain in a fog. The congestion had started Friday morning, and by the time I'd finished my deliveries that afternoon, I could barely stand upright. I had flopped into bed without even changing out of my clothes, desperate to try and sleep off whatever it was before I had to prep for the next week.

The thought of doing my job had never made me cry before. My heart tore in half as I sobbed into my pillow, overwhelmed and overwrought. Sometime between my emotional breakdown and when my coughing forced me into the kitchen for water, Van had called. I hadn't missed his first text an hour before, but I hadn't been in a state to form a coherent thought, let alone type a reply. The mere sight of his message had caused a fresh wave of tears because I hadn't heard from him since Wednesday.

Van's text messages and my lunchtime visits over the last few weeks had meant more to me than I could articulate. His care, his attention–they had made me feel seen in a way I had never been before in my adult life. And when he allowed the distance between us to grow, when he stopped reaching out and took hours to answer my texts, I had never felt so alone. And, even through the haze of the illness gripping me, I knew my thoughts were illogical. That I was giving him too much power and myself not enough. But, damn it, I was having the single worst week of my life and I fucking needed someone. And for the first time since I'd moved to the Bay, I hadn't wanted to lean on Preston. I wanted Van.

"Cami?" Parker's voice broke through my malaise, and I lifted my head from where it rested on my arms.

"Parker?" I croaked, then started coughing, nearly sliding off my stool.

"Shit," he muttered, rushing over to my side.

LB, his girlfriend, was behind him, a look of concern in her blue eyes. "Cami, honey, what happened?"

I shrugged. "Needed water."

She winced at my hoarse voice, then looked around. "Did you get it?"

Blinking, I slowly shook my head. I couldn't exactly remember what had happened between deciding I needed water and ending up on the kitchen stool. "Forgot."

"Ohhhkay," she said, her eyes wide. "Let's get you to bed. Parker, get her some water and put the kettle on."

"On it," he called, rushing over to the cabinet.

"Come on, hun." LB draped my arm over her shoulders, then wrapped hers around my waist. "Bedtime."

Wordlessly, I slipped off the stool and stumbled briefly against her before finding my feet.

"Thanks," I muttered, resting my head on her shoulder.

"Of course," she answered. "You're going to explain what the hell is going on and how you got into this state at some point, missy, but for now, I'm just going to help you get some rest. Van told Parker he'd sent a doctor over, so here's hoping he can help you feel better."

Van did what? I vaguely remembered Van mentioning a doctor, but most of our conversation was little more than a blur. LB helped me into my room, then eased me into a pair of sweats and a soft t-shirt. As I lowered my arms to slip them through the sleeves, the room started to spin and I could hear blood rushing in my ears.

"Gonna pass out." I quickly flopped over onto my pillow, not wanting to fall right off the edge of the bed.

In the distance, I heard male voices and footsteps, then LB saying something I couldn't understand. Then everything went dark.

———

I can breathe. As my awareness returned, I realized the heaviness that had settled into my chest had eased. I was comfortable and warm, snuggled into the covers. *And someone is stroking my hair. Wow, that feels good.*

Blinking the sleep from my eyes, I turned to face the presence at my back.

"Van?" I gasped, raising my head as I caught sight of him, brow drawn in concern.

"Settle, *bella*," he murmured, pressing lightly on my shoulder to keep me from sitting up.

"You're here," I whispered as I relaxed back into the sheets, dumbstruck.

"I am," he nodded, brushing the backs of his fingers over my forehead, then cupping my cheek in one large, warm palm. "How do you feel?"

"Why are you here?" I ignored his question, emotions bubbling up, hot and insistent in my chest.

He studied my face for a moment, then leaned down and pressed his lips to my forehead. "I needed to be here," he breathed against my skin. "For you. With you."

Tears gathered in my eyes as he straightened. "But you were with your family."

"I was. And now I'm here where I belong."

He gently wiped the tear that spilled from the corner of one eye as I stared up at him.

"But what happened?" I pressed through my tears. "Are they okay?"

"Calm, *fiorellino*. Mamma and my nieces were in an accident, but they're fine. They're safe." He stroked his fingers through my hair, teasing it back from my face. "I need you to be, too."

"You came back...for me?" My voice was trembling, as was the hand I reached out to clasp his.

"Of course." He turned to the nightstand, and I saw a steaming mug and bowl sitting there. "I made you tea. And soup."

There was no stopping the ragged sob that tore from my lips before I clapped a hand to my mouth. Van turned to me, eyes wide with concern.

"What is it, Cami?" he pressed. "Are you in pain? Dr. Landry said you shouldn't be hurting."

I shook my head, unable to speak as the sobs kept coming. Everything that had happened over the last five days crashed into me at once–the stress over work, the emotional turmoil over Van's sudden distance, the feelings of inadequacy in so many aspects of my life. And on top of all of that was the utter disbelief that Van had returned the moment he realized something was wrong. He arranged a doctor to care for me, then traveled across the country to make sure I was okay.

"You...you made me soup?" I gasped through my tears.

He looked at me, bewildered, and simply nodded. "White bean and kale. Parker said it was your favorite."

He asked Parker for my favorite soup? And made it? I wailed, burying my face in my pillow.

"Camellia, love, please," Van begged.

I heard rustling, then I felt his arms around me as I was lifted from the bed. I twisted in his hold to bury my face against him and wrap my arms around his neck. He settled back against the bed, and I melted against him.

"*Fiorellino*, what's wrong? Did I do the wrong thing?" His hand drew a soothing path up and down my back.

I laughed wetly, shaking my head. "No," I managed, my voice raw.

"Then what's the matter? I've been worried sick about you. You were sleeping so deeply," his voice trailed off and he sighed. "I hated it, but Dr. Landry said to let you. You were so still."

"I'm okay, Gio." My lips moved against his skin as I spoke, unwilling to put any distance between us.

"You are not," he admonished. "Dr. Landry said you were exhausted. He asked if you'd been eating and drinking, because you were dehydrated and running on fumes. And he said you have some form of viral pneumonia."

Well, shit. I thought back over the last 24 hours, then realized I had no idea what time it was. Sniffling, I went to sit up, but Van's arms tightened around me and held me flush to his body.

"No," he growled. "Not letting you go yet."

Fine by me. I relaxed against him again, ridiculously pleased by his satisfied grunt.

"What time is it?" I asked.

"About seven pm."

My face twisted in confusion. "I've only been asleep for a couple of hours?"

He scoffed. "It's Saturday."

"Oh," I squeaked.

"Mmhm." He kissed the top of my head. "Can you tell me why you're crying, please?"

I sniffled again. "Overwhelmed."

He just held me and rubbed my back, waiting. I heaved a sigh, gathering the fragments of my thoughts.

"When I was seven," I began, licking my lips and swallowing roughly.

"Wait, please," he said. "Water first."

I sat up and took the glass he offered, taking a long sip. Handing it back to him, I smiled my thanks before settling back against his chest, my face tucked against him.

"When I was seven, I got the flu. My mom had me stay home from school and made me tea and soup. My fever was so high and she was so worried. She was pregnant with Lani, so I was the only kid in the house. I felt awful for the day, but my fever finally broke that night." I took a deep breath, remembering. "She stayed with me all day and night, stroking my hair and reading to me. She brought me water and put a cool washcloth on my face when I overheated."

Slowly, I sat up. I was straddling his lap, staring into his eyes. Cupping his cheeks in my hands, I studied him.

"Two months later, Lani came into the world. And even though there were more fevers, more flus, more sick days...that was the last time she sat by my bedside." I rubbed a thumb over his cheekbone, marveling at how beautiful he was, still in awe he had come here for me. "Looking back, I think it was the last time I truly felt like a kid, like I had nothing to worry about because someone else was taking care of me."

It's strange how the veil of childhood falls away as an adult. Growing up, I felt like I owed my parents for all they did for me. My success was their success, so I had no choice but to do well in school and on the farm. But as I grew older and gained perspective, I realized how much of my childhood had been spent living up to their expectations, and how little of it had been about discovering my own. I'd been trying to give myself the space to do so ever since.

"Once Lani came," I went on, "I was the big sister–the helper, the responsible one. After, I had to help care for my siblings, for the family. And I never stopped."

His eyes were warm amber pools, inviting me to dive right in. Empathy shone in his gaze, and his lips quirked up into the slightest smile. "We both had to grow up young," he murmured, squeezing my hips in his big hands.

"We did," I agreed. "I've been taking care of the people I love ever since."

"I know what you mean."

"I know you do." I felt the tears welling again, felt them start to spill over as his expression turned concerned, then confused. "I haven't gotten to turn my brain off and just *be* since I was seven, Gio. Until now. Until you."

Understanding dawned on his face, and he wrapped his arms around me, pressing me to his chest. I clung to him, wiping my tears on his shirt and chuckling wetly.

"I'm sorry I'm so emotional–"

"Please," he interrupted. "You have nothing to apologize for. Thank you for telling me."

I tilted my face up and pressed my lips to his, going boneless in his hold as he leaned into the kiss. A feeling of rightness settled in my chest, warmth and contentment filling me. The worries plaguing me about our compatibility seemed so trivial in the face of Van's care. There was no reason for me to believe he wanted anything other than exactly what I had to offer, no evidence I should feel threatened by someone like Victoria. I couldn't imagine him comforting her, or dropping everything with the family he loved so deeply after a single video call. He may have been a man of few words, but his actions spoke so very loudly. *I'm listening, Gio. And I think I finally hear you.*

Chapter 27

Van

Something had shifted between us. There was an openness to Cami that hadn't been there before, a final protective wall removed. After she recovered from the emotions that overwhelmed her when she realized I came back for her, I convinced her to try the soup I had made.

Parker had proven quite helpful that morning, letting me into her condo shortly after my redeye flight had landed. He was clearly concerned about Cami, and had shared as much as he could about Dr. Landry's visit.

"She's going to be okay, right?" Parker asked, standing in the doorway of his sister's place after providing me the copy of the key I'd requested.

"He said she will be, but I'll be here to make sure."

He nodded, looking down the hall toward her room. I shifted, moving into his line of sight. He scoffed, shaking his head at me.

"I'd ask you for permission to speak freely, but I think we can both admit we're way past that," he quipped.

"We are."

"So you know that bullshit is unnecessary," he gestured toward me.

I shrugged, unapologetic. "Can't help it. She's mine."

"She agree to that?"

"In time," I replied, my voice a warning.

He eyed me, gaze assessing, then nodded. "You're a good guy, Van. She deserves great."

"I agree."

"If you hurt her..."

I shook my head. "I'll punish myself plenty if that happens, I assure you. And I won't make you a promise I can't keep."

His eyes narrowed as he regarded me.

"Relationships are messy," I continued. "It's impossible to expect there will be no hurt."

"You'll fix it, when you do."

"I will."

"Whatever it takes."

"And then some," I vowed.

He nodded, then looked toward the door. "I should go. It was a rough night."

"Parker, thank you. For being here, and helping her."

"Like I said, Van–she's family. You don't have to thank me." He clapped a hand to my shoulder, then turned and left.

After she ate her soup, I settled Cami in the shower while I changed out her sheets and started a load of laundry. When she emerged from the steamy bathroom, she offered me a tentative smile.

"Help me get ready for bed?" she asked.

My heart swelled in my chest. "Of course, *bella*." I was beyond pleased she appreciated those quiet moments as much as I did.

After I combed through her hair and smoothed lotion over her skin, I helped her into a soft, clean shirt I'd brought from home. She pressed her nose to her shoulder and inhaled, then sighed happily, her eyes closed as she swayed.

"Come on," I urged gently. "Lie down. I want to hold you."

"Yes, please," was her mumbled reply.

I shucked off my shirt and sweats, slipping under the covers with her in nothing but my boxer briefs. She turned and fit her soft body to mine, her head on my arm and one leg thrown over mine as she cuddled my bare chest. I laid there, my arm around her and resting in that captivating hollow by her hip, and listened to her breathe. My eyes fell closed as emotion rushed up in my throat, hot and potent. *This is where I belong.* As gratitude filled me, I drifted off to sleep to the rhythm of her in my heart.

————

It was early on Sunday when I woke to find her still nestled against me, my chest her pillow. The sense of rightness that had seized me the night before was still there, simmering just under the surface. Guilt tried to rise over my abrupt departure from home, but I pushed it back. *This is where I need to be.*

Cami stirred, her eyelids fluttering as they slowly opened. She nuzzled against me, squeezing me with one arm before her eyes popped open. Her gaze met mine, her smile blinding.

"I was worried it was a dream," she murmured, her morning voice adorable in its raspiness.

"What was?"

"You," she said simply, kissing my skin directly over my heart.

I chuckled and tightened my hold around her. "Not a dream, *bella*. Just me."

"Same difference." She shrugged.

Peering down at her, I soothed a hand over her back. "Are you ready to tell me what happened?"

Her expression turned sheepish as she looked up from

behind her lashes. She laid her arm on my chest and propped her chin on her wrist as she gazed up at me.

"Things got a little...wild...with the Kitchen," she muttered, briefly looking away.

My eyebrows lowered. "You said you were busy."

"Yeah, well, I might've left out the details about just *how* busy," she sighed, then explained how much overtime she'd put in to keep afloat under the deluge of unexpected orders.

Guilt prickled under my skin as I listened. The List had put her on the map, but I hadn't stopped there. A few well-placed comments and recommendations to certain people in the community, and word of Cami's business had spread through the Bay like wildfire. I had no idea she didn't have the systems in place to prevent the challenges she was describing.

"But why didn't you cancel some?" I asked, concerned and frustrated. Something as trivial as work should never take priority over her well-being.

"I didn't want to," she was quick to respond. "I've built my business on positive word of mouth, and I take customer service seriously. It felt like too big a risk to cancel after the automated system had already confirmed, especially as it was my error."

I huffed, the concern I'd felt for her rising to the surface. "Your health is more important than customer service, Cami."

"Hey," her voice was gentle, as though I needed calming. "I know that. I was doing the best I could with the situation, Gio."

"You could've asked for help."

Her brow furrowed, then she sat up. "I did. I called Preston, but there's only so much she could do from the south of France. Lani did way more than I should've asked her for, given it's harvest season. And I about tapped out my market connections–I couldn't dream of asking them to help with prep after they bent over backwards to deliver everything straight to me."

"You could've called me," I snapped, sitting up and leaning toward her. *Why didn't you call me?*

She leaned back, affronted. "You were gone, and not just physically. I barely heard from you, and when I did, every other message was about you needing to go. It was clear your attention was elsewhere, and I wasn't about to push."

The guilt roared back up, and I growled. "I would've helped if I had known."

"I get that, Gio," she said, as though she was explaining something to a wild animal. "You've proven as much now. I didn't know it on Tuesday."

"You know I have connections," I insisted. "You have to know I'd do anything for you."

Her lips parted as she stared at me. "Uh...well, I know now."

"Good," I gritted out.

Sighing, she rubbed her hands over her face. "If I'm honest, Gio...the emotional rollercoaster I was on after Napa was worse than you going dark on me."

My eyebrows drew together. "What do you mean?"

She looked up at me, then back down to her hands as they fidgeted in her lap. "This thing between us...it's still new. You've been so attentive, and we had an amazing time in Napa, and then..." her voice trailed off and she bit her lip. "Well, we saw your ex–"

"Victoria means nothing to me," I interjected fiercely. "You do." *You mean everything.*

Her lips twitched up in one corner. "I'm getting that now. Truly, I am."

Good. I nodded once, then motioned for her to continue.

"Anyway, then you were gone. And you weren't attentive anymore, and I didn't know what that meant for where we stood. Where *I* stood, I guess, on your list."

"My list?"

She nodded. "Of priorities."

"At the fucking top, Camellia."

I needed her to understand this wasn't temporary for me. It wasn't a good time for now, or a fling, or anything that could remotely be considered casual. As far as I was concerned, my heart now resided within her–matching tempo with hers.

She flushed, then shuffled forward on her knees before straddling my hips, her hands tight on my shoulders.

"I hear you," she said earnestly, looping her arms around my neck and leaning forward to kiss my nose. "You've been very clear since you've come back, and I appreciate that. I appreciate you."

Our chests pressed together, and I swore I could feel her heart beating against my skin. It resonated within me, echoing through me and encouraging mine to follow the same rhythm. I wanted to tell her how she made me feel, how worried I'd been, but I couldn't find the words. I could negotiate a ten-figure deal without breaking a sweat, but putting the emotions raging within me into something coherent felt about as achievable as walking on the sun.

As her fingers slid into my hair and she lowered her lips to mine, I knew there was nothing I wouldn't do for her. *Nothing.* From my knees, I had promised to burn the world down for her or lay it at her feet, and I meant it now more than ever. What-ever she wanted, whatever she needed, she would have. And I'd be damned if I stood by while she worked herself to the bone.

Dr. Landry encouraged me to ensure she took a full week off to recover. The sheer exhaustion of her work week ravaged her immune system, making it impossible for her to fight off something that should've been nothing more than a simple cold–if that. I still had to convince Cami to let me cancel her orders for the next week, but I was a persuasive man.

In the meantime, I had a few ideas about how I could help

ensure she never found herself in that position again. She built her business into something amazing, but I knew I could help her turn it into an empire. And I couldn't wait to show her exactly what we could achieve together. But first, I needed to use my body to say what I wasn't yet capable of speaking aloud.

Chapter 28

Cami

I f there was anything the last week had taught me, it was that Italian men were very giving in bed...though it was possible that was just a Van thing. *The man is insatiable, and I am so here for it.* I also learned being the sole object of Van's attention was as intoxicating as it was exhausting. After our morning heart-to-heart, he'd wrung several orgasms out of my body with his fingers and tongue, then told me I'd be recovering for the rest of the week at his condo.

"Duke will help me take care of you, and you won't be tempted to work," was his brilliant argument.

Before I could even think of protesting, he'd swept me into some sweats and down to his car. For the entire ride to his place, I tried to convince him to change his mind about the work thing, but he refused.

"I've gotten access to your password manager from Preston." Before I could panic completely over that bit of information, he held up a finger. "She agrees with me and *Dr. Landry*," he raised a pointed eyebrow, daring me to defy medical advice, "that you need a week off. I'm going to ensure you get it."

"But, Van, my customers–"

"Your business partner made a call while you were incapacitated." He leveled me with a stern look when I went to protest. "Not a negotiation, Camellia."

My core clenched at the demand and possession in his tone, but it was still my turn to hold a finger up in front of his face. "Fine. One week. *One.*" *And I'm not going to comment on how fucking hot it is when you boss me around.*

He simply nodded, and the rest of the week unfolded with him waiting on me hand and foot. Under his expert care, which included a generous schedule of daily orgasms, I recovered faster than expected and felt human again by the time my imposed rest period ended. It was amazing what my body was capable of when I didn't have to do anything other than enjoy my boyfriend's attention. We hadn't talked about labels yet, but I'd finally accepted that Van and I were far more than just a fling.

On Saturday morning, one week from when we'd struck our deal, Van announced we had somewhere to be. Without waiting for an acknowledgement or reaction, he hustled me into the car. He was buzzing with restrained energy, a sense of excitement tense between us.

"Where are you taking me, Gio?" I teased, sidling up to him in the back seat of his hired car.

"You'll see," was his cryptic reply.

It was blindingly obvious he was up to something. He just took my hand in his, brought my fingers to his lips to kiss the tip of each one, then tucked my hand into his lap and looked out the window. I followed his gaze and only got more confused as we pulled into the parking lot of a small, unmarked building.

"Come on," Van said, opening his door the second we stopped and tugging me after him.

I followed, looking around in interest as we walked up to the unmarked glass entrance. Interior curtains blocked the view into the space, so I remained clueless as to what was within. Van pulled a key from his pocket and unlocked the door, then pushed it open with a flourish. Giving him a puzzled smile, I stepped over the threshold.

We were in a small, hyper-modern cafe with a tiny seating area. There was a glass pastry case by the till that was covered in butcher paper, and an over-the-top espresso machine on the marble counter beside it. One wall boasted vertical dark green and white stripes, while the fixtures throughout were shiny chrome. It was clean and sleek, but a bit garish for my taste.

"Is this a new venture?" I asked Van, taking it all in.

"Of sorts."

His vague answer only served to unsettle me as we continued toward the back of the cafe. The place was almost clinical in design, lacking decor and all sense of character. Van stepped behind the counter and into the immaculate commercial kitchen, which was generously appointed.

"Wow." I dropped Van's hand to run mine along the top-of-the-line induction range. "This kitchen is drool-worthy."

Van's lips twitched into a smile. "Check the walk-in."

I shot him a curious look, then did as he suggested. The refrigerator was spacious and full of gorgeous fresh produce– easily my favorite part of the strange tour to that point.

"This is awesome!" I called back to him as I wandered into the depths of the space, finding a selection of dairy alternatives in one corner. "Hey, they use a lot of the same stuff I do. What a coincidence."

"Imagine that," Van muttered, watching me with rapt attention.

I paused and gave him a look. "I'm missing something. What is this place?"

He nodded toward a case at the front of the walk-in, and I peered inside. It contained compostable single-serving containers–a more expensive version of the ones I used–with dark green stickers on the lids. As I got closer, my stomach dropped. I reached out with a shaking hand to pick up one of the bowls, my mouth suddenly dry.

"Van..." I whispered, "what is this?"

There, on the sticker, plain as day, was my logo. I looked up at him, my heart rate increasing as I fought to ignore the rushing in my ears.

"Why do these say 'Camellia's Kitchen'?" I demanded, my voice wavering.

Van just grinned and grabbed my wrist. "Come on."

He spun back to the door, tugging me after him. I followed, almost stumbling, as I tried to piece together what was going on. Whatever it was, Van seemed inordinately pleased with himself. He brought me back to the front of the cafe, then tore the butcher paper off the pastry case to reveal my logo emblazoned across the glass.

"There's a delivery truck, too," he beamed. "It's out back. Just the one to start, but then–"

"What the fuck." I couldn't stop the words; they just tumbled free.

Van finally seemed to realize his surprise was not going over as well as he expected it to. "Cami, what's wrong? You're white as a sheet."

"What's wrong?" I cried, my voice several octaves higher than normal. "What is this, Van? What have you done?"

His brow furrowed, and his spine straightened. "Cami, this is a good thing. In this commercial kitchen, you actually have the space and resources to scale. There's no reason for you to be the one cooking every meal, anyway. And the team can't wait to meet you, they were so impressed by the recipes–"

I held up a hand, fire ants marching under my skin as the hairs on the back of my neck rose. "Stop. You hired a team?"

"Well, yes, to fulfill and deliver last week's orders."

My eyes bulged. "Excuse me?!" I yelled, throwing my arms wide as fury engulfed me. "What the fuck, Van!? You hired a team without telling me and just handed over *my* recipes? There have been complete *strangers* running my business for a week and you didn't think to tell me!?"

"You were recovering," he said slowly, his expression shuttering. "After you told me what happened while I was gone, I wanted to make sure you were never in that position again."

"That responsibility doesn't belong to you!" I shouted.

I wasn't the kind of person to raise my voice at anyone. But I was full-on yelling at Van, my face ablaze. I could feel the vein at my temple pounding as I tried to catch my breath.

"You are so far out of bounds you're off the fucking map, Van," I snapped, my voice shaking with the weight of my anger and disbelief. "I agreed to let you cancel my orders for the week. Not for you to come and turn my business into whatever the fuck this is!"

"Cami, I just wanted to help you be successful."

His words were a slap in the face. My father's voice filled my head in response, belittling my business and dismissing my dreams. I stumbled back, bracing one hand on the wall as I stared at the man I thought believed in me. *Boy, was I mistaken.*

"My business *is* successful," I declared, my voice level once more. Panic flared in his eyes as he realized what he'd implied, but I didn't give him the chance to acknowledge it. "I am successful. I never wanted *this*." I threw my arms out to indicate the cafe around us.

"Camellia, I understand this is a surprise–"

"No, Van," I interrupted. "It's a betrayal. My business is mine, and–"

"I'm not trying–"

"Interrupt me again and see what fucking happens!" I

snarled, holding my hand up.

Van's jaw snapped shut, his nostrils flaring.

"What was the plan here, huh? Just do all of this without my consent, step in and take over something I built with my own two hands, and tell me what to do with my business? My life? Was Preston part of this?"

He swallowed, his Adam's apple bobbing. "Preston didn't know."

"Well, at least my best friend wasn't in on this farce." I shook my head, anger and confusion waging a war inside me. "How did you think this was going to go? Did you expect me to be grateful you steamrolled the business I built from the ground up?"

He waited to be sure I was done speaking before answering. "After I contributed to the quantity of orders you received, I felt some responsibility to address the challenges you were facing."

And the hits just keep on coming. "Hold up. Repeat that. What did you have to do with my order volume?"

"I may have made a few calls," he said, then cleared his throat. "I didn't want the impact from the List to be temporary."

My jaw dropped. "You have got to be kidding me. Let me see if I have this straight. Your meddling put me into the situation where I 'needed' you to swoop in and be the hero, yanking my business out from under me in the process. That about sum it up?"

"I don't have any negative intentions, Camellia, I assure you. Your business is very much still yours."

"But it's not, Van," I pressed. "My business is produce I pick by hand from growers I've known my whole life. It's meals I make in my kitchen with my own two hands, because I love every second of doing it. It's greeting customers I know by name and getting to brighten their day with a meal I've poured my heart and soul into."

I looked around and scoffed, shaking my head. "This place is cold, corporate, and soulless. It might be cute for the right business, but it's everything Camellia's Kitchen isn't. And you'd know that, if you stopped for one second to ask me what I wanted."

He opened his mouth, then closed it, his lips pursing.

"I've spent my life being told what my future held." My voice was impossibly quiet, but it rang in the wake of my vitriol. "The Kitchen was the first thing I got to choose for myself. You were the second."

I met his gaze, my heart disappearing into a black abyss in my chest. Even though I felt hollow and stripped raw, I'd never been more sure of a decision in my life. Van had seemed too good to be true, and now I knew he was.

"Men have tried to screw me and my business over before, and I promised myself I wouldn't let it happen again."

His jaw ticked, and he took a half-step forward. "If you mean Gabriel, I–"

"It doesn't matter who, Van. That's not the point. The point is–*I trusted you.*" I fought back the tears that wanted to rise as I thought about how deeply that statement had been true just an hour before. "I trusted you, and you destroyed that trust. You blasted it to smithereens."

I rubbed a hand over my face. "I'm going to need the names and contact information of the people you hired."

"Cami, I can help–"

"You abso-fucking-lutely cannot. If there is anything you have done today, Van, it's prove you cannot be trusted with anything to do with my business. I need you to provide me the names and their employment details so I can start untangling this mess. And I need to know where and how you shared my recipes."

"They were printed out and taped to the prep stations during the week," he said, his voice flat.

"Maybe it would be best if you had someone at Athena write it all up and send it over to me," I suggested, swallowing the urge to sob. "I'm not exactly taking notes, and this shit is important."

I pulled my phone out of my purse with trembling hands.

"What are you doing?"

"Calling Parker."

Van's nostrils flared, and I glowered, infuriated by his possessiveness for the first time. I hadn't missed that the first move he'd made since I lost my temper was in anger over his own mention of Gabriel. That it was his possessiveness that goaded him into action, not my pain, was a level of toxic masculinity I did not find the least bit attractive.

"You have no claim on me, Van," I snapped, turning to walk out of the door. "Not anymore."

"Cami, please."

I paused, looking back over my shoulder as Parker's line rang. "I need space, Van."

"For how long?" His voice cracked, but I hardened my heart.

"As long as it takes."

"For what?"

"For the joy of being with you to outweigh the pain of what you've done." I took a steadying breath. "And for me to believe you see and respect me for who I am and what I want...because I finally believe I deserve nothing less."

He opened his mouth to reply, but Parker answered the phone as he did. I turned my back on Van Costa and walked out, asking Parker to come get me as the chasm in my chest swallowed me whole.

Chapter 29

Van

"You do know scowling at it doesn't make it go any faster, yes?"

I raised my eyes from the cup of espresso I had just brewed, turning slowly toward Miles, my entire body wired with tension.

"Oh, are you having one of your moody mornings?" He arched a brow, then pouted his lower lip and continued in a voice best suited for children or pets. "I forgot. All your mornings are moody, aren't they?"

On an average day, I would've rolled my eyes at him and gone on with my business. That was how our dynamic worked— he pressed all my buttons and I made a show of barely tolerating him. But I had no patience for our back-and-forth in the wake of the utter disaster of my weekend. I was an open wound, and his attempt at our twisted form of banter was nothing more than salt.

"Are you done?" I snapped. "Because if I have to listen to another second of your asinine drivel, I'm going to put a fist through the goddamn wall."

The low buzz of work happening around us dulled to

unnatural silence as I realized my voice had climbed to a near-yell. Miles stared at me in shock, his lips parted. I closed my eyes briefly and blew a slow breath out through my nose, then turned back to the espresso machine.

"Leave it, Miles," I muttered, taking the cup.

I could feel his eyes–and those of at least a dozen others–on my back as I left the kitchen and returned to my office. The door had barely closed behind me when it opened again.

"I told you to leave it," I bit out, not turning around.

"You told Miles to leave it," Lex's voice responded.

Sighing, I pinched the bridge of my nose. "You heard that, then."

"The whole office heard it, Van." There was the sound of her sitting on the couch, then the snap of her fingers. "Sit."

"You're about the only person in the world who could get away with snapping at me like a dog."

"I know," she said simply, watching as I followed her command. "Speak."

I glowered at the teasing look she sent me. "I'm not in the mood."

Her expression smoothed. "Frankly, I don't give a shit. Whatever is going on with you might be personal, but it stopped being private the second you verbally assaulted an employee. So I'm going to sit here until you work through enough of whatever shit you're processing because our team deserves better." She crossed her ankles and settled back. "And if you were in a remotely reasonable state of mind, you'd agree."

Groaning, I propped my elbow on my knee and lowered my head into my hand. "I hate it when you're right."

"No, you hate it when you're wrong." Her foot nudged mine. "Talk to me, Costa."

Talking was the last thing I wanted to do. Talking meant acknowledging, and I had been living in a firmly upheld state of denial ever since I watched Cami walk away. But Lex didn't play, and I knew she wouldn't leave until I gave her something. *And just maybe she can help.*

"Cami dumped me." It was the first time I uttered the words aloud, perhaps the first time I plainly stated what happened. I'd been avoiding everyone, my family and Cece included, because I was completely unwilling to admit to myself or anyone else that things had gone so terribly sideways.

"What did you do?"

I looked at her through narrowed eyes. "Why don't you sound surprised?"

"I'm not an idiot," she deadpanned. "You've been in one hell of a mood all week, and I don't think I've seen you utter a single word to Parker." She studied me. "You're stalling, Van. Start talking. What did you do?"

I threw my hands up and stood. "I tried to help!" Turning to the gap between the coffee table and the door, I began to pace. "She was sick, overworked, and I saw an opportunity to upgrade her operations so she wouldn't ever be in that state again."

As I explained how I'd transformed Camellia's Kitchen, I thought back to the look of horror on Cami's face when she realized the cafe she stood in was hers. Her reaction had truly baffled me. I was expecting excitement, perhaps a refusal to accept such a gift. Her flat out rejection of everything, including me, fractured something deep within and left me reeling.

"She asked you to help?" Lex clarified.

"No, of course not. She's got too much pride." I ran a hand through my hair, tugging on the ends harshly. "I wanted to surprise her, show her how good we could be together..." My voice trailed off as I met Lex's gaze and found her eyebrows furrowed.

I gestured toward her. "What is that face? Why are you looking at me like I'm dog shit on the bottom of your shoe?"

"Van, I know you mean well," she started, hand out in a calming motion as I felt my hackles raise in response to her tone. "But let me tell it back to you and don't interrupt me while I do."

Sweeping my hand out in front of me impatiently, I beckoned her to continue.

"You thought she was mismanaging her business." I opened my mouth to deny the claim because *no, I fucking didn't*, but she held up a finger to silence me. "You thought you could do it better, so you did. Without asking or discussing her objectives and goals, you made decisions to significantly change the nature of her business and its operations."

"When you put it like that, it sounds terrible."

"Well? Isn't that what happened?"

I rubbed the back of my neck, frustration pulsing hot and uncomfortable under my skin. "No, Lex. That's not what happened. You should have seen her! She was pale as a ghost, sleeping so soundly in that bed I thought she was dead. Do you know how many times I checked to make sure she was breathing?! And all because of something I'd done!"

"You thought you were atoning."

"I...yes." I paused, considering the word, then nodded. "Yes, I made a mistake. I needed to fix it. And there was so much unrealized potential!"

"She's not our client, and, as far as I'm aware, never asked to be."

"I know that." *Where is she going with this?*

"And I'm glad because just about any client would've fired us over the shit you pulled."

I reeled back, offended. "Excuse me?"

She sighed, crossing her arms. "What do we start with, every time?"

"Goals, objectives," I waved my hands through the air. "The client's why."

Nodding, she looked askance at me. "What's the why for Camellia's Kitchen?"

I almost scoffed, the answer obvious. "To grow."

"According to who–you? How would Cami answer that question?"

"I..." Flopping back into my seat, I rubbed my fingers across my forehead. "When did growth become a bad thing, Lex? What am I missing here?"

"You're a man."

I glared at her.

"And you're a hypocritical one, at that," she continued. "Explain to me, for a moment, how what you did to Cami is any different from what my father and brother have tried to do to me?" That eyebrow of hers rose imperiously. "They never believed I had what it took to be successful in the financial world, and they did their best to set me on a different path. They always claimed it was for my own good, too."

"I am nothing like those assholes, and you know it," I snapped. The male members of Lex's family were abhorrent, controlling misogynists who wouldn't know talent if it bit them in the ass.

"The actions are the same. You defined Cami's path for her with no consideration for what she had envisioned for herself and her future. Wouldn't you say her business is successful already? You may have put her name in the hat, but she earned Camellia's Kitchen a spot on the List."

"I know! And I've told her that. I believe in her and her potential. This was about what we could achieve together, nothing more." I felt agitated by the conversation, guilt nagging at me while my frustration won out.

"I'm sorry, Van, but that's bullshit." My nostrils flared as anger rose in my chest, but she stared me down. "I know it's hard to hear, but it's true. You didn't show her what you could accomplish together. You showed her that your vision was the only one that mattered. And you implied she lacked the skill and talent to be successful on her own."

How dare she. "Seriously? I am nothing like Nate or your asshole of a father, Lex. And I'm Cami's biggest fucking fan."

"You're willfully missing the point." She stood and walked to the door before turning back to me. "You're a good man, Van. Better than my father and brother combined. But you fucked up, and Cami deserves better."

Blowing out a sharp breath, I got back to my feet, stalking to my desk. I needed to run or punch something or find any outlet for the negative energy roaring through me. "My intent was to help," I gritted out through clenched teeth.

"I know. But your good intentions don't change the fact that you completely discarded her thoughts, opinions, and dreams in the process. She has every right to be angry. And if you want any hope of getting her back, you need to stop protesting and start listening."

"Right." I knew I was being dismissive, but I couldn't reconcile Lex's version of events with what I felt. My heart claimed Cami from that first moment, and with every interaction between us thereafter, I surrendered more of myself to her. Whether we discussed it or not, it was my responsibility to care for her, protect her. Even from herself.

Lex scoffed at my sullen response. "Stop pouting. You're in your fucking forties. Take the rest of the week off."

I looked up at her sharply, panic rising at the prospect of being alone with my thoughts. "Lex, that's not necessary."

"It is, and it's not up for negotiation." She studied me, her hard gaze unflinching. "I hear Ethan Masters is having a rough week. It appears his partners have ousted him from all three businesses for an ethics violation."

Anger washed through me at the mere mention of his name. "Good riddance. They did themselves a favor by taking out the trash."

She tutted at my impassive expression. "Are you going to ruin the career of every man who makes eyes at your girlfriend, Costa?"

"He did a hell of a lot more than make eyes, and you know it. He's lucky that was the extent of my retribution." I glanced down at the healing scrapes on my knuckles as I tried to control my temper. "He deserved far worse," I gritted out.

"Of course he did, but perhaps you could choose a more subtle form of revenge in the future." Her tone softened, teasing, but my body still vibrated with tension, my lips a firm line. Lex sighed. "Get out of here and take your attitude with you, Van. Come back when you have some perspective."

"Helpful," I groused, throwing a hand in the air in exasperation.

"You'll thank me," she insisted, turning to leave. "As soon as you get your head out of your ass."

Chapter 30

Cami

"You need wine."

A full glass appeared in front of me. I glanced up at Preston and smiled gratefully, taking it from her. She studied my face for a moment, then huffed and shook her head.

"Thank goodness I'm back."

I rolled my eyes as she flopped next to me on the couch, her glass equally full. LB sat on my other side, her socked feet tucked up under her.

"How's your week been, hun?" LB asked, taking a sip of her wine.

"You know what? It could've been worse." I nodded, mostly to myself. "It could've been a complete disaster, but it wasn't. I'm back in control of the Kitchen and the imposters were kindly and fairly shown the door. So I'm taking the win."

Preston snorted. "By that, she means she was either girl-bossing so hard she could barely think, or she was a puddle on the floor of her bedroom. Or my bedroom. Or the bathroom. Or the living room."

"Why are we glad you're back, again?" I snarked, throwing her some side-eye.

"Are you feeling better, though? I mean, after that whole exhaustion business," LB pressed, used to our antics.

Sighing, I turned to her. "For the most part. I've still got the sniffles and a lingering cough, but I'm pretty much back to normal."

"Hard to tell what's the pneumonia and what's the emotional turmoil, though," Preston quipped.

I grabbed a pillow and whacked her with it. "You try getting your heart obliterated, see how long you can go without bawling your eyes out!"

She squealed and threw her hands up to fend me off. "No thanks! I've seen the two of you go through the wringer plenty. That shit is *not* for me."

LB and I exchanged knowing glances. Preston was full of it, but we'd let her live with her delusions if they made her happy. Her time would come, I had no doubt.

"Okay, so you're not on your deathbed anymore–that's good," LB redirected the conversation. "Have you talked to Van, though?"

"No, she hasn't. And she better not." Preston pointed at me, her eyes flinty.

"I'm not ready to, regardless." I bit my lip, remembering the fire that had filled me as I stalked away from Van and his cafe. "It was the final straw, I guess. After years of hearing my father dictate my future, I thought I was desensitized to people running roughshod over my dreams. Gabriel certainly didn't care about my opinion on things."

The girls both listened intently. LB's expression was encouraging and kind, while Preston had a perma-glare in place over the mere suggestion I'd been hurt.

"I mean," I went on, "I just expected more from Van. But I guess I should've seen it coming. It's not the first time a man took advantage of me like that."

LB's brows drew down in concern. "Catch me up. What history am I missing?"

Preston grumbled and busied herself with her wine. Ignoring her, I turned to LB.

"Gabriel, my ex. We were best friends growing up, thick as thieves because our parents were close. I think they always expected the two of us to get together, and we both just kind of went with it?" Sighing, I rubbed my forehead. "We were just kids, but I always expected him to grow up, you know? To want something, anything, for himself. But he was content to take whatever anyone handed him."

"You mean he was happy enough to have you wait on him hand and foot while he did jack shit," Preston groused.

"You met him *once*, Pres." I rolled my eyes.

"But I lived with you for years!" She pointed an accusatory finger at me. "I listened to you complain about him while you were together and then lament this love you thought you lost, but that man never once reciprocated what you thought you felt for him. He was and is a useless, ambitionless leech of a human being."

"Wow, okay," LB turned to me. "We know how Preston feels about the ex."

"I mean, she's not wrong." I took a sip of my wine. "The straw that broke the camel's back was when he stole from me, took the entire nest egg I'd put aside to start Camellia's Kitchen a few weeks before I was going to open it. At the time, I believed him when he claimed he wanted the money for a new car mod or whatever, but looking back..." I sighed and closed my eyes. "Pretty sure he was just trying to keep me in Ukiah."

"Yeah, so he'd never have to figure out how to care for himself," Preston scoffed. "That boy was perfectly content letting you do literally everything for him. Fucking ingrate."

LB's eyes narrowed in disgust, and her lips twisted. "He sounds like a real piece of work."

"Yeah, you're not wrong. When I think back to our relationship now, I see all the ways he used me and never really cared, you know? My dreams were immaterial to him." Something heavy settled in the pit of my stomach and I licked my dry lips. "I never thought Van could make me feel the same."

"Hang on," Preston interrupted. "Let's be clear. Gabriel is a trash human, we absolutely agree on that. But he and Van are not the same, not even close."

I shifted, discomfort skating over my skin. "They both made decisions that affected my future without involving me, and completely dismissed my dreams in favor of what they wanted."

"I can see how it feels that way," LB said slowly, "but I get Preston's point. It sounds like Gabriel only cared about himself. Van clearly cares about you, hun. I've never seen a man as frantic as he was when you were sick. He was beside himself."

"That doesn't give him a pass," I grumbled.

"Oh, he fucked up," Preston confirmed. "One hundred percent, the man was an idiot. But his heart–and he has one, unlike shitstain Gabe–was in the right place."

"So, what are you saying? I should just forgive him?" I set my wine glass down on the coffee table, then crossed my arms as I sat back with a huff.

"Let me be very clear," Preston replied. "The man needs to grovel. I'm talking big time, on-his-knees, begging for your forgiveness while he makes all your dreams come true groveling. But you might also need to look in the mirror for a minute."

"I think what Preston is getting at," LB interjected, seeing the indignation rising in my chest, "is...did you ever talk to Van about the Kitchen? After all that business with the List, for instance. Did you tell him how that made you feel?"

Squirming in my seat, I shook my head.

"She likes to pretend things never happened, so she doesn't have to deal with the conflict. Ask her if she ever talked to Van about the multiple times he referred to her as his girlfriend and partner without asking."

I shot Preston a filthy glare, not appreciating her airing out my dirty laundry one bit, even if it was to LB.

"Well, no time like the present. Let's unpack this, shall we?" LB suggested brightly.

Before I could reply, Preston's phone rang. She frowned down at it as she checked the ID.

"It's the door. Give me a sec." She accepted the call, then barked a laugh. "You're not welcome here, Van."

I sat up suddenly, my eyes wide, and reached for the phone. Preston leaned out of my reach, then scrambled over the back of the couch to get away, glaring as she went.

"She's not ready to talk to you and you need to respect that," she snapped. "I understand you've never been told no before, bucko, but that's what's happening. No. I'm not buzzing you up, I'm not passing the phone to Cami, I'm not doing any of it. N-O."

"Preston, don't." Rising to my feet, I moved closer to her.

"Dude, are you hearing me? Do you care about anything other than your inflated ego and what you want?" Preston yelled. "No is a full sentence!"

I cast a desperate look at LB. "This isn't helping anything!"

She just shrugged. "I'm not about to get in the middle of all that." With a gesture at Preston, she settled back and took a long sip of wine. "I suggest you grab your glass and tune her out. She's right, you aren't ready to talk to him. And he needs to remember his needs aren't the only ones that matter right now, no matter how much he might want to see you."

"Fuck right off, Costa!" Preston ended the call with Van and turned to me. "Your phone. Now. Hand it over."

"Pres, come on–"

"Nope, don't even try it. You're weak on wine. Give it." She held her hand out, palm up. "Now, babe."

"Ugh, you're the worst." I handed her my phone, then followed LB's lead and took several large gulps of my wine.

"We're gonna need snacks," LB announced, jumping to her feet.

Preston snorted. "Check the fridge. Chef Rivera over here cooks when she's in her feels. We have enough hummus, falafel, baba ghanoush, and homemade gluten-free pita to feed a fucking army."

LB raised her eyebrows at me with a grin. "In a Mediterranean mood this week, are we?"

Yes, because that was the theme of our first date. "It sounded good," I mumbled, keeping the real reason to myself. Preston gave me a knowing look, reminding me that absolutely nothing got past her.

"Anyway," Preston drawled, clapping her hands. "Where were we?"

"Group therapy!" LB called from the kitchen as she dug through the fridge.

Preston's lips twitched into a smirk. "Goody."

I leveled a finger at her. "You're scary. I nominate LB for the role of therapist."

"I accept!" LB returned to the living room laden with Mediterranean appetizers and a plate of Italian wedding cookies. "The cookies seemed a little off-theme, but they looked too good to pass up."

"Off theme for the meal, but not the conversation," Preston sing-songed, not missing the symbolism.

"Can I kick her out before we start therapy?" I groaned to LB.

"Then it wouldn't be group therapy," Preston quipped,

flouncing back to her seat on the couch with a plate full of food. "Where shall we begin, doctor?"

"I'm glad you asked." LB settled into her spot, her plate on the side table next to her. She turned to me with a mock-serious look. "Cami, honey...how's your relationship with your parents?"

The three of us looked at each other for five seconds, then simultaneously burst into laughter.

"Oh, hell, I needed that," I gasped as the giggles and laughter-induced coughing subsided and I could catch my breath. "And you may have been teasing, LB, but you weren't far off. I have no doubt the pressure my parents put on me to take over the farm from the age of seven has played a big role in all of this."

"Wait...they want you to move back to Ukiah?" LB blinked, then looked at Preston. "How am I just hearing about this?"

Preston jutted her chin out at me. "Communication issues, remember?"

"Wait, does Van know?" LB looked at me with wide eyes.

Preston just cackled while I winced.

"No, I don't talk about it. And I didn't even think there was a reason to tell him because I had no idea what we were or what I was to him...until right before he ripped my heart out." I sighed, pushing back the hot pressure rising in my throat. "At this point, I think it's mostly denial. I don't want to think about leaving the Bay and all of you because I don't *want* to. Some part of my heart thinks I might still find a way out, even though my head knows I can't."

"For someone who is full of so much goddamn sunshine, you sure can be a downer sometimes," Preston accused. "Explain to us both why you can't find a way out."

"I can't just abandon my family, Pres."

"Because those are the only two options? Indentured servitude or abandonment?" Her face contorted in exasperation as she rolled her eyes. "Come on."

I opened my mouth to respond, then closed it. *Am I really being that myopic?*

"Have you told your parents how you feel?" LB's gentle question interrupted my thoughts.

"I mean, their expectations haven't changed. But they know I want the Kitchen."

"Do they?" Preston challenged. "Because I've never heard you tell them. Only that you'll be ready to be the dutiful little heir when your five years are up."

"Hmm," LB hummed. "I'm seeing a pattern here. I think you need to have a conversation with your folks and with Van. Let them see your side of things, then figure out what to do from there."

"You deserve to get what you want out of life, babe," Preston said, pushing against my thigh with her toes. "But you gotta tell the universe what you want to have any hope of it providing."

"At least you know what you want," LB chimed. "Figuring that out was a heck of a journey for me."

Preston barked a laugh and threw a carrot stick at her. "You put my brother through hell!"

LB just shrugged. "A girl's gotta do what a girl's gotta do, Pres."

"Van knows what he wants," I murmured, my thoughts a hectic jumble.

They both looked over at me. Preston's foot nestled against my thigh and LB scooched closer to lay her head on my shoulder.

"Pretty typical for a daddy his age," Preston offered. "They don't fuck around."

LB raised her head and looked at me with bright eyes. "Ooooh, Daddy Van. I love that for you."

Preston beaned her with another carrot stick. "She's not done processing. The daddy is still off limits."

"For now," LB muttered, sipping her wine innocently.

"Most guys my age have no idea what they want," I mused, ignoring their banter. "Gabriel only knew he wanted me because our parents told him so. They have this vision of us uniting the businesses and creating some sort of agricultural empire. Pretty sure that's the main reason he's still trying to get me back."

"Sounds a little too arranged marriage-y for me," LB said, sticking her tongue out like she tasted something sour.

Preston snorted. "You know what I want to see? A Gabriel versus Van cage match. It would be so entertaining to watch your hulking daddy eviscerate your ex."

"Why does your brain jump to cage fighting?" LB asked, bewildered.

"It's a violent place," Preston said with a shrug. At our blank stares, she elaborated, "My brain."

"Anyway," LB drawled, turning back to me with wide eyes.

"If you're looking for examples of guys our age, just look at my brother. He had no idea what he wanted out of life until this one smacked him in the face with it." Preston reached her foot over my lap to prod at LB.

"It's true," LB nodded sagely. "Poor boy was a lost little lamb."

We all giggled at that and I snuggled deeper into the couch, feeling warm and fuzzy from the wine.

"I want the Kitchen," I said definitively. It felt good to claim it out loud, and I felt a twinge of self-loathing that I hadn't done it before.

"Damn straight," Preston agreed, raising her glass to clink against mine. "Don't decide on Van yet. The man still needs to beg."

The mere mention of him filled my head with images of us. Van showed me what it was like to be cared for, to be cherished. It wasn't something I was ready to give up. "But I want to be able to turn my brain off, sometimes."

The girls glanced at each other, then me. "That's the dream," LB agreed.

"When was the last time you turned your brain off?" I glanced over at Preston.

Her cheeks pinkened the barest amount, and my eyebrows rose as she looked away and used her wine as a shield. "France," she muttered.

Before I could press her for details, LB sighed dreamily. "Last night."

"Ew!" Preston cried, chucking some pita at LB. "No more out of you!"

I squealed as I got caught in the crossfire of LB's retaliation, wiggling off the couch entirely to escape. After a few moments, they both joined me on the floor.

"You deserve to turn your brain off sometimes, Cam." Preston slung her arm around my shoulders.

"You do," LB agreed, resting her head on my shoulder. "If Van helps you do that, that's pretty big."

I just hummed in agreement, grateful for them both. Surrounded by their love and support, I made a silent vow to myself. *It's time to put words to what I want. No more being a passenger for my own life.*

Chapter 31

Van

Duke's gentle bark and excited circles were the only warning I got before Cece waltzed into my condo Sunday afternoon. She was impeccably dressed, per usual, and she swept into my kitchen without hesitation.

"Tea or coffee, love?" she called.

"Hello, Cece," I replied, heaving myself off the couch.

After Lex banished me from the office on Wednesday, I rattled around my condo, oscillating between righteous indignation and pitiful desperation. I tried to see Cami on Friday night, but her obnoxious roommate refused to buzz me in or pass the phone. Afterwards, I added "destructive anger" to the list of emotions.

"Pick one or I'll pick for you," she sing-songed.

"Coffee," I huffed, padding into the kitchen. I hadn't been expecting visitors, so I wore the athletic shorts from my earlier run with Duke and nothing else.

She eyed me. "It's unfair. Us girls go into a relationship spiral and we look downright terrifying. Puffy eyes, swollen face. Here you are looking like an underwear model."

"Who said anything about a relationship spiral?"

Her eyebrows climbed. "Oh, maybe the fact you've brought me more food than one person could eat in a month, let alone a week. I'm surprised I didn't find you in the kitchen."

I grunted, then pointed to the oven. "Pizzas will be done in two minutes."

"Of course they will." She walked over to the oven and peered in. "Looks delicious."

The comment didn't seem to warrant a response. I settled myself on a stool, waiting for her to explain why she was in my kitchen. I had an inkling, but I wasn't in the mood for guessing games.

"Are you in a better place than the other night?" she asked, busying herself with my espresso machine.

"I'm fine."

"What about the lamp in your guest room?"

"Not fine." *But that's a problem for future Van.*

She nodded as she set the cup of espresso in front of me. "What happened with Cami?"

"According to everyone, I fucked up."

"But you don't think you did."

I studied her for a moment, then shook my head.

"Alright. Why don't you tell me your side of things?"

Duke wandered over to headbutt her thigh, and she absently scratched his head. Perhaps indulging Cece wouldn't be the worst idea.

I moved to the oven and pulled out the pizzas, setting them on the rack to cool.

"I'm going to change. Make yourself at home."

"You know I will."

"We'll have lunch when I'm done."

"And talk?"

She crossed the room as I passed her with a grunt of

acknowledgement. I made my way to my bathroom as she headed to the couch with Duke close on her heels. While I appreciated Cece for caring enough to check on me, frustration percolated under the surface. I'd been feeling it for days–a persistent edge of discomfort niggling at me, wearing me down. Lex's accusations were insidious, burrowing into my psyche as constant reminders of my failure. While I still believed my actions were in Cami's best interest, it was clear I failed in the execution.

After an eight-minute shower and fresh clothing, my thoughts were still roiling. Cece sat on the couch with Duke beside her, his head in her lap while she stroked his head and ears. They both looked up as I entered, Duke's tail thumping against the couch.

"How many slices?" I asked from the kitchen, my eyes on the pizza.

"One will do."

I plated lunch, then brought them to the living room. At my pointed look, Duke hopped off the couch and wandered to his bed, settling in to watch us with pleading eyes. I handed Cece her plate, then sat on the couch opposite her.

"I would've shared with him," Cece muttered, taking her first bite of pizza.

"I know." My answering look was pointed.

Her eyes were spotlights on my face as I took my first bite. When her attention didn't waver, I set my food aside and leaned forward, elbows on my knees and hands clasped before me.

"Tell me, Cece, did you and your husband fight?"

She blinked, then chuckled. "All the time. His personality was even bigger than mine."

"Any themes to those fights?"

Her gaze drifted as she considered the question. "We both had strong opinions about most things, but his usually won out. It was typical for the time, but I never did like convention."

"He was controlling?"

"Sometimes. Dismissive, more often."

"And you loved him."

The smile on her face softened. "In my own way, I did. He didn't always deserve it, but that's the way of love, isn't it?"

Restlessness filled me, a persistent itch under my skin. "What made you forgive him?"

"Well, the benefit of time is distance. And with distance, I can recognize that I would do some things differently if they happened today. But relationships and human beings are flawed, Van, and they're unique in their instability. Comparison won't help you." She held my gaze for a long moment. "What answer are you looking for?"

I blew out a harsh breath and hung my head as I tried to piece together my feelings. "Grace is part of love, right? It has to be."

"Of course it is, when it's earned."

"So it's transactional? Enough grace in the bank and you're fine."

"Some context would help here, love," her voice gentled.

"I wanted to help Cami, amplify her business. It's what I do, Cece. My literal job."

"And you do it well."

I threw my hands up in the air and sat heavily back into the couch. "Apparently not well enough."

"Is it your ego that's bruised, or something else?"

My eyes narrowed. "I may be a hothead on my best day, but that's not the problem here."

"Then what is?"

My nostrils flared as I filtered through the events of the week. Lex's accusations, Preston's harsh words, my own self-flagellation...it all rose to the surface. I opened my mouth, and the last vestiges of the dam gave way.

"I was trying to help, to take care of the woman I love. I *love* her, Cece! Not infatuation or lust or convenience. Love. And I've loved her from the beginning. She's the sun, I've told her that, and I am helpless in her orbit. I want nothing more than to bask in her light and lift her up, make all of her dreams come true. I went about it wrong, I understand–I can admit my mistakes." Surprise filled me as I realized I was on my feet, my arms thrown wide. Some of the tension vibrating through me slipped away, and I caught Cece's gaze. "But I love her. And I have to believe that counts for something."

"It does, Van. It counts for a lot." Her eyes shone with emotion as she watched me. "You mentioned wanting to make all of her dreams come true. Tell me about them."

My breath was ragged as I tried to collect myself. "About what?"

"Her dreams."

"I..." my voice trailed off as I considered the question. "She loves her business, her family. Thinks the world of her friends and the people in her community."

"And what does she want from life, Van? From her business? From love?"

I searched her gaze as one of the missing pieces settled into place. "We haven't discussed those things specifically. Not big picture."

"Everyone appreciates feeling heard. This is still new for both of you; there are bound to be hiccups. But you might need to do a little more listening."

"All I want is to give her everything she wants."

"I believe you. But maybe she wants a partner in life more than a benefactor for her business, hmm? Seems like she's got that pretty well in hand if the profile in the Bulletin is any indication."

My eyes fell closed. "I never meant to suggest she wasn't successful. She's that and more. I just hated the part I played in her getting sick and felt compelled to do everything I could to prevent it from happening again. The thought that I was the one who hurt her was...devastating."

"I can imagine," Cece murmured. "I'm sure it was scary for her, too. I bet she was grateful for that week she was here."

My lips quirked into a smile. "Best week of my life, bar none."

A moment of silence stretched between us. Whether blinded by pride or pig-headedness, I hadn't fully confronted the role I played in driving Cami away. After she opened up to me and dropped the barriers between us, I acted as though she didn't have a voice or agency in her business. *God, I'm an asshole. Fuck. Lex was right.*

"And have you told her you love her? What she means to you?"

My eyes flew open and the vehement affirmation was at the tip of my tongue, but I swallowed it back. The way I saw it, I'd been telling Cami she was the one for weeks. I told her with the time I carved out for her each day, with flowers and notes, with passionate kisses and mind-numbing orgasms. But I had a feeling that wasn't what Cece was asking.

"Not in so many words, no."

"Might be time to fess up, love."

I scoffed, angry at myself. "If she gives me the time of day. I haven't given her much reason to."

Cece snorted. "You're a bull, Van. I have faith you'll rise to the challenge."

I eyed her. "Any more advice while I'm in a receptive mood?"

Her eyes twinkled. "What advice? I'm just here to listen."

"I should take notes," I chuckled dryly. "Seems like I need to do more listening."

"Might have to start with apologizing this time."

I hummed my agreement. "Any tips there?"

"I think you know her well enough at this point to know what she values. Diamonds always worked for me, but Cami doesn't seem like the type."

I agreed, but there was one piece of jewelry I couldn't get out of my head. Glancing up, I saw Cece's eager expression and raised my eyebrows in askance.

"What are you planning, hm? Can I help?"

"I think you just might." I stood, gathering our plates and taking them back to the kitchen. "I'll box up this pizza for you."

"Fine, but if you bring me anything for the next two weeks, it should be green."

"Pesto Napoletano and tagliatelle, of course."

Cece gasped. "The man has jokes!"

I handed the container of pizza to her with a wink, her answering grin indulgent.

"Go get her."

"I intend to."

She paused at the door and looked back at me. "You deserve happiness, Van, and you deserve it with someone who cares as deeply for you as you do for those you've chosen as family." Her smile softened and turned wistful. "I've seen how you both look at each other. You say more in those looks than some people manage to say in a lifetime. I know it feels uncertain now, but if you can weather this storm together...well, love, it's blue skies and infinite happiness ahead. I want that for you more than anything."

"Thank you, Cece."

"You're welcome. You'll tell me if you need help with your plans, yes?"

"I will."

She nodded, then let herself out of my condo. I pulled my phone from my pocket, eager to set a few things into motion. First though, I opened my messages app.

> Me: I was an ass.

> Me: I get it now.

> Lex: Good

> Me: I'm sorry.

> Lex: While I appreciate it, I'm not the one who needs to hear it

> Me: I know, I'm working on that.

She added a thumbs up emoji to my message.

> Me: I'll do something for Miles.

> Lex: You approved an off-cycle bonus on Friday, he was very grateful

I barked a laugh.

> Me: Strange, I don't recall.

> Lex: Asshole-induced fever dream, clearly

> Me: Thank you.

> Lex: You back to normal is all the thanks I need

> Lex: Fix it with Cami, though

> Lex: The team and I will thank you

Me: Am I that insufferable?

Lex: I plead the fifth

With a scoff of amusement, I closed out of our thread and opened the group chat with my siblings. I needed the whole family to support the plans forming in my mind. *Get ready, fiorellino. I'm coming for you.*

Chapter 32

Cami

"Whoa, this is quite the operation."

I glanced up and squealed in excitement, rushing over to embrace my sister. "You're here!"

"Yeah," Lani laughed, hugging me back. "Preston let me in. She was on her way to the gym or something? You didn't answer your phone."

"Ugh, sorry. It's been...wild."

"I can see that. Is it always like this?"

Sighing, I glanced around the kitchen and tried to view it through fresh eyes. Stacks of empty containers covered the table, waiting to be filled. Dishes full of the prepped components of the day's menu were strewn across the island. Bread for the next day baked in the oven, suffusing the space with the comforting scent of sourdough.

"Pretty much," I confirmed, walking back over to finish composing the quinoa bowls. "My order volume has been significantly different in the last couple weeks, though. Thanks for coming down to help on a random Tuesday."

"Of course." She shucked off her jacket and dumped it and

her purse on the couch. "It's nice to have a reprieve from the harvest."

"Mom and Dad were okay with you being away?"

She shrugged as she rounded the island to wash her hands. "They weren't thrilled, but there's not much they could say. I haven't taken any time off in months, and we have decent hired help this summer."

"Well, I'm grateful. Thanks for using your PTO on me."

"Believe me when I say it's my pleasure," she teased, stepping up next to me and bumping me with her hip. "What can I do?"

"There's a printout of the veggie burger recipe on the island over there, and all the elements are already prepped and labeled in the fridge. We need 20 for the day."

She whistled as she opened the fridge, recipe in hand. "Girl, you are so organized it's scary. Does that say tzatziki sauce?"

"Yeah! The cucumbers from Gloria have been super flavorful this season. Couldn't let them go to waste."

"Mediterranean vibes, I dig it." She set up across the island from me and started putting the first burger together. "Is this vegan feta?"

"It is! So's everything else." I grinned at her.

She tilted her head. "What's up with that? It's cool, but seems random 'cause I've definitely seen you go to town on a steak."

I chuckled. "So many people have allergies or restrictions, and so few businesses in the area cater to them. Seemed like an opportunity."

"It's obviously working out for you." I felt her eyes on me, assessing. "You look really happy, Cami."

"I am," I agreed, tossing her a playful smile. It faltered as I thought about how soon my five years would be up, and I turned away.

"What was that?"

"Oh, you know," I said with false brightness. "Got stuck in the future there for a second."

Companionable silence settled between us as we completed and stacked orders in the second fridge.

"Okay, sister, spill," Lani burst out. I looked up, surprised to see the stern look on her face. "What's so bad about the future in your head?"

Sighing, I stacked the empty prep dishes in the sink. "It's nothing new, Lani. I just don't feel ready to give up on the Kitchen and my life in the Bay. I want to talk to Mom and Dad about it, but I don't know how to."

She crossed her arms and lowered her eyebrows. "What's so scary about that conversation?"

"Uh," I scoffed an incredulous laugh, "have you met our parents? After the overwhelming disappointment, they'll probably disown me."

"Oh, whatever," she tutted as she rolled her eyes. "You're the golden child. You'll be fine."

My brow furrowed. "Golden child?"

Her eyes widened. "You're joking."

I frowned. "Lani, I'm no golden child. All I ever hear from them is how they're worried I'm not ready to take over and need to focus when my five years are up."

"Because you're not ready!" she barked, throwing her hands up. "The farm is way more than running the market and having connections with the community. I know you were once just as immersed in it as I am, but that was a long time ago, Cami. The drought has changed things. Some of our equipment is entirely new, and most of the crew wouldn't know you from Adam."

Defensiveness rose, but I fought it back. My sister and I rarely found time for open conversations and the last thing I wanted to do was shut it down just as it started.

"You haven't shared these concerns before," I noted.

She snorted, raising a sardonic eyebrow. "When would I have been able to do that, huh? This is the most one-on-one time we've spent together without interruption in literal years."

The truth of her statement made my chest pinch. "I'm sorry I haven't made more time for you, Lani."

"Cami, no," she stepped around the island and wrapped her arms around me. "You're the best big sister on the planet and I won't hear you ever suggest otherwise. Your life is just going in a different direction than certain people assumed it would. And that's okay."

After returning her embrace, I stepped back to meet her gaze. "It's never felt okay. It's always felt like I was running uphill while Mom and Dad held my tether."

"I have news for you," she whispered conspiratorially. "Our entire family is crap at communicating."

"You seem to be doing alright," I mumbled, shooting her a sideways glance as I turned back to clearing the island.

"I had some great mentors in high school." She shrugged. "And I had the benefit of our parents focusing most of their attention on grooming you and then raising Cris. Good ol' forgotten middle child syndrome."

Her grin hinted she was teasing, but I hated the suggestion. She read my expression and laughed.

"I'm good, Cam. Promise. But I think you need to be honest with yourself and our parents about where you want to be this time next year. And it's okay if it's here." She looked around and her smile turned proud. "Because I totally get it; this is fucking awesome. You're a badass."

I laughed wetly, gratitude and surprise welling up. "Thanks, Lani."

"And," her look turned sheepish, "in the spirit of open communication and all...I want the farm."

My mouth opened to respond, then closed as I processed her declaration. "You want the farm."

"Yeah. I do. I have, for years."

"Like, you want to run the whole thing and take over from our parents."

"Yes." She nodded emphatically. "Preferably without whatever weird marriage situation they tried to arrange with Gabriel and his parents, because fuck that guy, but the rest of it? I want it all."

I leaned back against the kitchen counter and blinked at her in stunned silence.

"I know. Total surprise, right? But it seems like a pretty decent idea, if I can pat myself on the back."

"You can. You should." I stared at her. "Leilani, holy shit."

She laughed. "Yep, yeah. I kind of expect our folks to react the same way, if I'm honest."

"You haven't told them?" I frowned. "Of course you haven't, they're still all over my ass." Looking back up at her, I put my hands on my hips. "Why haven't you told them?"

"Well," she drawled, dragging the word out. "I was kinda hoping you would?"

As I crossed my arms over my chest, I raised an eyebrow at her. "What was that about your stellar communication skills?"

"Ugh, of course you bring that full circle. Typical big sister move."

"Lani, why didn't you say anything?"

She fidgeted, weaving her head back and forth in a gesture of indecision. "Forgotten middle child, remember? Everyone was set on you being the one, and you never denied it or said you weren't going to. You just asked for an extension."

"True." I sighed. "What a pair we are."

"Yeah, but together we can do anything, right?" She

knocked her shoulder against mine and offered a hopeful smile, her brown eyes bright.

I chuckled. "Right. We can."

"It can always be better," she teased, echoing our dad.

Groaning a laugh, I threw my arm around her and squeezed her to me. "Okay, well, thanks for coming down to help and completely blow my mind."

"At least it's in a good way?" She grimaced as she turned back to the fridge. "What's next?"

"Just need to cross reference the order list with what was prepped. Make sure we've got everything we need for deliveries." I patted her shoulder as I walked past her toward my laptop. "And for the record, yes. My mind is blown in the best way."

Hope for the future–my future, one I defined–fizzed in my gut for the first time in years. If Lani took on the farm, I'd be free to focus on the Kitchen. I could stay in the Bay. *Why didn't I think to ask her before?* I wanted to kick myself, but I also knew I'd been protecting her and Cris in my own way. If our parents focused on me, my siblings would be free to choose their own paths. Realizing I'd limited their choices in the process was uncomfortable but felt necessary.

"Whoa, that's quite the declaration."

Lani's voice in my ear startled me, and I jumped. "What?"

She gestured to the laptop screen. "Van. That's the guy you brought to the market, yeah? Total hottie, scared the shit out of Gabriel?"

"Uh, yeah," I muttered, looking back at the screen.

Van's order was pulled up, having hit the system just before the cutoff. He hadn't ordered the day before, which I told myself was out of respect for my need for space after Preston chewed him out Friday. His orders for the entire week prior had been relentless, and I'd delivered them to Parker like a coward.

Bringing Lani up to speed on the whole situation was on my to do list, but it was admittedly toward the bottom. My heart was too raw.

"I didn't know you guys were at the declarations of love stage. You've been holding out on me."

"What are you talking about?"

She gestured to the notes section of the screen, which I'd ignored earlier. My eyes widened as I read what he'd typed.

"Farei qualsiasi cosa per te" means "I would do anything for you." And I will, Camellia.

My breath stuttered as I sat hard in the chair at my desk. There were so many things he'd uttered in Italian and never explained. Were they all like this?

"You okay?" Lani put a reassuring hand on my shoulder.

"Uh, yeah, sorry." I shook my head, then took a calming breath. "It's just...me and Van? We're not exactly talking at the moment."

"What did he do?" Her immediate scowl made me laugh.

"Down, girl, I don't need protecting. Van's a marshmallow."

Her eyebrows rose. "I mean, Gabriel would definitely disagree with you, and I've never seen another human put that buttface in his place, but okay."

I huffed a laugh. "Okay, so he's a marshmallow for me."

"And we're not talking to the Italian-speaking heartthrob who only goes gooey for you because..."

Now or never, I guess. As I closed Van's order and printed the details of the day's deliveries, I caught Lani up on Van's failed attempt to make my business successful.

"You walked out and haven't talked to him since," she reiterated, her tone surprised.

"Well, yeah. He hasn't even apologized."

"You haven't given him the chance."

"Wow. Tell me how you really feel, sis."

"Okay, okay, look," she held up her hands in a placating gesture. "Maybe I came on a little strong; let me try again. Van made some assumptions about what you wanted, then did everything he could to give that future to you. Yes?"

My brow furrowed. "I guess he might see it that way."

"Right." She nodded, then shrugged nonchalantly. "Nothing like you protecting me from a future dictated by our parents, even though it's exactly what I want. I mean, totally different situations."

My lips parted as I stared at her.

"If your beef is that he didn't talk to you about what you wanted and just acted anyway...then I guess I should give you the cold shoulder now?"

"Point made, Lani," I snapped, my gears spinning overtime.

"Yup, noted. Little sister shutting up now. Cool. So, uh, how do we get all this to your customers?"

As I walked her through the process, my brain kept replaying what she'd said. *Maybe Van's not the only one who needs to grovel.*

Chapter 33

Van

Patience was not my virtue. I'd made a good show of it for one week, but I couldn't wait any longer. After setting my plans into motion, I expected to hear from Cami. Maybe after a day or two, but the days had marched right along without a word. By the time I fed Duke his dinner on Saturday evening, the waiting became unbearable.

As rare as summer rain was in the Bay, the deluge fit my mood as I stood in front of Cami's building. My attempt to buzz her condo failed, so I decided to wait. She would enter or leave at some point, and we needed to talk. I was done keeping my distance.

Huddled under a small overhang, I checked my watch. *Who even am I?* Rain found its way around the shelter I stood under, and water dripped from my hair down my collar.

"Van?" Her voice was a beacon.

"Cami." I stepped toward her, reaching out a hand.

She stared up at me, surprise etched on her features. "What are you doing?"

"Waiting for you."

Her frown lanced straight through me. "It's raining."

"It is."

"You're soaked through. How long have you been out here?"

Two hours. "A while."

Her frown deepened. "You could've called."

"I tried to buzz in, but no one answered."

"Preston's gone for the weekend." She eyed me. "You're shaking."

"I'm fine. I needed to see you." Her gaze seemed to soften just a touch, and my heart swelled in response. "Camellia, I..."

She watched me expectantly, waiting, and I realized I was terrified. For the first time in my adult life, the future scared me. Because the only future I wanted revolved around her, and I didn't know if she felt the same.

I dropped to my knees. Cami gasped in surprise, stepping toward me. The water on the sidewalk instantly soaked through my jeans and seeped into my socks and shoes. The cold shock of it was grounding, keeping me there in the moment and not spiraling into the unknown.

"Please," I begged, gently taking her hand in mine. "I know I fucked up, made mistakes. I intend to make up for all of them."

"Van, get up, please," she insisted, tugging on my hand.

Refusing to budge and relishing the feel of her warm skin against mine, I continued. "I can't take the silent treatment anymore, *bella*. I'm not strong enough to exist in a world without you in it. Please."

Her lips parted as she listened, attention rapt. The tote on her shoulder swayed with her as she waged an internal battle, then huffed and muttered, "fuck it."

"Get up, Van, please. Come inside, get warm. Seeing you like this is hurting me. Please get up."

"I don't want to hurt you," I intoned, rising to my feet with her hand secure in mine.

"I know," she sighed, pulling me gently toward the door.

I followed her in silence, willing to let her lead now that we shared the same space again. The frenetic energy pulsing through me quieted in her presence, and I breathed easy for the first time in weeks.

When we reached her floor, a surprised grunt tore from my throat. Cami glanced back up and flushed.

"Yeah, um, Preston," she explained, shuffling past the obstruction nearly blocking our way.

Every single floral arrangement I sent over the last two weeks–roughly one daily, all full of camellias–sat dying and discarded in the hall. The cards were all removed, though. My eyes went back to Cami, drawn like magnets, as she led me to her door.

"Sorry," she grimaced, her cheeks bright. "She did it to help me stay strong."

"Why did you need strength?"

Her eyes found mine briefly as she opened the door. "To resist you."

"Then I hope your strength fails you, just this once. For my sake."

I followed her lead and toed off my shoes before joining her in the condo.

She handed me a towel from the bench by the door and looked up at me, her expression puzzled. "How are you still so disarming, Giovanni Costa?"

We were in her living room, a puddle rapidly forming beneath me. I peeled off my coat and hung it on the hook by the wall, then tossed the towel on the floor and fell to my knees before her once more, close enough to touch.

"Does this help?" I asked. "Am I less disarming when I'm on my knees for you?"

"No," she whispered, staring down at me. "Only makes it worse."

Her fingers flexed, as though she wanted to reach for me and stopped herself.

"I'm desperate." My voice was low, gentle. "I have so much I want to tell you, to ask you, *bella*. I'm not trying to disarm you."

Her chin trembled as she gave in and reached toward my face. The moment she was close enough, I pressed my cheek against her palm and inhaled her warm vanilla scent. She stepped closer, and I buried my face against her stomach, wrapping my arms around her hips and pulling her to me. Her gasp ruffled my hair as she stumbled, but I steadied her and refused to let go. The tote bag on her shoulder slipped off and thunked to the floor, the contents going ignored as they spilled and rolled away.

"Van," her hoarse voice cracked on my name. "What are you doing?"

The hint of her sob made me tighten my arms around her, desperate to comfort her even as my emotions overwhelmed me.

"I know we have to talk," I murmured against her, unwilling to lift my head, "but I just need to hold you. Can we set the rest aside for now? Please, let me hold you."

Her hand clutched my shoulders and my gut dropped, thinking she was about to push me away. But her fingers dug into my shoulders and she held me to her, folding at the waist as she embraced me back. I closed my eyes and released a shaky breath, tears forming.

I couldn't remember the last time I cried. When my papà died, I didn't have the time to cry—my madre and sisters did enough of it for all of us. What little energy I possessed was reserved for holding my family together; there was none left over to allow me to break.

In Cami's arms, on my knees and soaking wet, I broke.

The sob that cracked my chest rocked us both. Cami cried

in response and held me tighter, my name tumbling from her lips in reassurance.

"I'm sorry," I rasped. "I'm so sorry, Camellia."

Chapter 34

Cami

For all Preston's talk of groveling, I never imagined it would be quite like this. My head and heart were scrambled as Van huddled against me. He only sobbed twice, but it was enough to open the floodgates for my emotions. My knees weakened, and I let myself slide through his arms to nestle against his chest. He let me, sitting back on his heels and supporting me without hesitation. Rainwater from his clothes soaked through mine, but I barely noticed, too wrapped up in all that was Van. *I missed him so much.*

Between the Kitchen and Preston's vow to ensure I didn't talk to Van until I was ready, I'd been properly distracted for two weeks. As I gathered Van's shirt in my fists to hold us together, the depth of my longing washed over me. Even though we'd only met at the start of the summer, I craved him. Craved his scent in my nose and on my skin, his lingering touches and the casual way he focused on me every time we were in a room together. After the first order note I found with Lani, I ignored the notes section of the system completely, partly to protect my heart and partly because I wanted to hear him say the words.

"I know I have so much to atone for." Van's deep voice interrupted my thoughts.

I wanted to tell him it was all behind us, but the vow I made to myself to own my future was ever-present in my mind.

"You do," I agreed, sniffling.

I could feel him smile against my hair. "Where would you like to start? Do you want to tell me how you feel?"

I raised my head, looking at him in surprise.

"Or would you like me to go first?"

The Cami who had yet to live this summer would absolutely pick the latter option. But that felt like the cowardly choice in the wake of how much I'd grown.

"I'll start."

"I'll listen."

I sniffed again, then sorted through my thoughts. *Start at the beginning, Rivera.* "When you put me on the List without talking to me about it, I felt blindsided and inconsequential to my own business." I paused, waiting for a protest or to feel his body tense, but he was still. Bolstered by his silent encouragement, I continued, "It was a dream and a goal of mine and I'm grateful to be honored, but I wanted to be part of the process. I could've learned a lot."

"That's fair," he nodded.

"And when you started telling people I was your girlfriend and partner, without even asking me, I felt like an object. Like I was something you decided to have, and I didn't have any choice in the matter. It was dehumanizing."

His eyes flashed as his arms tensed briefly around me. "That's the last thing I want you to feel."

I searched his face, finding nothing but support and openness. "I appreciate that. And then you left without a word, and I was back to feeling inconsequential, but this time to you." My voice dropped. "It was the worst."

"It sounds terrible," he agreed, tone earnest.

The anger that still stirred in my gut when I thought of his failed surprise rose. "And then the cafe. How dare you just go and decide on the future of my business? Does my opinion mean nothing to you?!"

"Your opinion means everything to me."

"Well, you have a weird way of showing it," I snapped, crossing my arms. *Preston would be proud.*

"You're right."

I narrowed my eyes. "Are you just saying that, or do you believe it? You're awfully calm."

His lips quirked up in one corner. "I'm still in listening mode, unless you're ready for me to start to atone?"

"It can be your turn, but start by answering the question."

"I can do that."

He shifted, taking me with him as he stretched his legs out, then leaned back against the couch. Opening his arms, he arched a brow to invite me to get comfy. I turned and leaned my back against him, melting against his chest. His arms closed around me, his cheek pressed to my head.

"My sisters–"

"Elena and Lucia, I remember."

He kissed my hair. "I asked them for advice."

I glanced at him over my shoulder. "What kind of advice?"

"I explained what I did, and asked them what they'd want if they were in your shoes. Their answers varied more than I expected, but they both said I should listen and acknowledge your emotions."

"Smart sisters," I scoffed, amused.

He hummed. "To answer your question, I didn't just say what I thought you wanted to hear. Validating emotions might be a new concept for me, but I see its merits."

I twisted around to face him. "Are you ever going to stop surprising me?"

The most beautiful smile I'd ever seen broke across his face. It brought out his laugh lines and made my toes curl. "I certainly hope not," he answered, his voice a low rasp.

Shivering, I sighed. "Back to atoning, mister."

"As you wish," he chuckled. His expression sobered as he went on. "I apologize for making assumptions about what you want for your life, Camellia. Only you can decide what's best for you, I know that." He took my hands in his, smoothing his thumbs across my knuckles. "I should have told you about my idea for the List. If it's something you want to pursue again in the future, I'd love to help."

"Thank you," I murmured.

"I see how I was blinded by my care for you when I bought the cafe."

"You *bought* it?!"

He smirked again, eyes twinkling. "I did. Haven't decided what to do with it yet, but if you want to help with that decision, I'd welcome your thoughts."

"Too soon, Costa," I grumbled, but it lacked bite.

"I'm sorry I overstepped and didn't ask you what you wanted."

I gazed up at him and shrugged. "I should've told you how I felt long before it got to that point. I'm sorry, too."

He took a deep breath, some of the tension in his shoulders draining away as he did. "Did you get my notes?"

Heat rushed to my cheeks, and I groaned. "I only read the first one you sent in with your Tuesday order, and Preston confiscated all the ones with the flowers."

His look turned a touch feral, and my pussy took notice. "I'm glad. I'd rather tell you in person, regardless."

I licked my lips, my nipples pebbling under his focused attention. "Why are you looking at me like that?" I whispered.

"My sisters told me I needed to grovel. Have I groveled sufficiently?"

"I could think of a couple more things that might help," I retorted, my voice thready.

"Do those things require you to be naked, *bella*?"

I nodded, suddenly desperate to have his hands, mouth, skin on me anywhere, *everywhere*. Goosebumps rose as he growled in approval, then surged forward to gather me in his arms and lift me as though I weighed nothing.

"What about the notes?" I gasped, clinging to him as he started walking toward my room.

"I'll tell you what they said," he promised. "I'll paint the words on your body with my tongue."

I groaned, the intimate knowledge of how talented his tongue was making it a filthy promise. He tossed me on the bed the moment we burst through the door.

"Strip," he commanded, following the same order with quick precision.

I ripped my dress off over my head and shimmied out of my bra and thong as fast as I could. He was down to just his boxer briefs, his hard cock poking out from the band. With my eyes on him, he slowly lowered himself to his knees.

"You want me to grovel, *bella*?" His voice was a thick rasp. "Tell me how."

Holy fucking hell, that's the sexiest thing a man has ever said to me. Swallowing the urge to whimper in response, I demanded, "I want your mouth on me."

His eyes darkened in approval as I sat on the edge of the bed, then he walked forward on his knees. "Where?"

I spread my legs, placing my hands on my inner knees and pushing them wide. "Here."

312 ASHLEY JACOBS & S. S. RICH

His groan made my core clench on nothing. I only had a moment of wanting before he surged forward and buried his face between my legs. He took a deep breath, a rough moan on his lips as he savored my scent.

"You smell like heaven and sin," he purred, before flattening his tongue against me and licking a long stripe up my labia.

I moaned and fell back against the bed, losing myself in the sensation of him. He gripped my hips and yanked me closer to the edge, giving him better access. His tongue found my clit and circled it slowly before he sucked it roughly into his mouth. I writhed, jutting my hips toward his face. He brought me right to the edge, my breathing fast and my body one taut line, then drew away. I whimpered as he trailed wet kisses along my inner thigh, then he started to whisper—each word separated by a nip, lick, or gentle press of his lips.

"*Farei qualsiasi cosa per te,*" he breathed. "I would do anything for you."

"More," I begged as my heart panged.

"How many?" he asked, stroking a finger through my folds as he watched my face. "How many times do you need to come?"

It was an impossible question. I wanted to answer "as many as you can" but I knew he'd take it as a challenge and I wasn't sure I'd survive. "Three," I gasped, squirming under his light touch.

"Hmm, too low," he murmured, pressing his mouth back to my pussy as he slid two fingers inside me.

My back bowed as I drove closer to him, seeking more. He found my G-spot and stroked back and forth to the same rhythm of his tongue on my clit, coaxing me higher.

"Oh!" I gasped, the wave of pleasure gathering with unstoppable force. "Oh, Gio, right there. Please, don't stop..."

He listened, increasing the pressure inside me right as I got to the edge. The suction on my clit increased as I clamped around him, crying out as the wave of my orgasm crashed. Words fell from my lips, nonsense and praise, as he continued to stroke me through the aftershocks. My body was tingling, my legs twitching, when he pulled back from my core just enough to speak again. His mouth was close enough for his warm breath to tease my clit.

"*Ho bisogno di te,*" he murmured, "means I need you."

My heart swelled at the gravity of his statement. He wasn't delirious with need; I'd seen him like that enough to know. His tongue slipped out and curled around my clit again, teasing ever so gently, as he pulled his fingers from inside me.

"Hmmm," he hummed, "I want to lick you off me. But I have a better idea."

His fingers slipped down to my ass, spreading my cum along the tight ring of muscle. I jumped, the sensation both foreign and arousing. A growl rumbled against my clit and a second orgasm rushed up as my body tightened, not quite breaking.

"May I?" he asked, tapping on my ass. "Just to play, *bella*. For now."

I bit my lip and nodded, then remembered my words. "Yes."

"*Brava ragazza,*" he hissed. "Good girl."

He sucked my clit back into his mouth as I came, the combination of his praise and the simultaneous stimulation pushing me out into the abyss. As my body relaxed in the post-orgasm haze, his finger pressed in earnest against me.

"Relax," he soothed, then thrust his tongue into my pussy.

I ached to be filled with more of him, but before I could ask for what I wanted, his finger slid past my tight ring of muscle. Gasping, I raised my head and looked down at him, shock and excitement coursing through me. Slick pleasure soothed the burn as he returned his attention to my pussy. He pressed a thumb to my clit, rubbing gently as he fucked me with his tongue.

Losing myself in the cacophony of sensation, I relaxed back against the bed. Van hummed his approval, his lips vibrating against my clit. Tension gathered once more, the muscles in my stomach almost painfully tense as anticipation filled me. I teetered on the edge, bliss just out of reach.

Van slipped his finger further into my ass, and the third wave started to crest. My legs shook violently as my release washed through me, warmth suffusing my limbs and my body melting into the mattress. Van's magic tongue didn't stop as he slipped his finger from me, my body feeling simultaneously used and bereft.

He pulled back, a lascivious smirk on his lips. "Fucking delicious."

Throwing an arm over my eyes, I huffed a tired laugh, absolutely spent. I heard him head to the bathroom, then return a few minutes later. Lifting my arm, I squinted up at him.

"Hi," I muttered, my breathing finally regulated.

His chuckle felt like a caress. "You okay?" he asked gently.

"Mmhm," I nodded. "That was new."

A pleased, possessive sound rumbled from his chest as he crawled up onto the bed. "I'll take every first you have to give." His voice oozed smug satisfaction and gentle command.

He paused at the juncture of my thighs, kissing my pussy lightly, then trailed his lips along my lower stomach.

"*Al cuore non si comanda. È dato,*" he murmured, looking up at me with his cheek flush against my body. "It means the heart cannot be commanded. It is given."

His tone was reverent, and tears welled in my eyes. He continued his slow, sensual progression up my body, reducing me to little more than a puddle of emotion and whimpering need by the time his lips touched mine.

We were facing each other on our sides, bodies flush. Van had shed his briefs and his erection stood hot and heavy against me.

"What do you need?" he asked, kissing my neck.

"You, inside me," I pleaded, reaching down to stroke him.

"Where?" He licked the hollow of my throat, sending a shiver down my spine.

I lifted my leg up onto his hip, guiding the head of his cock to my pussy. "Here."

He pressed his forehead to mine, eyes closed, and pushed slowly forward. I kept my fingers in place, guiding him into me. My eyes rolled back as he seated himself and I pulled my hand away, heat blooming across my body at the welcome stretch.

"I missed you," he breathed, fingers digging into my ass cheek as he drew back and surged forward.

"I missed you, too," I managed, my voice falling into a moan as his pace quickened.

He adjusted my leg on his hip, making sure I was secure, then brought his hand up to my cheek to bring my eyes to his.

"*Il mio cuore è tuo*," he rasped. "My heart is yours."

I whimpered as he pressed his lips to mine, his slow, forceful thrusts gradually dismantling the last vestiges of defense around my heart. Van captured my lips with his, his tongue diving into my mouth as he plunged into me.

When our lips parted, I teetered on the edge. "More," I begged, pulling him closer, wanting him on top of me.

He rolled me onto my back and braced himself over me. "Brace your hands against the headboard."

I did, my heart thundering in my chest and my pussy tightening in anticipation. He groaned, his eyes wild with lust.

"Hold on," he growled, then pistoned into me with force.

Pleasure exploded in my core, the head of his cock brushing my over-sensitive G-spot with every movement. My back bowed as I started to shake, the rush of pleasure blossoming deep within and radiating through me. Van shouted his release as I clamped down around him, my pussy fluttering wildly as my climax multiplied. Waves of bliss that felt like miniature orgasms kept washing through me.

"I will never get enough of seeing you shatter, Camellia," Van whispered. "Never."

I wrapped my arms around him, anchoring us together, and sighed in contentment when he relaxed against me. I loved the weight of him, loved that I had to work to breathe with him on top of me.

"*Sono tuo*," he murmured. "I'm yours."

My eyes squeezed shut on the tears his words summoned. Too soon, I felt him slip from me. But before I could protest, he shifted to free me, then sat back on his heels, pushing my knees apart.

"Sexiest thing I've ever fucking seen," he crooned, eyes locked on my pussy. "All pink and swollen, my cum all over you."

He reached forward, pushing his release back inside as he met my eyes. "Can't waste a drop, *bella*. Want you full to bursting."

I couldn't help my whimper as he slowly dragged his fingers out of me, then offered them to me.

"Taste us."

He bit his lip and groaned as I obeyed, taking his fingers into my mouth and licking the mess. The moment I released him, he kissed me, his tongue tangling with mine as the flavor of us overwhelmed me. As we parted, he gave a pleased hum and pressed his lips to my forehead, then relaxed against the bed and pulled me to rest against his chest.

After a few minutes, he asked, "Where did Preston hide the cards from the flowers?"

I looked up at him in confusion. "Her top right dresser drawer."

He frowned. "Is it safe to go in there?"

"Just socks in that one," I giggled. "Why?"

He sighed in relief, then stood. "I'll be right back."

Yanking on his briefs, he disappeared out of my room and down the hall. I sat up, confused. He returned a moment later, one envelope in his hand.

"They're still sealed."

I shrugged. "She's a big believer in boundaries. Opening something personal would violate mine."

"Admirable." He sat next to me, our sides flush. "I sent something with the last one. Didn't want to lose it."

He handed me the envelope. I could feel something within, a lump warping the thick paper.

"Open it," he encouraged.

I did. My heart froze, then began to gallop as I stared at the stunning, art deco style antique ring in my palm. An emerald shone at its center.

"It was my nonna's," he murmured.

"Gio..."

"We are the only ones who can decide what's best for us," he said, his palm settling under my open hand as his gaze met mine. "I've known you're the best thing for me for a while. And after you asked me for space, well..." His sigh was deep, almost tortured. "I realized I never put into words what you mean to me. I let you question us, question your importance in my life."

He closed his hand around mine, the ring encased by our fists. "I don't want you to question how much I value you, Camellia. I want you to know, without a doubt, that I will always put you first." He nodded toward the note. "Turn it over, please."

I turned the card over in my other hand, my fingers trembling as I read the message.

Ti amo oggi più di ieri ma meno di domani.

Van spoke the words in Italian, his deep voice filling the room and resonating in my chest.

"What does it mean?" I breathed.

His eyes shone, a soft smile curling his lips. "I love you more today than yesterday but less than tomorrow."

I laughed through my tears, stunned. *How is this real life?* "You love me?"

He leaned his forehead to mine, our hands still clasped. "I do."

"But that's a ring, Gio."

"It is. A meaningful one."

"Are you asking me to marry you?"

The smile on his face was unlike any I'd seen before–unrestrained, joyous. "Would you? Someday?"

I laughed at the innocent hope in his expression and threw myself at him. "I don't know what to say."

"It's not a real question, *bella*." His arms were tight around me, our cheeks together. "Not yet. Not until you want it to be."

"Then, what is it?"

"A promise. You are and always will be at the top of my list."

Chapter 35

Cami

I writhed in my dream, my mouth parting on a soft moan as Van's tongue lazily circled my clit. My fists clenched in the sheets as I extended my head back, my eyes screwed shut. Dream Van ran a hand up the center of my body, putting light pressure on my stomach to keep me still. He ducked a shoulder, shoving my leg out of the way as he thrust his tongue into me.

My whimper made him groan, and the vibration on my clit had me shivering all over, my feet twitching. He licked up my slit, then sucked my labia into his mouth, his teeth scraping along the flesh. The slightest hint of pain set my nerves on fire and I bucked my hips, seeking more. Always more of him.

Dream Van refocused his attention on my clit, then stroked one finger along my pussy lips, teasing me. I tried to move, to impale myself on him, but his other hand held me still. My frustrated whimper jolted me, my eyes fluttering as I realized I was no longer dreaming. *Was it ever a dream?*

Van, in real life and between my bare thighs, sucked my clit greedily into his mouth as he stroked my channel with his finger. I gasped, my back bowing as awareness rushed in and pleasure spiked through me. Heat gathered fierce and heavy in my pussy, behind my clit, building with a rare intensity. Van crooked his finger inside me, stroking, and the heat intensified as my orgasm rushed up.

I cried, body strung taut, as the most exquisite ache bloomed through me. It was extreme and prolonged, the strange heat dissipating slowly as the aftershocks continued. My eyes were closed once more as my body melted into the mattress, my limbs boneless and my lips numb as I gasped to catch my breath.

Van's dark chuckle sent goosebumps along my skin as he slowly withdrew his fingers. I pried my eyes open by sheer force of will and looked down my body to find him staring at my pussy, my cum visibly dripping from his gorgeous face.

"Good morning, *fiorellino*," he rumbled, his voice pure sex.

"Morning," I breathed.

"Tell me, Camellia, have you done this before?"

My brows drew together as I propped myself up on my elbows. "Done what?"

He grinned at me as he sat up, gesturing to my lower body. I slowly sat, then gaped at the massive wet spot on the bed.

"What the hell?!"

His smug chuckle filled the room, and I smacked him. He caught my wrist and pulled me into his body, kissing me soundly. The flavor of me was still all over him, and it was hotter than I wanted to admit.

"I take it I can claim another first?" he murmured against my lips, clearly pleased with himself.

"That is not from me," I denied, shaking my head.

"It is," he retorted, eyes sparkling. "I watched it happen. *Bellissima.* I can't wait to see it again."

Heat flared in my cheeks as I pushed at him, still in denial. He chuckled again and wrapped his arms around me.

"Your body is stunning in all it does and is capable of. *You* are stunning," he insisted.

Pouting, I leaned into his chest and ignored the sheet situation. *Thank goodness for waterproof mattress covers, I guess.* Van kissed my neck before resting his head against me, breathing me in.

"Did you sleep well?"

I smiled and nodded. My sleep was sound and my dreams calm until the dream-that-wasn't woke me. "I haven't slept that peacefully in weeks."

"Same for me," he murmured against my skin.

"Do you have any plans today?"

"Be with you." He took my left hand in his, this thumb stroking the ring he'd given me.

I bit my lip. Sensing my hesitation, he lifted his head and looked down at me, then brushed the hair out of my eyes.

"What is it?" he asked, reaching out to gently free my lip from my teeth.

"Well, I was planning to work the market today."

"Can I help?"

My tummy flipped as I smiled hesitantly at him. "You want to?"

"I enjoyed our market day. I would be happy to learn and be helpful."

I grabbed his face in my hands and kissed him, a grin on my lips. He returned the smile, the laugh lines I loved appearing as he did.

"Thank you. I'll take you up on that soon, but I need to talk to my dad today."

"Everything okay?"

"I'm hoping it will be." I looked up at him as nerves churned in my gut, and I fiddled with his ring on my finger. "There's something I want to tell you." *Now that it's very clear there's nothing temporary about us.*

"I'm listening," he murmured.

"Well, my parents expect me to uh...take over the farm."

A small smirk appeared on his lips. "I may have picked up on that from your family's website. I did wonder why your face was so prominent when you own a business down here, so far away."

My jaw dropped as I stared at him, then laughed. "You looked up my family's farm?"

"You shouldn't be surprised." He kissed my forehead. "When I'm interested in someone, I want to know everything about them. And I've never been more interested than I am in you."

Ignoring the flush that immediately rose in my cheeks as his tone dropped, I pressed on. "Well, they expect me to take over in a few months."

Van's eyebrows climbed. "I assume that would require you to move back to Ukiah." His gaze unfocused as he looked off to the side, and I had the sense he was plotting.

"Before you make an offer on anyone's farm, mister, hear me out."

He huffed a laugh as his eyes met mine. "Apologies. Go on."

As I explained Lani's interest in the farm and my plans to discuss it all with my father, Van listened. He asked a few questions, all in the vein of ensuring I was pursuing the path I wanted. My heart swelled in my chest as he smiled warmly at me, expression full of something like love and pride.

He rubbed his hands along my upper arms. "Thank you for telling me, *bella*. I'm here for you, however you want to use me— even if just to listen."

"Your sisters did a number on you with their advice, didn't they?" I teased.

"I think they were so shocked I came to them, they missed the opportunity to mess with me."

I snorted. "Not one to ask for help, eh? Shocking." *What a pair we are.*

Van just tightened his arms around me. "Can I make you breakfast?"

"There's quiche and fresh orange juice in the fridge, and I think there are a few raspberry coconut scones left."

"I'll take that as a yes." He kissed me thoroughly, then slipped from the bed.

I watched him unabashedly as he pulled on his briefs, enjoying the unobstructed view of his thick thighs. The vision of spending every morning just like this, waking in Van's arms and sharing in the small intimacies of life, filled my head. *Yeah, I could get used to this.*

———

Van dropped me off at the market a couple of hours later. He needed to take Duke for his run, then would be back to meet my dad and pick up a few things.

Cris, Dad, and I had been at it for a few hours and the crowds were dwindling. I walked over to where Cris was stacking crates near the back of the stall and sidled up to him.

"Think you can handle things for a bit?" I asked. "I need to grab Dad for a few minutes."

"Do I have to?"

"Please?"

He sighed and moved reluctantly toward the front of the stall. I squeezed his shoulder in thanks as he passed, then turned to my dad.

"Hey, can we chat?" I gestured to the back of the stall.

He studied my face, then motioned for me to lead the way.

"What's this about, Cami?" he asked as we stepped out of the flow of foot traffic.

"Well," I swallowed, steeling myself. "I know you and Mom have been worried about my readiness and commitment to the farm."

"We have," he agreed, crossing his arms.

"It took a frank comment from Lani for me to realize you had the right to be. When I asked you for time to see what I could build here in the Bay, I always thought it would be temporary."

He grunted. "So did we."

"I know, and I should've said something sooner. It's taken a lot for me to be ready to have this conversation, but I want to talk to you about the vision I have for my future."

He tilted his head. "Go on."

I suppressed the urge to fidget. "As hard as it is to admit, I don't think taking over the farm is the right path for me. I've built a life and a business here in the Bay, and I want to see it through."

He furrowed his brow. "Cami, I don't understand. Your business isn't temporary?"

"It started that way," I conceded. "But it's grown a lot in the last five years. So have I. It feels like a disservice to myself not to see where I can take it."

"And what about your responsibility to the family? To the farm?"

"I'll always be part of this family, regardless of where I work. And the Kitchen has never stopped me from supporting the farm."

He tossed a hand up in frustration. "That's not entirely true, is it? You've been more distant lately, far more in need of support than giving it."

His words felt like a physical attack. I swallowed roughly, choosing not to rise to the bait. "Dad, I've spent the last four and a half years building the Kitchen by myself, while doing everything I could to meet your and mom's expectations. There's a lot I haven't shared with you about what I've done because I honestly didn't think you'd care."

"We've been nothing but supportive, Cami. Giving you five years–"

"Respectfully, Dad, that's not true." I fought to keep my voice steady, my hand shaking slightly as I settled it on my hip. My father's nostrils flared as he crossed his arms. "You've never once asked about the Kitchen or my goals. If you had, you'd know I've created a community of growers and local restaurateurs in the Bay. We fundraise to support farms in need and provide educational materials and programs to local schools. Just last year, the Kitchen sponsored the launch of a composting program for offices downtown. The Bulletin even did a story on it."

His brows furrowed. "Why didn't you tell us?"

My lips quirked into a small smile, a heavy breath leaving me in a rush. "It's always been the farm between us, even when I was a kid. As proud as I am of myself for being on the Best in the Bay list this year, none of my news ever felt significant enough to warrant your attention."

His eyebrows rose comically high at my mention of the List. "We would've appreciated the opportunity to know, to be proud of you," he insisted, heaving a sigh. "I *am* proud of you. You really did all that?"

I nodded with a shrug. "All that and a lot more, Dad. I'd love to tell you about it sometime."

"I'd like that." His voice was rough. "But that doesn't solve the challenge that your absence will cause at home, Cami."

Taking a deep breath, I walked right off the hypothetical cliff. "Dad, have you ever asked Lani what she wants to do long term?"

His expression turned thoughtful. "Can't say I have."

"Well, she wanted me to tell you that she sees a future on the farm and in Ukiah. She wants it and she's committed to it. I know I'm the oldest, but I don't see why she shouldn't be the one to take over from you and Mom."

"Is that right?"

"It is."

"Hm," he regarded me. "Lani has stepped up a lot in the last couple of years. She's got a knack for reading the land and managing the crew." He huffed a wry chuckle, looking off into the distance with a shake of his head. "You girls sure do like to keep me on my toes. That's a lot to think about, Cami."

"I know it is, and I'm sorry it's taken me this long to be upfront about it."

"You know your mom and I just want you to be happy, right? We took over the farm from my parents because we wanted to build something lasting for you kids. If your life takes you elsewhere, we'll support you. But if you want the farm, it'll always be there for you. As will we."

My lips curved into a soft smile. "I know, Dad. Thank you. And I'll do everything I can to support you and Lani, the family. I don't want to let you all down, but I don't want to let myself down, either."

"You could never. We're proud of all you kids, you know that." His voice was gruff.

"I do now," I murmured, squeezing his hand.

He nodded at me, then jutted his chin toward the stall. "Better go save your brother."

"If you know he hates it, why do you make him come on market days?" I asked quietly.

"There's growth in discomfort. Builds character."

I shook my head and walked over to tap Cris on the shoulder, sending him to handle stock while I took over the register.

We only had a few more minutes before Van would be back to pick me up.

As though thinking of him conjured him from thin air, my tall, tanned, brooding man appeared. He strolled up the aisle, his amber eyes locked on me. The claim in his expression was absolute, and I was seized with sudden clarity. Despite all odds, it turned out our worlds were as compatible as we were. Van's ring on my finger was a promise, yes, but the strengthening connection between us was a contract. One I finally felt willing to sign, without reservation.

My father saw my expression and paused, then followed my gaze. "Friend of yours?"

"Started that way," I replied, stepping out from behind the register. "But now he's part of my future."

Glancing back, I giggled at the surprise on my dad's face.

"Hi, *bella*," Van greeted, reaching for me.

I stepped into his embrace eagerly, then leaned up to press a chaste kiss to his lips. When we parted, my dad had stepped around to join us, an assessing look in his eye.

"Mr. Rivera," Van said, offering a hand. "I'm Giovanni Costa."

"Call me Miguel, please."

"Miguel." Van nodded, slipping an arm around my waist. "Cami's told me so much about Ukiah and your farm. I'd love to see it someday."

"You know your way around a farm?"

"I know to listen to those who do."

My dad grunted approval, then nodded to me. "You can go, enjoy the market. It's slow enough that we can manage."

"Oh, Dad, it's okay, I can stay."

"Don't need to," he insisted. "We've got it, Cami. Thanks for telling me about Lani. Your mom and I will discuss it with her"

Why did I avoid this conversation for so long? "Thank you. Travel safe home, okay?"

He waved me off with a grunt and a nod at Van, then stepped back into the stall. Van tightened his arm around me.

"Want to grab your purse, then tell me what gorgeous vegetables to buy?" he teased.

I hip checked him with a laugh, nodding. As we wandered through the aisles, greeting my suppliers and friends while we filled Van's market bags, my vision of the future crystallized. I saw weekend brunches at Van's condo with Preston and Cece, Parker and LB stopping by when they could. Van wrapped around me in his kitchen as I tried new recipes, unable to keep his hands to himself. Duke at my feet as I read in the living room, Van a warm presence against my back.

Before that summer, I let the ticking clock of obligation steal my joy for what was to come. Reclaiming my optimism felt both empowering and inevitable, especially with Van by my side.

I leaned into him as we turned for the exit, bags laden but my heart feeling lighter than air.

"Thank you."

Van looked down, his smile indulgent. "For what, *fiorellino?*"

"Reminding me some things are worth fighting for. Even me."

His arm tightened around me and he kissed my head, breathing me in. "Always you, Camellia. *Sono tuo.*"

That's one I don't need translated.

"I'm yours, too."

Epilogue

Cami

My phone buzzed on the counter, and I snatched it up.

> Gio: Home in 10.
>
> Gio: Been thinking about your ass in those leggings all day.
>
> Gio: Can't wait to taste you.

Anticipation tingled in my core and I bit back a grin. Marriage hadn't dulled the fire between us one bit.

> Me: You'll have to find me first

I giggled at the devil emoji he sent in reply. Adjusting the sign on the island, I made sure it was visible from the entryway. The arrow pointed toward the oven, where a fresh brioche bun awaited discovery. *I couldn't pass up the opportunity for a food-related pun.* Glancing down at the test stick on the counter, I placed a hand on my belly as excited disbelief danced in my gut. Ever since moving in together a month after Van put his nonna's ring on my finger, he'd been feral over the thought of getting me pregnant. *He's going to lose his mind.*

After those two little lines appeared that morning, I asked Cece to take Duke, so I'd have Van's undivided attention when he got home. She'd been all too happy to oblige, especially when the ask came with an invitation to join us for brunch on Saturday. She and I had become close in the months since I'd moved in, and she even signed as a witness at our small courthouse wedding over Christmas.

The speed of our relationship surprised me at first, but once we gathered our closest family and friends, I knew it was meant to be. Our journey was ours alone, and true to Van's promises on the night that changed everything, only we could decide what was best for us. Besides, Van desperately wanted to show me off as his wife at the Athena holiday party; marriage was really our only option.

Our families traveled to the Bay to celebrate with Van and me over the holidays. Our condo was overrun, full to bursting with laughter, shrieking children, and the comforting scent of his mom's baking.

An amused Lex gifted us a lovely dinner and open bar in lieu of a formal reception, and we got to see our family–relative and found alike–together for the first time. That night, from Preston teaching Van's youngest niece self defense to our brothers bonding over a shared distaste for people, would live rent-free in my head for the rest of my life. And watching Van with his nieces and nephews had shown me what a patient, supportive, and loving father he'd be, nearly reducing me to tears.

I tucked the positive test into the pocket of my cardigan, then walked slowly down the hall, trailing flower petals in my wake. The path would lead Van from the kitchen to our room, where I'd set up a surprise. One early morning call to Preston to determine how to tell Van had resulted in a delivery at our door a few hours later.

> Pres: I was searching baby shit for you and it was too perfect

> Pres: figured it could help the surprise?

> Pres: it's okay if you hate it

> Pres: am I nailing this godmother thing yet?

> Me: you're ridiculous

> Me: I love it, love you

> Me: thank you 🥹

A white crib stood in one corner of our bedroom, the green and yellow blanket Van's mom had gifted us at our wedding draped over the edge. She'd called it a subtle hint, then patted my cheek with a wink.

The noise of the condo door opening sounded faintly and I jumped, rushing to our bathroom to check my hair. I was still wearing the leggings Van had admired at lunch, with a loose tank under my cardigan.

"Where are you, *fiorellino*?"

I giggled nervously as my belly swooped, nerves and excitement bubbling over. My fingers fidgeted with the test in my pocket as I walked back to the bedroom, listening to Van move through the condo.

"And what's this, hm?" He projected his voice so I could hear. The sound of him opening the oven was faint but identifiable. "Smells delicious."

His footfalls drew closer. "I wonder what she has in store for me..."

Placing the pregnancy test in the crib, I turned it to make sure the positive result was facing up. Then I slipped into our walk-in closet, hiding just behind the door. The crib was still in view, so I'd be able to see his face when he entered the room.

Moments later, Van walked in. He was looking toward the bathroom, so it took him a beat to notice the new furniture in the corner. When it registered, his entire body froze.

"Camellia..." he breathed, transfixed by the sight.

I bit my lip as my eyes filled, my emotions amplified tenfold. Between pregnancy hormones and the complete emotional kryptonite of my imposing, 6' 5" giant of a husband's eyes glistening with tears, I was a complete goner.

Van stepped up to the crib and lifted the blanket, brushing a reverent hand over the monogrammed "C" on one corner. Just as I slipped through the closet door to join him, he caught sight of the pregnancy test. I watched, almost in slow motion, as he reached over the rail to grab the test, then slowly dropped to his knees.

I rushed over to him, my movement catching his attention as he lifted his face to mine, eyes glassy and lips parted.

"You're sure?" he whispered, jaw slack.

I could only nod, tears stealing my voice. He reached out and seized my hips, pressing the side of his face against my belly as he laughed in disbelief, his shoulders shaking. When he caught his breath, he sat back on his heels and gazed at my abdomen, as though he could see through to my womb by sheer force of will.

"*Ti amo oggi più di ieri ma meno di domani,*" he vowed.

Those words were written on my soul–I no longer needed him to translate. He whispered them every morning, texted them when we were apart, and reminded me of their truth through his care and support each day. *I love you more today than yesterday but less than tomorrow.*

"Was that for me or your baby?" I murmured.

His gaze rose to mine as my favorite smile–the one that brought out his laugh lines and lit me up in seconds–burst across his lips. "Both. For you and *our* baby."

He looked back down at my belly, gathering my shirt and lifting it so he could kiss my skin. "We're having a baby."

"We are."

"We're having a baby!"

Suddenly, he was on his feet and I was in the air, his arms wrapped just under my ass. I shrieked a laugh, grabbing onto his shoulders as I looked down into his joyous face. He grinned up at me and spun us around slowly, then walked over to the bed. Cupping his cheeks in my palms, I leaned down and kissed him deeply.

When we parted, he turned and set me on the bed, more gently than usual, and crawled up after me, as I settled back onto the pillows. He pushed my shirt up again and laid his cheek against my belly, then wrapped his arms around me. I threaded my fingers through his hair, gently scraping his scalp, as we cuddled in silence.

Van kissed me gently, his lips lingering, then looked up at me. "I can't wait for you to start showing."

I laughed, bright and loud. "That's what you're looking forward to?"

He nodded, not lifting his head. "You're always gorgeous, but you're going to be so fucking sexy all big and round. I can't fucking wait."

He kissed me again as I giggled at him and his caveman antics, enjoying the moment. It didn't take long for his kisses to turn teasing and goosebumps to rise across my body as he nipped and licked a path up to my breasts.

"I hear," he murmured, pushing my loose tank up to bare my chest completely, "that pregnancy makes these particularly tender. Shall we test that theory?"

I shivered, my nipples already drawn into taut peaks, and nodded. "Only one way to find out."

He hummed in approval. He leaned down to lick one nipple, causing my back to bow, as I arched into him at the intensity of the sensation. When he drew back, his eyes were wild.

"I want to fill you up," he growled, "want you dripping with my cum."

Arousal pulsed through me, but I couldn't pass up the opportunity to tease. "You already put a baby in me, Gio."

His eyes flashed as he leaned down to scrape his teeth along my nipple, wringing a whimper from my throat. "Practice makes perfect, *bella*. Can't lose my touch."

I laughed, breathless, as happiness and gratitude filled me to the brim.

One reservation for a lifetime of this, please. Costa, party of three...and counting.

––––––

The fun for Van and Cami doesn't stop here. Picture this: Van's determined to pamper Cami within an inch of her life on a Mediterranean island for their babymoon. Think they'll get up to all kinds of filthy shenanigans? Get the bonus scene free when you register for our mailing list.

GET THE BONUS SCENE
http://bit.ly/sbb-2-bonus

———

Wondering who at Athena Ventures gets their HEA next? Read on for chapter one of *Succumbed*!

Excerpt from Succumbed
South Bay Billionaires Book #3
Chapter 1: Declan

The last time I saw her, I was a fool. A stupid, trusting fool who put my future in the hands of someone woefully undeserving. Seeing her striking face again brought it all back to the surface–the humiliation, the anger, the overwhelming need to tear it apart just to rebuild it better.

"Dec, are you watching this?" My brother's voice interrupted my rage-fueled thoughts.

I looked up at him and the phone he thrust toward me. There she was again, impeccable as before, the interview playback a few minutes before the version still running on my screen. Linc looked down at my phone and grunted, pocketing his as he plopped next to me on the couch and watched over my shoulder.

"Shane!" he hollered, eyes glued to the interview. He knocked my shoulder with his. "Pause it for a sec, yeah? Maybe start it over."

My narrowed look went unnoticed as he glanced back over the couch and gestured urgently.

"C'mon, man, you gotta see this."

Shane, my best friend and business partner, rounded the couch and took the open spot beside me.

"Seriously?" I grunted, gesturing at the immense amount of available space around me. "This fucking thing seats twelve. Why the hell are you two in my lap?"

"You're fine." Linc waved his hand at my phone. "Start it over, Dec."

"Here." Shane plucked the device from my fingers, ignoring my frustrated exclamation, and tapped the screen.

Before I could ask him what the hell he was doing, the video appeared on the television mounted across the room. We all stilled, watching the woman who had tossed us out without remorse as she smirked.

"It's an honor to have you both here." The interviewer, Cass Thompson–startup and tech reporter for the Bayview Bulletin–nodded to the two women seated opposite her.

"Thanks for inviting us," Preston Brooks replied. She was a society darling and angel investor, well-known in the Bay. "I relish any opportunity to talk about the importance of women-led businesses."

Lex Livingston, owner of Athena Ventures and arguably the most powerful businesswoman in the state, nodded once. "Agreed. Empowering female founders, particularly in the male-dominated tech space, is something I'm fiercely passionate about."

"That passion is well-documented, and a big reason we're so pleased to have you and Preston co-hosting our annual Bay's Brightest luncheon to honor women in the startup community." Cass tilted her head to the side, her brows furrowing minutely. "Your own path to success has had its own share of challenges, hasn't it?"

Lex's eyes flashed with something unreadable. "It certainly has. And that's a big part of why I've invested my time, energy,

and funds into causes like these. I don't want the next genera-
tion of female leaders to face similar hurdles."

"Could you share an example with us?"

Lex's lips twitched up ever so slightly at the corner as she
glanced down. "What I've always been most offended by, if I'm
honest, are the women who climb up by stepping on others.
While I'm not the type of person to preach sisterhood–"

Preston snorted, then covered her mouth with wide eyes as
she held back a laugh. Lex just smirked and pressed on.

"I do believe every woman who has a seat at the table should
save one for another."

"Preach, sister," Preston agreed, raising one hand toward the
ceiling.

Lex chuckled as she glanced at her, then refocused on their
interviewer. "I'll share a specific example from several years ago.
My business partner, Van Costa, and I were waiting to hear a
pitch from a promising young startup."

"Oh shit, here we go." The proximity of Linc's voice was
jarring, and I flinched.

"Why the hell are you still on top of me?" I demanded,
leaning away from him only to find Shane hovering by my other
side. "Seriously, you two have zero fucking physical
boundaries."

They glanced at each other over my head, then shrugged in
unison.

"You're both impossible," I muttered, turning my attention
back to the interview.

The three women were laughing, Preston's eyes bright as
she looked between the other two. "Sorry, Lex, couldn't help it.
Please, continue your story."

Lex inclined her head, then turned back to Cass. Her
expression hardened as she spoke, her features sharpening.
"One of the four startup founders was a woman who has since

made quite a name for herself in this community. She waltzed into the conference room as Van and I stood to welcome them, but she went straight to Van."

Her eyes unfocused and she gazed into the distance, then huffed a laugh. "She shook his hand and introduced herself, then looked me dead in the eye and said, and this is a direct quote, 'I take my coffee black and a water would be great, thanks. Can I also grab the wifi password? We've got a lot to cover with Mr. Costa.'"

"Like fuck she did," Preston hissed, her expression murderous.

Cass cleared her throat and shot the mouthy brunette a pointed eyebrow. Preston winced in response.

Undeterred, Lex continued. "She did. I'll never forget it."

"What did you do?" Cass asked.

The smile that settled slowly onto Lex's face was cold, calculating. Something stirred in the pit of my stomach in response. "I got her a black coffee, then sat down with Van and listened to her pitch. Neither of us said a word."

"Oh, you're good," Preston praised. "You let her set up her own fall."

Lex's nonchalant shrug was impossibly elegant. "So to speak. When she finished, her business partners knew something was off, but she was too arrogant to notice."

"Tell me you eviscerated her." Preston leaned forward eagerly.

"That chick is bloodthirsty," Linc laughed. "I fucking dig it."

"Shut up." Shane snapped his fingers, then pointed at Lincoln, his gaze never leaving the TV.

My brother's lips parted, then pursed and drew into a frown as he crossed his arms and sat back against the couch with a pout. *I am surrounded by children.*

"I didn't eviscerate her, no. But I was honest. Their tech was promising–incredibly so–but they didn't have enough hard evidence to back up their claims. I was skeptical from the start, and shared that, but her failure to know her audience? That was unforgivable."

"Say more about that. Why was that your takeaway?"

"She and her business partners came to my firm to ask for my investment. It was their job to know us and what we cared about, and tailor their pitch accordingly. She should never have stepped foot in Athena without knowing who I was. Mistaking me for an assistant should've been an impossible mistake for her to make. The fact that she made it?" Lex tutted.

"It was lazy. And if you're not willing to put in the effort, you're not worth my time. Because if it's easy, you're doing it wrong. I don't tolerate laziness or lack of preparedness because I've found both to be at the root of most avoidable failures."

"You should teach a masterclass, seriously."

Lex chuckled at Preston and shook her head. "I don't have time for that. But I make time to coach every female founder on our roster."

"Sounds like she missed out on more than just your funding," Cass quipped with a wry smile.

"She did, but I doubt she'll ever realize it. When someone is focused on their own success without consideration of others, their aperture becomes incredibly narrow. That's risky for the business and society because people making decisions from a narrow perspective are rarely going to make the right choice. And one terrible decision can negatively affect us all, especially when it brings a magnifying glass to a group that is anything other than white and male–female founders in the tech startup world, for example."

"Dec, that's our sign. If we went back–"

"Quiet," I snapped, refusing to look Lincoln's way.

"What would you say to her if your paths crossed again?" Cass asked.

The answer was immediate.

"Not a word. If she approached me to make amends, I'd listen. Otherwise, there are other women in this industry who are far more deserving of my attention." She gestured toward Preston. "Take this brilliant young woman, for instance."

The brunette basked in her peer's praise for a moment, then grinned at her. "Is this the part where I'm supposed to demure and say you're too kind?"

"I hope you don't. Own your brilliance, Ms. Brooks. It suits you."

Preston turned to Cass. "You've given her all the best lines! It's really not a joint interview at this point. Don't get me wrong, I'm here for it. I'm basically the president of the Lex Livingston fan club."

As the women laughed and Cass turned to question Preston, I leaned back against the couch. I could feel Lincoln's eyes boring a hole into the side of my face, but I didn't turn toward him. A few years ago, we fucked up. *I* fucked up. And I wanted nothing more than to make it right and restore our business and reputation. Well, that and one more thing.

"Linc's right, Dec. We should approach her." Shane's voice was steady and sure.

"I'm still not convinced."

"What more do you need, though? A flashing neon sign?" Lincoln threw a hand toward the television as the women chatted, the young brunette talking animatedly. "You know we can't do this alone. We need help. We need *her*."

"Like fuck we do." I scowled at him.

"Don't be blinded by your pride," Shane intoned.

I glanced over at him, ready to defend myself. But he was the picture of relaxation, arm flung over the couch as he kicked his legs up on the coffee table. *How is he always so goddamn calm?*

"I'll think about it." I stood, needing space from them and the reminder of past failures.

"Think quickly."

My eyebrows rose as I turned back to Shane. "What's your rush?"

His eyes flashed to mine. "The backstabbing bitch is close to launching. She goes live before we make our move, and it's all for nothing." He looked back at the television. "Who knows how many lives are at risk. And over a decade of work, Dec. Gone."

I looked back to the screen a final time. Lex was speaking again, but I tuned out her words and studied her face. Her light green eyes were fierce and glittering. Experience and knowledge were heavy in her gaze and in the intentional way she spoke. Frustration welled in me, and I huffed, stalking from the room.

Time hadn't dulled the sting of betrayal or the weight of responsibility that settled on my shoulders. I was reticent to trust anyone other than Lincoln and Shane with our business, but the need for retribution was a persistent drumbeat in my skull.

As much as I wanted to focus on building our business into what we envisioned, I couldn't ignore the siren song of revenge.

Get the rest of the story in March 2024. Preorder available now: https://books2read.com/succumbed

Glossary

Van is Italian American and a second-generation immigrant whose family hails from Naples. We've done our best to do the language justice and appreciate your grace for any creative liberties we may have taken. Find Italian-to-English translations below.

If something seems off, please contact us: hello@shelfindulgences.com. Thank you!

Al cuore non si comanda. È dato. – The heart cannot be commanded. It is given.

Bella – pet name; "beautiful"

Bellissima – extremely beautiful

Brava ragazza – good girl

Buongiorno – good day

Farei qualsiasi cosa per te – I would do anything for you

Fiorellino – pet name; "little flower"

Ho bisogno di te – I need you

Il mio cuore è tuo – my heart is yours

Il tuo futuro marito – your future husband

Sua regina – his queen

Nessuna donna è mai stata così perfetta – no woman has ever been this perfect

Senza di te, la vita non ha significato – without you, life has no meaning

Sono tuo – I'm yours

Tesoro – term of endearment, "treasure"

Ti amo oggi più di ieri ma meno di domani. – I love you more today than yesterday but less than tomorrow.

Ti voglio bene – non-romantic phrase for "I love you"; literal translation "I want you to be well"

Ti voglio bene anch'io – non-romantic phrase for "I love you, too"

Acknowledgments

Well, that was fun! And a little spicier, eh? 🌶 We hope you enjoyed Van and Cami's story as much as we did. These two had such clear personalities from the beginning, and it was delightful to see their love story develop on-page. We'd love to hear your thoughts! Your honest reviews on all platforms are greatly appreciated (and you can tag @ashleyjacobsssrich on Instagram and TikTok).

This indie author thing takes one heck of a village, and we're fortunate to have an incredible one. Thank you to the husbands for keeping us hydrated and fed, reminding us that sleep is a good thing, and serving as our eternal sounding boards.

Endless gratitude to Dawn for alpha reading, and to our beta team: Anh, Cassie, Clary, Courtney, Jessica, Kimberley, Laura, Natasha, Paige, Sara, Vanessa, and Zoë. You were all so enthusiastic, patient, and kind.

Thank you, too, to /u/Caratteraccio for consulting on Van's Italian heritage and language use (and forgive us the creative liberties we took).

And to the supportive, amazing communities in BookTok Baddies, Cliterature, and Spicy BookTok on Facebook–your passion and voracity is terrifyingly wonderful. We're grateful for every last one of you.

On to the next!

If you want updates on our plans for the Bay or the–ahem, *cough* dark mafia *cough*–series to come after that, you should join our Facebook reader group, <u>Ashley Jacobs & S. S. Rich's Billionaire Babes</u>.

'Til next time!

xoxo

ashley & s

About the Authors

Ashley Jacobs is a contemporary romance author. She loves to write alpha billionaires and the strong women they fall for. She lives in the United States with her golden retriever husband and goldendoodles. When she isn't spending time with fictional characters, she's busy hunting for the perfect croissant.

An avid reader from an early age, S. S. Rich grew up on old school sci fi and fantasy. Now, she enjoys creating strong female characters and the growly alphaholes who melt for them. Getting to do it with her bestie is the icing on the cake. When she's not writing, you can find S. chasing her children and dogs, enjoying the Pacific Northwest, obsessing over special edition books, or feeding her wanderlust.

Find out more and sign up for our newsletter at shelfindulgences.com.

Made in the USA
Coppell, TX
10 March 2024

LJR10206